**Margaret Daley**, an award-winning author of ninety books (five million sold worldwide), has been married for over forty years and is a firm believer in romance and love. When she isn't traveling, she's writing love stories, often with a suspense thread, and corralling her three cats, who think they rule her household. To find out more about Margaret, visit her website at margaretdaley.com.

**Jessica Keller** is a Starbucks drinker, avid reader and chocolate aficionado. Jessica holds degrees in communications and biblical studies. She is multipublished in both romance and young adult fiction and loves to interact with readers through social media. Jessica lives in the Chicagoland suburbs with her amazing husband, beautiful daughter and two annoyingly outgoing cats, who happen to be named after superheroes. Find all her contact information at jessicakellerbooks.com.

# Heart of a Cowboy

## Margaret Daley

## &

# Home for Good

## Jessica Keller

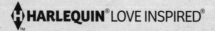

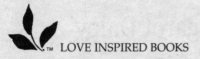 LOVE INSPIRED BOOKS

PLEASE RECYCLE · THIS PRODUCT IS RECYCLABLE ·

Recycling programs
for this product may
not exist in your area.

ISBN-13: 978-1-335-00665-3

Heart of a Cowboy and Home for Good

Copyright © 2017 by Harlequin Books S.A.

The publisher acknowledges the copyright holders
of the individual works as follows:

Heart of a Cowboy
Copyright © 2010 by Margaret Daley

Home for Good
Copyright © 2013 by Jessica Koschnitzky

www.Harlequin.com

**Printed in U.S.A.**

# CONTENTS

# HEART OF A COWBOY

Margaret Daley

To Ashley, Alexa, Abbey and Aubrey

The Lord is good, a stronghold in the day of trouble; and He knoweth them that trust in Him.
—*Nahum* 1:7

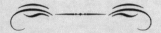

# Chapter One

The horse in the corral reared up, jerking the rope from his wrangler's grip. Standing next to the hood of her car watching the interplay, Jordan Masterson stiffened. The animal's hooves plunged down toward the man. Barely missing him.

She gasped. Even from a distance the flare of the animal's nostrils indicated agitation. She glanced at her ten-year-old son as he climbed from her yellow Camaro.

*Nicholas can't ride. He could get hurt.*

The horse's whinny drew her attention to the corral again. The huge black animal backed up, lifting its head as it stared wide-eyed at the cowboy.

"Whoa, boy. Easy, Midnight." The soothing cadence of the man's deep, husky voice eased the mounting tension in Jordan as well as the horse.

The animal slowed its backward steps. Its dilated pupils contracted. The man moved in closer, all the while saying, "Easy, boy. You're okay," until the horse stopped. The man raised his hand inch by slow inch. Finally his fingers grazed the horse's neck. He reached out and grasped the rope.

Something stirred deep in her memory. The cowboy's back was to her, but Jordan noted the breadth of his shoulders, the narrow hips, the long legs, clad in dusty jeans and his worn brown boots. She ran her gaze up his well-built body to his nape where his sable hair curled against the collar of his white shirt.

"Mom, did you see that?"

"Yeah," she whispered, more to herself than anyone.

The cowboy turned partially toward them, and Jordan drew in a deep breath and held it. His square jaw, his alert stance prodded a memory forward—one she wanted to forget. She zeroed in on his face, but his black cowboy hat shadowed most of his features until he lifted his head enough for her to see the firm set of his full lips, the tic in his jawline, the frown that graced his expression. Panic seized her, tightening its squeeze on her lungs. A panic that had nothing to do with the temperamental horse in the corral.

*Zachary Rutgers.*

Her high school sweetheart. The man who broke her heart.

His sea-green gaze zoomed in on hers. Suddenly Jordan was whisked back eleven years to the last time she saw that scowl that now transformed his tanned features into a hardened countenance. Even from yards away the tension that poured off him blasted her.

Breath trapped, Jordan pivoted away, gripping the frame of the car door. "Nicholas, maybe you shouldn't learn to ride right now." She schooled her voice into a level tone while inside her heartbeat galloped like a runaway stallion.

"Ah, Mom, you promised I could when we moved here."

"But…" *I can't do this. We can't be around Zachary.*

"I really want to ride."

Her son's intense stare drilled into her, reminding her yet again of the promise she'd made. One she needed to break.

"You said I should do something physical."

Her own reasoning was going to come back and bite her. Nicholas was a child who would stay buried in his books if she didn't get him out of the house and doing some activities. He was ten but was more comfortable around adults. His genius-level IQ often made him the butt of other kids' jokes. Something she had hoped would change when they'd moved back to Tallgrass. It hadn't.

"Hon, let me ask around. I'm sure there are other places you can get some riding lessons." Just not at this ranch. Not with this cowboy.

Her son swiveled toward the corral and grinned at Zachary, who was striding toward them.

"Jordan, I didn't realize you were back in town."

*I didn't realize you were, either.* "Yeah, I moved back a few weeks ago. When did you and your wife move back?"

"Wife? I'm not married."

He looked from her to her son. "What can I do for you?"

*Not married?* But he had been engaged.

"Aunt Rachel said you give riding lessons out here." Nicholas straightened his shoulders. "I want to learn to ride. Maybe be in a rodeo one day."

Rodeo? Where had that come from? Jordan's panic, centered on Zachary, suddenly shifted to her son. Participating in rodeos was dangerous.

Zachary pushed his hat back from his forehead. "Well, partner, the only lessons I give are for the kids in the Helping Hands Homeschooling group. Are you part of that?"

Nicholas threw a glance back at her. "Mom?"

*A homeschooling group?* Jordan heaved a sigh and slammed the car door, then rounded the front of her Camaro. "No, we aren't. Sorry to bother you." She had intended to grasp her son's hand and get out of there as quickly as possible. Before any questions were asked. Why hadn't her sister and mother told her Zachary was living in Tallgrass?

Nicholas stepped out of her reach and even closer to the fence that separated him from Zachary. "May I see some of the horses? I've never been on a ranch." His grin grew to encompass his whole face. "I've read all about how a ranch works and how to train horses."

Zachary slid a glance toward her, his gaze boring into her for a full minute. Behind the hard glint a hundred questions lurked—ones she didn't want to answer. Her own anger bubbled to the surface and shoved the panic down. He was the one who had gotten engaged so soon after their breakup.

"Please, mister."

Zachary wrenched his attention from Jordan. His face relaxed its harshness, and he actually smiled clear to the green depths of those eyes that had captured her interest when she'd been a junior in high school.

"Tell you what. I have three kids coming out to ride. They should be here soon. If it's okay with your mother, you can join them this time."

*No, it isn't okay.* The words screamed through Jordan's mind while her son swung around with that puppy-dog look that turned her to mush.

"Mom, may I please?"

Only her son would ask and be grammatically correct. Zachary's gaze fell on her, too, and she resisted the urge to squirm. In the end he was the one who had walked away from their relationship. And she wasn't going to let him make her feel guilty.

Jordan tilted up her chin and looked Zachary square in the face. "That would be fine. I appreciate your making an exception this once. Shouldn't you run it by your boss first, though?"

He lowered his hat to shield his eyes. "I own the Wild Bill Buffalo Ranch."

His answer really didn't surprise her since Zachary used to spend time at his uncle's ranch in southern Oklahoma. Had he fulfilled his dream of being a bull rider on the rodeo circuit? What happened to the woman his mother said he was engaged to? There was so much she didn't know about him now—purposefully.

"C'mon. I'll get you hitched up with a horse and give you a few pointers before the others arrive." Zachary moved a few steps to the gate of the corral and opened it. "I'm Zachary." He held out his hand toward her son, ignoring her.

Jordan's throat tightened. She swallowed several times, preparing herself for an onslaught of questions—possibly accusations—if her son gave his full name.

"I'm Nicholas." He fit his small hand in the large one.

"It's good to meet you, Nicholas. Let's go. I think I've got the perfect little mare for you."

As her son followed Zachary toward the barn, relief fluttered down her length. Nicholas's undersize frame fooled many people into thinking he was younger than ten. In this case, she was glad because it gave her time to decide what to do about the fact that she and Zachary now lived in the same town again.

"So you and my mom know each other."

"Yeah, a long time ago. We went to school together." Zachary glanced back at her.

His limp as he entered the barn caught her attention. A riding accident? The second the question popped into her mind, she shook it away. She didn't want to know the answer to that query. She didn't want to have anything to do with him.

At the entrance Nicholas stopped and waited for her to catch up. Reluctantly she hurried toward him. Why out of all the activities and sports she had mentioned to him did Nicholas pick riding horses? Why had she listened to her sister and come out here? She suspected she knew what Rachel was up to and would have a word about her meddling.

No matter how much she berated herself and the circumstances she found herself in, she would have to deal with Zachary—at least for the next hour. After that she could hightail it out of here—before he found out Nicholas was his son.

Ever since Zachary had come back to Tallgrass, his past with Jordan would sneak into his thoughts, his dreams. He'd found himself wondering about her more and more. Now she was here at his ranch. He hadn't been prepared for her surprise visit. Memories—both good and bad—overwhelmed him as he glanced back at Jordan with her son. Her life had gone on just fine without him.

Her son was what? Around eight? Obviously Jordan hadn't wasted any time finding a replacement for him. His gut solidified like the hard ground when he was thrown from a horse. His leg aching more than usual, Zachary stalked toward the stall to fetch a horse for the boy to ride.

Zachary led the mare into the center of the barn. He certainly had a right to be mad at her. She'd left him. Not the other way around. When she'd received the scholarship to the art school in Savannah, he'd tried to be happy for her. But there was a good one within a few hours of Tallgrass, and yet she'd decided to go to the college in Georgia. He'd given her his heart, and she'd left it to spend four years at a place halfway across the country.

The night before she'd left for Savannah, they had a huge fight. Their views of their future together had been so different, and she'd decided to break it off with him. They needed their space. He'd waited two months for her to change her mind. Then when he couldn't stay in Tallgrass another moment, he'd joined the army. He'd needed to get away to decide what he wanted to do with the rest of his life.

And he'd never heard from her after that—until now. Eleven long years later. Too late for them.

## Chapter Two

"**M**om, are you okay?" Nicholas asked as he stood in the barn entrance.

Jordan cut the distance between them, the odors of dust and musky grass squeezing her throat. "Seeing that horse in the corral reminded me how dangerous riding can be." But even worse was seeing Zachary again. Now she was faced with several dilemmas. The first being should she tell Zachary he was Nicholas's father and change everything? It had been so long. She didn't know if she could.

"I'll be all right. I'm tougher than I look." Her son puffed out his chest.

"I know, honey, but this really isn't a good idea. Let's thank him and leave."

"Mom, you're babying me again. I'm ten years old."

Jordan's gaze zoomed in on Zachary leading a horse out of a stall, hoping he hadn't heard how old Nicholas was. She couldn't have the conversation she knew she now had to have in the middle of a barn with her son looking on. This wasn't the time or the place—if ever there was one. But she would have to soon on her terms. After all, Zachary walked away from her, refusing to return her calls.

"Fine. But if I think it's getting too dangerous, you'll get off immediately and that will be the end of riding." A few years ago, she'd almost lost Nicholas. She wouldn't lose him now.

"I know what you're thinking. My atrial septal defect has been fixed. My cardiologist says I'm fit as a fiddle. While I never thought of a fiddle as especially being fit, the point he's making is I'm fine now."

Jordan shook her head. There wasn't much she could get past her child. She flitted her hands. "Go. Have fun." For now. She'd find something else he'd enjoy that would give him some physical activity to make him forget about the horses.

"I will." Nicholas covered the short distance to Zachary, who had the chestnut mare already saddled and ready to go.

"There's a mounting block outside that you can use." Zachary led the horse out the back double doors, never once looking her way since he'd left her standing by the corral.

Jordan trailed after the pair, wanting to be close for Nicholas but far away because of Zachary and his possible questions. *Lord, what do I tell him? He wanted nothing to do with me after we broke up that summer after graduation.*

Before she knew it, her son was sitting on a horse that was huge. If he fell off, the ground would be a long way down and the impact would be hard. As Zachary gave Nicholas a few instructions on how to sit properly in the saddle, use the reins and get the animal to do what her son wanted, Jordan stepped a little closer to the paddock where they were. Zachary walked beside Nicholas and the mare as they circled the corral.

The deep timbre in Zachary's voice as he explained to her son what to do flowed over her, prodding memories forward of those fun times they had shared before everything had fallen apart. The memory of the feel of his long fingers as they combed through her hair or the brush of his lips over hers sent her heart beating faster.

She jerked back from the fence, putting some space between them. She would not fall for Zachary Rutgers again. Even if he was Nicholas's father and not married now, she would keep her distance. If she never told him about Nicholas being his son, then it would be easy to keep away. If she did, they would be connected always.

Zachary glanced toward the entrance into the barn. "Ah, I see the others are here." As he peered away, his look brushed over her, reminding her again of the soft feel of his lips grazing hers. "Sit here for a few minutes, partner. I'll be right back."

After tying the horse to the fence, he passed her striding toward the large double doors. His gaze homed in on her, his eyes narrow, his mouth set in a tight line. The we'll-talk-later stare held her rooted to the ground although her first inclination was to whirl around and flee. Again her anger flooded her. He acted as if he hadn't done anything wrong. She refused to break the visual connection first.

He looked toward the barn when a child called out his name. His steps lengthened, and he quickly disappeared inside. Jordan let out a long breath and sank against the fence post nearby, her legs weak, her hands shaking.

"Isn't this cool, Mom?"

Her son's question forced her to pull herself together.

She was discovering how much anger she still had toward Zachary for leaving her when she'd needed him the most.

"You might hold the saddle horn." She moved toward the mare. If he fell, maybe she could catch him before he hit the ground. She'd remembered Zachary once having a broken arm from being thrown from a horse, and then there had been the accident at the Oklahoma Junior Rodeo Finals. Him lying crumpled in the dirt. The dust created from the horse finally settling around Zachary's prone body. Whatever had possessed her to agree to come out here in the first place? She hadn't really thought the riding lessons out.

Zachary approached with three kids. "Nicholas, this is Jana, Randy and Ashley. They'll be riding with us."

Her son greeted each one as they led their horses out of the barn to mount. His grin spoke of his joy and pushed Jordan's fears to the background. She'd be right here as he rode around in the paddock. She'd be right here to make sure he didn't go faster than a walk.

"Uncle Zachary, can we go for a ride to the stream?" Ashley sat atop her mare, her dark brown hair pulled back in a ponytail.

Randy swung up into the saddle. "Yeah, it's getting hot today. It'd be fun wading in the water. Can we?"

"I don't know. Nicholas is just learning." Zachary rubbed his hand along the stubble of growth on his jaw.

"But I did my first time riding." Jana took off her cowboy hat and fanned her face.

"I'd love to go for a ride. Please." Her son threw in his own plea.

"Let me get my horse." Zachary started for the barn.

Jordan stepped into his path. "Nicholas doesn't know

how to ride. He can't go." Over his shoulder, she could see the hopeful look on her son's face fall.

The intensity in Zachary's eyes bored through her as though it could make her move away. "He'll be okay. But he's your son."

Yes, he was. She'd been in labor for thirty-six hours alone. She'd raised him alone. Watched him go through the surgery to repair his heart defect alone. "He'd never been on a horse until fifteen minutes ago." She hated the fact she felt as though she had to justify her stance.

"If I remember correctly when I taught you how to ride, we went riding in a meadow not long after that. Doing it in a paddock isn't what I really call riding."

She remembered one time when they had ridden across a pasture, galloping, the wind blowing through her long, loose hair. And they had ended up kissing for the first time under a large oak tree when they had finally stopped. Heat flushed her cheeks at the remembrance of his lips on hers.

"He'll be okay, Jordan. Nothing ever happened to you riding."

"But it did to you."

"If it'll make you feel better, come with us." His voice held no emotion. It was as though she were a stranger to him.

"I haven't ridden in years."

"It'll come back to you." He skirted around her and strode into the barn.

Chewing her bottom lip, Jordan peered at her son, who patted his mare. Should she go?

When Nicholas stared behind her, his face brightened. Jordan swept around and saw Zachary leading two horses out of the barn. He handed the reins of one to her, their hands brushing against each other. His eyes widened for a few seconds as he peered down at where they had briefly connected. With a shake of his head, he quickly stepped away and swung up into the saddle of his mount.

He'd felt the electric jolt just as she had. She massaged her fingertips into her palm, trying to erase his touch. It had been nearly impossible as a teenager and still was.

She glanced at her son then at the mare next to her. "Okay, I'll come along."

"Yippee!" Nicholas shouted, pumping one arm into the air.

Ashley rode in the lead with Jana next to her. Randy followed with Nicholas slightly behind him and to the side. Zachary waited for Jordan to go next then took up the rear. As they crossed the meadow, heading toward a grove of trees, the feel of Zachary's gaze zapped a fiery trail down her spine. In less than an hour in his presence, he tempted her to forget eleven years of heartache. No, she wouldn't let him get close this time.

She listened to her son talk with the other children, who willingly answered his questions about Key Elementary although all of them were homeschooled. Nicholas had only been attending the school for ten days. He hadn't said much to her, but she sensed the same teasing was happening there that had at his previous one in South Carolina. Her son was a scholar and a pacifist besides being a grade ahead and small. She'd questioned him on the way out to the ranch about how school was going, and he had gone silent. A sure sign something was wrong with her talkative son.

"He'll be all right." Zachary came alongside her.

She slowed the horse's gait and let the kids get a little farther ahead because she didn't want Nicholas to overhear anything that might lead to questions—at least not until she knew what she was going to do about Zachary. She'd tried to tell him about Nicholas, but when he hadn't returned her calls, she'd decided she could do it without him. She would never force anyone into a relationship he didn't want. "Who?" she finally asked although she knew he was referring to her son.

"Nicholas."

She wasn't so sure Nicholas would be all right. A couple of kids at his last school had been awful to him, making his life so miserable that she decided to move back home before school started in August. She was tired of doing everything without any family support, and her mother had said she needed help with Granny. Now at least she had her mother, grandmother and sister here. In all those eleven years, she'd only returned to Tallgrass a couple of times, the last time two years ago when her sister's husband died unexpectedly from a heart attack.

"He's a natural when it comes to riding. He knows instinctively how to flow with his horse."

Jordan studied Nicholas for a moment and had to agree. He was a natural—like his father.

"Are you always this uptight or is it just around me that you get that way?"

"Uptight?"

He gestured toward her hands gripping the reins. "Relax. Maybelle is sensitive to her rider."

"Do you blame me? We didn't exactly end our relationship on a good note."

He nodded his head toward Nicholas. "It looks like

you found someone to replace me pretty fast. What's your son? Eight?" A tic twitched in his jawline, its strong set strengthening even more.

"How about you? I thought you would be married by now." The last time she'd called Zachary's mother to get hold of him, she would never forget the news the woman imparted before she could tell Zachary's mom about the baby. He was engaged to someone he served with in the army, and he was still stationed overseas. His mother might as well have said, "Out of your reach."

"No. Where's your husband?" His gaze held hers captive, a hard glitter to his eyes.

*What happened to your fiancée?* She bit the inside of her mouth to keep the words inside. She wouldn't let him know how much that had hurt her when she'd discovered he'd moved on only seven months after they had broken up. "I'm not married."

"What happened to Nicholas's father?"

"He hasn't been in the picture for quite some time."

"Sorry to hear that—" he paused for a long moment "—for your son's sake."

*But not mine.* His unspoken words cut her to the core. The pain sliced through her in spite of her efforts to distance herself. Anger rose. "How long have you been back in Tallgrass?"

"A couple of years. Becca found this ranch for sale for me. The deal was too good to turn down."

"How's your sister?" Becca had been the first one she'd talked to when she'd called after the doctor had told her she was pregnant. She'd only been at art school in Savannah for two and a half months. The news had rocked her world, and she hadn't known what to do. She'd desperately needed to talk with Zachary, but he'd enlisted in the army and was at boot camp. Becca had promised her she would tell Zachary to call. He never did.

"She's still married to the same man, and they have three kids. They live here on the ranch, too. Ashley is the oldest."

Jordan glanced toward the children. Zachary's niece slid from her horse and tied its rein on a tree limb. Jordan nudged her mare to go faster as Jana and Randy dismounted, too. Her son started to bring his leg over and drop to the ground.

"Hold it, Nicholas," she shouted, mentally measuring the long distance from the horse to the patch of grass below the mare. "I'll help you."

"Jordan, he's doing fine. Let him do it himself. That's the way he'll learn."

She slanted a look toward Zachary. "But…"

"See." Zachary pointed toward her son, who'd slipped to the ground and like the others was tying up his horse. "Why are you so protective?"

"That's how mothers are supposed to be." She'd come so close to losing Nicholas. She didn't know what she would have done if he'd died. He was her world.

"Yes, protect but not smother."

"What do you know about being a parent?" Her hands curled around the reins, and she pulled harder than she should have to halt the mare. He hadn't wanted children, or at least that was the impression she'd gotten when they had talked about the future right after high school graduation. At the time, his dreams had centered around the rodeo—not having a family.

A flicker of pain glinted in his eyes before a frown descended. "You're right. I don't have personal experience raising a child, but I was a boy once. I know he needs a little breathing room."

He dismounted and strode away from her before she could think of a retort, some kind of defense for herself. She shouldn't have lashed out at him. He was right. Nicholas had told her that on more than one occasion, especially when she'd wanted to march up to the last school and face those kids who'd teased Nicholas and made fun of him. If it had started again, she would have to do something different. She wouldn't let her son be miserable for another school year.

Zachary stood at the edge of the stream that ran through his property and watched the kids wade across it. Their giggles peppered the air and brought a smile to his mouth. He'd enjoyed living near his niece and nephews, but at night he always went home to an empty house with no child's laughter to fill it or bedtime stories to tell. And yet, Jordan had moved on with her life and had all of that with Nicholas.

The boy captured his attention as he bent down and stared at something on the ground. He picked it up and straightened. When he saw Zachary staring at him, Jordan's son crossed the creek and approached him.

"Look what I found. This is a *Terrapene carolina triunguis*." Nicholas held it up for Zachary to see. His expression must have conveyed surprise because the child added, "A three-toed box turtle. They were common where I used to live. They eat insects, worms, fish, berries, snakes."

"Did you have one as a pet?"

"No. They're better off in their natural habitat. I have a dog named Tucker."

What eight-year-old kid knew the scientific name of a turtle? At least he assumed that was what the child spouted off. "Do you like science a lot?"

Nicholas shrugged. "It's okay. I really enjoy math the most. I've been working on algebra, but tell you a secret—" he leaned toward Zachary "—Mom's not very good at it. I have to teach myself."

"Teach yourself? That's mighty ambitious."

"I love to learn." Nicholas set the turtle on the ground.

*Like his mother.* Jordan had always been a good student while he'd been more interested in sports, especially riding. She'd helped him with his classwork and he'd taught her to ride. For a brief moment he allowed himself to recall some of the good times he and Jordan had in high school—when she'd helped him cram for a test and he'd made an A or when he'd worked odd jobs to save enough to buy her a necklace the first Christmas they'd been together. The glimpse of her smile had made it all worth it. Randy's voice calling Nicholas pulled Zachary away from the past—thankfully. He didn't need to remember.

Jordan's son flashed him a smile. "Gotta go." He whirled and raced toward the other kids.

Zachary watched the children talking. Nicholas pointed at something in the creek and Jana squealed, ducking behind Randy. A brown, foot-long snake slithered through the water. Zachary slid his attention to Jordan. Her eyes grew round, and she backed away from the stream. She never did like snakes.

He chuckled, remembering that time he'd found one on her porch. She'd jumped into his arms so fast he'd staggered back, almost losing his balance. But he'd recovered and tightened his embrace, cradling her against him. The onslaught of memories cracked a fissure in the wall about his emotions.

Those carefree days were over. She'd walked away from him and never looked back.

"We better get back to the barn." Zachary started for his horse.

"Do we hafta, Uncle Zachary?"

He glanced at his niece. "Yeah, Alexa will be here to pick up Jana."

Nicholas had already crossed the stream while the other three were still on the opposite side. They reluctantly followed. For a few seconds a yearning for what he didn't have inundated Zachary. But he pushed it aside. He just had to be satisfied with having a niece and two nephews. And staying out of Jordan's way.

## Chapter Three

Sore, Jordan slid to the ground back at the barn half an hour later, keeping her eye on her son to make sure he dismounted okay. He did, almost like a pro. She had to admit everything Nicholas did he did well. He was quick to pick up things. But usually they weren't physical activities.

Jordan caught sight of Zachary taking a few extra moments to explain to her son how to take care of his horse after a ride. Nicholas absorbed what Zachary told him with his usual intense concentration. She knew that after this he wouldn't have to be told again. Zachary patted him on the shoulder. The smile her son gave Zachary right before he strode away to tend to his gelding stirred doubts in her that she hadn't made a good choice all those years ago.

That brief scene confirmed she had to tell Zachary about Nicholas soon. There was no way she could keep her secret if they were both living in such a small town. He was bound to find out some way or another. She still didn't know how she would break the news. Tell Zachary first or Nicholas? She felt in over her head.

But maybe this was one of the reasons she'd finally come home. She wanted Nicholas to be surrounded by family—even Zachary's. It would be to her son's benefit, and maybe for once, she wouldn't feel so alone in this world. Yes, she'd always had the support of her mother, grandmother and sister, but long-distance support wasn't the same as immediate face-to-face interactions. And yet, for years she'd lived far away from that support because of her feelings toward Zachary.

Could she really tell him? If she kept quiet, she wouldn't have to see him. She could even leave Tallgrass. He never had to know. That idea suddenly appealed to her because every time she thought of telling him about Nicholas, her stomach coiled into a hard ball.

"Hi. Jana told me your son had his first riding lesson today." A young woman with long, curly mahogany hair and soft, dark brown eyes stopped next to Jordan. "I'm Alexa Ferguson, Jana's stepmom."

Jordan shook the hand the twentysomething offered her. "Nice to meet you. My son enjoyed getting to know Jana and the others. He can be shy around new kids."

"So can Jana, but this year she's come a long way."

"How so?"

"The best thing my husband did for Jana was take her out of school and teach her at home. She'd developed separation anxiety when her mother divorced Ian and left. She was afraid she was going to lose him, too. She needed that time with her father. I don't advocate that for every child because a school placement is right for a lot of them, but some need something else. Jana was one of those."

"So you think homeschooling is a good option for some?" *Is that what Nicholas needs?*

"Jana has blossomed since she's been at home. When I'm not taking classes, I help Ian teach her. This past couple of weeks, I haven't had a chance as much since I'm doing my student teaching, and to tell you the truth, I miss working with her."

"So it's been a positive experience?"

"It's been great. I'm finishing my elementary education degree, so it's a good experience for me. She's bright, and we've had so much fun." Alexa hiked her large purse up on her shoulder.

"But you know what you're doing." She didn't know the first thing about homeschooling. What if homeschooling was the answer if Nicholas continued to have problems at school? She'd never studied to be a teacher like Alexa. How could she teach her child with his high IQ? But she should check into it.

"The beauty of being part of the Helping Hands Homeschooling group is you have support from other parents who are doing the same thing and have probably gone through the same problems. Most of them don't have formal educational training."

"Zachary mentioned something about being involved with the organization."

"Are you thinking of homeschooling your son?"

Jordan searched the area and found Nicholas talking with Randy, both boys relaxed, grinning. "I never thought about that option for him until now." She didn't know what to do. Going up to the school, talking with the teacher and principal really hadn't taken care of what Nicholas had needed at his last school.

"Why don't you come to an HHH meeting this week and talk with others who've been involved a long time. I've only been doing it since January."

Jana ran up to Alexa. "Can Ashley come home with us today?"

"Sure. Your dad is working on the bench for your room so he'll be busy in the garage." After Jana whirled around and raced to her friend, Alexa returned her attention to Jordan. "I hope I'll see you Wednesday night. I'll introduce you to some of the others." She rummaged in her big purse, pulled out a pad of paper and wrote an address down on it. "This is where we have our meetings."

Jordan stuffed the note into her jeans pocket. She just might take Alexa up on her offer, especially if her son continued to have social problems. Yesterday morning, his second Friday, he hadn't wanted to go because of a stomachache, but today he'd had a great time interacting with the kids at the ranch.

After Alexa gathered Jana and Ashley to leave, Jordan called out for Nicholas to get into the car. Then she crossed to where Zachary stood by the corral with the horse that had been frightened earlier. He glanced at her when she came up to the railing next to him.

At the stream after he'd stomped off, they hadn't said a word to each other, but she needed to thank him at least. Soon enough their rocky relationship could be even rockier if she told him about Nicholas. "Thanks for letting us stay and for giving Nicholas a riding lesson."

"No problem." He kept his arms resting on a slat of the fence, his gaze trained on the horse in the paddock. "Even though I don't have any children, I love having them here at the ranch."

Ouch! The jab at her earlier statement scored a direct hit, especially when he did have a child although he didn't know it. "I'm sorry I said that. It's obvious children respond to you. The kids enjoyed the ride today, especially Nicholas."

"And that's why he's welcome to come out here and ride. He doesn't have to be part of the homeschooling group for him to be included. I saw how much he enjoyed it." His tightly clasped hands attested to how much that invitation had cost him.

"Can I get back to you on that?"

"Sure. I'm here most days." He shoved himself away from the railing and turned toward her. "For the lessons you can just leave Nicholas and come back in an hour. Most parents don't stay."

There had been a time they had spent every possible moment together. Now it was obvious he didn't want to have anything to do with her. Which was the way she wanted it. What would he do when or if he discovered Nicholas was his son? For a few seconds she considered telling him and just getting it over with. The words were on the tip of her tongue. But she peered to her left and saw her son making a beeline for them. She didn't want everything to change with that revelation. She needed to do some thinking, praying.

"Thanks for the riding lesson. I haven't had that much fun in a long time."

If she had been thinking of refusing Zachary's invitation, her son's declaration stopped that.

"You're welcome to come anytime."

"Really? Great!" Nicholas beamed. "Mom, can I come next Saturday? The others will."

"We'll see. Right now we need to get home. Nana's gonna wonder where we disappeared to." Jordan started for her car.

"But Aunt Rachel knows. She'll tell her." Nicholas

halted his progress toward the Camaro, swung toward Zachary and waved. "Bye. See you Saturday."

Jordan wanted to tell Nicholas no, but she knew she couldn't deny him an opportunity to ride, especially since it was his father who would be teaching him. As she pulled away from the barn, she glimpsed Zachary leaning back against the railing, studying her with those intense green eyes.

His last expression, totally unreadable, stayed with Jordan the whole way home. Twenty minutes later she pulled into the driveway of the two-story house where she'd grown up. Her sister lived down the street. After years away, she and Nicholas were finally surrounded by family members—more than she'd counted on when she'd decided to return to Tallgrass.

"I need to take care of Tucker. I'll be out back." Nicholas hopped from the car and raced toward the backyard and the dog that had been his companion through his ordeal to fix the hole in his heart.

Inside she found her mother lying down on the couch in the den with a cold pack on her forehead. Jordan started to back out of the room when her mom shot up.

"How did it go riding?"

Jordan sank into a chair, her muscles protesting the afternoon ride, her head pounding with tension from dealing with Zachary. "Why didn't you or Rachel tell me Zachary owned the ranch?"

Her mother's eyes widened. "Maybe your sister knew, but I didn't. I'd heard he was back in town, but that's all."

"Well, then, why didn't you tell me that at least?"

She swung her feet to the floor and faced Jordan.

"Because I was afraid you wouldn't come home. Isn't he the reason you've stayed away?"

"My work kept me in South Carolina."

"Your graphics design business can be done from anywhere. You had a few clients there, but you've managed to serve them from here, haven't you?"

"Okay, you're right. Most of my clients are from all over."

"See, I knew it."

Jordan removed the rubber band that held her hair off her neck. She shook her curls loose, running her fingers through them. "It's hot out there."

"It's August in Oklahoma. That means hot. And you're avoiding talking about your encounter with Zachary."

"I didn't know that was what we were talking about. Why the cold pack?"

"Your grandmother is driving me crazy." Her mother frowned. "And you're doing it again. It's obvious you ran into Zachary. How did it go?"

"I've been manipulated by my son into taking him back out to the ranch for more lessons with Zachary as the instructor. Not something I'm looking forward to."

"Are you going to tell him about Nicholas?"

The question shot Jordan to her feet. She hurried to the entrance and checked to make sure her son wasn't anywhere he could overhear, then moved back to the chair and plopped down. "I don't want Nicholas to know until I'm ready to tell him. He thinks his father didn't want to be involved with us." Which was what she had convinced herself of. Now she wasn't so sure of anything. Even if Zachary found out about Nicholas, he might not want to be in his son's life, but after today she realized she probably should have pursued getting in touch with him more than a couple of times. But her feelings had been so hurt she couldn't bring herself to make another call that might go unreturned.

"He never questioned you about his father?" Her mother schooled her voice into a whisper.

"Sure, when he was young. I think he saw how upset I got by the subject that he decided not to ask any more questions."

"So what are you going to do?"

"That's a good question. One I need an answer to."

"Hon, you've got to figure that out yourself. I know it's been rough raising Nicholas by yourself, especially with his heart problem, but the doctor said he was fine now, that the surgery was a success. You've done a wonderful job with him."

"But, Mom, I've made some big mistakes." She was blessed to have Nicholas in her life and wouldn't trade him for anything. But a mistake she had been paying for these past eleven years was believing that she and Zachary would be together forever and giving herself to him before they were married.

"We all make mistakes. Remember Christ was the only person who walked this earth who was perfect. I'm not perfect. You aren't. Zachary isn't."

"I know, but in South Carolina I could forget that Zachary was the other half of Nicholas. Here I can't. I discovered that today. My past has caught up with me."

"Then you need to tell Zachary right away."

"I've got to find the right place and time. I want to tell Zachary before I say anything to Nicholas. I owe Zachary at least that much. I'm giving myself some time to figure it out. What to say. Where to say it. I'm not rushing into it. I've got to do it right."

Her mother pushed to her feet, clutching the cold pack. "You always have to analyze everything. You never rush into anything. Don't wait too long, hon. The truth needs to come from you and frankly Nicholas looks a lot like Zachary."

Her son's features were similar to Zachary's, but Nicholas's hair was blond and his stature was small like hers.

"As sharp as your son is, he might figure it out if given the time and given the connection between you two."

Jordan stood. "Okay, you've made your point." She couldn't have that. She needed to decide how and when.

"Now if I could only make my point with your grandma."

"What's going on with Granny?"

"She has a date tonight."

"What's wrong with that?"

"Don't you think eighty is a little old to start dating after being a widow for twenty-five years?"

Jordan chuckled. "It's wonderful. Where did she meet him?"

"At church. He's a widower. Doug Bateman lives down the street. She can barely walk without her walker, but I think she's been sneaking out to meet him in the park."

"She's an adult. I think she can do what she wants."

Her mother snorted, rounded the coffee table and crossed the den to the doorway. "I'm gonna see if I can get more support from your sister," she mumbled as she left the room.

Jordan eased into the chair again. The throbbing beat of her headache pulsated behind her eyes. She buried her face in her hands and massaged her fingertips into her forehead.

*I need help, Lord. I don't know how to tell Zachary or Nicholas. Everything will change if I do.*

"Ashley told me a new kid named Nicholas joined them today riding and his mother is Jordan. Do you have something to tell me?" Becca approached Zachary not an hour after Jordan had left the ranch with her son.

Zachary slanted a look at his sister standing on the other side of the corral fence with her hand on her hip. "Nope."

"The other day I heard *Jordan* Masterson came back to town. Was that her?"

"Why didn't you tell me she was back?" He removed his hat and tapped it against his jeans. "I don't like surprises."

"I didn't think she would come out here."

"So it was okay not to say anything to me? I was bound to meet her sometime in Tallgrass. We have a number of the same friends, and I'm sure she'll get reacquainted with them."

His older sister studied him. "I thought you had moved on."

He'd thought so, too. Until he'd seen Jordan and all the old hurt came back. His gut burned as if acid eroded it. "As much as I'm enjoying this little chitchat, I've got to train this horse." He gestured toward Midnight, warily watching him on the other side of the paddock.

Becca huffed, her mouth pinched into a frown. "If you need to talk, you know where the house is."

As his sister left, Zachary made his way toward Midnight. He'd wanted a family, children, and couldn't have any now. But in spite of the rodeo accident that snatched away his dream he'd carved out a life here in Tallgrass, and Jordan had come back and disrupted everything.

Why couldn't she just stay away? Leave him in peace? All those years ago he'd fled his hometown because every place he'd gone reminded him of Jordan. Even when he had joined the army—anything different to take his thoughts off Jordan—in the back of his mind he'd clung to the hope she would call and come back to him. She never did, and he was left to pick up the pieces. When he had patched his life back together, he'd vowed she would never break his heart again.

And now he'd gone and agreed to teach her son to ride. Now he would have to see Jordan once a week. He didn't want a weekly reminder of what could have been.

"Ms. Masterson, Nicholas seems to be having a hard time adjusting to this school. He knows the rules, and yet he snuck into the school at lunchtime when he was supposed to be outside on the playground. His teacher found him sitting at his desk when she came in after eating lunch."

Seated in front of the elementary school principal on Wednesday, Jordan crossed her legs, shifting to try to make herself more comfortable. But there was no way around it. She felt as though she'd been sent to the principal's office, rather than her son. "Was he disruptive or doing something he shouldn't in the room?"

"No, but that's not the point. He wasn't supposed to be there."

"Did you ask him why he came inside early?"

"He wouldn't say why." The principal scanned a piece of paper. "And I've got a report from the nurse that he's going to her almost every day complaining of a stomachache or something else being wrong. Have you taken him to the doctor to make sure he's all right?"

"Last week and he's fine." Jordan rose, gripping her purse in front of her like a firewall. "I'll talk with him." It was the same situation as his last school. He didn't fit in easily. She needed to do something to make his learning years more enjoyable.

As the older woman came to her feet, she leaned into her desk. "Maybe he shouldn't have skipped a grade."

"That's something the school in South Carolina did to keep him interested in his studies. The curriculum was too easy for him. Is he having problems academically?"

"On the contrary, his grades so far are excellent, but socially…" The principal averted her gaze for a moment then reestablished eye contact and said, "Frankly, he doesn't interact with the other children much. I'm concerned about him."

"Thank you. I'll talk with Nicholas today about following the rules." Her son always followed the rules. Which made this new behavior troubling.

When Jordan emerged from the principal's office, Nicholas pushed himself off the wall and trudged toward her. With his head down, she couldn't see his expression.

"We need to talk in the car." She didn't want others to overhear their conversation. She was determined to get to the bottom of what was happening to Nicholas.

Five minutes later with the air-conditioning cooling the interior of the car, Jordan sat behind the steering wheel in the parking lot of Key Elementary, Nicholas in the front seat next to her. "What's going on at school?"

"I don't understand the other guys' fascination with video games and football."

Well, neither did she but that didn't solve the problem her son had. He was more comfortable with adults. "Are they making fun of you?"

"I'm supposed to play dumb." Nicholas looked directly at her. "I can't do that. If some of them would do their homework, they could answer the teacher's questions. I'm bored and miserable."

"How about the enrichment class?"

"It meets twice a week for an hour. I need more. Randy was telling me about being schooled at home. May I try that? That way the class won't hold me back. I can learn at my own rate."

And going up another grade wasn't an option. "I'll think about it. I'll even go to the Helping Hands Homeschooling meeting tonight and see what they have to offer." Jordan pulled out of her parking space and headed to the street running in front of the school. "Because, Nicholas, I'll need help, and I want to make sure I can have opportunities for you to socialize if I homeschool you."

"I don't think like kids my age."

"You seem to like Randy, Jana and Ashley."

"Yeah, they're different."

Maybe if she could get Nicholas to socialize outside school, it would work better for her son. She was glad the HHH meeting was that evening, but she needed to know more before she committed to homeschooling. Was that the best option for her son? Could she provide him with the needed academics as well as opportunities to be with other kids?

Would Zachary be there? He'd said something about going because he was involved in the planning of an HHH Junior Rodeo Event at the ranch. She'd tried calling him several times since Saturday to set up a meeting with him, but each time she'd hung up before the phone had even rung once. The thought of seeing him that evening sent her pulse racing through her body. Should she even go?

When Jordan and Nicholas arrived at the Tallgrass Community Center where the Helping Hands Homeschooling group's meeting took place, the first person she saw was Zachary standing near his older sister, Becca.

"Mom, I see Randy. He told me to join him when I came."

"Fine." She couldn't take her eyes off Zachary.

He lifted his head and fastened his gaze on her. For a brief moment she was swept back to the time he'd approached her after a football game for the first time. Her heart reacted as it had then—tapping a fast staccato against her rib cage.

Something akin to that look they had exchanged all those years ago flickered into his eyes. Then suddenly he banked the fiery gleam. Even from across the large room she saw the tensing of his shoulders, the hardening of his jaw as though he gritted his teeth.

She tore her attention away. Not far from her, Alexa stood with a tall man who wore wire-rimmed glasses. Plastering a smile on her face, Jordan headed for the young woman she'd met at the ranch. Maybe she could work her way toward Zachary and casually find out about his work schedule.

Because her mother was right. She couldn't postpone this discussion concerning Nicholas much longer. If she told him, she needed to do it soon. The longer she waited the more she would have to explain.

"It's great seeing you at the meeting. Are you thinking of homeschooling?" Alexa asked after introducing Ian to Jordan.

"I'm thinking about it. I wanted to find out what resources were available to someone like me who doesn't have any training in teaching."

"Dr. Nancy Baker, the founder of HHH, is a professor at Tallgrass Community College. She has a lot of materials and books available that you can access."

"Before you two talk shop, I see Zachary. I need to see him about the HHH Junior Rodeo Event. Nice meeting you." Ian nodded toward her, squeezed Alexa's hand, then weaved his way through the throng toward Zachary.

For a few seconds Jordan's gaze followed Ian's path until he reached Zachary, who caught her looking. She quickly averted her eyes. "I'd like to check into homeschooling. Nicholas isn't doing as well as he should at school right now. He's so bright, but his potential isn't being met. I'm not sure, though, I can do any better. He's been studying algebra on his own with some help from me, but it's been a while since I did it. I'm having a hard time keeping up."

"Ian is starting his second math group involving algebra for homeschoolers next week. We have a medical doctor in this group who teaches a different science course every three months—human anatomy starts in

September, too. Those courses are part of the co-op classes some of the kids tap into."

"So I don't have to teach every subject? Because there are a few I'm not good at."

"No one is. If you have some kind of expertise, you might want to offer a course for the group, but it's not a requirement."

"My job is a computer graphic designer. It might be fun doing something with that. I'll have to think about it."

"Let me introduce you to Nancy before the meeting begins." Alexa searched the large room. "Ah, I see her talking to Ian and Zachary." The young woman started for them.

Jordan braced herself with a deep breath and followed Alexa. Maybe no one else sensed the tension flowing from Zachary as she and Alexa joined the small group with Ian and Nancy, but Jordan did. That tic in Zachary's jawline jerked.

"This is Jordan, Nancy. She's thinking about home-schooling her son." Alexa stepped next to Ian, who slipped his arm around her shoulder.

Nancy shook Jordan's hand. "Great. If you need any help, there are plenty of us to ask."

"I wondered if I could come look at your materials. Nicholas needs a lot of enrichment, and I want to make sure I can give it to him." Jordan shifted from one foot to the other, conscious of Zachary next to her. Only inches from him, her arm prickled as though there was a physical connection.

"Fine. How about we set up a time to talk, and then you can look through the resources? Say tomorrow morning at eleven?"

"I appreciate that. I don't want the situation at school to go on too long."

"Then I'll see you at eleven. Now if you all will excuse me, I need to get this meeting started. We've got an HHH Junior Rodeo Event to plan for in October." Nancy walked toward the front of the room.

"What's going on at school?" Zachary's deep voice, with a husky edge, broke the momentary silence.

Suddenly Jordan faced him alone because Ian and Alexa moved off to sit in a row not far away. "He's teased a lot because he's smart. He has trouble socializing with some of the kids his age. But mainly Nicholas isn't being challenged enough in school." She didn't want to go into too much detail. That could lead to questions she wasn't prepared to answer.

He scanned the group of children filing into the room off the main one. "It looks like he's getting along great with Randy." He gestured toward Nicholas, who was laughing and talking with the boy as they trailed behind the group of kids. "I know that Randy wanted to learn to ride as much as your son did. Nicholas will be a good addition to the Saturday riding group. They both have a fascination with the rodeo."

"Nicholas said something to you about that?"

"Yes, he wanted me to teach him to ride a bronco."

"That's not gonna happen."

"He could learn some of the less risky activities like barrel racing."

*Racing! Falling off a horse going fast!* She ground her teeth and kept those thoughts to herself. As Nancy started the meeting, Jordan realized they were the only two not sitting. Two chairs nearby seemed the logical choice for them to sit in, but she didn't want to be seated next to Zachary. How in the world was she going to handle him being in Nicholas's life as his father?

## Chapter Four

Why was he sitting next to Jordan at this meeting? The question needled Zachary with pinpricks of awareness of the woman who was only inches away from him. The hair on his arm near hers actually stood up as though at attention. He'd suffered through the past hour while the group planned the HHH Junior Rodeo activities scheduled to be at his ranch, but he'd hardly heard what had been said. The turmoil in his mind drowned out the voices. Worse, when he'd been called on to give his opinion, he'd barely been able to manage a coherent sentence in answer.

Since he saw her on Saturday, he hadn't been able to get the blonde dynamo out of his thoughts. She'd plagued his awakened moments and his sleep until exhaustion clung to him like sweat on a hard-ridden horse. She had no right to turn those dark brown eyes on him as though they hadn't parted ways after a nasty fight that had left him reeling eleven years ago. She'd been angry when she'd seen him in the corral a few days ago, as if he'd been the one who'd fled Tallgrass and hadn't looked back. He'd stayed around two months waiting for her to come to her senses. But not a word from her.

If his dream had been fulfilled, they would have been married, possibly with two or three kids by now. He hadn't wanted children right away, but he'd always wanted to be a father someday. But instead he'd decided to get as far away as possible from Tallgrass because of the constant reminders of what he and Jordan could have had.

After nine years he'd returned home, ready to put his life back together. He was through running from the home he'd loved and needed to put down roots. He was ready to complete one of his dreams—to own a ranch and raise horses, some of which were used in the rodeo. That was about the only way he was going to participate in the sport he'd loved after his injury in a bull trampling two years ago.

Suddenly, he noticed the people surrounding him and Jordan rising. The meeting was over? He blinked, wondering where the time had gone and what he'd agreed to as far as the HHH Junior Rodeo.

Zachary shot to his feet, needing to escape before Jordan totally befuddled him. He started to hurry away when her hand clamped on his arm and that tingling awareness became a flash through his body. Sweat beaded his brow. She'd always had that effect on him.

"I need to talk to you. Can we get together sometime soon?"

Her question threw him off-kilter. Talk to him? Get together? Why? He wanted to stay far away from her until he could tamp down the lingering feelings he had for her. Because being rejected by her once was enough.

"I'm busy." For a second his gaze clung to her full lips—lips that he'd one time loved to kiss.

"This is important."

He dragged his focus to her chocolate-brown eyes, concern in their depths that tried to wheedle its way into his heart. "Is this about Nicholas?"

She blinked, her face going white. "Yes, how did you know?"

"Let me assure you I meant what I said on Saturday. He can still take riding lessons even if you don't decide to join this group. I don't go back on my word." Realizing she still clasped his arm, he shook it free. "Now, if you'll excuse me, I've got to go."

"But…"

He didn't wait for her to say anything else. Quickening his step, he escaped outside and drew in deep breaths of the hot summer air. The light breeze cooled his cheeks.

Nicholas. The boy's name flitted through his mind. She'd moved on without him, had another man's son—loved another man. He'd tried to move on and for a short time had even become engaged to a girl after he'd been on the rodeo circuit a few years. After his bull riding accident, she'd left him. Audrey had wanted to have children, and he wouldn't be able to give her any. No, he'd decided not feeling anything was so much better for him. He had his ranch and was doing what he loved to do, raising horses. That was his life now, and he wasn't going to let Jordan's return change his plans nor the memories of their good times together.

Jordan looked up from working on her laptop to see her sister come into the kitchen. "Have you been hiding from me?" She clasped the edge of the table.

Rachel poured herself some coffee and sank into the chair next to Jordan. "Granny told me I'd better come down or you were going to send out a search party."

"Yeah, I have a beef with you. You sent me to Zachary's ranch last Saturday and now I'm stuck taking Nicholas there tomorrow. What were you thinking?" She couldn't keep her rising ire from resonating in her voice.

"That you two needed to work the past out."

"Have I interfered with your life?" Rachel had never been able to resist meddling.

"Only because you've been in South Carolina until four weeks ago. In time you'll be right in the middle like you were as a child."

"Me? Telling you what you should do? You've always done that. Don't. I can live my own life now." The words exploded from Jordan's mouth like compressed soda in a shaken bottle.

"I'll always care about you. I can't stop being your big sis."

"Sister, not mother."

Rachel's gaze connected with Jordan's. "I'm sorry."

Her apology deflated Jordan's annoyance. She couldn't stay mad at her sister for long. Growing up, Rachel had protected her. She'd listened to her. She'd been there through the pain of her breakup. "I know," she murmured, her tone a ragged stream.

Rachel took a sip from her mug. "Hmm. Your coffee is so much better than Mom's."

"How do you know I made that?" After Jordan closed down the program she was working on, she pushed her laptop to the side and lifted her mug to take a drink.

"Because you got Granny's cooking genes. Mom didn't. I didn't."

"Speaking of Granny, who is this Doug person?"

"A sweet man who is seventy and taken with our grandmother."

"Seventy! She's robbing the cradle."

Rachel raised her forefinger to her lips. "Shh. Don't let her hear you say that. She'll probably outlast Doug by years."

She wished she were as together as her sister or Granny. "Rachel, I need help. What am I gonna do?"

"Tell Zachary about Nicholas?"

"Do you know what that will do to me?" Jordan bit down on her thumbnail, then suddenly realized she'd reverted to a bad habit and said, "See what I'm doing just thinking about the havoc that will cause in my life. It took me years to break myself of biting my fingernails. Now I'm doing it again. Home less than a month."

"Zachary has a right to know whether he wants to be in Nicholas's life or not. It's his choice. Not yours. I told you years ago that you needed to get in touch with him."

"I know I need to do it. I just don't know how. I can't march up to him and say 'Nicholas is your son.'"

Rachel winced. "No, you need to cushion the news a little."

"Like you did when you told me Zachary owned the ranch?" The urge to chew on her fingernails inundated her. Jordan sat on her hands instead.

"Just do it. The longer you think about it the more upset you're going to be. Quit analyzing the problem to death."

"I can't change who I am."

"Oh, but you have. You used to take risks. Now you think everything to death."

"Yeah, well, finding out you're pregnant with a child

whose father doesn't want to have anything to do with you can go a long way to curing you of taking risks."

Rising, Rachel finished her last swallow of coffee and strolled to the sink to set her mug in it. "I'm going back into hiding. Let me know when you tell him."

"*If* I tell him," Jordan couldn't resist saying to her older sister's back as she left the room.

Jordan slid into the pew at the Tallgrass Community Church between Nicholas and her sister.

"I'm glad you could make it," Rachel whispered.

She smiled sweetly at her only sibling. "With the move I've been swamped, but I'm working to strengthen my faith. I'll admit I let life interfere in South Carolina."

"Did you tell him yesterday when you went to the ranch for Nicholas's lesson?"

With a glance at her son, she bent toward Rachel and lowered her voice to the barest level. "No and don't bring it up."

At that moment the music began to play, signaling the service would begin in a few minutes. Jordan bowed her head and folded her hands together in her lap.

*Lord, I'm here like I promised, but I'm still clueless what to do. Yesterday I couldn't have gotten the words out to say anything to Zachary if my life depended on it. Where do I start? How do I do it? Please help me. Amen.*

A commotion behind her drew her attention. First Becca then Ashley, Mike and Cal entered the pew. Next came Becca's husband, Paul, with Zachary on the end, right behind Nicholas.

Her son twisted around and grinned at Zachary, waving his hand. "Howdy."

Howdy? Her son had never said that word in his

whole life. She groaned and kept her gaze focused straight ahead. But the hairs on her nape tingled.

"Mom, Zachary is behind us."

Every nerve ending was acutely aware of that fact. "Shh, hon. Church is about to start." Which thankfully it did with the choir marching in singing "Onward, Christian Soldiers."

Zachary rose as the rest of the congregation did to sing the opening hymn, but he could hardly concentrate on the words of the song. Not with Jordan standing within arm's length of him. So close he could tug her into an embrace. That thought sent panic coursing through him. He should have expected her to show up at church with her family attending the same one as he did and prepared himself better—hardened his defenses against Jordan, who had always managed to get under his skin like a burr in a saddle blanket.

After seeing Jordan with Nicholas yesterday at his ranch, he didn't know if he could continue teaching her son how to ride. The boy reminded him of Jordan. He liked him a lot—probably too much.

When he looked at Nicholas, all he could think about was the child he never would have. The boy should have been his with Jordan. That had been his plan all those years ago. They would marry. He would make his living on the rodeo circuit until he had enough money for a ranch. Then they could start a family. He had his ranch thanks to a fruitful career on the rodeo circuit for five years. But now he couldn't have any kids—not since the accident in the National Finals in bull riding. It had left him lame and unable to father the children he'd always wanted.

He sat again after the song, his hands clenched at

his sides. There were a few days imprinted in his mind forever—when he first met Jordan, when they broke up and when he'd nearly died in the ring, riding a two-thousand-pound bull.

The longer he stayed in the pew behind Jordan the tenser he became. When the service ended an hour later, his muscles ached like they did when he was trying to rein in an untrained horse.

Nicholas turned toward him. "I didn't know you go to this church. That's neat. I had a great time yesterday."

"I'm glad. Before long you're gonna be riding rings around the others." There was no way he couldn't teach the boy how to ride. He had to find a way to stay away from Jordan and still help Nicholas. But he was beginning to think that would be impossible.

Nicholas beamed. "I want to be the best."

Jordan angled toward her son. "The best what?"

"Rider. I hope to participate in barrel racing at the HHH Junior Rodeo."

Jordan's eyes grew round. "You do?" Then her mouth firmed into a thin line.

"Yes. If I'm good, Mom, then you won't worry about me."

"Hey, Nicholas, want to join us?" Randy called from the aisle.

"Okay, Mom?"

"Fine. We'll be in the rec hall," Jordan said while the rest of her family filed out the other end of the pew.

Leaving Zachary practically alone with Jordan. Even his own family had abandoned him. He faced her, the muscles in his neck tightening even more than before until he didn't know if he could speak, which reminded him of the time years ago when they had first talked.

He'd been sweaty, tired and tongue-tied, but he'd needed to make sure she was okay after her fall while cheer-leading at the game.

"All the way home yesterday Nicholas couldn't stop talking about his lesson. I wish I had stayed to watch it. I had an errand to run, but I'll stay next week."

"Don't," slipped out of his mouth before he could stop the word.

Her forehead creased. "What do you mean?"

"I think the less we're around each other the better it is. Let's face it. The time when we were friends is past. You go your way. I'll go mine." There was a part of him—a desperate part that couldn't believe he was saying that to her. But it was true. Their time together was in the past.

"But Nicholas—"

"He's a joy to teach. He's welcome to come for the riding lessons. But I want you to drop him off and come back to pick him up." Because if she stood around watching, that would be all he would focus on. And he needed to concentrate on working with the kids, not on Jordan. She distracted him more than he wished. "Now if you'll excuse me, I need to find my family."

Striding away before she wanted to talk more, he scanned the near-empty sanctuary, surprised that most of the churchgoers had left. That was Jordan's effect on him. She had the ability to wipe away his common sense. He could still remember that time years ago when he had been competing at a rodeo and Jordan had been late arriving to watch him. When he saw her sit in the stands, he kept his attention on her a few seconds lon-ger than he should have. He ended up on the ground, his arm broken, berating himself for losing his concentration. He wouldn't let her get close enough to do that again. Too dangerous.

On the following Tuesday Jordan parked in front of the barn in nearly the same place as she had on Saturday for her son's second riding lesson. This time Nicholas wasn't with her. This time she was on a mission: to find Zachary, get him alone and tell him about his son.

She knew she had to and waiting would only make it worse. Knots riddled her stomach, and she hadn't eaten much in the past twenty-four hours. For a moment at church on Sunday, she'd contemplated telling him then, but he'd hightailed it out of the sanctuary so fast she hadn't had a chance. It probably hadn't been the best place anyway. They needed to be totally alone.

She saw the same black pickup as she had Saturday. She hoped that meant he was inside. Trudging toward the entrance, she surveyed the ranch. Several corrals with some horses surrounded the black barn. A little farther away were green pastures with groups of horses, some with colts and fillies. His place had a well-tended look about it, which didn't surprise her because that was the kind of person she'd known as a teenager. He took care of his own.

Inside, the hay-scented air cooled a couple of degrees. She peered down the long center of the cavernous structure with stalls on each side. "Zachary," she called out.

A short wrangler stuck his head out of an open door. "You just missed him. He's at his house."

"The blue one by the road?"

"No, ma'am. He lives due west. A small white place.

You can't miss it if you stay on the dirt road that runs in front of here."

She smiled although the corners of her mouth quivered. "Thanks." Seeing him at his house would be perfect. They could talk without being disturbed.

A few minutes later, she pulled up to a one-story white house, again well tended with a small vegetable garden to the left and a flower bed running the length of its front. Exiting her car, she inhaled a calming breath, full of the scent of the recently mowed grass. A swing hung from the ceiling of the wraparound porch, offering a comfortable haven at the end of the day. A sense of peace enveloped her as she took in her surroundings.

That peace was shattered a few seconds later when the front door opened and Zachary emerged from his house with a scowl on his face. She stiffened. The carefully prepared speech she'd rehearsed for hours wiped completely from her mind as he descended the steps and strode across the lawn toward her. His features were schooled in a neutral expression.

"What brings you out here?" His voice remained flat like the prairie around them.

Seeing him suddenly made her want to postpone telling him. Forever. The muscles in her throat convulsed. She backed up a few steps until she bumped into her car behind her and she couldn't go anywhere else. Trapped.

*I need to leave.* How could they work together for Nicholas's benefit? "I have to talk to you."

"What do you want?"

"A glass of water."

His brow crinkled. "What?"

"Water. I'm thirsty." Anything to delay what she needed to do.

"You came all the way out here for water?" He threaded his fingers through his hair.

"No, but I could use some first."

Several heartbeats later he shrugged. "Suit yourself." He spun on his heel and marched toward his place.

Jordan fortified herself with another deep breath and trailed after him.

He banged into the house, closing the door on her.

The barrier didn't bode well for the conversation she had to have with him. She sought the comfort of the porch swing and sat. *Lord, I need your help. Please give me the right words to say to him.*

The door opened, and Zachary came outside holding a tall glass with ice water in it. He handed it to her then lounged against the white railing and folded his arms over his chest.

Her hand trembling, she sipped several gulps of the cold water although it did nothing to alleviate the tightness in her throat. "Thank you. That hit the spot."

His biceps bunched. "Why did you come all the way out here, Jordan? What's going on?"

"I needed to talk to you in private. I thought this might be a good place and time."

His jaw clenched. "For?" He crossed his legs, totally closing himself off to her.

Her heart pounded so fast and loud she wondered if he heard it. Perspiration broke out on her forehead, upper lips and her palms. "Nicholas…" Her son's name came out in a whispered rush, the air sucked out of her lungs.

"Is this about homeschooling? I don't know anything about that. Talk with Becca if you want. She could answer your questions."

She put the glass on a table near the swing before she dropped it, then ran her damp palms on her capri jeans. Her chest rose and fell with the deep inhalation. "No, I went by and talked with Dr. Baker last Thursday. I've decided to take him out of school and teach him at home. I've got to do something different because what he's doing now isn't working." The sense of doom and the sensation of being cornered besieged her as though she were under attack.

"Then what is it?"

*Tell him. Before you lose your nerve.* "Nicholas—" The blood rushed into her ears. She gripped the edge of the swing, her fingernails digging into the wood, her breath trapped in her lungs. "Nicholas loves coming out here, and I want to thank you again for giving him lessons."

A sigh blew out between pursed lips. "What is it you're avoiding? This isn't like you not to come to…" His gaze latched onto hers. She could almost see the wheels turning in his head. He shoved away from the railing, not one emotion on his face. "How old is Nicholas?"

"He turned ten in April. He's small for his age. He was born a month early. Nicholas is your son."

He slumped back against the wooden post, clutching it. The dark stubble of his beard accentuated a gray pallor. His eyes fluttered. A flush of excitement glimmered in his expression. But quickly joy morphed into a bitter twist like a bundle of barbed wire. "You kept my son from me?"

She nodded slowly—all words lumped together into a huge knot in her throat.

His gaze clashed with hers. He opened his mouth to

say more but snapped it closed, his teeth clicking from the force. Pivoting away, he clamped his hands on the railing and leaned into it. With his shoulders slumped forward, he dropped his head.

She collapsed back against the swing, twisting her hands together in her lap. She should have eased into the news. Cushioned the blow. But it wouldn't have really made a difference. It wouldn't change the fact Nicholas was his son.

Finally he turned slowly toward her. The painful look in his eyes tore down all her reasons for never telling him and made a mockery of the hurt she'd experienced at him not contacting her. Then a shutter fell over his face. He wore a cold mask as though they were strangers—adversaries, and she supposed they were now.

"Why didn't you tell me this eleven years ago? Even a week ago?"

The lethal quiet of his words sent a chill down her spine. He wasn't innocent in this whole affair. She'd given him two chances, and he'd ignored her—hurt her and left her to deal with Nicholas's birth and illness by herself. She'd learned the hard way to rely only on herself and God. No one else. Certainly not him.

"I called you and left several messages. You never called back."

He fisted his hands. "I never received any messages from you."

"But I talked with your sister once, then later when I called again, to your mother. I asked her to have you call me. That it was important. In spite of the fact she informed me that you were engaged and happy, I was going to tell you I would be having a baby within two months. Your child." For a few seconds the memory hurled her back in time. A bone-deep ache overpowered her.

"I dated some but nothing serious. I didn't get engaged until after I left the army."

"Then I would have a talk with your mother." Her anger seeded itself in her heart, and she bolted to her feet. "I'm not the villain here. I tried. I decided while I was having Nicholas three weeks after that call that I would never force a man—you—to be his father."

He uncurled his hands then curled them again. Taking two steps, he cut the distance between them and thrust his face close to hers. "After calling twice, *you* decided I didn't have a right to know I had a child. That I couldn't be his father. Who are you to make that decision for me?"

"I'm Nicholas's mother. I'm the person you told that if I left Tallgrass that it was over between us. I'm the one who stayed in the hospital chapel on my knees praying to God to let my son live when he was struggling to stay alive. It was your mother who took pleasure in telling me you had a new woman in your life."

"Leave. You've done what you came to do."

He stalked to the front door and yanked it open. The sound of it slamming shut reverberated through the air. Jordan stared at the barrier between her and Zachary, her brief fury deflating. He had a right to be angry. But so did she. Why hadn't his mother told him?

She started to knock on his door, stopped and decided to leave as he asked. Emotionally she didn't have the energy to talk to him anymore. She still needed to tell Nicholas. Tonight when her mother took Granny to church. Nicholas and she would have the house to themselves. She hurried toward her car to put as much distance between her and Zachary as possible. Maybe then the pain would go away.

Numb, Zachary stood in the middle of his living room, staring at the floor as though that would help him to understand what had just happened. His mind swirled like a dust devil on the prairie. He couldn't grasp a thought beyond he had a son. Nicholas.

How could Jordan keep something that important from him? He sank into the chair next to the phone, his legs weak, his heart hammering so hard it hurt.

And his mother had kept Jordan's call from him. He flinched at the double whammy. If only he'd known about Nicholas, everything would be different.

No, he couldn't change what Jordan had done all those years ago, but he needed to know the truth. His hands shook as he reached for the phone to call his mother, who now lived in Arizona. He had to hear from her that she had kept Jordan's phone call from him. Even if his mom had, it didn't excuse Jordan. He hesitated with the last number. What good would it do to know his mother had kept a secret from him? He loved his parents, hated for anything to come between them. And yet, she'd had no right.

He moved the receiver toward its cradle. He halted in midair. No, he needed the truth—all of it. Then he would deal with the fact he had a son, that between Jordan and his mother he'd lost over ten years with his child. A child he'd dreamed of having but with the rodeo accident had been wrenched from his grasp. Was this a second chance? He pressed the last number.

When his mother answered, his tight grip on the phone shot pain down his arm. "Jordan Masterson has returned to Tallgrass. She just left here. She told me she asked you to have me call her that spring after we broke up. Did she?"

"Becca told me she was back home, that you two have seen each other several times."

"Mom, did she leave a message for me?" His heartbeat thundered in his ears as though a storm crashed against his skull.

"She called in March. You'd just finished boot camp and had been sent overseas. You talked about having met a girl you liked and had even gone out on a few dates. I didn't want you to be hurt again by Jordan so I didn't tell you."

He clamped his teeth together and watched the second hand make half a circle on the kitchen clock before saying, "That wasn't your decision to make." Somehow his voice only held a hint of the turmoil he was experiencing.

"That was more than ten years ago. Why are you bringing it up now?"

"Because Jordan just told me I have a son." A son! His insides felt as though a tornado raged within him.

The sound of a swift intake of air followed by a long silence greeted Zachary. He collapsed into the chair at his round oak table, holding the phone in one hand while kneading his temple with the other. He was ecstatic; he was angry.

"Are you sure he's your son?"

His mother's question sucker punched him. Pain radiated throughout his body as the fact he was a father finally sank into his brain. Really. Thinking back to what Nicholas looked like—the same eyes and set of his chin with a cleft—Zachary closed his eyes. How could he have missed it? "Yes, Mom, Nicholas is my son." *I have a son after all these years.*

"I have another grandchild? How could she keep something like that from you, from our family?"

"She called right before he was born to let me know she was pregnant." Part of him wanted to take back his defense of Jordan, but there were so many good memories tangled up in the bad ones that he couldn't totally put the blame on her.

"She should have said something to me. I'd have told you if she had mentioned she was having your child."

The accusatory tone sliced across his chest, a band drawn taut. "She said something about you telling her I was engaged. I guess that stopped her."

"Oh, that." His mother sighed. "That still doesn't excuse her for not saying something to you."

*No, it doesn't.* She should have called back. Everything would have been different if she had.

"She was wrong, son."

A long, long silence stalked her last words. He shifted in the chair.

"I'm so sorry I didn't say anything. I didn't want you to get hurt again. I don't know what else to say."

The anger he felt toward Jordan eclipsed any he could have toward his mother. Jordan should have called and called until she had spoken to him personally. How could he ever trust her again? How could he forgive her for stealing ten years of being a father from him?

Jordan downed the last swallow of her fifth cup of coffee in the past two hours. She had to tell Nicholas as soon as her mother and grandmother left for church.

After her encounter with Zachary today, she couldn't put it off any longer.

Her grandmother shuffled into the room, wearing a pink chiffon dress, with makeup on her face, and her short gray hair done in soft curls.

"You look great. What's the occasion?" Jordan rose and started to help Granny into the chair she'd been sitting in.

Her grandmother shook off her assistance. "Child, I wish you would stop listening to your mother. I can manage by myself." She sank into the chair and waved Jordan toward the one next to her. "Doug's going to be at the Prairie Pride meeting tonight. I finally talked him into being part of the group at church."

"You really like him?"

A twinkle entered her eyes, and her mouth tilted up in a huge grin. "Yeah. And I don't care what Eileen thinks."

"Mom will come around. Give her time."

"Time isn't my friend. I'm going to grasp the brass ring while I can still reach for it."

Jordan chuckled. "I love you. After the day I've had, you still manage to make me laugh."

"You finally told your young man about Nicholas? I know you've been praying about it."

She chewed on a fingernail then realized what she was doing and dropped her hand into her lap, grasping both of them together to keep from doing it. "Zachary isn't my young man, but yes I did today." Seeing him earlier had renewed feelings she wanted—needed—to deny, especially when she discovered that Zachary hadn't known about the calls all those years ago.

"I imagine he wasn't too pleased."

"That's putting it mildly."

"And now you need to talk with Nicholas?"

Jordan nodded. "I've made a mess of everything. I wish I'd never run into Zachary." At least a part of her wished that, but another part wondered if she and Zachary could put the past behind them and start over.

Her grandmother cocked her head and studied Jordan with those sensitive dark eyes that could see right through her. "Do you really? You don't think this is for the best in the end?"

Her clasped hands squeezed until her fingers tingled. "You always did like Zachary."

"He's a likeable young man. But what I feel isn't the point. This is about Nicholas and you, and your son deserves to know."

Jordan dropped her head and stared at her hands twisting together. "I'm afraid I'm gonna have to get used to seeing Zachary."

"Good. It's about time. I hated seeing you two break up."

Jordan looked at her grandmother. "You never said anything before. You sound like Rachel."

"It was your mistake to make."

"Mistake? It wouldn't have worked back then. I wanted different things than Zachary."

"How about now?"

"I don't know him. I realized that when I saw him."

Jordan's mom came into the kitchen. "There you are. We need to get going or you'll be late."

"And we wouldn't want that." Her grandmother winked at Jordan then rose slowly, peering at her. "I suggest you get to know him."

"I was looking for your walker. Where is it?" Eileen scanned the room.

"I put it away."

"You can't."

"I can do what I want. I don't need it." Her grandmother hobbled toward the back door, saying, "Let's get going. I don't want to be late," then disappeared outside.

Her mom huffed and stalked past Jordan. "See what I have to put up with."

"See you in a couple hours."

Jordan pushed to her feet and took her mug to the sink. For a few seconds the dark out the window enticed her attention. Anything to prolong going to Nicholas's room. Anything to prolong having the conversation about his father. Anything to rewrite the past. Not possible. A long breath hissed from her lips.

She moved toward the hallway. The doorbell rang. She quickly diverted her path to the front foyer, eager for the interruption. She swung the door open. All eagerness vanished.

Zachary stood in the entrance. His commanding presence stole her breath and her thoughts.

## Chapter Five

"**W**hat are you doing here?" Stepping out onto the porch, Jordan closed the door behind her. Blocking the entrance to the house, she faced Zachary, his expression totally closed.

"I'm here to see my son."

"You can't. I haven't…" Panic choked off her words.

He moved closer. "I'm not leaving until I see Nicholas."

She backed up. "I haven't talked with him yet."

"Good." Taking another stride, Zachary stood in front of her, invading her personal space. "I want to be there when you tell him. I'm his father."

"No!"

A tic in his jawline was the only sign he didn't like her answer.

The slashing line of his mouth underscored his anger. "Jordan, I want to be in my son's life. I think you at least owe me that."

"I know my son. You don't. I can't—"

"The only reason I don't know Nicholas is because you didn't tell me I had a son. I want to change that. I've lost ten years with him. I'm not losing another day." He thrust his face close.

The scent of his peppermint toothpaste taunted her, sparking a vivid memory of the first time he'd kissed her. She slammed the lid quickly on that thought. She needed all her wits about her. Squaring her shoulders, she met his pinpoint gaze. "He's also my son."

His lips pressed together. "I want to be with you when you tell him."

A constriction about her chest pulled tight. She grappled for something to say, but all she could think of was he was Nicholas's father. She was no longer the only one in her son's life. She would have to share him with Zachary. This was exactly what she'd been afraid would happen. "Fine." She drew in a composing breath. "But I'm the one who tells him."

With a nod, he backed away several steps.

Jordan took another deep breath, trying to fill her oxygen-deprived lungs. Pivoting away from Zachary, she fumbled for the handle then shoved the door open. As she crossed the foyer toward the stairs, she slung a look over her shoulder. He hung back for a few seconds, surveying her home.

His harsh gaze returned to hers. "At least some things haven't changed." He strode toward her.

This was the house she'd grown up in, and Zachary knew this house. He'd spent a lot of time here while they had been dating in high school. "If my mother has a say in it, they will. She wants to redo the whole place."

"Where are your mother and grandmother?"

"They're at church. They won't be back for a few hours." She mounted the steps, feeling Zachary's eyes on her back.

The walk down the hallway to Nicholas's room took seconds, but all she could think about was the eternity she'd endured during her son's heart operation while she waited to hear from the surgeon. The same empty feeling in her stomach. The same chill blanketing her. The same numbness as if what she was experiencing wasn't real.

At Nicholas's door, she knocked then pushed it open. Her son sat at his desk in front of his computer.

He twisted toward her, an excited smile on his face. "Mom, I figured out this problem." He tapped the screen. His attention shifted to Zachary, who appeared behind Jordan. "Hi, Zachary. What are you doing here?"

The very same question she'd demanded only ten minutes ago. "We have something to talk to you about," she said, not wanting Zachary to answer.

"Is it about the riding lessons?"

"No, hon." She moved into the room and sat on Nicholas's bed before her legs gave out.

"Oh. What's wrong?" Nicholas scooted around to face her, but his gaze strayed to Zachary for a few seconds before returning to her.

"Nothing is really wrong." *Who am I kidding? Everything is wrong.* The words she needed to say stuck in her throat, burning a hole. She swallowed once. Twice.

Zachary stepped toward Nicholas.

"Mom?" His eyebrows slashed down.

"Remember when I told you that your dad didn't want to be involved in your life?"

Nicholas nodded.

"Well, I was wrong. He does." A fortifying breath did little to fill her lungs. Zachary opened his mouth.

Alarm dislodged her clogged words, and she blurted out, "Zachary is your father."

Nicholas's jaw dropped. He peered at her for a brief moment, then fastened his stare on Zachary. "You are? Why didn't you say something when I was at the ranch?"

Zachary spread his arms wide, palms outward. "I—I didn't—"

"He didn't know." When Nicholas looked at her again, her stomach clenched into a hard ball.

Nicholas's confusion ripped her composure. She wanted to hug him. To hold him in her arms until everything was back to normal. To soothe his turmoil until the shadows faded from his eyes.

She'd handled this all wrong. She should have told her son first by herself no matter what Zachary had insisted. The minute he'd entered the picture all the carefully planned words she'd rehearsed evaporated like water in Death Valley. "I never told Zachary about you."

The furrows in her child's forehead deepened. "Why not?"

She threw a glance at Zachary, catching the same question in his eyes. "I tried. I called him several times to tell him, but he wasn't there and he never returned my calls." All of a sudden, even to her own ears, the reason wasn't strong enough. "I was nineteen. Hurt he hadn't called me back. I…" She couldn't tell her son it was pride that had kept her from trying to get in touch with Zachary again. Pride and fear of rejection.

"I never received the messages to call your mother. Through a series of unfortunate incidents, not your mom's fault, I didn't discover you were my son until today when she told me."

Surprise flitted through her. *Not my fault?* That wasn't what he'd implied earlier.

Zachary covered the few feet between him and his son. "That's why I'm here tonight. We have a lot to catch up on. It looks like you're working on algebra. I didn't do algebra until I was fourteen."

Nicholas studied Zachary's face for a long moment. "We look alike. I should have seen it."

"If you aren't looking for it, you wouldn't notice." Zachary returned his son's intense survey. "But you're right. We have similar features." He sat on the long chest at the end of the bed, his legs spread, his elbows on his thighs, his hands loosely clasped. "Tell me about what you're doing on the computer."

With a narrowed gaze thrown her way, Nicholas scooted his chair over a few inches to give Zachary a better view of the screen. Then her son launched into his plan to have calculus mastered by the age of fourteen. She prayed that Nicholas would talk to her about what he was feeling after Zachary left, but if that glance was any indication she was in for a rough night with her son.

After listening to the boy's explanation of what he wanted to study, Zachary examined Nicholas's—no, scratch that, his son's—bedroom. It was nothing like his when he was growing up. On a wall was a detailed map of the solar system while on the opposite one was a map of the world with red and blue pins stuck in it—probably at least fifty. Another poster listed the periodic table. The full double bookcases next to his desk held volumes of books that an adult would have—not a child of ten. When he skimmed over the other titles, his gaze lighting upon *War and Peace,* questions flooded

Zachary's mind. How smart was his child? How was he gonna relate to him? The fact he'd missed the first ten years struck him like a punch to the gut. He was out of step with his son and didn't know if they would ever have anything in common. His one chance to be a father.

"So you really enjoy math?" He'd hated the subject in school.

"Yes, sir. It comes easy to me."

Zachary heard the creak of the bed as Jordan stood. He slipped a look toward her, hoping she would leave him alone with Nicholas, but she remained nearby. The feel of her gaze on him made him clutch his hands together. "What don't you like?"

"Really not much. I guess writing. But I love to read, especially history and biographies. You can learn so much when you read about a famous person."

"What was the last book you read?" Zachary couldn't remember the last one he'd read—had to be years ago.

"A six-volume series by Winston Churchill concerning World War II. Next I want to read about Hitler to get a better sense of what happened at that time."

Zachary's mouth hung open. Quickly he snapped it closed. *I should have seen the resemblance. Figured it out. But I never thought Jordan would keep something like that from me.* The anger, just below the surface, surged to the foreground along with self-doubt. *I'm so not prepared to be a father.*

"I find it's necessary to read both sides of an issue or topic. Don't you think?"

"Yeah. What about you, Jordan?" Zachary swung his attention toward the woman who'd not readied him for this moment. He'd enjoyed history in school while

Jordan hadn't. Maybe he could find a common bond with his son after all. He could go to the bookstore, find some books on World War II.

"Sure, both sides are important."

The uncomfortable look on her face didn't vindicate him. For his son's sake he would be tied to Jordan, and he needed to make this work, somehow.

"Mom, what are we having for dinner?"

"Dinner? Uh…" Her mouth twisted as she shot a glance toward the door. "I guess I can fix some sandwiches."

"Will you stay for dinner?" His son clicked off the computer.

Zachary didn't know if he could sit at a table with Jordan and act as if everything would be okay. It wouldn't be. And yet the eagerness in Nicholas's expression prompted him to say, "Yeah, that sounds nice."

"Fine. Why don't you come help me?" Jordan stared right at Zachary.

"My idea of fixing a meal is opening a can of soup."

She blew a breath out, her gaze darting between Zachary and the doorway. "It shouldn't take me five minutes. Nicholas, make sure you wash up."

After she hurried from the room, Nicholas checked his watch. "She'll probably have it done in four."

"Why do you say that?" Zachary asked, amused for the first time that day.

"She's afraid to leave us alone."

"Very perceptive."

"Not really. She's just very obvious. What happened with you and Mom?"

It was his turn to squirm. "You don't pull any punches. How old are you?" He knew, but the question just slipped out because the more he was around his son the older he seemed.

"Ten but sometimes I feel a lot older. I was sick a lot when I was younger and I spent a lot of time reading books. At least with them I could go places, do things I couldn't otherwise. That's what those pins on the map represent. Blue are my first choices of where I want to go. Red are the back-up ones."

Suddenly Zachary looked hard at his son. He hadn't had a chance to be a boy. Maybe that was what he could do for his son. Teach him to play, have fun. "Then maybe I can do something about that. You said something about being interested in the rodeo."

His face brightening, Nicholas straightened. "Yes. I've read some books about it."

"Books are good, but experiencing it firsthand is so much better. I started participating in rodeo events for kids when I was your age. Actually earlier."

"Then I could, too."

Zachary wanted to say yes—should have the right to since he was the child's father—but caution made him murmur, "We'll have to run it by your mother first."

His son frowned. "She'll never let me. She gets scared that I'll get sick or hurt myself."

"The first thing you need to do is learn to ride well. Then we'll see after that."

"Nicholas, dinner is ready," Jordan shouted as if she stood at the bottom of the stairs.

"Let's go wash up, partner." Zachary rose. "I hear your mom is gonna teach you at home."

"Yeah, tomorrow is my last day at school and I'm so glad. It takes Mom a while to make up her mind."

His son lowered his voice and bent closer. "She doesn't like change."

He settled a hand on his son's shoulder as they headed for the bathroom. "What's been going on at school?"

Nicholas shrugged. "Just the usual."

In the hallway Zachary faced the boy. "Are you being teased?"

He hung his head. "Yes. I don't fit in. I don't understand them. Today I was the last one to be picked for a team. That happens all the time. Then another kid laughed in class when I had to write an answer on the board."

Nicholas's injured tone magnified Zachary's anger at Jordan. "Why?" He could have been there to help his son—if only he'd known about him.

"My handwriting isn't legible. I've tried to make it better, but my fine motor skills aren't good."

Would he ever not be amazed what came out of his son's mouth? Nicholas was nothing like his niece and nephews. Zachary lifted his son's chin. "You have nothing to be ashamed about. You're smart. You have a lot to offer a friend." He started again toward the bathroom. "I can help you with that."

The dinner had been a disaster. Jordan carried the plates to the sink while Nicholas snagged Zachary and took him outside to show him his telescope. She'd wanted to follow, but after being excluded through most of the meal, it was obvious her son only wanted to spend time with his father.

During the meal Zachary and Nicholas had talked horses and riding, leaving her out of the conversation. What if she hadn't gone to the ranch that Saturday? Or come back to Tallgrass? Then she wouldn't be facing this problem. But remembering Nicholas's joy-filled expression and his laughter during the dinner made her realize telling Zachary had been for the best.

She sank into a chair at the kitchen table, placed her elbow on its top and cupped her chin. Tapping her finger against her cheek, she visualized Nicholas on the back of a horse, racing across the meadow. The next image of him flying over the animal's head and crashing into the hard ground sent alarm through her.

She bolted to her feet and marched to the back door. She was joining them whether they liked it or not. He was her son, too. She'd been his parent for the past ten years and wasn't going to turn the reins over to Zachary just because she'd made a mistake and hadn't told him about Nicholas.

Because now she realized she'd been totally wrong not to. Somehow she had to make sure that Zachary understood she regretted the decision she made all those years ago. That they should work together.

She flung open the door and stepped out onto the deck. Both Zachary and Nicholas glanced toward her then her son returned to showing Zachary how to adjust the telescope—one she'd spent a bonus on to get her son two Christmases ago. At the time the telescope had been taller than Nicholas. He spent hours outside watching the sky at night. He was determined to discover something new, and if she knew her son, he probably would one day.

"What are you all looking at?"

Zachary peered at her. "The rings of Saturn. I can't believe I'm actually seeing them."

She recalled the first time she'd seen them or the

craters on the moon or Mars. "Yeah. They're neat." She watched father and son, and her heart expanded against her rib cage. She still needed to talk with Nicholas without Zachary around, but looking at them together firmed the rightness of her decision. "It's getting close to your bedtime."

"Ah, Mom."

"You've got to get up early for school. I'm sure you and Zachary will spend a lot of time together in the future. You need to take your bath—"

In the dim light from the kitchen, Nicholas pivoted, his arms straight at his sides, his hands balled. "I want to spend time with him *now*."

Stunned by the angrily spoken word, Jordan took a step back. "Nicholas."

"Partner, I need to leave, but why don't you and your mother come out to the ranch tomorrow after school. I want to introduce you to my sister and her family. You've already met Ashley, but I have two nephews, too." Zachary stood behind her son—their son—his face in the shadows.

"But—but…" spluttered out of Nicholas's mouth before he closed it and stalked toward the door. Its slamming vibrated through the clear night air.

Jordan flinched, her eyes shutting as she scrubbed her hands down her face.

"Do you blame him?"

Zachary's quiet question chipped away at what composure she had left. "I blame you for not letting me prepare him for the news."

"Oh, I see. I was supposed to wait some more time to get to know *my* son while you come up with a way to explain why you never told me or him about who I am. Let's face it. There's no easy way to tell him you kept the truth from him and me."

Anger and guilt tangled together to form a knot in her throat. And now she had to deal with the consequences of that decision. How could she have thought that she could come home and continue merrily along with her life as she had for twenty-nine years? Because she hadn't known Zachary was in Tallgrass.

"I'm going, but I want my family to get to know Nicholas. He wants to come to the ranch tomorrow and meet them."

"If *your* family had given you my messages all those years ago, we wouldn't be standing here like this." She'd been wrong—but not the only one.

He drilled a look through her. "Touché. I'll give you that, but it still doesn't excuse what you did." Skirting her, he descended the steps to the deck and made his way around to the front of the house.

Jordan sank against the lounge chair near her, clasping its back to keep upright. Zachary's intenseness had sucked the energy from her, and she would need all she had to speak with Nicholas before he went to bed.

She would love to postpone this conversation. Forever. But she couldn't.

*Lord, I know I was wrong. Please help me to fix this with Nicholas. I need You more than ever.*

Shoving away from the chair, she headed for the door, then up the stairs toward her son's bedroom. She and Nicholas had always been close. This wouldn't change that. She hoped.

She rapped on his door, then entered, expecting him to be at his computer since he hadn't been in the bathroom. Instead the chair was empty. When she scanned the room, she discovered him already under the covers, his head barely peeking out. He always prolonged going to sleep, hating to miss anything.

"Nicholas."

Nothing. Not a word. Not a movement, as though he had fallen asleep in that short amount of time. She knew better.

"Nicholas, we need to talk."

"I don't want to talk to you."

## Chapter Six

Nicholas's words hurt, a pang piercing through Jordan's heart. As much as she wanted to leave and never have this conversation with her son, she crossed the room to his bed and sat. "Hon, I know you're angry at me, and I can't blame you."

His back to her, he hunched his shoulders, pulling the blanket up around his neck even more. "Why didn't you tell me?"

"I really don't have a good defense for that. All I can tell you is what I was feeling when I was young. I was scared, alone and determined that I could raise you by myself. After trying to call Zachary, I decided I couldn't force him to be involved in our lives if he didn't want to. I figured I could be enough for you."

Nicholas twisted around, his eyes red from crying.

The pain in those eyes amplified her own. With her hand trembling, she placed it on his blanket-clad leg. "Your father had joined the army and was posted overseas. I didn't know where. Then you came more than a month early. It was all I could do to handle that. I was wrong and I'm so sorry about that. I should have told him. I should have tried harder to track him down somehow. I should have told you, but I honestly didn't think Zachary wanted anything to do with me." *Which is still true. But he did want to be involved with Nicholas. I can't deny him that.*

Her son's forehead scrunched. "I don't know what to think anymore."

"I can understand that. Can you forgive me?"

He turned away. "I'm tired."

What a mess she'd made of everything because of pride. Zachary was furious with her, and worse, her son was disappointed in her. She'd seen it in his eyes. That look tore her heart in two with guilt.

*Lord, what do I do?*

But no ready answer came to mind. She sat for another minute staring at her child's rigid body beneath the blanket. All she wanted to do was gather him into her arms and hold on to him as she had when he was a little boy. Instead, she settled for leaning over and kissing his cheek.

He shrank away and pulled the blanket totally over his head.

With a deep sigh, she shoved to her feet and trudged toward the hallway. Coming back to her hometown was supposed to be a good move for her and Nicholas. But now her life was in more of a mess than ever before.

The next afternoon before Jordan went to pick up Nicholas from school and go to Zachary's ranch, she strolled down the street to her sister's house and rang the bell.

"I wondered if you would stop by today," Rachel said as she stepped to the side to let Jordan inside.

"Who called you? Mom?"

"This morning I got a call from Granny, then an hour later one from Mom."

Jordan plopped down on her sister's pristine white couch in her formal living room off the foyer. How she managed to keep her home so clean with three kids was a marvel to Jordan. "Where are the twins?"

"At Mother's Day Out at the church. I have to pick them up in half an hour." She sat across from Jordan in a wing chair.

"So I'm assuming you know all the gory details?"

"Yep. What Granny left out, Mom was able to fill me in on. Your usual talkative son didn't say a word to you this morning before school."

Jordan shook her head. "What do I do? You've had more experience than me. I'm desperate."

"I'm not so sure I'm the one you should come to. I'm having problems with Taylor, and I don't see an end in sight. She's thirteen, and we're butting heads."

"What if Nicholas wants to go live with Zachary?" There. She'd said her greatest fear.

"You're going to have to share your son now."

Jordan's fingernails gouged her palms. "If you hadn't sent me to the ranch…" She couldn't finish the sentence. A lump jammed her throat.

"Zachary should be in Nicholas's life."

Jordan stared at her feet. "I know. I should have listened to you."

"Yeah, but then I've been telling you that all your life."

"You never regretted telling Taylor she was adopted?"

"No."

"Does she ask about her biological parents?"

"No, she knows that her dad and I really wanted her. And Nicholas knows how much you love him and wanted him. He'll come around when the newness wears off. Be patient."

"Patient? I'm not very good at that."

Rachel chuckled. "Boy, do I know. That's one of the reasons I sent you to the ranch. It would have only been a matter of time before you and Zachary ran into each other. This way it's over with, and you won't continue to run away from what you should have done eleven years ago."

"A warning would have been good."

"And you wouldn't have gone. I'm not stupid."

Rachel was her big sister but had always been a friend and confidant. The only thing they had ever really argued about was Zachary. "You know Zachary didn't purposefully ignore my calls back then."

"I figured as much. He's a good man. A tad stubborn but then you can be, too."

Jordan pushed to her feet. "I can tell I'm gonna get no sympathy from you."

"When you need it, I'll be here, little sis."

"I'd better go. If I'm late to pick up Nicholas, I'll really get the cold shoulder."

Rachel walked her to the door. "Give it time and pray about it. Nicholas will come around. You two have been through a lot, and he knows you'll always be there for him."

Fifteen minutes later Jordan picked up Nicholas at Key Elementary then headed toward the ranch. Her stomach roiled from the silence in the car. Her damp palms slipped on the steering wheel.

Halfway to their destination, she asked, "How was the last day at school?"

"'Kay."

"Any trouble?"

A grunt was the only answer to that question.

"After we go to the ranch, I thought we would stop and have dinner at The Green Shack. I know how much you've enjoyed it the couple of times we've gone."

Not a peep out of the child who often talked nonstop, especially when he was excited.

"Are you worried about today?"

He shook his head. She would have missed his answer if she hadn't glanced at him.

When the ranch entrance came into view, she wiped her hands one by one on her jeans, then gripped the steering wheel tighter. Sweat popped out on her forehead and upper lip. Maybe Nicholas wasn't worried, but she was. The only good thing about the day was that Zachary's mother wouldn't be there. If she'd only given him Jordan's message, she wouldn't be in this pickle. Then she remembered the first time she'd talked with Becca, who had promised to pass the message on to her mother. She'd only been there visiting. Had Becca done as she promised or had she kept it to herself?

Not sure where to go—the blue house, barn or Zachary's place, Jordan drove past his sister's and the barn. She stopped outside Zachary's white home. The second she parked, Nicholas leaped from the car at the same time the front door swung open. Zachary came out onto the porch, smiling at his son as he raced toward the steps. Nicholas threw his arms around his father's waist.

The sight of their embrace slammed into her chest. This was how it could have been if they'd stayed together. Only, she'd be part of that hug, as well. The scene before her faded away as if she were in someone else's world. Slowly she climbed from her Camaro and strode toward the house, nearly stumbling when Becca came outside. Right behind the woman was Ashley and two younger boys. Lastly Becca's husband appeared, a broad grin on his face as he shook her son's hand.

She'd hoped Zachary would ease her son into his family but most of them were here now. The only thing missing were his parents. Already overwhelmed, she checked behind Becca's husband to make sure no one else was there.

Almost to the bottom stair, Zachary disengaged himself from his family. "You all go on inside. It's a scorcher out here."

Somehow she ended up at the bottom of the steps. She put her foot on the first stair.

Zachary stood before her. "If you don't want to stay, I can bring Nicholas home later this evening."

Meeting his gaze that had softened for a few seconds, she planted her feet on the next step. "That's okay. I don't mind staying." She forced a smile that quivered and fell.

"Suit yourself." He opened the screen door and headed inside.

Leaving Jordan standing on his porch by herself. She wasn't welcome at this little family party, but she didn't care. She was crashing it anyway. She wouldn't lose her son to the Rutgerses.

When she entered the living room, crammed with Zachary's family, she found Nicholas on the couch between Becca and Zachary. The only place for her to sit was a lounger set a little ways from the others—

as though she were purposefully being excluded. She eased into the recliner, its worn comfortableness luring her into relaxation after getting almost no sleep the night before.

She looked around her, caught sight of a magazine about ranching, opened on the table near her elbow. When she drew in a deep breath, she thought she could smell Zachary's earthy scent embedded in the brown leather of the chair. The sense of him surrounding her zapped her. Her heart pounded against her chest. She was tied to Zachary now whether she wanted to be or not. She swiped her hand across the beads of perspiration on her upper lip. All the good times they'd spent together as teenagers paraded across her mind, taunting her with what she'd missed out on.

Becca rose from the couch and approached Jordan. "Would you help me get some drinks in the kitchen."

Jordan peered at her son, laughing at something Mike, Zachary's nine-year-old nephew, said. She nodded and rose, trailing behind the woman toward the kitchen. At the entrance into the room she glanced toward Nicholas. Zachary's pinpoint gaze snared hers and held it for a long moment. The sense of trespassing bathed her in a cold film.

"Which would Nicholas like—apple juice or lemonade?"

Becca's question dragged Jordan from the connection with Zachary. "He loves apple juice."

"So does Ashley but Mike and Cal like lemonade. That's why Zachary keeps both here. My children visit him a lot. This is a second home to them." Becca withdrew glasses from the cabinet. "What about you? Which would you like?"

"Neither."

Becca surveyed the contents of her brother's refrigerator. "There's tea in here, too. I have to admit little else, though."

"I'm not thirsty." Jordan stood in the middle of the kitchen. When Becca retrieved a small tray from a drawer, Jordan wondered why she was there.

"Can you fill those with ice?" Becca gestured toward the tumblers on the counter.

"Sure." Jordan didn't know Zachary's sister very well. When they had been dating, Becca had already been married a year and lived in Oklahoma City. That was why Jordan had been surprised that Becca had answered the phone when she'd called right after she'd found out she was pregnant.

"I thought you could use a breather."

"What do you mean?"

Becca lifted her shoulders in a shrug. "I figure this isn't easy for you."

Zachary's sister's words took Jordan by surprise. "You aren't mad at me?"

The woman paused and studied Jordan for a long moment. "No, not really. I should have asked you some questions when you called all those years ago. I could hear how upset you were. I should have made sure my mother gave Zachary the message."

Becca hadn't kept her call from Zachary. Somehow that comforted Jordan. "Why didn't she?" It might have changed everything.

"When I talked with her last night, she kept telling me she thought she was protecting Zachary from further hurt." Becca gave her a thin smile. "That's Mom for you. She-bear extraordinaire."

But Zachary's mother didn't have the right not to give her son the message. "Your brother doesn't care that I tried calling him."

"He's upset he didn't know about Nicholas until now. He'll get over it."

"I'm not so sure."

"Give him time. All of a sudden he's a father. It's a lot to take in. And you know men. They don't like to deal with emotions. They don't take them out and examine them to death like we do."

Jordan's tension eased. She relaxed against the counter. "He wasn't very good at telling me his feelings when we were teenagers."

"That hasn't changed in eleven years."

That was the crux of the problem. Even if Zachary could get past his anger at her, they had changed quite a bit from when they were two teenagers in love. They were really strangers who shared a son. She suddenly realized she wanted to get to know the man who was her child's father. Maybe there was hope for them.

"Thanks for letting me know not everyone in his family is mad at me."

Becca finished pouring the drinks and put the pitchers back in the near-empty refrigerator. "Nicholas is part of our family now, and you're part of his. I want this to work for everyone. Forgiveness is the only way to go. The Lord has it right. If we don't forgive, all we do is live in the past. I'm a present kind of gal." After handing Jordan two glasses of apple juice, Becca lifted the tray of lemonades. "Those are for Ashley and Nicholas."

Back in the living room, Jordan gave her son and the young girl their drinks, then took her chair again. This time calmness—a remnant from earlier in the kitchen—

cloaked her. Forgiveness. Would Zachary ever be able to do that? Would she, for that matter? She still held scraps of anger toward him, especially when she thought about the pain of his rejection—being scared and alone, waiting for his calls that never came. But then she remembered he'd been clueless about her calls and what little anger was left melted away. She couldn't blame him for something he didn't know.

"We're gonna grill hamburgers for dinner up at our house. I hope you brought a big appetite, Nicholas." Becca set her glass on a coaster on the coffee table.

"I don't eat meat."

"You don't?" Zachary glanced from his son to Jordan. "Are you a vegetarian, too?"

"No, I'm not a purist like Nicholas. I occasionally eat meat."

"Mom tries to support my beliefs as much as possible."

"Okay—" Zachary ran his hand through his hair "—I'm sure we can find something for you to eat."

"I've got peanut butter," Becca piped in.

"I like that."

Mike studied his cousin. "Do you eat pizza?"

"Sure, cheese and a vegetable one."

"Yuck! I hate vegetables." Six-year-old Cal squirmed on the floor by his dad's feet.

"Mom makes a great one." Nicholas peered toward her. "She's the best cook."

Jordan released a slow breath. He might be upset with her right now, but his comments gave her hope she would be able to make it right with him soon. She needed to give her son time to bond with Zachary and his family. She owed Zachary that much.

Rising, she said, "I'll leave you all to enjoy your dinner. Zachary, what time should I come back to pick up Nicholas?"

"I'll bring him home."

"Fine." Overwhelmed by the past week, Jordan hurried from the house, fighting tears just below the surface. At her car she hesitated, staring at Zachary's home. For her son's sake, she and Zachary needed to get along. Could they come to an understanding?

*My life is a mess, and I only have myself to blame.*

Zachary pulled to a stop in front of Jordan's place and glanced at his son in the front seat of his truck. "If your mom says okay, grab your pj's and some clothes for tomorrow. We'll do some riding before some kids come for a lesson."

"Super."

He started to say, "Let me talk with your mother first," when Nicholas hopped down from the cab and raced toward the house.

As Zachary ambled toward the porch, his son announced his plans to Jordan, then scurried away—presumably up the stairs to get his stuff to stay overnight with him. When he mounted the steps, she came out onto the porch.

The light from the house illuminated her concern. Her beauty, which had plagued his dreams many nights, touched his core, tempting him to forget the last eleven years. "I get it that you want to make up for lost time, but you don't have to cram it all into the first few days. Nicholas has a habit of tiring himself out, then he gets sick."

He came to a halt a couple of feet from her, close

enough to get a whiff of her vanilla scent. At least that hadn't changed in eleven years even if just about everything else had. Her fragrance stirred memories best left locked away. Zachary backed away to give himself some space. But he couldn't forget the times he'd held her close, enveloped in the vanilla-laced fragrance. "I'll make sure he doesn't overdo it. He asked if he could. He wants to see what I do. I didn't see any reason to say no."

"How about the fact that I was starting his home-schooling tomorrow?"

"One of the nice things about teaching your child at home is that your schedule is flexible. You decide the when and where."

"I know we have to work out some kind of arrangement, but please run things by me before you say anything to Nicholas. He's been through a lot in his short life." Her voice quivered.

He could never resist the urge in the past to soothe away her concerns. This was no different. "Are you talking about the surgery to repair his heart defect?"

She nodded. "What did he tell you?"

"That his doctor says he's fine now. Fixed."

"That doesn't mean he shouldn't be careful."

"He'll be safe. I just found my son. I'm not gonna let anything happen to him, but I have a lot of catching up to do." He wanted this to work out for Nicholas's sake.

Tears misted Jordan's eyes. "I want this to work out for Nicholas. In order for that to happen, we need to be a team. Can you put aside your anger at me so we can work together for—our son?"

## Chapter Seven

Jordan's unshed tears nearly undid Zachary. His gut tightened as though preparing to be hit. "You want the honest truth?"

"Always."

"I don't know. Yesterday morning I knew nothing about having a son. Then you appear and tell me Nicholas is my child. I'm still trying to digest what you told me. I need time."

"Fair enough." Jordan closed her eyes for a few seconds, a tear leaking out and running down her cheek.

The sight of it jolted him back to another time when they had fought and parted—her going to Savannah while he stayed in Tallgrass licking his wounds. Where would they be now if they had never fought that day or his mother had told him about Jordan's calls?

"Nicholas's welfare is the most important thing to me, so I want this to work. If we fight all the time and use him as a pawn in some game, he'll be the one who ends up hurt the most."

"Agreed. Let's start over. I'm Zachary Rutgers. I raise quarter horses and have a small herd of buffalo on my ranch." He held out his hand, shoving his anger away. He'd loved her at one time—knew she had a good heart. Working as a team—as Nicholas's parents—was what was best for their son.

She fit hers in his grasp and shook it. "I'm Jordan Masterson. I have a graphic design business and as of today I'm homeschooling my child and terrified I'm going to mess it up."

The warm feel of her fingers seared his palm. It took every ounce of willpower not to drop her hand, not to react to her touch, the softness of her skin against his work-toughened flesh. "I'll try to help with the home-schooling. I've picked up some things from Becca. And I know my sister would help you." Releasing her, he inhaled deeply. He could do this—be on friendly terms with Jordan—but he would make sure he guarded his heart. He wouldn't let her hurt him again.

"It'll be all I can do to stay one step ahead of him, especially in math."

"Check with Ian Ferguson about his math group. I know Ian and Alexa are planning to leave after the New Year, but until then it could be a solution to Nicholas's math needs."

"I'll do that. Nancy Baker said something about that when I met with her last week."

The door opened behind Jordan, and Nicholas exited. "I've got everything."

"Let's go, partner."

Jordan stopped their son and hugged him. "I love you, Nicholas. I know you'll behave." She kissed his cheek.

"Ah, Mom." He tugged away and hurried down the stairs toward Zachary's truck.

The crestfallen look on Jordan's face prodded Zachary to move closer and touch her arm. "Just exerting his independence."

"I wish he'd wait a few years. I'm not ready for him to grow up."

At least she'd had the first ten years with Nicholas. Her words drove home the fact he'd lost out on so much of his only child's life. He stepped back from Jordan, stomping down the rising anger. A team—him and Jordan. He would make it work somehow. For their son.

"What do you want for breakfast?" Zachary looked in his refrigerator and saw the few food provisions he had. He should have gone grocery shopping, but he hadn't originally thought that Nicholas would spend the night. "I've got some milk. We could have cereal." He took the carton, opened it and smelled. The rancid aroma of sour milk accosted his nostrils. "On second thought, maybe we could go out for breakfast." He glanced toward his son standing by the kitchen sink.

"That's okay." Nicholas rubbed the sleep from his eyes. "I'll go get dressed."

"Thanks, partner." When his son left the kitchen, Zachary massaged his temples. What else was he forgetting? He wasn't starting out very good as a father. *Note to self: get food in the house. See what Nicholas likes. Find out everything I can from Jordan about him.*

When he heard a knock at the front door, he made his way toward it. Jordan stood on his porch with a sack full of food in her arms. The beat of his heart sped as if he was settling on the back of a bull in the chute— seconds before the gate opened. He moved to the side and allowed her into his house, actually pleased at her appearance.

"I saw your empty refrigerator yesterday and figured you might not have much for breakfast, so here I am. I can make both of you buttermilk pancakes. Okay?" She turned in the foyer and waited for his answer.

She was trying to make the best of their situation. He needed to meet her halfway. "I haven't had pancakes in a long time."

"And you used to love them."

"Still do."

"So does Nicholas." She started for the kitchen.

Zachary followed her and watched from the doorway while she made herself at home, taking the food out of the sack and putting some of it away while setting the rest on the counter to use. The sight of her in his kitchen reconstructed some of his past dreams when he'd thought they would marry. He couldn't emotionally afford those dreams, and yet she fit well into his kitchen.

"Blackberries are in right now. I use them as a topping. Remember that time we went blackberry picking? That snake that slithered among the bushes?" She opened a cabinet and withdrew a mixing bowl, then threw a glance over her shoulder.

"You couldn't move fast enough."

"Right into your arms. All I could think about was getting my feet off the ground," she said with a laugh. "That seems to be my reaction when I see a snake."

The sound of her merriment drew him forward. Crossing the kitchen, he kept his gaze on her. All of a sudden he was whisked back to when he was eighteen, in love with her, spending a morning picking blackberries because she asked him sweetly to help her. Her grandmother was going to make her blackberry jam and needed some fresh ones. He'd been on top of the world, in spite of the snake that had quickly slid away, probably because of Jordan's loud scream.

"I never did get a jar of the jam." He stopped a few feet from her, their looks still entangled together.

"Neither did I." She blinked and averted her head.

"Yeah, you left for art school three weeks later."

The air thickened with charged emotions. Recalling that time brought bittersweet memories to the foreground. Zachary clamped down on his jaw to keep the words from boiling to the surface. Words of recrimination. If only the past had been different, they would be a couple now. If only… He had to stop feeling this way. He needed to live in the present.

"Mom, what are you doing here?"

Jordan whirled around, a grin on her face. "Rescuing your dad with breakfast."

*Your dad.* Zachary liked the sound of that.

Nicholas checked out the ingredients on the counter. "Buttermilk pancakes?"

She nodded.

His son pumped his arm in the air. "Wait till you eat them, Dad."

*Dad!* That was the first time Nicholas had said it. The best sound in the world. It filled him with joy. "Can I do anything to help?"

She waved her hand. "No, you two go somewhere and get to know each other. I'll call you when I've got it fixed."

He studied Jordan for a moment. What was this Jordan like? She wasn't a teenager anymore. He suddenly wanted to know the woman standing before him. Maybe then they could be the team Nicholas needed. "We'll be out on the porch."

"Great. It'll be about fifteen minutes."

Outside Nicholas sat on the top stair next to Zachary. His son set his forearms on his thighs just like him, clasping his hands loosely.

"Did you ask Mom to come?"

"No, but I guess yesterday she saw how pitiful my food supply is."

"She's perceptive like that."

"Yeah, and better organized than I am."

"I find if you're organized it saves a lot of useless time looking for things you've misplaced."

Zachary chuckled. "You're one hundred percent right. You two will have to rub off on me."

"How did you and Mom meet?"

The question flooded him with memories—all good ones. "I was on the football team in high school. A fullback. It was the first game, and not far from where I was sitting on the bench waiting for the offense to get their turn to play, I spied your mom cheering. She was the new one on the squad. I caught her gaze. As we were staring at each other, she missed her move and the girl next to her ran into her. She blushed a nice shade of red. Matched her uniform. Of course, after the game I had to apologize."

"So you two started dating?"

The journey into the past prodded good memories into his mind. But she wasn't the same. He wasn't the same, either. Zachary kneaded the cords of his neck. Too tight—tight as the cinch on a saddle. "Well, not exactly. It took me a few weeks to wear her down. She was embarrassed in front of the student body. A piece of advice for the future. Not the best way to meet a gal."

"You played football. I don't know anything about the game. Isn't it just a bunch of guys trying to hurt each other?"

"I can see where you might think that. When I played, I learned teamwork."

Nicholas's gaze skimmed down his length. "I'm too small to play football."

"The game isn't for everyone. There are other sports if you want to do something like that. Soccer doesn't depend on size. Have you thought of that?"

His son shook his head. "I'm not very coordinated."

"I could work with you if you want to practice handling a ball." Zachary placed his hand on his son's shoulder. "But you don't have to. It's your call. Just know I'll help you any way you want."

Nicholas flashed him a huge grin.

In that second a bond formed between him and his son. Emotions he'd guarded welled up into his throat, sealing words inside—words he wasn't good at saying.

"Breakfast is served." Jordan stood at the screen door.

Zachary swallowed several times and breathed in the coffee-laced air. "You fixed coffee, too?" The wobble in his voice hung suspended for a few seconds between them.

"Sure. I know how you like it. I pitched yours." She winced. "I'm gonna have to teach you how to brew a good cup."

She'd always been a good cook. "I may take you up on that." Zachary rose, brushing his hand down his jeans.

Nicholas did the same thing, dust flying everywhere. Zachary needed to sweep his steps. His son began coughing. Jordan started toward him but stopped halfway there and remained still.

"Did you bring apple juice?" Nicholas asked after sucking in several deep breaths.

"Your dad still had some left from yesterday. I poured you a glass. It's on the table."

Nicholas hurried into the house while Zachary said, "Housekeeping has never been my forte."

"To tell you the truth it isn't mine, either. Give me something to cook and I'm happy. Give me a dust rag and I find a way to get out of it."

Zachary swiped a hand across his forehead. "Whew, I'm relieved. It's bad enough I don't cook well, but I hated to fall short in every area."

Jordan paused in the foyer. "This isn't a competition."

"I know but I've spent a good part of my life competing—first on the football field and then in the rodeo ring."

"What did you two talk about?"

He grinned and winked at her. "How you and I met."

A faint blush tinted her cheeks, again reminding him of their first encounter. "Did you mention I fell flat on my bottom in front of a stadium full of people?"

"Sort of, but I took full blame for the accident."

"Oh, that is so reassuring." Jordan marched past him.

He admired how cute she was when she blushed. Putting the brakes on the direction his thoughts were going, he shook his head then proceeded into the kitchen a few steps behind her. Friends—that was all they could be now.

"Where have you guys been? I'm starving."

"Did you wash your hands?" Jordan asked as she sat across from her son.

Zachary diverted his path to the sink and made sure he did exactly what Jordan had asked Nicholas. He had to set a good example for his son.

"Yes, I did. I know how important good hygiene is. So many of our germs are spread by hand contact. That's why they stress washing so much during flu season."

Zachary listened to his son launch into the health risk when people didn't follow that simple rule, even quoting a medical source. That was when he knew he was in over his head and drowning.

Two days later on Saturday afternoon Jordan turned into the ranch to pick up her son after he'd spent another night at Zachary's. When Nicholas had returned home after the first time, all he could talk about was how neat it was to own a ranch. He had her take him to the library and he got every book he could find on the subject of horses. As she pulled up next to Zachary's Ford F-150 truck near the barn, she wondered how the joint grocery store trip went last evening. He had wanted Nicholas to go with him so he got all their son's favorite food.

As Jana strolled with Alexa toward an SUV, Jordan climbed from her Camaro and waved. With quick steps she covered the area between them. "I'm glad I caught you before you left."

Alexa grinned. "I hear you're taking the plunge and homeschooling Nicholas."

"Yeah, and I'm suddenly freaking out. What if I don't

do a good job? What was I thinking that I could teach my child? I haven't had any training at all. This week was my first, and I felt so out of my comfort zone."

"You aren't alone. Ian told me he felt the same way when he first started. Probably still does."

"But he has you. You're almost through with your education degree."

Alexa leaned close as Jana climbed into the front seat of the SUV. "I have my doubts at least once a week. It's a big decision to become solely responsible for a child's education. The fact you don't take it lightly means you'll do fine."

"I was hoping to catch you today. I want to sign Nicholas up for Ian's new class."

"Great. I'll tell him. It starts next week on Wednesday at one."

Releasing a sigh, Jordan relaxed. "At least that's one worry taken care of. But then I'll have to relearn algebra all over again in order to help him. I bought a book this morning. It's been years since I had any."

"If you get stuck, I'm sure Ian will help you." Alexa opened her door and settled behind the steering wheel. "You could even take the class with Nicholas."

"Thanks. I'll think about that." Jordan headed forward. That was one problem she could mark off her long list. She'd started reading the curriculum she'd borrowed from Nancy. If it fit Nicholas, she would purchase the books and use them as a framework to teach him. Having a structure at least made her feel better— like a pilot having a flight plan.

Inside the barn she paused at the entrance to scan the area for her son. Out the back double doors she glimpsed him with Zachary. As she ambled toward them, Zachary demonstrated how to rope a steer by using a bale of hay with a cow head made of plastic stuck in one end.

When Nicholas took his rope and swung it over his head from right to left, Zachary said, "Keep swinging, but bring it out in front of you and remember when you release it to point your finger toward the steer."

Nicholas let go and the loop landed on the hay. "I don't think I can do this."

"Yes, you can. It just takes practice." Zachary released his rope, and it sailed over the horn and around the fake steer's head.

"And why would you want to do it?" Jordan asked as she came up to the pair.

Eyes round, Nicholas stared at Zachary. "It's part of being a cowboy."

"A cowboy? Since when did you want to be one?" The last time she'd talked with her son, he'd wanted to be an engineer. Of course, that was before he'd found out Zachary was his father.

Her son straightened, his shoulders back. "I want to help Dad on the ranch. I've got to know these things."

The second Nicholas said *Dad* Zachary beamed, crinkling the corners of his eyes. "I was showing him how to throw a rope. He was asking me about some of the activities I've done in a rodeo."

"Rodeo! No, sir. You won't go near a rodeo."

"Why not? Once I learn to ride, I can do all kinds of things. I've seen some videos on the internet. There's barrel racing, for one."

There were those words again. What was it about dangerous sports and men? The time Zachary had flown off his horse, racing, and crashed into the dirt flashed through her mind. For long seconds he hadn't moved, and it seemed as if her heart had stopped beating for that time. When he finally had stirred, he'd broken his arm. Jordan stuffed her hands into her jeans pockets to still their trembling. The image of Zachary injured blurred with a similar picture of her son, lying still, in pain. She couldn't separate the two in her mind. The insight stunned her. Did she still have deep feelings for Zachary?

He clasped Nicholas on the shoulder. "I think that's enough practice for today. Why don't you go say good-bye to Chief?"

Her son peered from Zachary to her then back. "Sure. I'll mosey on over to the paddock. Let me know when you two finish jawing."

Jordan's mouth fell open at the sound of Nicholas trying to imitate some cowboy from a B movie. "What have you done to my son?"

"Nothing. He wanted me to show him the ropes of being a rancher today. He rode with me to check some fences, helped me fix one section. We stacked hay bales. He learned to muck out a stall."

"Muck out a stall? Nicholas?" He rarely got down and dirty.

"Yep, little lady, you've got that right." Hooking his thumbs in his waistband, Zachary winked at her.

"I can't believe…" Her words spluttered to a halt like a runaway calf roped by a cowboy.

Nicholas was a scholar. He lived in books and loved to read and study. Yes, he should do some physical activity, but mucking a stall and stacking hay bales was hard work. Filthy work. "I agreed that my son could learn to ride a horse, but that was all. Nothing else beyond that and certainly nothing that might lead him to believe he could perform in a rodeo. Look what happened to you." She gestured toward Zachary's leg that had been broken while riding a bull, bred to buck and twist and trample anyone in its way. At least that was what Nicholas had told her.

"I zigged when I should have zagged." Although he shrugged, the set of his shoulders sank back into a tensed stance. "It happens sometimes to a bull rider. I knew the risk when I took up the profession." If he'd known what he could have lost—his ability to have children—would he have still risked riding a bull? He'd loved the thrill. For eight seconds on the back of a bull, he'd come alive. He hadn't felt that way—like anything was possible—since he and Jordan had dated. Now he knew anything was possible only through the Lord.

"My son isn't gonna do anything remotely like that. Is that what you want for Nicholas?"

He pressed his lips together for a few seconds, causing a quiver in his facial muscle. "I don't know my son well enough to start dreaming his future. I do know I will not dictate what he does but guide him."

She stepped back. "Ha! This from a man who has been a father for half a week. Walk in my shoes for a few years or for that matter months then tell me you won't worry about his choices and try and change the ones that aren't good."

"Hey, guys, you're shouting," Nicholas yelled from the fence.

She moved within inches of Zachary and lowered her voice. "He's fragile. He gets sick easily and doesn't need to do a lot of physical activity. Just a little."

"Why? He was fine today. I thought his heart defect was fixed." Was there something he didn't know? He was discovering so much about Nicholas—and Jordan. What had made her so afraid of life? He wanted to know. He wanted to get reacquainted with Jordan. Stunned by the thought, he curled his hands into fists and jammed them into his pockets.

"It is, but we still go to the cardiologist for checkups. He has one with his new doctor in a week in Tulsa."

Zachary folded his arms over his chest. "I'm going with you. Let's talk to his doctor about how much activity Nicholas can do and what kind. Let him decide." Nicholas was his one chance at being a father. He had to know his son would be okay. He narrowed his look and dared her to take the challenge.

"Okay. A deal. If the doctor says he can do more, I'll consider it."

The second she agreed, he thought of being in a car for two hours with Jordan. He didn't like the emotions Jordan stirred alive in him. He didn't want to remember the past, to care for her. That gave her the power to hurt him all over again. "No, Nicholas will then have the choice. He's my son, too." His gaze strayed to their child. "I'm warning you now that Nicholas wants to ride in the barrel race during the HHH Junior Rodeo competition next month. He's asked me to help him. There are two events set. One for beginners and another for advanced riders. He'll be able to do the beginner one. He's a natural when it comes to riding."

"Why can't he run in some other race like the fifty-yard dash?"

"Because he told me he doesn't run fast and isn't strong. I think he believes being on a horse makes him more equal physically to the other kids. It requires a certain amount of skill, which he thinks he can learn."

"He probably can if he sets his mind to it."

"Speaking of mind, just how smart is Nicholas?"

"When he was tested, his IQ was one hundred sixty-two."

Zachary whistled. "I'm gonna have to hustle to keep up with him."

"Welcome to my world. There are words he'll throw out when telling me about something he's read that I've got to go and look up their definition."

Her chuckles sprinkled the air with her amusement. The sound reminded Zachary of a time when they had been carefree teens dating, falling in love. He couldn't shake the question: what could have happened between them if he'd received her messages?

But he hadn't. She was a good mother—a bit overprotective but Nicholas was a fine young man. Jordan had always wanted three or four children, and she should have them. He couldn't give her what she always talked about. He had to accept that fact and try to keep his distance.

## Chapter Eight

"Hi, Granny. What are you doing out here?" That evening Nicholas plopped down next to his great-grandmother on the porch swing.

"Enjoying the beautiful evening while waiting for my friend. How did you enjoy your day with your dad?"

"I'm learning everything I can about ranching. Did you know that Dad has a pregnant mare? She should give birth any day. I hope I'm there when she does. I've seen videos, but I'd like to see it in real life. The more I'm around the animals the more I'm thinking of being a vet instead of an engineer."

"That's a wonderful profession. So you don't have dreams of going on the rodeo circuit like your dad?"

Nicholas shook his head. "Me? I found a clip on-line of when my dad got hurt at the National Finals." A shudder rattled down him as if he was in his dad's truck bumping over rough terrain.

"Did your mom see it?"

"No. She would freak out. It made me think twice about learning to ride. But then he was on a bull. A horse is different." Nicholas remembered the feel of power beneath him, the sense of freedom when he'd ridden. "I like how I feel when I'm riding."

Granny patted his leg. "Well, a word of advice, don't let your mom see that clip. She *will* freak out. She used to when Zachary was in a rodeo when they were in high school. She hasn't totally learned that the Lord is in control. She still tries to control everything."

"I know." Nicholas leaned against the side of the swing, fitting his chin in his palm. "Dad told me how he met Mom today. When he talked about it, he smiled. There was a look on his face that makes me think he still likes Mom even though they fight."

"They're fighting?" One of Granny's penciled-in eyebrows rose.

"I heard them today, fighting over me. I don't want to be the reason they're arguing."

"Then we need to do something about that."

"What?"

"How about we give them something else to think about? It's time those two got together for good. They're meant to be a couple. They just don't know it."

Nicholas angled toward Granny. "Fix them up? I like it. What can we do?"

"Well—" she rubbed her chin "—let me think a second. Maybe you could have them both take you somewhere."

"Dad's going with us to Tulsa this week to see my cardiologist."

"Good. That's a start." Granny snapped her fingers. "I've got it. Homecoming at Tallgrass High School is in two weeks. Get your dad and mom to take you to the game. You know your dad played football?"

"He told me. I guess I could. I've never understood

the lure of the game, but maybe if I went with Dad, I could see what the big deal is."

"Yeah, a lot of folks around here live for the games on Friday nights."

"We'll be in the middle of a lot of people in the stands. How's that going to help?"

"Time spent together is good. They need to get to know each other again. A lot has happened in eleven years." A brilliant smile lit his great-grandmother's face, the dark twinkle illuminating her mischief. "And I'll get them to take Mr. Bateman and me to the Alumni Homecoming Dance the following night."

"You're going to a dance?"

Straightening, she peered down her nose at Nicholas, both eyebrows lifting. "I'll have you know I'm eighty years young and can still dance."

"I think this can work. I'll say something on the trip to Tulsa." Nicholas hugged Granny, kissing her cheek. "You're the best."

Two patches of red colored her face. She looked beyond Nicholas. The impish gleam metamorphosed into a sparkle of delight. "My date is here. Help me up."

As Nicholas assisted his great-grandmother to her feet, a thin, balding man with a matching glimmer in his brown eyes ascended the steps to the porch. "Do you want me to get your walker?"

"I've hidden that thing. I'm perfectly fine getting around on my own. And don't you forget it, young man."

"I won't, Granny."

After finishing her meal, Jordan sat back in her chair at the Osage Restaurant within Gilcrease Museum and stared out the floor-to-ceiling window that afforded a panoramic view of the surrounding hills. Across from her Zachary savored his last few bites. He glanced up and found her staring at him. She quickly returned her attention to the beautiful scenery outside. She enjoyed watching Zachary. Always had.

Nicholas stuffed the last of his cheese pizza into his mouth then finished off his milk. "May we stop by the museum gift shop before we leave? I want to see if they have any books about the tribes that settled in this area. I haven't read much on them yet, but don't you think that should be something I study, Mom? Oklahoma is unique. Over half the state was Indian Territory until the early twentieth century."

"I remember once in elementary school we reenacted a land rush like they did to settle part of Oklahoma." Jordan sank back in her chair, relaxed despite Zachary being so close. The visit to the cardiologist had gone well. Nicholas was happy. Today for a short time at the doctor's she'd felt as though they were truly a family. She'd liked that feeling.

"Some people cheated and jumped the gun. They snuck onto the land ahead of time and staked their claim. Those folks were called Sooners, and that's where the name Sooner State came from." Zachary lifted his iced tea and took the last few swallows of it.

"Isn't the University of Oklahoma's football team called the Sooners? They have a good football tradition there."

Surprised by her son's comment, Jordan stared at him. "I didn't know you followed college football."

"I haven't, but Granny told me football is important to this area so I've been reading about it. I think I have most of the rules figured out, but I'd like to go to a game. Granny said something about Tallgrass High School where you two went is having its homecoming game next Friday night. Will you take me?" Nicholas swung his gaze from her to Zachary. "It would be fun to go together."

The last sentence thrown out so casually made Jordan shift and study Zachary's suddenly unreadable expression. Going to a football game with Zachary would certainly bring back memories of how it had once been between them. Was that wise? "I don't—"

"Please, Mom, Dad."

"Sure, why not. I had planned to attend, and it would be easy for me to swing by and pick up you two."

"That's fine with me." There was no way she would be the one to say no, not with her son looking eagerly at her. But the idea of football and Nicholas didn't go together. She would go for no other reason than to make sure her son didn't decide he should play the game like his father had. Picturing kids twice Nicholas's body mass barreling into him sent a shudder through her. But she was concerned visiting their old high school haunts would make her dream of a future with Zachary. A risk she would have to take.

"I do have a question." Nicholas's forehead crinkled. "How come it's called football? From what I've found you use your foot more in a game like soccer than you do in football."

"You're right. And in other parts of the world soccer is called football."

"It makes more sense," Nicholas said in a serious tone.

"What would you call it?" Zachary took out his money to pay the check.

"Tackleball. It seems like that is the focus of the game."

Leave it for her son to question the name of a national sport. "I think you have something there."

"Ready to go to the museum shop?" Zachary rose.

Nicholas hopped up and hurried ahead of them out of the restaurant.

"I guess he's ready," Zachary said, the laugh lines at the sides of his eyes deepening.

"Dangle a book in front of him and he can move fast." Jordan paused outside the gift shop in the museum hall. "You aren't gonna encourage him to play football, are you?"

"No, in fact, we talked about it last week. I suggested if he wanted to play a sport soccer might be a better fit. But ultimately I want Nicholas to do what he wants. If his heart isn't in it, it's a waste of time."

"A parent has to sometimes say no to certain activities."

"True, but there's nothing wrong with soccer. Yes, he could get hurt, but he also could crossing a street." His gaze fastened onto hers, narrowed slightly. "But soccer isn't what you're really worried about. You think he'll want to participate in rodeo events like I did."

"Just because the doctor said exercise would be great for Nicholas doesn't mean he should do that." Zachary's triumphant expression at the cardiologist's office played across her mind. She drew herself up taller.

He cut the space between them. "Do you think I'd purposely put our child in danger?"

The low rumble of his voice rolled over her. "Well, no."

"A lot of events in a junior rodeo are safe. As safe

as any other sport. You won't always be able to protect him. What parents do is prepare their children the best they can and then leave the rest in the Lord's hands. What are you really afraid of?"

*Being on the outside looking in. Losing Nicholas to you. Losing control of my life.* But she couldn't tell Zachary that. When she'd nearly lost her son, she'd clung to anything that she could control. She set up a routine for herself and Nicholas, and it had worked until she'd moved back to Tallgrass. Now she was struggling to fit homeschooling into their lives. And to fit Zachary into their lives. "What any mother would be afraid of."

As she started for the gift shop, he stilled her movements with a hand on her arm. "I want what is best for our son, too."

She could barely concentrate on what Zachary was saying. His touch branded her his. She was going to get hurt.

"I'm just finding out how bright he is. But I also see his shortcomings. He isn't comfortable with his peers. He's even told me that. Thankfully he and Randy have hit it off, but then Randy is a smart kid, too, so they talk the same language. He has trouble doing things with his hands like tying a knot for his rope. He isn't in the best physical shape. He probably sits too much at a computer. He needs to be more active."

His words slammed her defenses in place. "He's not playing video games. He's researching. He uses the computer for just about everything because his handwriting is not legible." Needing to sever their physical connection, she pulled her arm from his grasp and backed away. This way she could think straight while around Zachary.

"I'm being realistic here. I'm not putting him down. Like everyone, he has strengths and weaknesses."

She knew that. And what Zachary said was true. Her son needed to work on his social skills as well as his fine motor ones. He needed to become more physical.

Zachary moved again into her personal space and glanced over her shoulder into the store before he returned his gaze to her. "I may not have the book smarts like Nicholas and you, but I can help our son. Let me help him become more active. Get more involved in life and the people around him."

For a moment she wanted to protest. She was doing a good job with her son. Then she remembered the doctor had suggested he do more physically, that he was perfectly healthy now. Finally she said, "I'm doing the best I can."

"And anyone who sees you two together sees the bond you all have. I'm continually amazed at how smart Nicholas is, and you've cultivated that. You're willing to give up your time to homeschool him because he isn't thriving in a public school. No one doubts the type of mother you are."

His praise lifted her shoulders, raised her chin a notch. He thought she was a good mother. That meant a lot—perhaps too much.

"But I want to be his father. I want to share equally in raising him. But you're still holding on so tight."

His words deflated her, lashing like a whip against a horse's flank. She blew a breath out. "You don't pull any punches, do you?"

"No, this is too important. I'll make you a promise. I won't let Nicholas do anything he isn't prepared to do. He's too important for me to do that."

"I'll try my best. Now I'd better go get Nicholas. It's gonna be late when we get back to Tallgrass." Needing some distance from him, Jordan quickly entered the store. Each day she was with Zachary more of her heart surrendered to him. And that scared her.

Zachary stayed in the hall, waiting while Nicholas paid for a book he wanted to buy. This was his one shot at being a father. He didn't want to screw it up.

*Am I doing the right thing, Lord? How does a parent know if he is?* He felt like the first time he rode a bull: ill prepared. In over his head, careening toward disaster.

"Look at the book I got, Dad. It's all about the tribes that settled this part of Oklahoma."

His son's contagious smile warmed Zachary. He'd make mistakes—what parents didn't—but Nicholas would always know he loved him. "My great-grandmother was part of the Osage tribe."

"Really? Then that's the first one I'll research."

"C'mon. We need to get on the road. I have a pregnant mare to check on."

"Will you let me know when she's going to give birth?"

"Sure."

Nicholas turned toward his mother. "Then you can bring me out to the ranch. Maybe I can be there for it. It could be a biology lesson."

Jordan nabbed Zachary's look. "If it's okay with you."

"It could be in the middle of the night. I try to bring my pregnant mares into the barn and keep an eye on them when their time gets close. Usually there isn't a problem, but my stock is important to me. I like to be there if something goes wrong." He held the door open for Nicholas and Jordan at the exit to the museum.

"That's okay with me. I can sleep the next day." Nicholas clutched his book to his chest.

"How about you, Jordan?"

"Sure. I'll have you call my cell so it won't disturb Mom or Granny. I'll warn them about what's going on so they won't worry if we aren't there in the morning."

So much for his vow not to spend time with Jordan. First the football game next Friday and now the birth of a foal. He found it hard to separate his feelings for his son and Jordan. And worse, her appeal was as strong as it was when he was a teenager. He wasn't the best man for Jordan. He couldn't give her what she wanted or needed—the same as in the past. She'd fled Tallgrass because she'd wanted something different. What was stopping her from doing that again? Fear and doubts intruded into his thoughts. Although he couldn't keep his distance, that didn't mean his heart would be involved.

"So how has it been so far?" Rachel sat where Zachary had been before halftime of the homecoming game on Friday night.

"Lonely." Jordan sipped her soft drink, watching the band march off the field.

"You've got thousands of people around you."

"Yeah, but Zachary and Nicholas deserted me to go to the locker room during halftime."

"I guess it pays to be male and know the head coach."

"I forgot that Zachary was good friends with him in high school."

"Feeling left out?"

Jordan slid a glare at her older sister. "Well, no, but

even when I was cheerleading I didn't particularly like the game. At least with them here, the time goes fast."

"Ah, who are you missing more, Nicholas or Zachary?"

Heat scored Jordan's face. She gave Rachel another glare, hoping the set of her features conveyed the topic was off-limits.

Her sister held up her hands, palms outward. "Hey, it was just a question. A valid one at that."

"Don't you have to get back to the concession stand or something?"

"I only had to man it for the first half. I can join you all and watch the game." Rachel tucked her purse down by her feet. "I'm not into football much, but my daughter, believe it or not, is and I had to bring her. She's off with her friends right now. You know how thirteen-year-olds are. They want nothing to do with their moms. I offered to work concession as an excuse to be near Taylor."

"Ha!" Jordan waggled a finger at her sister. "I'm not the only one who overprotects their child."

"I have good reason. Taylor tends to get into trouble all the time. When has Nicholas?"

"He forgot to shut the gate last week, and Tucker got out of the backyard."

"I wish that was the worst thing my daughter did."

Jordan studied her sister's worried expression, eyebrows drawn together. "Can I help?"

"Actually I'm thinking of looking into homeschooling if things don't turn around at school for Taylor. She had to serve detention yet again—four times so far this year. I don't know her anymore."

"Since I haven't been doing it long, I would suggest

you talk with Dr. Baker or even Zachary's sister. They know a lot more than I do."

"I thought homeschooling was going okay for you."

"It is. I think. Never thought I would be sitting in on a math class again. But when Nicholas is taking algebra at Ian's house, I'm right there, too."

"Maybe once he learns it, he can help Taylor, who is struggling in math."

Jordan caught sight of Nicholas running out onto the field with the football team. Zachary trailed behind him, talking with the coach. Her son's grin could be seen all the way up in the bleachers where she sat near the top.

"Nicholas looks happy. Zachary has been good for him," Rachel said.

*Yeah, he has.* "I just wish things were better between us."

"You two been fighting? I thought you told me you were working as a team."

"Yeah, but there's still a barrier between us. I don't think he's ever going to forgive me for not telling him about Nicholas."

"Give him time."

"You know me. Impatient. I want to control everything." Jordan tried to laugh it off, but the sound came out choked. She wanted more from Zachary. She didn't want to be just friends. She nearly dropped her soda. The realization astounded her. The intensity that cinched her insides chilled her. If she wasn't careful, she would fall in love with Zachary all over again.

"I hear Granny and Doug are double-dating with you and Zachary tomorrow night."

"Have you ever felt manipulated by our grandmother?"

Rachel smiled. "All the time. She's a pro."

"She didn't say anything to me. She asked Zachary when he brought Nicholas back home a few days ago. Granny said something about Doug's car not working or some such excuse that she and her beau needed a ride to the Alumni Homecoming Dance. And how going to the dance with me and him would be perfect. I could have died from embarrassment."

"But Zachary is taking you? Have I misunderstood?"

"Only because Granny worked her wiles on him. He could never resist her."

"So you're not looking forward to tomorrow night?"

Jordan watched Nicholas and Zachary making their way toward her in the stands. "I've already had several friends from high school ask us if we're dating again. It'll be far worse at the dance."

"Which is worse? It's not an actual date, or that your friends think you two are dating again?"

Thankfully Zachary and Nicholas arrived before Jordan had to answer her sister's question. She hated to admit out loud it was because it wasn't an actual date— one that Zachary had thought to ask her on.

"Mom, did you see me with the team?" Her son held up a football. "They all signed it for me."

"That's wonderful," Jordan said as Nicholas sat on the other side of Rachel and Zachary folded his long length in the place next to Jordan.

Zachary bent close to her ear. "You don't have to worry about him wanting to sign up for football tomorrow. He told me he was having a good time, but there was no way he would stand in front of a guy larger than him and let him mow him down. Football is not a sensible game to our son."

His breath tickled her neck. She shivered. How was she going to make it through tomorrow night?

Later that night, Zachary laid his son on his bed in his room. Nicholas stirred, his eyes fluttering open for a few seconds then closing. Rolling onto his side, he hugged his pillow.

Zachary sat beside Nicholas and untied his tennis shoes. "He wants a pair of cowboy boots." With a glance toward Jordan behind him, he gauged her reaction to that statement. A flicker of something blinked in and out of her eyes. A composed expression fell into place. "I told him I would take him to buy them."

Her neutral facial features didn't change. "That makes sense if he's going to be at the ranch a lot. He already has the cowboy hat. He might as well have the boots."

When Jordan approached the bed, he could smell the vanilla scent she always wore. Memories rushed forward. He shook his head and rose. Inhaling cleansing breaths, he watched Jordan bend over, kiss Nicholas and then pull a blanket up to his shoulders. Tender caresses. Loving gestures. Remembered ones.

She turned on his night-light and switched off the overhead one. "He's gonna sleep soundly tonight. He's exhausted."

"Yeah. One minute he was talking in the backseat and the next he was conked out."

"That's our son. One hundred percent whatever he does." Jordan descended the stairs to the first floor. "He really enjoyed meeting the team."

*Our son.* They shared a child. The idea still amazed him. He'd given up hope of ever having a child. "And now you don't have to worry he's gonna play football anytime soon. Did you see him wince every time the quarterback got sacked?"

As she ambled toward the front door, she threw him a grateful smile, a shade of relief leaking into her eyes. "Yeah. I'd forgotten how much I hated seeing you play. I held my breath whenever you were tackled."

"That's part of the game."

She tsked. "Men and their sports."

"Women play sports, too."

"We're not generally out on the football field tackling each other."

"True." He stepped out onto the porch and swung around to face her. "It's nice to see some things haven't changed. You're still a softie."

"And proud of it."

The tilt of her lifted chin, the sparkle in her eyes brought back more memories. Ones he couldn't hold at bay. Her challenging him to a horse race she knew she would lose. She'd only been riding a few months, but he had most of his life. Or the time she'd played a practical joke on him that had backfired. She'd laughed at herself, drenched with water, her long blond curls limp about her face, her dark eyes dancing as she had backed away from the hose.

"Oh, that reminds me. Nicholas wants to bring Tucker to the ranch next time he goes. He thinks his dog will enjoy the space to run." She shifted from one foot to the other.

"Sure, we can try it. If Tucker gets along with the other animals, he'll be fine."

Jordan moved out onto the porch, the light from the

foyer not quite reaching her face. "Are you all right about taking Granny and Doug to the dance?"

"Are you kidding? I can't wait to see your grand-mother dancing."

"She told me once she was quite a ballroom dancer, but since she has trouble walking, I don't think she'll do much tomorrow evening."

"I have a feeling your grandmother can do just about anything she sets her mind to."

Her laughter echoed in the night. Its sound washed over him in more remembrances of shared amusement and lured him closer to her. He cupped her face still hidden in the shadows and wished the barriers between them were gone. He couldn't trust the feelings stirring deep in his heart.

"You do realize Granny manipulated us into tak-ing her?"

Her question came out in a breathless rush that jolted his heartbeat into a faster tempo. "Yes, from the begin-ning. This isn't really a double date."

Beneath his palm she tensed. "Yeah, we're just—" there was a long pause "—friends."

Her words unsettled him. He wanted more and couldn't risk it. Nicholas was not enough of a reason to take their relationship any further than friendship. And there were barriers to anything more. "Just friends," he repeated as though he needed to emphasize it to him-self rather than Jordan.

She began to pull back. His hand tightened. She stilled, the rapid rise and fall of her chest attesting to her charged emotions. Ones that mirrored his. He wanted to kiss her. To feel one more time her lips against his. For old times' sake.

## Chapter Nine

The direction of Zachary's thoughts brought him up short. Falling back into that old pattern wouldn't be good for either one. They had their chance once, and it hadn't worked out. He had to remember that.

He backed away, his hand dropping to his side. "I'd better go." Another foot back. "I'll see Nicholas for his riding lesson. There's a place I wanted to show Nicholas and the others." His palms sweaty, he buried them into the depths of his front pockets. "You can come if you want. You might enjoy seeing the place."

"What is it?" Jordan moved into the stream of light from the foyer.

He still wanted to kiss her. His gaze fastened on her lips. "My secret."

She flinched when he said the word *secret*. That evasive flicker he'd seen a moment before blazed a second. Died. "I can't. Alexa is taking Nicholas for me."

"How about I bring him home when I come to pick you and Granny up tomorrow evening?" Disappointment edged his voice. He heard it and prayed she didn't. "He can help me get ready. I've got to find my suit."

"At least you don't have to go buy a dress. Rachel has decided to give me her expert advice after looking through my closet and declaring I have nothing to wear."

Her full lips, set in a slight pout, enticed him. "See you tomorrow." He spun on his heel and hurried toward his truck before he changed his mind and dragged her into his arms.

Slipping into his cab, he gripped the steering wheel. He hadn't thought much about the dance until now. Even if Granny had manipulated him and Jordan into taking her and Doug, this was a date in everyone's eyes—even his. The implications quaked through him. He shored up his defenses against Jordan's lure. He didn't want to be hurt a second time by her.

"Mom, why do I have to do schoolwork?" Nicholas shouted from the den where he sat at his grandmother's desk. "We have to go to the ranch in an hour."

Jordan entered the room with a refreshed glass of iced tea. "Then you have an hour to finish the essay."

"But it's Saturday."

"The beauty of homeschooling is we have the freedom to work anytime we need to."

"I hate writing."

"I know. That's why we're working on it."

"But, Mom—"

"We can skip the riding lesson today if you need more time."

"I can tell you the strengths and weaknesses of the North and South during the Civil War. I'm a lousy speller. You know how long it takes me to find a word."

"All I want is your rough draft. Then Monday we'll edit it together."

Nicholas sighed loudly, the sound expelled from his pouting lips. And just in case she didn't hear the first one, he did it again. He stared at the computer screen and typed a few words then resumed staring.

"I'm leaving with Aunt Rachel. We're taking Granny with us shopping. Alexa has volunteered to take you with them to the ranch. I'm letting Nana know you can't go if you don't have your essay done."

Nicholas grumbled something under his breath.

Jordan decided to let it go. He did just about everything easily and well except writing. Grammar and spelling came hard to him. Putting his ideas into words on paper was a long-drawn-out process. Like other activities involving his fine motor skills, he avoided writing if at all possible.

After Jordan told her mother about the assignment that Nicholas needed to finish, Rachel arrived to take Granny and her shopping. Their grandmother insisted on not using her walker. She did take her cane.

"My flowered dress is perfectly good for the dance." Granny sat in the back with her black purse on her lap.

"Don't you want to look your best tonight for Doug?" Rachel pulled out of the driveway.

"Nonsense. I could come in a sack and Doug wouldn't care."

"Granny, you might as well give up if you're going to cling to that attitude. Rachel is on a mission to outfit us for this dance." Jordan turned around and looked at her grandmother. "Remember this evening is your idea."

"One I'm starting to regret. All I wanted to do was get you and Zachary together."

"Granny!" Jordan mocked a severity she didn't really feel. How could she be upset when she herself was starting to want more from Zachary than friendship?

"Oh, hush, child. You knew exactly what I was up to from the beginning. Someone had to shake some sense into that young man of yours."

"Zachary isn't my young man."

"Yes, he is. He just doesn't know it. We'll get him to see it."

"We will?" Jordan swallowed hard.

Granny waved her hand in the air. "You two were meant to be together eleven years ago, but pride and stubbornness got in the way. That needs to change. Neither one is good for a relationship. Remember I was married for thirty-seven years. Happily, I might add."

"I think Zachary might have something to say about your matchmaking."

"Child, he'll come to his senses soon enough."

*Will he?* Jordan remembered how he backed away the evening before. She'd been sure he was going to kiss her and he hadn't. She'd wanted him to, and when he hadn't, frustration had deluged her.

Dressed in a classic black sheath with three-inch-high heels, Jordan descended the stairs at her house on Saturday night. Her gaze connected with Zachary's as he stood at the bottom waiting for her. When he smiled, all she could think about was her senior prom and the same look of admiration that glimmered in his eyes. Her legs weakened. She gripped the railing to keep herself from melting at the heart-stopping expression on his face that for an instant wiped away eleven years. This wasn't prom—just the Alumni Homecoming Dance.

They weren't teenagers in love. Sadness pricked her for a brief moment.

He held out his hand to her, and she settled hers in his. "You look beautiful."

She took in his dark Western-style suit with a black string tie and cowboy boots. "You don't look half bad yourself."

He tipped his Stetson toward her. "Well, thank ya, ma'am."

Nicholas escorted Granny from the back of the house where her bedroom was. He grinned from ear to ear as though he held a secret no one knew.

Zachary gave Granny a wolf whistle. "You're gonna wow all the guys tonight."

A blush painted the older woman's wrinkled cheeks pink as she slowly moved forward in a floor-length royal-blue gown with long sleeves. "I bet you say that to all the gals."

"No, ma'am. Only the special ones." Zachary winked at Granny.

The color deepened on her face to a bright red. "He's a keeper, Jordan."

When the doorbell rang, Nicholas hurried toward the foyer and let Doug inside. The man dressed in a tux stared at Granny for a long moment as if no one else was around, then approached her.

Carrying a box, Doug opened it and slipped a corsage on Granny's wrist. "These roses pale in comparison to you."

A noise behind Granny intruded on the romantic moment. "Mom, I found your walker. Someone hid it under your bed." Jordan's mother rolled it toward Granny.

Her grandmother's lower lip protruded. "That some-

one, as you well know, was me. I'm not using it." She
slid her arm through the crook of Doug's. "I can hold
on to him and be perfectly fine."

"Then at least use your cane. I'll go get it for you."
Jordan's mom whirled around and went in search of it.

"Let's get out of here *now.*" Granny began shuffling
toward the front door, dragging Doug with her.

Jordan pressed her lips together. "We'd better leave.
Knowing Granny, she'll start walking toward the school
if we don't get out there." Grasping her son's arms,
she drew him to her and kissed his cheek. "Take care
of Nana. She isn't gonna be too happy we left without
the cane."

Nicholas giggled. "I'll challenge her to a game of
chess and let her win tonight."

"She'll know."

"Yes, but it'll take her mind off the fact Granny is
out dancing."

Hearing her mom's footsteps coming down the
hall, Jordan grabbed Zachary and hurried out the entrance. When she descended the porch steps, she realized she still held Zachary's hand and started to drop
it. He squeezed her fingers gently and kept the connection intact—all the way to his sister's SUV. Then
he opened the front passenger door for her to slip inside. Like a date.

*But this isn't a date.* She had to remember that.

Granny thumped the back of the driver's seat. "Get
moving, young man. Eileen's on the porch with that
cane."

"Yes, ma'am." Zachary threw a glance at Jordan, a
smile deep in his eyes, as he started the car. "This is
gonna be an interesting evening," he whispered.

"You think?"

"What was that, young man. Speak up? I don't hear as good as I used to."

Jordan twisted around. "We were just commenting on what a fun time we're gonna have."

Granny grinned. "I intend to cut a rug, as we used to say."

An hour later, true to her word, Jordan's grandmother was out on the floor with Doug dancing. The twinkling lights and candles lent a romantic air to the evening. The music played was a combination of several decades for the alumni who attended—none Granny's but that didn't stop her, although she confined herself to slow dances.

Leaning close, Zachary handed Jordan a cup of punch and said, "I hope when I'm her age, I enjoy life half as much as your grandmother."

"Yeah, she has a unique outlook." His nearness doubled her heartbeat like the tempo of a fast song.

They had talked with several old friends, watched Granny and Doug on the floor, but he had yet to ask her to dance.

She turned toward him, using that motion to step back and give herself some breathing room. "Nicholas wanted me to ask you to Sunday dinner tomorrow night."

"He mentioned something about it being Granny's birthday."

"She doesn't believe in celebrating her birthday, so we can't mention why I'm baking a double-chocolate-fudge cake."

He tossed back his head and laughed. "So, no presents?"

"Oh, no. She's told me she's got all she needs. She doesn't want another trinket or something she would have to dust."

"Does Doug know?"

"Yes. I've invited him, but he promised no gifts."

"What time?"

"Six."

"Then I'll be there." He inched nearer, taking her elbow.

Her heartbeat pulsated a salsa. His fingers on her skin branded their imprint into her brain. Goose bumps covered her bare arms. "Remember, just a regular old family dinner."

"Yes, ma'am. I wouldn't want to be on your grandmother's bad side."

"Are you kidding? You can do no wrong."

Another slow dance began. "Let's give it a try. I hate to think an eighty-year-old woman is putting us to shame."

Jordan swallowed several times to clear the tightness in her throat. Although the leisurely rhythm vibrated through the air, her heart still picked up speed. "Are you sure?"

His gaze linked with hers. "Yes." He drew her out onto the gym floor and into his embrace. "It's been a while, but I think I remember."

As his arms wrapped around her, she'd come home. She couldn't fight her feelings any longer. She loved him. And no amount of telling herself not to was going to change that.

Zachary shouldn't have asked her to dance. That was his downfall. But he'd taken a look at her, the dim lighting adding a certain intimacy to the air, and the invitation just tumbled from his lips. Then once he'd put his arms around her, thoughts of their senior prom all those years ago attacked his defenses, tearing them down.

Tomorrow he would regret this—opening this door to the past—but for the time being he would enjoy having her close to him. Feeling her heart thumping against his chest. Touching her warmth. Smelling her vanilla scent.

When the music stopped, with all the barriers gone he framed her face in his hands and stared into her dark-chocolate gaze as though he were a teenage boy again and in love for the first time.

People left the dance floor, but he couldn't move. Transfixed by the smile that brightened her eyes, a smile that coaxed his heart to forget and forgive, he didn't want to be in the middle of a crowded gym. He wanted her alone. With that thought in mind, he grabbed her hand and tugged her after him.

"Where are we going?"

"A surprise."

"What about Granny and Doug?"

"We'll be back before the dance is over."

He exited the building, his destination before him—a hundred yards away. Crossing the parking lot, he slowed his step to allow her to keep up. When he reached the gate to the football stadium, he punched in a code and opened it.

"How do you know how to get inside?"

"I've helped Coach out some in the past, and he hasn't changed it in the last few years. Probably a quarter of the town knows how to get in here." Zachary mounted the steps to the stands and stopped when he reached the row right under the press box. "Remember?"

"Yes, this is where you asked me to go steady." Her words came out in a breathless, halting gush.

Whether from his fast pace or from something else, he didn't know. For the evening he wanted to forget all his fear and doubts and just enjoy her company—like in the past.

He pulled her down next to him on the bench, slung his arm around her shoulders and pressed her against his side. "This used to be my favorite place. My thinking place."

"It's not anymore?"

"No. Now I usually just go riding."

She shivered.

"Cold."

"A little."

He shrugged out of his coat and gave it to her.

"Thanks." She snuggled into its warmth.

And he wanted his arms around her—not his coat. He stared at the dark field below then lifted his gaze to the nearly full moon in the clear sky. Its radiance gave them enough light to see by. He inhaled a deep breath of the recently mowed grass. Silence surrounded them, except that his heartbeat throbbed in his ears, drowning out all common sense.

He shouldn't be here with Jordan.

He should leave—he shifted toward her. Their gazes bound across the few inches that separated them. His throat went dry. Thoughts fled his mind. His blood rushed to his limbs.

He leaned closer and brushed his lips across hers. Drawing her totally to him, he fenced her against him and deepened the kiss until he became lost in the sensations bombarding him—her heady scent, the feel of her mouth on his, the little gasp of surprise that had come from her when he first made a tactile connection.

When he pulled back slightly, she murmured, "Why did you kiss me?"

"Can you deny you haven't thought about how it would be after all these years?"

"Is that all it was to you? A way to satisfy an itch?"

Her questions sobered him—propelled him into the present. He shouldn't have kissed her. Too much stood between them. He rose. "We'd better get back. I wouldn't want your grandmother to worry."

She removed his suit jacket and thrust it into his hands. "I don't need this anymore." Whirling around, she started for the aisle.

He let her go, following a few paces behind her. Her stiff arms at her sides and long strides announced to the world she was upset.

Just friends. There could be no in between for them. Friends only.

Okay, so now that he'd gotten the kiss out of his system, he could move forward. Cement his relationship with Nicholas and keep Jordan at arm's length.

*Yeah, right.*

Nicholas opened the front door. "Dad, you're here. Mom said you might not come."

"Sure. When does a guy turn down a home-cooked meal?" Sunday evening Zachary stepped through the threshold into the best-smelling house on the planet.

Aromas of baking bread, pot roast and spices assailed his nostrils. Mingling among those smells he caught a whiff of coffee. His stomach roiled, protesting his hunger. He'd worked nonstop from right after church to thirty minutes ago. He refused to let the previous night intrude into his thoughts, but if he stopped for any amount of time, he began to think about the kiss.

He followed his son into the den and found Granny, Doug, Eileen, Rachel and Jordan sitting and talking. Everyone stopped and stared at him when he came into the room.

Awkward, he covered the distance to Granny and presented her with a bouquet of flowers. "For the prettiest gal here."

A flush stained her cheeks, much like it did Jordan's. "Who told you it was my birthday? Nicholas?"

His son shook his head.

Her sharp gaze landed on Jordan. "You?"

"Yes, and I made you a chocolate cake. If you don't watch out, I'll put eighty-one candles on it."

"Not unless you want to call the fire department, child."

Jordan stared at Zachary. "What about 'Don't bring a gift' did you not understand?"

He slunk to the nearest chair and plopped down onto it. "I didn't think flowers would be considered a birthday present."

"Dear, why don't you want to celebrate your birthday?" Doug looked at Granny. His white mustache framed his pinched lips.

"Because I've given them up. I did when I turned sixty."

"What if I said I picked these from Becca's garden?" Zachary still held the bouquet in his hand.

Jordan stood and took the flowers from him. "I didn't know your sister has a rose garden."

"She doesn't. The only one she has is a vegetable garden," he said in a low voice for her ears only.

"Well, since he went to the trouble to get them, you might as well stick them in some water and put them in the dining room. And I thank you kindly, Zachary." Granny angled toward Doug on the couch next to her, plastered her biggest smile on her face, her wrinkles deepening, and patted his hand between them. "Your presence is all I need on my birthday."

Zachary surged to his feet. "I'll help you, Jordan."

In the kitchen, he blew a breath out between pursed lips. "I messed up."

"No, you didn't. Granny loves flowers, but she couldn't make a big deal out of it because she has insisted for years nothing special on her birthday."

"Where did Nicholas disappear to?"

She waved her hand toward the kitchen door. "He's out back with his cousins. Taylor's helping him fix the fence where Tucker keeps digging out of the yard."

"Beagles love to escape. I had one when I was a boy that was a master at climbing the fence. Tucker did like the ranch, especially the squirrels and birds he ended up chasing around."

After filling a glass vase with water, Jordan put the yellow roses into it one by one. "Dinner is about ready."

"Can I set the table?"

"Done, but you can put these flowers on the sideboard in the dining room." She held the vase toward him.

He clasped it, their fingers brushing against each other. He locked his gaze on hers, and all the sensations from the night before when he'd embraced her, kissed her, washed through him anew. He jerked back as though shocked by their touch. The glass vase crashed to the tile floor, shattering between them, shards flying everywhere.

"I'm sorry. I didn't mean to pull back." Staring down at the mess, he almost didn't hear her reply.

"Yes, you did. What's going on between us?" She dragged the trash can to the broken vase and stooped down to pick up the pieces.

Bending down next to her, he helped clean up the mess. "Nothing."

"Oh, I see. That kiss meant nothing to you."

"I shouldn't have done that. I got caught up in the moment, remembering the time when I had asked you to go steady sitting in that very spot."

Emotions—hurt, sadness and finally irritation—flitted across her features. Her eyes downcast, she continued to work, but he'd seen the misty look in them.

He seized her wrist. "I made this mess. I'll take care of it. You get dinner on the table. Where's your broom and dustpan?"

"That's okay. I'd rather you go get Nicholas and the other kids. I need space." She compressed her mouth into a thin line, but her eyes still glistened.

"Fine." He rose and headed toward the back door.

Space was a good thing. Because for a few seconds, he'd wanted to sweep her into his arms and take away that hurt look inching back into her expression. But he couldn't. He'd loved two women in his life and had discovered he couldn't trust either one not to trample his heart. His fiancée had walked away after his bull-riding injury. And he'd been left alone with his grief—again.

Between Jordan and Audrey, he'd decided to live a life without emotional entanglements. Much easier on him—until Jordan turned up again.

"Do you want to go out and look at the stars with me?" Nicholas asked Zachary after the dishes were done that evening.

"Sure."

"How about you, Mom? The moon is full. You'll be able to see the craters."

Jordan put the dish towel over the handle on the stove. "I don't—"

"Please. We should be able to see Venus, too."

"Okay. For a few minutes."

Out on the deck, Nicholas removed the covering over his telescope and began adjusting it to view the moon.

"Nicholas, can you come in and help me with something?" Granny stood at the kitchen door, her expression hidden in the shadows.

"Yes. I'll be back. I think it's set up." He pointed up into the sky to the left. "Venus is that way. Low on the horizon." As he hurried away, her grandmother backed away to allow Nicholas inside.

The click of the door resonated in the quiet. Jordan peered at the telescope then Zachary. "You go first."

While she waited for her turn, music drifted outside from an open upstairs window in her son's room. Words from "Sealed with a Kiss" sounded, competing with Tucker's howl.

Zachary straightened and glanced toward the window. "What's that?"

"Granny has a CD with love songs on it that she plays occasionally."

In the light that streamed from the kitchen Zachary's forehead creased. "Isn't that our son's room?"

"Yes. He's at it again with some help from Granny."

"It's in His Kiss" followed next.

He burst out laughing. "What's next? 'Then I Kissed Her'?"

"Actually I think 'Something's Gotta Hold of My Heart.'"

"Yeah, heartburn."

Jordan chuckled, catching sight of Nicholas peeking out the kitchen window with Granny next to him. "Don't look now but they are spying on us."

He grabbed her and drew her to him. "Are you game for a little fun?"

"What?"

Her pulse thudded against her neck. He plastered her against him, then dipped her backward while he planted a kiss on her mouth. Her head spun, especially when he came up, dragging her with him. Dots before her eyes danced to the rhythm of the music.

"Do you think those two are still looking?" he said against her lips, his warm breath caressing them.

She leaned back and glanced up. "Yep, now they're blatantly standing in the window."

Zachary pivoted around, shoved his hands to his hips and asked, "What do you think you're doing?"

Nicholas stuck his head out the kitchen door. "Granny wanted to hear her CD."

Jordan stepped around Zachary. "She might but the whole neighborhood doesn't need to be serenaded. Nor do we. Close your window and get ready for bed."

"Ah, Mom."

"It's getting late and there's no more entertainment

out here for you to see." She crossed her arms to emphasize the point.

Evidently Nicholas decided not to argue, but instead did as she asked.

"Someone needs to talk to him." Zachary raked his hand through his hair. "He needs to understand about our relationship." Again his fingers combed their way through his dark strands.

*Explain it to me.* She clamped her lips together to still those words. "Then I suggest you have a father-son talk with him."

His eyes widened. "You don't want to do it?"

"I don't think I could explain it well." *Since you're sending me mixed messages.*

"Okay, I'll tuck him in tonight and have that talk. I'll take care of everything."

"You do that." Jordan marched toward the back door and entered the kitchen, not caring if Zachary followed her or not.

He was going to hurt her and there was nothing she could do about it. She'd had her chance years ago and Zachary wasn't going to give her a second one—no matter how sorry she was concerning not telling him about Nicholas.

## Chapter Ten

Half an hour later Zachary sat on Nicholas's bed, staring at his son's expectant face. Zachary gulped. He'd only been a father for less than a month. He wasn't ready for a father-son talk about the opposite sex, even if it had only to do with him and Jordan. When he thought about it, he'd probably never be.

"Nicholas, your mother and I are only friends."

"I saw you kiss her."

"I was playing with you." And shouldn't have done it. What was it about being around Jordan that made him forget his common sense?

"Why can't you two marry?"

"Marriage is serious and can't be taken lightly." *You have to trust each other.* But he couldn't say that to his son.

"I'm not. I want us to be a family."

"We are a family. You'll always be our son."

"That's not what I meant." Nicholas frowned, folding his arms over his stomach.

"I know. Your mother loves you and I do, too."

"But you don't love each other?"

He wanted to say no, but the word lodged in his throat. He swallowed hard, but the lump was immovable. "I'll always care about her," he finally murmured.

His son's frown evolved into a scowl. "That's not…" He pulled his cover up to his shoulder and twisted away. "Oh, never mind."

"Good night, son." Zachary bent forward and kissed him on his side of his head.

When Zachary descended the stairs a minute later, he found Jordan sitting on the bottom one, her head hanging down, her hands loosely clasped between her legs. He settled beside her. "I told him, or rather I tried to."

"I heard."

"You listened?"

She slanted a look at him. "I'll have to pick up the pieces after you leave. I needed to know what you two talked about."

"What a pair we make. Suspicious of each other."

"You don't know Nicholas like I do."

He surged to his feet, curling and uncurling his hands. He didn't like all these emotions flooding him. Life was simpler when he didn't feel so intensely. "And whose fault is that?" His hurried strides chewed up the distance to the front door. Out on the porch, he paused, tried to compose himself. Couldn't.

On the long drive to his ranch his gut kicked like a bucking horse. How was he supposed to forgive Jordan for robbing him of ten years with his child? The only one he'd ever have? He'd missed so much already. Every time he was with Nicholas that was reinforced. And yet, she'd tried to tell him once—thought she'd been rejected by him. What a pair they were!

When he drove down the gravel road that led to his

place, he saw the light in Becca's kitchen still on. He swerved his truck and parked behind her house. He didn't want to be alone with his thoughts. She'd been there after his rodeo accident and helped him adjust.

He knocked on the door, and a few seconds later it was opened by his older sister. He tried to smile a greeting, but it died instantly on his lips.

"Your dinner at Jordan's didn't go well?"

He shook his head. "Nicholas keeps trying to fix us up." He trudged into the kitchen and sank into a chair at the table.

"Ah, that's cute."

"No, it isn't."

"Why not? You loved Jordan once."

His gut constricted even more. "It's not that simple."

Becca sat across from him. "I feel bad about not saying something directly to you about her calling eleven years ago. If I had, this would be a moot point."

"It's not your fault."

"I can understand why you're angry with her, but you've gotta let it go. It will eat you up inside. Color your relationship with your son."

"How's this any different than if we were married and divorced?" He set his elbows on the table and steepled his fingers.

"It's isn't really. Most children want to see their divorced parents back together."

"I think Granny is encouraging him to get us together. Actually there is no 'think' about it. I know."

"Knowing Jordan's grandmother, you aren't gonna change her mind. She's like a pit bull. She isn't gonna let it go."

He rubbed his hands down his face. "I'm gonna have to stay away as much as possible."

"How's that gonna help you get to know your son better?"

"I thought I'd have Nicholas go camping with us next weekend. Getting away from Tallgrass will be good."

"You mean running away. Your problems won't disappear. Face them. As a teenager, you had deep feelings for Jordan."

Zachary pushed to his feet. "Yeah, a long time ago. Not now. The best we can be is friends for Nicholas's sake." If he said it enough, he would come to believe it.

He strode from his sister's place and headed toward his own. Answers still eluded him like the grand prize now in a rodeo competition. When he pulled up in front, he stared at his dark house. Once he'd dreamed of having a home full of children, a loving relationship—with Jordan. Then when that blew up in his face, he slowly rebuilt his dream with Audrey, who had left him because he couldn't be the father of the children she'd wanted. There wouldn't be a third time.

*At least I have one son. Thank You, Lord, for that.*

Early before dawn the next morning after Zachary had called Jordan, Nicholas rushed into the barn. "Has Buttercup had the foal yet?"

With his hands clasped, his forearms on the stall door, Zachary peered toward Nicholas and her coming toward him. "Nope. But she's getting close."

"Can I see? Can I see?" Nicholas hopped up and down.

Zachary passed Jordan going to the tack room. "I'll be right back."

After the evening she and Zachary had, the timing of the birth of the foal wasn't good. During the middle of her sleepless night, she'd come to a decision. If being his friend was the only relationship she could have with Zachary, she would try to make it work. Which meant she had to tamp down her feelings for him. He'd broken her heart once before. She rubbed her hand over her chest. She was afraid that it was too late this time, as well. It hurt to be in love with a man who didn't feel the same.

"Here, son, use this." Zachary put a stool in front of the stall door.

"Can't we go inside?"

"I don't like to unless there's a problem."

Zachary stood on the left side of Nicholas while she took up her post on the right.

Nicholas squealed. "Look. I see a leg."

Seeing the joy and wonder on her son's face made the uncomfortable feeling okay. She would do anything for Nicholas.

"If you decide to be a vet, you could work with large animals. There are plenty of ranches around here." Zachary's gaze slipped from their son to Jordan. The tired lines about Zachary's eyes underscored his sleepless night, too.

Groans from the mare filled the air. Jordan thought about when she'd had Nicholas, alone because he was a few weeks early. Zachary had been on the other side of the world, oblivious to the fact he was becoming a father. As though he were thinking the same thing, his lips disappeared beneath his tight expression. He turned away, keeping his full attention on the drama occurring in the stall.

"Guys, the head is out." Nicholas pointed at the dark, wet foal.

The mare strained, her stomach rising and falling. Buttercup struggled to her feet, twirled around, then plopped down on the hay-covered floor.

Nicholas's eyes grew huge. "Is everything okay?"

"Yeah, she's doing fine. The foal's coming out the right way. Sometimes the mama gets a little restless, impatient."

*Like a lot of mamas around the world.* But she kept that to herself, not wanting to remind Zachary he hadn't been at his son's birth.

When the baby came completely out, Nicholas jumped up and down, clapping his hands. "This cinches it. I want to be a vet. I'm going to have to really get into science now. When we get home today, let's work on that first."

"First, we're going over your essay. Then we can do science. Your anatomy class with Dr. Reynolds should be helpful."

"We're studying the heart and its function right now. I already knew quite a bit because of my problem. I've read a lot about it."

Jordan captured Zachary's look, trying to gauge his reaction to his son's words. His closed expression told her nothing of what was going on inside him until his jaw twitched.

"I thought this next weekend you could go camping with me and Aunt Becca's family. Would you be interested, Nicholas?"

Her son whirled around on the stool, nearly toppling over. After steadying himself, he radiated his joy. "I've always wanted to go camping. When?"

"We'll leave Saturday morning and come back Sunday evening."

"Mom?"

She wished she'd had some warning about this. Biting down on the inside of her mouth, she kept the first words that came to mind inside. After last night she didn't need any more tension between her and Zachary. "That sounds fine to me," she finally said when her son gave her a quizzical look.

"Mom, you should go, too. We've never been camping."

With the bugs and snakes? Her idea of roughing it was a two-star hotel. "I don't know."

"Please. It will be fun."

*It is if you like to get dirty and sleep on the ground.* She peered at Zachary, who remained stony quiet. When she swept her attention back to Nicholas, he studied them, his expression hovering somewhere between a grin and a frown. "I'll have to think about it, but that doesn't mean you can't go, hon."

The foal finally made it to its wobbly legs while Buttercup licked the baby. When it started nursing, Nicholas hopped down. "Can I go in now?"

"Sure, but don't interfere with the foal nursing." Zachary opened the stall door.

"I won't. I know how important it is for the mama and baby to bond."

Nicholas moved in slow motion inside, his eyes as round as wagon wheels while he took everything in. He began talking softly to the two animals. The mother's ears cocked toward him.

Zachary's hand clamped around hers, and he tugged her back toward the middle of the barn. "You can come if you want, but unless you've made an about-face on the idea of camping, you'd be miserable."

"Is that why you planned the outing? To exclude me?"

"No, I just want to get to know my son. I'm having to make up for lost time. When he talks about his heart defect, he's so matter-of-fact, but it couldn't have been easy. I wish I could have been there for him, held his hand, let him know I loved him."

Tears gathered in her eyes. "Are you ever going to forgive me?"

"That's what the Lord wants." He dropped his hand away from hers—sadness shadowing his eyes. "I'm really trying, Jordan, to do what's right."

But he hadn't forgiven her yet. He'd all but said that. His unspoken intent hurt more than she wanted to acknowledge. She saw out of the corner of her eye Nicholas watching them. She stepped closer, Zachary's male scent vying with the odors of the barn—horse, hay, dust. Tilting her chin, she averted her head so her son couldn't see her expression. "So am I, Zachary." She sucked in a stabilizing breath. "And I haven't changed that much. I'm still not gung-ho about camping."

"Well, that's reassuring. Not everything has changed." He strode toward Nicholas.

"Child, what are you doing here? You should be getting ready to go camping with Nicholas and Zachary." Granny shuffled into the kitchen not half an hour after dawn peeked over the horizon on Saturday morning.

Jordan nursed a large cup of strong coffee. She hadn't slept a wink last night. Each time she'd started to nod off, visions of her lying on the ground with bugs and spiders and snakes crawling all over her intruded. The picture destroyed her peace.

"I'm not wanted," she said in a self-pitying tone that even made her hunch her shoulders.

"Oh, my, you've got it bad. You're too busy feeling sorry for yourself. If you want the young man, you need to get up and do something about it. Sitting here moping won't change the circumstances." Granny eased down beside her and took her hand. "When you were a teenager, you still had a—" she thought for a few seconds "—a lot of growing up to do. You were used to getting your way, especially with Zachary. You thought you could go away for a couple of years and come back here after you'd done what you wanted and pick right up where you two left off."

"No, I didn't...." Yes, secretly she had thought that. She'd wanted to go away to see what was out there and art school in Savannah gave her the means. She'd been eighteen and not ready to settle down even in a year like Zachary had thought. "Okay, maybe I did."

"But Zachary didn't stay here waiting for you. And when you found that out, you were hurt and angry. Then Nicholas had problems, and you had your hands full. You grew up fast. You aren't that same young girl, and Zachary isn't that same young man. Get out there and get to know him in his element. Go camping. Your son asked you again before he left to go spend the night at the ranch. Give you three a chance."

Jordan pulled her hand free and wrapped her fingers around the warm mug, drawing in the fragrance of the coffee. The best smell in the world. "I'm not the one who's fighting us being together as a family."

"Do you blame Zachary? You can be so stubborn at

times." Her grandmother snorted unladylike. "To paraphrase the words of one of my favorite Gene Pitney songs, 'only love has the power to fix a broken heart.' Give him a reason to fall in love with you again."

"But he doesn't trust me."

"When he does love you, his trust will come." Granny struggled to her feet, steadied herself by gripping the table's edge. "I took the liberty of borrowing Doug's sleeping bag and small pup tent. In the hallway by the front door. Now get before they leave without you."

Her grandmother was right. She would have to fight for Zachary's love. She'd learned to fight when Nicholas got so sick. Jumping up, she kissed Granny on the cheek and hurried toward her bedroom.

Zachary leaned against the fence of his largest corral and watched Nicholas, on the back of Chief, gallop to one end, round the barrel and race back to the other one making a figure eight. His son was improving every day.

Nicholas trotted to him. "I did it."

When he held his hand up, Zachary gave him a high five. "Let's try it one more time before we leave for Prairie Lake."

"May I take my rope with us? I'd like to practice while we're camping."

"Sounds good to me. The HHH Junior Rodeo is only a few weeks away. Practice is the key to getting better."

"Maybe I'll rope a bear."

Zachary laughed. "I hope not. But maybe a tree stump."

Nicholas maneuvered his horse around so he could start the run again. He nudged the gelding.

As his son shot forward, the sound of a car pulling up drifted to Zachary. He glanced sideways and tensed. What was Jordan doing here? Turning back toward Nicholas, he prepared himself for a confrontation over the fact their son was racing around a set of barrels.

He heard her approach. The hairs on his nape stood up. He stiffened as he pushed off, his fingers grasping the wooden slat. She stopped right behind him on the other side. A fence between them. A past between them—a past he kept dredging up.

Nicholas finished his figure eight. "Hi, Mom. What are you doing here?"

"I decided to take your father's invitation up and come camping with you all."

Zachary strode to the gate and opened it for Nicholas to leave the corral.

"That's great!" His son loped toward the entrance to the barn and dismounted.

"Is the invitation still open?" Jordan came up to Zachary as he latched the gate.

*No, I didn't mean it. I need to stay away from you. You're too tempting.* Zachary pivoted and faced her, forcing a smile to his lips. "Sure. You do understand we'll be outdoors with everything you get squeamish about?"

"If Nicholas enjoys it, I want to be able to share it with him."

"Suit yourself. You were warned."

Her eyes became round, her eyebrows raised. "It's just a few bugs."

"Yeah, just a few," he murmured and started for the barn.

She hurried after him. "Nicholas is riding well."

"Yes. I told you I wouldn't have him do anything he's not ready for. You need to trust me on that."

She grasped his arm and stopped him. When he glanced back at her, she asked, "Is that a two-way street?"

Trust didn't come easily to him anymore, partially because of this woman who moved to stand in front of him.

"Zachary, I know you have a good reason to be leery of me, but we both have our son's well-being in mind."

"So I should trust you, no questions asked, because of Nicholas?"

She lifted her chin. "Yes."

He shook free. "We need to meet Becca at her house in twenty minutes."

He continued his path toward Nicholas cooling down his gelding. *It's gonna be a long weekend, trying to avoid Jordan. I thought I could be friends with her and not care beyond that. But I don't think that's possible.*

Jordan plopped down on a fallen log by a stream that fed into Prairie Lake, not far from their campsite. If she didn't know better, she was sure that Zachary picked the most primitive area for them to set up camp. And then on top of that, he'd insisted she put up her own tent as the others were doing. She had—or at least she thought it would stay up even if it did lean a little to the left.

She wouldn't say a word. She was determined to do this with a smile on her face.

A whiff of grilled hamburgers wafted to her. Her

stomach rumbled. She rose and gathered up her bundle of firewood and headed toward the sound of voices through the trees.

"I caught a fish today." Nicholas ran over to her and held up his hands to indicate a foot. "I threw it back, but I enjoyed fishing. Dad said tomorrow we can go early in the morning and will probably catch a lot more."

"That's great, hon. I hope this will be enough wood." Jordan dumped her armful onto the pile not far from the fire pit.

"So long as we have a big enough fire to last the whole night, we should be fine." Zachary clamped his lips together.

"Fine? What do you mean? It shouldn't get too cold with our sleeping bags." Jordan dusted off her jeans.

"I'm not talking about the cold. It's for the bears, bobcats and coyotes."

"Bears? Bobcats…" Her voice faded as a twinkle danced in Zachary's eyes. She punched him in the arm. "Funny. So what's the fire really for?"

"We're gonna roast marshmallows and tell scary stories," Nicholas piped in and returned to Becca.

"I know I'm not much of a nature buff, but I can tell scary stories. You're not gonna sleep at all tonight." She winked at Zachary and sauntered past him to help Becca with dinner.

"We'll just see who's up the whole night, too scared to sleep," he said behind her with a chuckle.

She was afraid it might be her. Not that she would let Zachary know she didn't get any sleep.

After helping Becca with the dinner, Jordan sat down with her plate, piled high with a thick, juicy hamburger, baked beans, macaroni and cheese, and cole slaw. The heat from the fire that Zachary and Paul, Becca's husband, had built warmed her. Now that the sun had disappeared behind the tall pines, scrub oaks and hackberry trees, the temperature had dropped a few degrees.

"How early are you and Nicholas going fishing tomorrow morning?" Jordan asked when Zachary took a seat near her.

"Crack of dawn."

"That early?" Who was she kidding? She wouldn't probably close her eyes all night so why not get up and join them. "I'd like to go with you two. Is anyone else coming?"

"Nope. Paul and I have a challenge going. He has a favorite fishing hole and I have one. We're gonna see who can get the most. He's taking his boys."

"Then I'll even out the numbers. Three to three."

His brow wrinkled, he looked sideways at her. "Then you want to fish?"

"Why not? If you and Nicholas are gonna, I might as well try."

"You'll bait your own hook?"

"Fine. Isn't it just rubbery things?"

He grinned. "Live worms. They come in dirt."

"I know how worms come."

"Just wanted you to know all the details."

"Okay, so I'm a girly girl."

His smile broadened, reaching deep into his eyes. "I've been impressed so far."

"Yeah, well, wait. It isn't totally dark yet."

His robust laugh echoed through the woods encircling them, bouncing off objects and returning to enclose them in an intimacy. For just a moment. "We still have the scary stories," he said, cutting through the emotion-packed tension.

"I have a better idea." Jordan turned to the rest of them around the fire. "Why don't we play charades?"

"Yeah, I like that game," Ashley said opposite Jordan.

"I'm good at it." Nicholas jumped to his feet and threw his plate away, then grabbed a brownie.

Zachary rubbed his chin. "That's actually a good suggestion. Charades it is."

An hour later with darkness surrounding them like a black curtain and their stomachs full of chocolate and marshmallows, the fire the only bright spot, Jordan sat with Becca and Ashley across from Zachary, Mike, Cal and Nicholas. Paul held the tin container out for Jordan to draw her final selection for charades. She read it and gulped then handed it to Paul, who showed it to the guy team.

She unfolded her hands to resemble a book then turned her hand in a full circle.

"A book and movie," Becca shouted.

She held up seven fingers, then indicated the second word. Without roaring, she gave a fierce face and acted as if she pounced on prey.

"Bobcat," Zachary said with a laugh.

Swinging around, she glared at him.

Becca snapped her fingers. "Lion."

Ashley bounced up and down on her seat. "Oh, oh. It's *The Lion, the Witch and the Wardrobe.*"

"Yes!" Jordan high-fived Ashley. "Way to go."

Next Zachary stood, groaned when he read his pick, *The Princess Diaries,* then faced his team to begin. He started to do something, scowled then walked to Paul and whispered something to him. "Ah, okay," Zachary said and came back to the center.

He pantomimed it was a movie and three words. He paused, thought a few seconds then pranced around the fire as though he wore high heels, then eased daintily into a chair. His team looked at him as if he were crazy.

For the next few minutes Zachary tried to coax the title out of the three boys. When he opened his hand like a book and pretended to write in it, Nicholas finally said, "Journal."

Zachary smacked his palms together and shouted, "Close."

"Hey, no talking." Jordan pointed toward Zachary. "That should be a thirty-second penalty."

"Time, without even adding a penalty. Girls win three to two."

Mike stuck out his chest, a pout on his face. "We had harder ones. That's the only reason you all won."

"Mike, they won fair and square." Paul put the tin container back with the other dishes. "It's bedtime. We need to get up early tomorrow. Got a challenge to win."

After standing, Jordan stretched and rolled her head to ease her tight muscles. Exhausted, she covered her open mouth. "I don't think I'm gonna have any trouble sleeping tonight."

"Well, don't let the bed bugs bite." Zachary winked and headed with Nicholas to the tent they were sharing.

Jordan watched everyone scatter to their respective tents. How did she get stuck by herself? *'Cause you don't belong. This is Zachary's family, not yours.*

Flipping back the flap, she crawled inside the small space where she would sleep. After snuggling into the warmth of her bag, Zachary's comment about the bed bugs came back to haunt her. She switched on her flash-light and checked everywhere around her for any sign of an insect or any other creepy, crawling critters. When she thought it was safe, she relaxed and zipped her-self in.

That was when the sounds intruded. The constant chatter of the crickets with an occasional bullfrog taunted her with the idea of sleep—just out of her reach. She stared into the darkness. The hoot of an owl nearby made her gasp. She hunkered down into her bag and squeezed her eyes closed. Sleep finally descended when she relaxed her tense muscles enough to allow it in.

Only to be jerked wide-awake by a howl. She bolted upright, flinging her arms out, connecting with the side of the tent. Canvas swallowed her in its clutches, trying to smother her rather than shelter her. Trapped. With a shudder, she squirmed in her sleeping bag, fighting with the zipper while shoving at the walls of the tent that had fallen on her. Twisting to the side, she searched for an opening and rolled down a small incline, ending up at the bottom in a tangle.

Her heartbeat thundered so loud in her ears she barely heard Zachary call her name. Then suddenly he freed her from the canvas and knelt down next to her.

"What happened, Jordan?"

"My zipper is stuck," she said between pants. She needed to get out of the confining sleeping bag.

He placed a calming hand on her. "Let me."

Five seconds later he liberated her totally. She sat up and inhaled deeply of the oxygen-rich air. Another howl reverberated through the woods. "What's that?" She threw herself into his strong arms.

For a moment he held her before saying, "It's a coyote." He helped her up, stooped and grabbed the tent and bedding. "We're safe."

"How do you know that?"

"I've been camping here many times and a coyote hasn't bothered me yet."

"There's always a first time." The trembling in her hands quickly overtook her whole body.

He tossed the items on the ground not too far from the fire then drew her into his embrace again. "You're all right."

She laid her head against his chest, feeling the steady beating of his heart beneath her ear. "You said a coyote hasn't bothered you. Has something else?"

"Raccoons. That's why our food is locked away in the car."

"Oh." Although she didn't want to encounter a raccoon, it sounded better than a coyote. From the dim light of the dying fire, she noticed the time on her watch was four in the morning. Even though her body didn't feel like it, she'd gotten a few hours of sleep. "I think I'm done for the night."

"Dawn is still a couple of hours away."

"I know but I'm not wrestling with my tent again."

"I can stay out here. Why don't you sleep with Nicholas?"

"You'd sleep out in the open?" His warmth encircled her and lured her into a serenity she wished she could maintain.

"I've done it before." His fingers skimmed down her spine.

She pressed closer. The thumping of his heartbeat increased. A sudden intake of air attested to her effect on him. She smiled. Hope blossomed within her and spread through her.

He stepped back. "I'll use this sleeping bag. You can use mine. That way we won't disturb Nicholas."

Still keyed up with her fight with her tent, she moved toward the glowing embers of the fire and sat. "I might take you up on it, but right now I can't sleep a wink."

He sank into a lawn chair nearby. "I probably can't, either."

"Ha! We have something in common."

His chuckles tickled down her spine like the feel of his fingers seconds ago. "Besides Nicholas. Yeah, I guess we do."

"Well, certainly not camping. I suck at it."

"Nicholas is having a good time."

"That's your genes. Not mine."

"But studying and the love of books are yours."

"He's a little bit of both of us and a whole lot of his own."

Zachary crossed his right arm over his chest while stroking his chin with his left hand. "Aren't most children?"

"Probably. I'd love to find out. I never pictured being a mother of one child. Growing up I enjoyed my relationship with my sister." The second she admitted that to Zachary she chanced a peek at his face.

His earlier neutral expression morphed into a frown, the cleft in his chin prominent.

"How about you? You were engaged once. Did you two talk about having a family?"

He blinked. The silence stretched between them.

"I'm sorry. I had no right to ask." What had happened

to Zachary from the time she'd left to when she'd come back to Tallgrass?

"Yeah, I wanted a family. Being around my nephews and niece made me realize that."

"That's the way I feel about Rachel's family. Every year she and Mom would drive across country and visit Nicholas and I for a couple of weeks. We spent time at the beach, seeing the sights. The time we went to Jamestown and Williamsburg was so much fun. Nicholas was four. Before he got so sick he couldn't go far from home. I think that trip sparked his love of history."

Zachary's intense gaze trapped hers. "At four?"

"He was reading by three, calculating addition, subtraction and even multiplication in his head."

"What an unusual son we have."

For a long moment a bond sprang up between them. He'd roped her as if he'd taken her into his arms again. She wished he would.

Finally he turned his head, poking the fire with a stick they'd roasted marshmallows on. "What happened when he got sick?"

"His health began to deteriorate until finally his doctor heard his heart murmur and referred us to a pediatric cardiologist. They put a catheter in to repair the hole. It's like a plug. But it became infected and they had to repair it surgically. He almost died. It took quite a toll on him." *And me, but my son's alive through the grace and power of the Lord.*

He folded both arms over his chest. "I wish I could have been there for him."

"I wish you'd been there, too." It should have been that way. If only… The brief connection she'd experienced with Zachary came crashing down about her. Her memories and emotions—mostly sadness—swamped her, sagging her shoulders. She pushed to her feet. "I think I can sleep now."

As she made her way to the tent where Nicholas was, Zachary's continued silence emphasized the distance between them. She wanted his forgiveness and trust. Neither of which she had. If she ever wanted that family she'd told him she wanted, she needed to move on. Why hadn't she while she lived in South Carolina? Her excuse had always been Nicholas. But now that she was back in Tallgrass she realized it was because she'd never stopped loving Zachary, even when she'd felt rejected by him.

When she settled next to Nicholas, weariness surrounded her like the sleeping bag. But Zachary's distinctive male scent ridiculed her thoughts of slumber.

Nicholas chattered most of the way back to the ranch from the lake the next evening. Zachary tried to follow what his son said, but his mind was filled with images from the weekend camping trip. Lying in the sleeping bag where Jordan had been moments before—her vanilla fragrance taunting him. Her trying to bait her hook with a wiggly worm. Her glee at reeling in a fish only to have to throw it back because of its small size. The sleepy-eyed look she'd given him that morning when she'd crawled out of the tent behind Nicholas.

And if truth be known, he'd enjoyed himself and believed she had, too. What would it have been like if he'd known about his son from the very beginning? Would they have a parcel of kids by now? Would he have become a bull rider? Had the rodeo accident? That day changed so much for him. His career was over. His fiancée walked away because he couldn't give her what she wanted—a family. *Like Jordan wants.*

The thought she wanted more kids marked his heart like a branding iron used on horses. It was too late for him but not her. Even if he could put aside his mistrust, how could he ask her to give him a second chance when he couldn't give her any more children?

"Dad?"

"Huh?"

"Who's that at Aunt Becca's?"

Zachary swept his attention toward the blue house as he passed it. Stiffening, he sucked in a sharp breath. "My parents." He'd avoided having any real conversation with his mother about Nicholas and what had happened eleven years ago. He should have known she wouldn't be put off for long.

He slid his gaze toward Jordan in the front seat. Her ashen features spoke of her own turmoil at his parents' visit.

## Chapter Eleven

When Zachary pulled up behind his parents' car, Jordan sank lower in the seat, her hands clenched beside her. *What do I say to the woman who kept my calls from Zachary, Lord? Things would be so different if she hadn't.*

"They're my grandparents?" Nicholas pushed open the back door of the truck and jumped down. Without waiting for a reply to his question, he darted across the yard toward them.

Zachary sent her a look full of concern. "I can understand if you'd rather not talk with my mom."

"I imagine she's not too happy with me, and I'm certainly not with her." Jordan stared out the windshield at her son, who embraced his grandparents as though he'd known them all his life. Didn't he realize that woman was the reason he didn't know about his father?

"She shouldn't have kept the message from me, but she was doing what mothers do—protecting their children."

She knew she wasn't being fair but the past month had been hard for her, her son and Zachary. Yes, she was to blame as well as his mother, but she'd been young, hardly an adult thrust into an adult situation she didn't know how to handle. "So you can forgive her but not me?" Finally she swung her full attention toward Zachary, narrowing her eyes when she saw the deep furrows on his forehead, the muscle in his cheek twitch, the flare of his nostrils.

His grip on the steering wheel whitened his knuckles. "You can't compare apples to oranges. The two situations are not the same."

"Yes, I can. She lied to me." Jordan shoved open the door. "It seems to me you have a double standard. I'm getting my car and leaving. I'll stop by and get Nicholas. He needs to go home. He's had a long, tiring weekend."

She started for the barn where she'd left her car parked and had only taken a few steps before Zachary blocked her path. "Nicholas can stay the night with me. He needs to spend some time with his grandparents."

Moving into his personal space, she shoved her face close to his. "No. He can visit tomorrow after he's rested and done his schoolwork."

His glare drilled through her. "I'll bring him home early tomorrow afternoon. This isn't a request. He's my son, too."

The stubborn set to his jaw declared his intention to fight for Nicholas to stay and frankly at the moment she was exhausted from the weekend's ups and downs. Her anger and energy siphoned from her. She stepped back. "Fine, but I need him home by noon. He has his anatomy class tomorrow at one."

Skirting around him, she marched down the road toward the barn. Pinpricks ran down her spine. She wouldn't look back at Zachary. She didn't need to see that he watched her.

* * *

"Mom said you're upset." Rachel came into the kitchen where Jordan was working on her laptop the next morning.

She twisted toward her older sister. "Zachary's mother is at the ranch."

"And Nicholas is out there?"

"Yeah, but it's not so much that as what she did to me."

Rachel crossed to the coffeepot and poured her some in a mug, then sat across from Jordan. "You're having a hard time forgiving her."

"Yes." She pushed her laptop to the side and cradled her coffee, the warmth from the drink doing nothing to take the chill from her fingers. "Everything would be so different if she hadn't kept my calls from Zachary."

"If you can't forgive her, how can you expect Zachary to forgive you?" Rachel sipped her drink.

Her sister's question threw her off balance. She stared down at her mug, trying to come up with an appropriate answer. She opened her mouth to say something. The situation between her and Zachary's mother was different, wasn't it?

But it wasn't. *The Lord forgives us, but He expects us to forgive others in return. How can I not?*

"I know it won't be easy, but don't you think you should make the first move? Show Zachary you can forgive."

Jordan shook her head. "I don't know if I can."

"Just think on it. We can't expect to receive forgiveness if we can't forgive."

"How did you become so wise?"

"It's the duty of an older sister." Rachel took another swig of her coffee.

Jordan shut down her laptop, her sister's advice nibbling at her defenses. "I think I'll pick Nicholas up at the ranch before anatomy class. Maybe by then, I'll know if I can forgive her and what to say."

Rising, her sister hugged her then took her mug to the sink. "I know you'll do the right thing."

With her chin cupped in her hand, Jordan stared at a spot across the kitchen as Rachel left. *Lord, I don't have to ask You what You think I should do. I know, but I don't know if I can do it. Please give me the strength and words to forgive Zachary's mother.*

Later after Jordan called Zachary to let him know she would pick up Nicholas, she headed out to the ranch early, hoping to catch his mother at Becca's. She took Tucker. Her son's pet had been missing him and moping around. When she parked behind the Rutgerses' car with an Arizona license plate, she kept the car windows down enough for Tucker to poke his nose out. Then, climbing from the Camaro, she fortified herself with a deep, cleansing breath and mounted the steps to the porch.

Becca answered her knock. Moving to the side to allow Jordan inside, Zachary's sister welcomed her with a smile. "Nicholas is at the barn with Zachary."

"I'm here to see your mother."

Her grin vanishing, Becca glanced toward the kitchen. "She's in there doing her daily crossword puzzle. Should I referee?"

"No. Your mom and I need to come to an understanding."

"Agreed." Again Becca made another quick look toward the kitchen. "She was thrilled to meet Nicholas yesterday evening. They're planning on staying the whole week and hope to spend as much time with him as possible. Dad's down at the barn with him and Zachary."

Jordan slowed her steps the closer she came to the kitchen. She wasn't sure how to begin a conversation with Zachary's mom. When she entered, the older woman looked up. Her sixty-plus years carved deep lines into her face. Lines at the moment that stressed her ire.

"You're early. Nicholas is at the barn." Putting her pencil down on the newspaper, Mrs. Rutgers pinched her lips even tighter together.

The cold thread that ran through her voice chilled Jordan, but she was determined to have this meeting with Zachary's mother. Before she'd left home, she'd read several passages in her Bible on forgiveness, trying to shore up her fledgling resolve to do what was right in the eyes of the Lord. "I know he's at the barn. I came early to talk to you."

"Why?"

Jordan sank onto the chair across from Mrs. Rutgers. "Don't you think we should talk with all that has happened? We owe it to Nicholas and Zachary."

Her eyebrows beetling together, she stared down at the crossword puzzle. "I suppose so. You kept our grandson from us for ten years. That was so wrong." Her voice strengthened its forceful tone as she spoke.

"And it wasn't wrong that you kept my calls from Zachary? If you had told him, you would have known."

"Why didn't you tell me that day why you were call-ing?"

Her words hit her like icicles piercing her flesh. "I wanted Zachary to be the first to know. I owed him that."

"Something you didn't do. Did you?"

She sucked in a deep breath, the hammering tap of her heartbeat pulsating against her rib cage. "I thought I was. I didn't know you wouldn't pass the message on. After you went on and on about him being engaged and then he didn't call, I thought he didn't want to talk to me." Remembering the pain and conflict that assaulted her at that time brought tears to her eyes. She might for-give Mrs. Rutgers, but she didn't want to break down and cry in front of the woman.

"You should have known he would want to know about his child."

"There was a part of me so hurt by his rejection that I convinced myself he wouldn't want to know." When Mrs. Rutgers started to say something to that last state-ment, Jordan held up her hand. "But there was a part of me that knew he would and couldn't bring myself to tell him. I'm sorry for what happened here, and I hope we can get past this for Nicholas's sake." *And mine. I'm tired of past events dictating my future.*

Mrs. Rutgers snorted. "I'll be civil to you when my grandson is around, but that's all I can promise." Bend-ing over the puzzle, she picked up the pencil and jotted down some letters in the squares.

Jordan stared at the top of her silver hair. Rising, she clutched the back of the chair. "I forgive you for not tell-ing Zachary about my calls, for lying to me about him being engaged. That's what I came to tell you. I can understand you wanting to protect your son. That's how I feel about Nicholas. Good day." Her rehearsed apology rolled from her lips like tumbleweed on a deserted road.

She marched toward the front of the house, not stopping to say anything to Becca. Tears burned her eyes, and she needed to get outside before she cried. On the porch the late-September air cooled her heated cheeks. The scent of honeysuckle along the front of the house floated to Jordan, reminding her of Granny's favorite fragrance. Thinking of her grandmother's parting words from Ephesians calmed her nerves. *And be ye kind one to another, tenderhearted, forgiving one another, even as God for Christ's sake hath forgiven you.*

She'd done what she'd come to do, and now she would pick up Nicholas and take him to his anatomy class. Peace settled in her heart as she headed to her car and drove toward the barn.

Nicholas stood on a fence slat, leaning against the top rail. He watched Zachary in the corral getting ready to mount a chestnut horse with Mr. Rutgers holding the animal by the halter. Jordan parked next to Zachary's black truck and approached her son.

Nicholas peered at her, saw Tucker following her and hopped down. He stooped to pet his dog. Its tail wagged against his leg. "Dad's riding this horse for the first time. He's been working with the gelding getting him used to him being around the saddle, but he's still a bit skittish."

Jordan peered at Zachary in the ring. He talked to the animal in a soft, soothing tone as he held the reins in his left hand tightly. After putting his foot in the stirrup, he swung up onto the gelding's back in one fluid motion, putting his weight in the center of the horse's back. His father had backed off toward the fence where she and Nicholas stood on the other side while Zachary continued to murmur to the animal. The gelding pranced back for a few steps then settled down.

Tucker barked. Zachary glanced toward them, zeroing in on Jordan. For a few seconds their gazes locked.

Suddenly the dog slipped from Nicholas's grasp and darted into the corral, yelping. He crossed the paddock, heading near the gelding and Zachary in his pursuit of a cat that raced from the barn toward a large oak shading part of the paddock.

The horse jumped and sidestepped, then began bucking. In a split second, Zachary flew off the animal's back and landed with a thud on the dirt ground a few feet from the gelding. Jordan gasped. Tucker yapped at the bottom of the tree where the cat had disappeared. The loud sound echoed through the yard. The horse reared up and his hooves came down toward Zachary. He rolled, but one hoof clipped him on the leg.

Nicholas started to climb through the slats to get to his father while Nicholas's grandfather hurried out to the middle.

"Stay put," she said to her son and rushed to the gate into the corral. "Don't come in here. Get Tucker. Calm him down."

With her heart pounding, she dashed to Zachary while his father approached the horse cautiously. "Are you all right?"

"Yeah," he said, pain etched into his tanned features. "Don't, Dad. I'll take care of it. Leave him to me." Zachary rubbed the calf of his leg then struggled to stand.

Jordan put her arm around his middle to help him. He allowed her to for a second, then shrugged from her.

"Keep Nicholas out. You get out. And keep Tucker quiet." He hobbled toward the frightened gelding.

Jordan moved to the gate, but her attention focused fully on the scene in the corral. The horse's nostrils widened, pupils dilated. Out of the corner of her eye Jordan noticed Nicholas scoop Tucker up into his arms and quickly walk away from the oak. Blissful quiet reigned again except for the horse's snorts.

With his arms out in front of him, his hands up, palms outward, Zachary slowed his steps, saying, "Easy. Everything's okay. Easy. No one is gonna hurt you."

Jordan pictured again that time Zachary had fallen off the horse in the rodeo and broken his arm. It could have happened today, or if she hadn't been here, Nicholas could have been out in the middle of the corral before his father noticed. The gelding could have charged...

*Don't go there. It didn't happen. Lord, how do I turn control over to You and stop getting so worked up over anything out of my control?*

She splayed her hand over her chest as she inhaled then exhaled.

Finally Zachary led the gelding toward the gate. Jordan backed away with Nicholas plastered against her side. Her gaze never left the horse as Zachary limped toward the barn with his dad next to him.

"Did you see Dad? Nothing scares him."

These past six weeks she'd felt as though she'd had no say in what was going on around her. She wasn't even sure her homeschooling with Nicholas was working out. Was she doing it right? What if her son lost ground in his education because of her?

Nicholas started forward.

"Where are you going?"

"To make sure Dad's okay."

"First let's put Tucker in the car. We don't want any more problems."

Nicholas slumped toward the Camaro and settled his dog in the front seat. "He didn't mean to cause trouble."

"I know, hon. I shouldn't have let him out, but he was so lonely for you." She strode toward the barn, keeping a grasp on her son's shoulder.

Zachary released the gelding into a pasture with other horses, and he immediately ran off. His father said something to Zachary, then hurried away, nodding to her and Nicholas as he passed.

"I'm sorry about Tucker," Jordan said when she reached Zachary.

"Bad timing. It happens. No problem." He took a step and winced.

"You're hurt."

"I've been hurt worse before, and I doubt it will be the last time. This is nothing. A cowboy is used to bumps and bruises."

Nicholas puffed out his chest. "Yeah, Mom. I fell off a horse and hurt my bottom. I was sore a few days, but it was no big deal."

"You fell off a horse?"

"Yeah. Didn't I tell you about it? It was last week. I was trying to open the gate to ride through it. I held on to it too long while Chief went on into the field."

"No, you two neglected to mention that."

Zachary compressed his lips, his nostrils flaring like the agitated gelding. "For this very reason. Nicholas is okay and learned a valuable lesson."

"It was one thing that it happened and an entirely different thing when I'm not kept informed."

Nicholas took his dad's hand. "I didn't want to worry you. You worry too much."

Father and son strolled toward the barn, leaving Jordan to stare at them. Her heart constricted at the thought she was losing her child. He might be her only one, because no matter how much she tried to move on after Zachary she hadn't been able to and now she knew the impossibility of that relationship.

She hurriedly followed the pair into the barn, catching Nicholas before he went into a stall. "We have to get going. You have a class today."

Her son's face brightened. "I almost forgot and I really want to hear what Dr. Reynolds has to say about the heart."

She wouldn't be half-surprised if Nicholas already knew most of what the doctor would impart to the students today. When he'd discovered what was wrong with him, he'd delved into everything he could get his hands on concerning his heart. If it had been too hard for him to read, she had read aloud for her son. It hadn't taken him long before she didn't have to.

Nicholas started for the double doors.

Zachary chuckled. "I once asked him to tell me about his heart defect, and it took all my willpower to keep my eyes from glazing over as he explained."

"Dr. Reynolds has been particularly patient with all Nicholas's questions during class."

"Do you stay?"

"No, I run errands, but I can tell by what he and Nicholas have said that he asks a lot of questions."

Nicholas placed his hand on his hip. "Mom, we're going to be late."

"At least I feel good about his math and science. The rest of the subjects I'm not so sure about." She strode away before Zachary had a chance to ask what she meant. She shouldn't have confessed her doubts about homeschooling Nicholas. Doubts she had to work through.

"How was class today? Did you learn anything more about the heart?" Jordan asked as she picked up Nicholas at the doctor's office where he held the biweekly classes.

"Yeah, a couple of things. Class got me to thinking. I need to be studying the anatomy of the different animals to help prepare me to be a veterinarian. There'll be similarities but also differences between species. When I'm older, I can help out at a vet's office. What do you think?"

"You've got some time before that."

"Dad said he would introduce me to his vet. I hope I can start taking college courses by age fifteen. You can help me plan that. Now that I'm being homeschooled, I can go at my own rate. I don't have to hold back."

"You've been holding back?"

"Some. I didn't like the other kids making fun of what I knew. I never felt like I could be myself around my classmates."

After pulling into the driveway at her childhood home, Jordan shifted toward her son and took in his serious expression. "Hon, it's okay if you're a kid and you have fun."

"I am. I love going to the ranch, helping Dad with the horses. One day I'll be able to do what he does."

"Fall off a horse? Didn't you already?"

"Dad's like a horse whisperer. I want that kind of connection. I've been working with Tucker on that."

College in five years? Her son had his whole life mapped out while she was still struggling with hers. "Oh, I almost forgot to tell you, I got you signed up for art lessons."

"Do you think a cowboy would draw?"

"Excuse me?"

"Maybe I should do photography or learn how to play the harmonica."

"I thought you liked to draw and wanted to learn more."

"That was last month. Do you know that Dad plays the fiddle?"

"A violin?"

"No, it's called a fiddle. He took it up when he was on the rodeo circuit. Some of the guys had an informal little band." Nicholas tapped the side of his chin. "Yep, I'm thinking the harmonica would complement a fiddle. I'll ask Dad."

Had her son been watching a lot of old Western movies or something like that? Before she could say another word, he pushed open the car door and raced for the porch. She felt as though a tornado had flattened her. Her child was changing into someone she didn't know. Becoming more like Zachary.

Her stomach knotted as she trudged toward the house. Scratch the drawing lessons. Where could she find someone to teach her son the harmonica? Maybe photography would be a better choice. It would be easier to find a class for that.

When she entered the foyer, she called out to Nicholas. He came to the top of the stairs and peered over the banister.

"We need to get to work. I'll be up there in a minute. This week's essay is an expository one."

Nicholas groaned.

"You'll need to pick a topic and explain in detail about a certain event or situation. No editorial comments. Facts and other people's views."

"Anything I wish?"

"Yes, if it fits the type of essay."

"Great!" He fled down the upstairs hallway, the sound of his pounding footsteps resonating through the house.

The words *great* and *writing* never went hand in hand with Nicholas. She strode into the den where Granny usually was at this time of day to let her know they were home—which obviously she'd already heard—and see if she was okay. Granny had had a headache earlier, and when she'd left for the ranch, her grandmother was lying down in her bedroom.

Five minutes later Jordan entered Nicholas's room and came to an abrupt halt. A video clip of Zachary on the back of a bull at a rodeo bombarded her. When she saw him tumble to the ground as the horn sounded, the next few seconds snatched her breath.

# Chapter Twelve

Nicholas glanced back at Jordan, then quickly clicked off the video.

She held up a trembling hand and pointed at the computer. "Where did you get that?"

"I found it online. I have all the rodeo clips of Dad, at least the ones I could find."

The image of the bull trampling Zachary shook her as though she had been there and seen the horrific sight of his battered body lying in the dirt. "I don't want you watching that or any ones like it."

"My essay is going to be about the rodeo. I was doing research." Nicholas turned totally around in his desk chair and faced her.

She folded her arms across her chest. She couldn't shake the picture from her mind. Zachary hurt. Not moving. "Find another topic."

"I know what happened to Dad that last time he rode. He told me about it. I'm not a baby. Quit trying to protect me."

*Remain calm.* Yes, she'd known an accident had caused Zachary's limp, but she'd never thought it had been as bad as what she'd seen. She waited half a minute to answer her son. "What do you suggest I do? Let you do whatever you want?"

He straightened his shoulders. "What are you afraid of? That I'll go out the first chance I get and ride a bull like Dad? I love riding horses, but I know I don't have what it takes to ride a bull. I don't want to learn. You can quit worrying about that. But I want to learn everything about something my father loves. He spent many years participating in the rodeo. A lot of the horses he raises end up in the rodeo. So what are you afraid of?"

A pressure in her chest expanded to encompass her whole body. She stared at her son and tried to come up with an answer to his question that didn't expose her fears. She couldn't. "I'm afraid of losing you." *I'm afraid I'll be alone.*

"To Dad?"

Tears lumping in her throat, she nodded. She'd centered her life around him for so long she didn't know what she would do if something happened to Nicholas. That one time waiting for him to come out of surgery had given her a glimpse of the fear that gripped her in a stranglehold. *How do I turn that over to You, Father?*

Nicholas leaped up, raced across the room and threw his arms around her. "You aren't going to lose me. I love you, but I love Dad, too. Can't I love both of you?"

She buried her face in his hair. "Yes. I haven't had to share you for ten years. Give me some time to get used to the idea."

"Sure." He leaned back, still clasping her. "But I want to learn about the rodeo. I already have a thesis statement."

The excitement in her son's voice wiped away her

concerns. She'd never heard him so eager to write a paper. She had to trust in the Lord. "What happened to your father that last rodeo?"

"Have him tell you. I always believe in going to the primary source, so ask him."

"I will. I need to understand, too." She ruffled his hair. "So you've already got a thesis statement. This is a first."

Grinning from ear to ear, he moved back to the computer and brought up a blank screen. "Yes, but I want to do a lot more research. But the idea of a cowboy is disappearing and I think the rodeo is one of the last bastions of the cowboy ideal. Rugged. Fearless. Skilled."

Jordan swallowed several times. These thoughts hadn't just formulated in the past fifteen minutes. Nicholas had been thinking about it for a while. "Let me know when you're through with your research. We'll work on the rough draft together."

"I'd like to write the rough draft by myself first before we work together."

"Okay. I'll leave you to write."

Jordan left her son's bedroom and headed downstairs to the kitchen where she had her laptop. She would do her own online search of Zachary's name and see what video clips were posted. When she'd told Nicholas she needed to understand, she'd meant that. What had made Zachary get on the back of a two-thousand-pound bull? Take risks in his professional life but not his personal one?

"Mom, what are you doing here? I was coming up to Becca's in half an hour." Zachary moved out of the way to allow his mother into his house.

"I thought we would talk a few minutes before the barbecue. Before Nicholas and—" she tensed, her mouth firming in such a thin line her lips vanished.

"—Jordan arrive. I think it's about time we talk, too."

"You do? You've been avoiding me all week."

He rubbed his nape. "I know. I haven't figured out how I feel about anything. Everything has happened so fast these past weeks."

His mother strode into the living room and took a seat on the couch. "But we need to talk about what I did all those years ago. Avoiding the subject won't make it go away."

Restless energy surged through him. He remained standing. "Why didn't you tell me about Jordan's calls? I know you said you were protecting me…" His words trailed into the silence. Were his mother and Jordan alike—protecting their sons?

"Ever since she came to see me last Monday, I've—"

"Wait, you talked with Jordan on Monday?"

"Yeah, she came to tell me she'd forgiven me. Can you believe that? She forgives me while she's the one who kept the fact you had a son from us."

"She did," he murmured, sinking onto the chair nearby, the spike of energy suddenly siphoning from him.

"I told her how I felt."

"How?"

"I'm angry like you. We missed ten years of Nicholas's life. Ten!"

*But I'm not angry anymore.* That realization settled over him, calming his restless spirit. "She had her hands full with Nicholas's illness and raising him alone."

"That was her choice."

"True. But she was hurt when I didn't call. She thought I didn't want to have anything to do with her. You told her I was engaged when I wasn't."

"Are you defending her?" Anger sparked his mother's eyes and deepened the lines on her face.

"I'm trying to understand her. I'm trying to make this situation with Nicholas work."

"She did you wrong. Stay away from her."

Zachary bolted to his feet and paced. "I can't. I have to think about Nicholas now." Pausing, he rotated toward his mother. "Why didn't you tell me she called?"

"I told you I was protecting you. She hurt you bad. I still remember how you were after you two broke up. You needed to get on with your life without her."

The similarities hit him full force. So like Jordan with Nicholas. "I needed to know I was having a child." His hands balled at his sides. So many emotions swirled around inside him like a dust storm on the prairie.

"I did what any mother would do. Looking out for the best interests of her child, no matter what."

"Including lying?"

Her face pale, she stared down at her hands twining in her lap. "I wouldn't have kept anything like Nicholas from you if I had known." When she lifted her head, tears shone in her eyes. "I would have done it differently. Given you the messages. But she didn't tell me."

His mother's words cut through his heart like a piece of barbed wire. He had enough turmoil in his life without adding conflict with his mother to the list. "Let's just drop this. It's in the past. We can't change it now."

She rose. "I agree."

"But I need you to be civil to Jordan at the barbecue for Nicholas's sake."

"I'll do my best. But why does she have to come to a family dinner?"

"Because she's my child's mother. Becca and her have become friends. And Nicholas wants her there."

She tilted her head and pinned her gaze on him. "But not you?"

"I want her there for all those reasons." He evaded what his mother really wanted to know because he didn't have an answer. Ever since Jordan had returned to Tallgrass, his emotions had been bound in knots— ones he couldn't slip loose easily.

"I'm gonna miss Grandma and Granddad when they return to Arizona in a couple of days." Nicholas squirmed in the front seat of Jordan's Camaro the closer they got to the ranch.

"I'm glad you're enjoying their visit." But thinking about her talk with Zachary's mother made her tighten her hands about the steering wheel.

Jordan pulled into the gravel road that led to Becca's house. The closer she came, the more her stomach constricted and roiled. She wished she had her son's excitement about this barbecue.

When she parked in front, Nicholas leaped from the car, raced toward the porch and disappeared inside. The sound of voices, a laugh, floated to her. This was Nicholas's family. Not hers. She should have stayed home. And yet, she and Zachary needed to do things without Nicholas—get to know each other as adults. Maybe she should ask him to go on a picnic like they had as teenagers.

But first she had to get through the barbecue with his mother.

Dropping her head on the steering wheel, she closed her eyes and prayed for strength and patience to get through this afternoon. *I can do this.* Then she remembered Mrs. Rutgers's words and the chill that emanated from the woman when she'd talked with her in the kitchen the other day. The chill enveloped her as she sat in the front seat.

A rap on her window startled her. She twisted around. Zachary's handsome face filled her vision. The ice that encased her melted away.

He opened the door. "Are you okay?"

The concern in his voice soothed some of her tension. *I can do this for Nicholas.* She relaxed and smiled. "Just working myself up to see your mother again."

"Ah." He straightened. "She'll behave herself. She promised me."

"I wish you hadn't had to ask." She climbed from the car.

"Me, too. But I imagine you can understand her feelings since you're a mother."

Jordan started for the house, hoping the next few hours sped by in a blur. When she neared the porch, laughter wafted to her from inside. She slanted a look toward Zachary next to her. "Does Becca need help in the kitchen?"

He chuckled. "A strategic escape. Not bad. I'm sure she would enjoy your company."

When she entered, she said hi to everyone then made her way toward the kitchen. At the door she peered back at Zachary's mom, who nailed her with a sharp gaze. What was the woman thinking? She shouldn't have accepted the invitation.

"I'm so glad you came, Jordan." With her hands full,

Becca shut the refrigerator with a push of her hip. "I could use you to put the potato salad together. The potatoes are cooked, but that's as far as I've gotten."

"I'd be glad to."

"It'll beat playing soccer." Becca gave her a knife and cutting board.

"Soccer?"

"Yeah, Zachary and Paul thought it be would a great idea to have an impromptu game. Of course, they didn't take into account I don't play and neither does Mom. I hurried in here to finish making the dinner and left them to pick teams."

"So your mom is going to join us?"

Chuckling, Becca shook her head. "Dad and Mom are gonna be cheerleaders."

"Nicholas doesn't know how to play." Jordan began dicing the potatoes.

"My youngest doesn't, either. Nicholas will learn. Zachary is a great teacher."

"Speaking of teaching, how do you homeschool three children? I feel like I'm in over my head half the time. I've been doing it a month, and I don't know if I'm doing it the right way."

"There's no one right way. What you do will depend on your child and how he learns. In Nicholas's case, he loves to learn. A lot of what he does will be self-directed whereas with Mike I have to be on top of him every step of the way. For Nicholas, you'll have to make sure he covers all he needs and doesn't get stuck on one subject. I know he's great with math, and from what Zachary has said, he doesn't like to write. You'll have to make sure he does it."

Jordan took the boiled eggs and began chopping

them to add to the large mixing bowl. "Yeah, I've been doing that. He whines when I make him write, even using the computer. With everything else he doesn't give me any problems."

"When it doesn't come easy or they don't like it, they balk at doing it. You should see Ashley with math. She hates it. There are times I've lost my patience with her, and I don't like doing that. Frustrating." Taking a wooden spoon, Becca stirred the brownie mixture.

"I know what you mean. He's so smart, but he gets frustrated with himself when he starts putting his thoughts down on paper." After adding the pickled relish, Jordan sliced a red onion. "Except with this newest writing project. He's really gotten into it."

"What's it about?"

"An expository essay about the rodeo. He told me he was almost through with the rough draft. I've seen some of it. It's the best writing he's ever done."

"That's my brother's influence."

Jordan cocked her head, thinking back over the past weeks and the changes she'd seen in Nicholas. "Yes, it is. Until Zachary, I didn't realize how much my son needed a father. It's always been just the two of us and that has seemed fine. But it wasn't really."

After pouring the chocolate batter into an oblong pan, Becca stuck it into the oven. "Kids do best when they have a stable environment with two loving parents."

Jordan paused in cutting up the onion, her eyes watering from its strong odor. If only she had swallowed her pride and hurt years ago, Nicholas could have had that kind of environment. *Lord, I've been so wrong. How do I fix this?*

"You okay?"

She brushed her hand across her wet cheek. "It's the onion." *It's me. I messed up.*

The chatter from the living room died down. The bang of the front door—more than once—echoed through the house.

"I guess they decided on their teams. Want to go be a cheerleader?" Becca laid the dish rag she'd used to clean the counter into the sink.

After scraping the onion pieces into the bowl, Jordan started on the celery. "I'm almost finished. You go ahead. If we arrive together, they'll want us to be on a team."

"Yeah, you're probably right, except I doubt any of them would want me." Becca patted her stomach. "I've really got to start exercising." Before she left, she added, "Jordan, you're doing fine. A lot of homeschooling moms ask the questions you are. Am I providing the best education? Am I missing anything? As you've been discovering, the Helping Hands Homeschooling group is a great place to get support and help. You aren't alone in doing this."

Jordan sighed as Becca strolled from the kitchen toward the front of the house. She felt confident in her work as a graphic design artist and even felt good about the job she'd done raising Nicholas to be a responsible young man. But she still wrestled with what was best educationally for her son. It was a comfort to know that other parents went through the same dilemma.

After putting all the ingredients for the potato salad in the bowl, Jordan stirred them together then put the dish into the refrigerator. The scent of chocolate permeated the air and made her stomach gurgle with hunger.

She took a few moments to clean up, trying to delay going outside as long as possible, but when Zachary appeared in the entrance, she knew she couldn't any longer.

"I came in to make sure you hadn't gotten lost finding your way outside." He rested his shoulder against the door frame.

"No," she said with a laugh. "I'll be there in a few minutes."

"We kinda need you now."

"Why?" She turned to face him fully, the mischievous sparkle in his eyes accelerating her heartbeat.

"Paul talked Becca into playing. We need another player to even out the teams. Mom and Dad are even participating."

Placing her hand on her hip, she gave him a pout. "You know how I am when it comes to sports."

"I know how you used to be. I'm not sure now." The gleam in his expression brightened.

"Well, let me reassure you, I'm lousy at anything having to do with a ball. And if I'm not mistaken soccer has one."

Zachary closed the distance between them and grabbed her hand. "Come on. It's about time you got over your fear of being hit with a ball."

"Hey, I've been hit with one and let me tell you it hurts." As he urged her toward the front door, she tried to frown, but her mouth refused to cooperate. "How in the world did Paul talk Becca into playing?"

"I'm not one hundred percent positive, but I think it was something about if my mother could do it, she could, too."

As Zachary dragged her laughing out of the house, Jordan decided playing a game of soccer could be fun— that was until she saw Zachary's mother. Her scowl darkened her eyes, and the older woman turned away. Jordan didn't know what would be worse, being on the same team as Mrs. Rutgers or the opposite one.

Later that day, the scent of hamburgers grilling saturated the fall air. A crisp breeze cooled the evening. A door shutting drew Zachary around. Jordan crossed the yard with a large platter.

"Becca said to put the burgers on this when they're done." She placed it on a table near the barbecue grill and turned to leave.

He didn't want her to go. He hadn't talked to her much since the soccer game earlier. "Stay. Keep me company. You've been awfully quiet. That's not like you."

"It's been a bit awkward."

"Because of Mom?"

"You are perceptive."

"Ouch. I think I hear a touch of sarcasm." He began flipping over the thick patties. "Mom hasn't said anything to you."

"No. But…" She snapped her mouth closed and averted her gaze.

"But what?"

"It's obvious I'm not wanted here and that makes it uncomfortable. If we'd been playing football, I think she would have tackled me, and I was on her team."

"Give her time."

"You aren't the least bit angry at her for not telling you I called?"

Zachary set the spatula on the platter and faced Jordan. "I'm not happy it happened, but she thought she was doing what was best for me."

She started to say something, shook her head and turned away. Walking to the edge of the patio, she stared at the horses in the pasture behind Becca's house. A strong urge to hold her and take away the hurt he'd seen flash into her eyes overwhelmed him. He stiffened, resisting Jordan's lure.

When she spun around, a neutral expression descended over her features. "Are you still mad at me?"

Was he? "No, not really. For Nicholas's sake, I let go of my anger. It doesn't do any good now, and like we talked about before, we need to be a team for our son."

"Then I have a proposition for you. I think we should spend some time together alone getting to know each other better to see if we can find a common ground."

"You want us to date?" The idea should have sent him into a panic. Surprisingly it made sense.

"No. Just two people getting to know each other better. For Nicholas's sake."

"Sure. Do you have something in mind?"

"As a matter of fact, I do. How about next Friday afternoon? We'll have a picnic lunch. My treat."

"Hey, Zachary, the burgers are smoking," Becca yelled from the back door stoop.

He whirled around, snatched up the spatula and scooped up the patties before they became charred. Jordan had always had the ability of taking his mind off what he should be doing. What in the world had he agreed to?

\* \* \*

"I want everything to be perfect today." Jordan finished packing the picnic basket with a container of peach cobbler on Friday.

"Child, you're gonna need a forklift to pick that thing up." Granny waved her hand toward the wicker basket.

"Didn't you tell me the way to a man's heart was through his stomach?"

"That I did. That's how I got your grandpa. Now with Doug, he cooks as good as I do. It's kinda nice having a man cook for me. In fact, we've got a date tonight."

"You two are getting mighty serious."

"We don't have the luxury of a long-drawn-out courtship. Time is a-ticking." Granny snapped her fingers several times as she spoke. "Remember that, child. You don't have the luxury, either. You and your young man have been apart long enough. Nicholas needs a whole family."

"I'm thinking about it."

"So where are you going today?"

"To Miller Falls."

"Ah, good thinking. Very romantic."

That was what she was counting on. Miller Falls was one of the places they had gone to as teenagers. It held special memories for her, and she hoped for Zachary, too. If there was to be anything between them, maybe they would discover it there.

The doorbell chimed. Jordan hefted the basket from the table, leaned down and kissed Granny on the cheek then started toward the foyer. "Have a great time with Doug."

Granny chuckled. "I will. And when I get back this evening, I want to hear all about your date."

At the entrance into the kitchen Jordan glanced at her grandmother. "Shh. Don't say that. It's not a date."

"Keep telling yourself that and maybe you'll really believe it."

By the time she reached the foyer, Nicholas had opened the door and let Zachary inside. "Are we going to practice tomorrow during our riding lesson for HHH Junior Rodeo?"

"Yep. We have only a week to go." Zachary tousled his son's hair.

Jordan set the heavy basket on the tile floor. "Don't forget your assignment for anatomy class. Aunt Rachel will be taking you this afternoon."

"I've already done it." He swung back to Zachary. "Dad, don't leave yet. I've got something for you." He raced up the stairs.

"Do you know what?" Zachary asked.

"You've never been good about surprises."

"You aren't, either."

"I've got a pretty good idea, but I'm not telling."

He frowned but didn't put much into the expression. "Is where we're going a surprise?"

She gestured toward the basket at her feet. "We're going on a picnic."

"Where?"

"Sorry. My lips are sealed."

Nicholas hurried down the stairs with a manila envelope in his hand. When he gave it to Zachary, her son thrust his shoulders back and lifted his chin. "I wrote this."

Zachary started to open the envelope.

"No, read it later." A blush stained her child's cheeks.

"Okay," Zachary said slowly, glancing between them. "Are you ready?"

She nodded.

He picked up the basket and stepped out onto the porch.

When she joined him outside, she stopped him with a hand on his arm. "I'm driving."

"Are you going to blindfold me, too?"

"What a great idea! Then where we're going will really be a surprise. Let me go back inside—" she pivoted toward the front door "—and get a scarf to use."

"By the time you get back out here, I'll be halfway down the street heading home."

With both hands on her hips, she faced him. "You aren't playing fair."

"I really don't like surprises."

"Okay, no blindfold, but I'm still driving."

"Then you'll have to use my truck. It's parked behind yours in the driveway." He descended the porch steps and tied down the basket in the back of his pickup.

When Jordan approached the driver's door, he tossed her the keys and rounded the front to slide into the passenger's seat. She backed out onto the street and headed toward the highway outside of town.

"You're the first person I've let drive my truck."

"I am?" She glanced at his white-knuckled grip on the handhold above the side window.

"Yep, and I still have two years of payments left on it."

She laughed. "Are you, in your not-so-subtle way, telling me I better not have a wreck?"

"Yes, ma'am."

"Then why did you let me drive?" The idea he had warmed her.

"I thought it was time."

At a stop sign, she fixed her attention fully on Zachary. "Time for what?"

"To give you a little trust."

"With your truck?"

"With my life."

Their gazes locked together. Jordan couldn't look away. Her throat contracted, and suddenly she wished they were anywhere but on a road waiting to pull out onto the highway. A blare of a horn behind her startled her. She dragged her attention away from Zachary and faced forward.

"To reassure you, I haven't had a wreck or a ticket. I'm a very good driver, but if I remember correctly when we were going together, you had one wreck and two tickets for speeding."

"But not in years. I'm a changed man."

Yes, he was different. More serious. Reserved. And when she caught a certain glimpse of Zachary when he wasn't looking, she saw a hint of tragedy in his eyes. Was she the one who had put it there? Or was it someone or something else?

After traveling five minutes north on the highway, Zachary said, "I know where we going. The south end of Prairie Lake."

"Nope."

She continued past the entrance to the park he mentioned. Another ten minutes and she turned down a narrow two-lane road.

"Miller Falls," Zachary murmured almost as if to himself.

"Yep. I thought it would be nice to visit somewhere we had good times at. We didn't just date. We were friends. I want us to capture that again."

"Is that the truth?"

The skepticism in his question hurt. "Yes. Part of the reason we broke up eleven years ago was because we stopped communicating with each other. We both got wrapped up in our own world and forgot the other's. You spent that last summer going to rodeos, and I went to the Sooner Art Institute for a month."

"I remember. We saw each other in passing until the middle of August. I was trying to make some money to help us get started."

"I know but every time you rode in the ring I could hardly breathe until you were finished. There were times I wouldn't even watch. As you got more and more involved in bull riding, I got more scared."

"Why didn't you say anything to me?"

Jordan pulled into a small gravel parking lot not far from the creek and waterfall. Angling toward Zachary, she looked right at him. "Because you loved doing it. I didn't want to be the one to take that away from you. I thought if I got away and could get some perspective on our situation it would be okay."

"Then we fought and broke up."

"You didn't understand my art and I didn't understand your need to participate in rodeos. I didn't like football, but I would have preferred you taking that football scholarship offered to you."

One corner of his mouth lifted. "Don't tell anyone around here, but I didn't care that much about playing football. I certainly didn't want to in college."

"No, your heart was somewhere else. So why didn't

you just go on the rodeo circuit rather than join the army?"

He stared out the windshield, his mouth lashing into a tight-lipped grimace. "I was a fool. I started going out with the guys, partying. Anything to forget you. Two of us enlisted after drinking. I thought if I could see the world some, get away from Oklahoma and all the memories, even the rodeo, that everything would be all right. When I realized my mistake thinking that, it was too late. I was in basic training. I haven't drank since then."

"How many years were you in the army?"

"Four. I got some training, I saw the world and I went to school." He opened the door, hopped to the ground and reached back to get the basket.

She knew after he'd left the army that he'd become a professional bull rider for five years and was world champion for three straight years before his accident. Although she couldn't bring herself to watch that video again, she did watch others where he'd ridden to victory. Seeing him talk after getting his first world championship helped her to understand a little of the lure of what he did. His face had shown excitement and a sense of accomplishing something important, the same expression she'd seen when he had finished his ride and left the ring.

He came around and opened her door. "Ready?"

She climbed down and pocketed his keys. "I wish it was warmer. We could have gone swimming like that one time."

"This would be a fun place to bring Nicholas, especially next summer."

"Once he learns to swim."

Halting, Zachary rotated toward her, both eyebrows raised. "He doesn't know how to swim?"

She shook her head. "He was sick for a long time. We didn't have access to a pool in South Carolina. I lived in a little house, but there was no neighborhood pool."

He started forward. "Well, that's gonna change. He might not always swim in a pool here, but places like this are great in the summer."

"Up until a couple of years ago, he didn't have the energy or desire. Now Nicholas is wanting to do all he's been missing."

"Like learning to ride?"

"Yep. That was top on his list when we moved here."

Looking back seven weeks, she wondered if her sister had told her the ranch she was sending her to was owned by Zachary if she would have come that day. Probably not. Actually, definitely not. But now she saw where the Lord was leading her. She needed to make amends to Zachary and bring them together as a family—at least Nicholas and his father, if not her, too. This outing renewed her hope it was possible.

"There's still so much I want to know about Nicholas." Zachary set the basket down on the ground under a large oak tree near the waterfall.

The sound of its water pouring over the rocks above and crashing down into the pool echoed through the small glade and faded into the woods that surrounded the place. Sunlight dappled the glittering surface like sparkling diamonds strewn across a pale blue carpet. The scent of pine and earth hung in the air.

Jordan opened the basket and withdrew the blanket. As she spread it under the oak, she gestured toward the manila envelope. "I suggest you read his essay as a start."

Stretching out on the blanket, he withdrew the papers and began reading. Intense concentration creased his forehead. Then slowly his expression went from surprise to awe.

When he finished, he peered at her sitting next to him. "He thinks the cowboy is the epitome of what this country stands for. He even draws parallels between the jousting of knights in medieval times to the contestants in a rodeo, competing for the prize. A lot of thought went into this."

"It's a tribute to you. He watched hours of videotape, mostly of you, before he wrote this. I didn't help him hardly at all, which is most unusual when he writes."

Zachary swallowed hard. "I didn't know he was doing this. He asked me some questions this past week about what I did, how I felt, but I just thought it was his curiosity."

"He wanted to understand what drove you to risk your life each time you got on the back of a bull."

"He obviously listens well."

"Until I read this last night, I didn't have a clue why you did it."

"'The thrill and adrenaline rush is unbelievable, but what really got me back on a two-thousand-pound, bucking bull each time was the faith of totally putting myself in God's hands' was the answer three-time world champion Zachary Rutgers stated when asked why he was a bull rider." Zachary lifted his gaze from the essay to look into her eyes. "That was my answer word for word and he didn't even write it down. Amazing."

She smiled. "Yes, Nicholas is amazing."

"Tell me about his heart defect, his surgery. I know you've told me some, but that had to be such a difficult time for both of you. I need to understand like you and Nicholas did about my bull riding."

"When he started school, Nicholas caught everything. He was always sick—small for his age. Finally our family physician diagnosed Nicholas with atrial septal defect. Usually it's repaired with a catheter. Nicholas got one, but then it became infected. He almost died. He was put on long-term antibiotics, lots of blood work, doctors. The catheter had to be removed and repaired surgically. All of this took a toll on Nicholas."

"And not you?"

Thinking back to that time brought a rush of memories of the hospital, long hours of doubt if Nicholas would be all right, sleepless nights, worry, prayers, tears. Her stomach still clenched anytime she visited someone in a hospital and got a whiff of that antiseptic scent. "Once Nicholas started recovering, I was fine."

Zachary clasped her palm. "You were? You're still scared for him and try to protect him."

She yanked her hand away. "What you really mean is that I'm overprotective."

He indicated an inch with his forefinger and thumb. "Maybe a little. The doctor said he is fine now. As I've said, a boy has to have breathing room."

"And guidance."

"Are you ready for him to compete in the HHH Junior Rodeo competition?"

"Barrel racing?"

"Yes, that's one thing."

"Do you really think he's ready?"

"I was doing what he's doing at six."

"And look what happened to you." She pulled her legs up and clasped them to her chest.

He lifted his shoulders in a shrug. "I survived, and I'm now doing something else I wanted to do—raising horses." Rubbing his hands together, he grinned. "I don't know about you, but I'm starving. What do we have for lunch?"

"A couple of your favorites. Or at least they used to be." Jordan scooted toward the basket and dug inside, bringing the first container out. "Fried chicken, extra crispy. Then I have a cucumber-tomato salad as well as a pasta one, slices of homemade bread and butter and for dessert peach cobbler."

Zachary peeked beneath the foil at the chicken and picked up several pieces. "Don't tell Nicholas how much I love this."

"Oh, he knows. He helped me with this lunch."

"I still can't believe I have a son who is a vegetarian."

"He isn't your usual child."

"I'm discovering that every time I'm with him." He finished loading his paper plate with the various dishes.

After she selected what she wanted to eat, she bowed her head and blessed the food. "Dig in. What you don't eat you can take home with you if you want."

Several bites later, he looked straight at her and said, "A guy sure could get used to food like this. This is delicious."

"You can thank Granny for teaching me how to cook."

"I'll do that. Your grandmother is quite a character. How are she and Doug getting along?" He took a sip of his bottled water.

"According to my mother, too well. She thinks Granny is too old to carry on like a twenty-year-old."

"Your mom doesn't want to see your grandmother with a man?"

"I think she's jealous. She's been divorced for more than twenty years and has dated off and on over the years, but she never has found anyone who interested her. Lately she has declared she isn't going to date anymore. She loves her life like it is."

"And you don't believe her?"

"Nope and neither does Rachel. My sister has even tried to fix her up with a couple of older men who were friends of her husband's. It didn't work out. Rachel has decided matchmaking isn't for her."

"Contrary to a certain grandmother and young boy."

Again Zachary's gaze snagged hers from across the blanket and held her linked to him. She swallowed her bite of salad past the lump in her throat. The intensity in his eyes heated her cheeks. For a moment she felt as though she were the most important person in his life. The warmth from her blush spread through her body.

"They don't seem to be too bad lately," she murmured, wetting her dry lips.

"Maybe they've given up on us."

"Maybe." Was there any hope for them? Had Nicholas and Granny realized there wasn't? "But I have to warn you, usually Nicholas is relentless and determined when he is after something. It's those qualities that helped him through his illness. He rarely cried when he was hurting. He was so brave." Tears sprang into her eyes when she thought back over that time, the pain he was going through evident on his face even though he tried to mask it. She closed her eyes, a wet drop dripping out and coursing down her face.

Zachary leaned close, wiped his thumb across her cheek, then cupped the back of her neck to draw her nearer. "You aren't by yourself with Nicholas anymore. I'm here to help."

His murmured words spoken into her hair as he hugged her against his chest made her almost believe there was a chance for her and Zachary. Then she remembered the invisible barrier always in place even when he held her close. As though he kept a small part of himself from her and that no matter what she did that wouldn't change.

With his thumb under her chin, he raised it so she stared into his eyes. "You've done a great job with Nicholas."

The compliment washed over her. She snuggled closer, wanting so much more than Zachary was willing to share. And it was her fault the situation was like that.

"If I could change what happened eleven—"

He settled his mouth over hers, stealing the rest of her sentence. For that brief moment when his lips connected with hers, all her doubts fled. Only possibilities lay ahead. Her heartbeat kicked up a notch, matching the faster tempo of his that she felt against his chest.

When he moved back, framing her face in his hands, his dazed expression vanished to be replaced with uncertainty, his eyebrows slashing downward, his gaze narrowing. "I shouldn't have done that. It only complicates things."

He surged to his feet and stuck his hands into his front pockets. "I'm sorry. That won't happen again."

Striding away, he headed for the pool and stood on its edge, staring at the waterfall.

Jordan curled her legs up against her body, hugging them to her and laying her forehead on her knees. She'd crashed from a high plateau into a bottomless pit. Just as she thought she might be breaking down the barrier between them, Zachary pulled back and erected the wall even higher.

## Chapter Thirteen

What had he been thinking? Kissing Jordan like that? Zachary plowed his hand through his hair, trying to bring order to his reeling thoughts. Today as she'd talked about Nicholas being in the hospital and having surgery, all he could think about was he should have been there. Then he saw her tears and all common sense evaporated.

As he listened to the creek plunging into the pool from above, the sound calmed him enough to turn back toward Jordan and cover the space between them. She'd put away the food except the peach cobbler and had a sketch pad out. Her head bent over the sheet, he couldn't see what she was drawing until she peered up at him. A shadow darkened her eyes and constricted his gut.

*Lord, how do I maintain my distance from her and stay on friendly terms for Nicholas's sake? I'm not doing a good job of it. I've hurt her. And I don't like that.*

"I shouldn't have kissed you." He eased down on the blanket at the other end from her.

"Then why did you?"

He waved his arm around the glade. "This place. Isn't

that why you brought me here? To have me remember how it once was between us?"

She stared at her sketch pad with the beginnings of a portrait of him. "Yes," she whispered, a raw edge to the word. When she reestablished visual contact with him, the shadow was gone. "But you don't need to worry about me doing anything like this again."

"I owe you an explanation."

"Isn't it obvious you can't forgive me?"

He ignored her question and said instead, "I never told you everything about my accident that ended my career as a bull rider."

"I saw it on the video. Nicholas showed it to me."

He sucked in a ragged breath. "I've never brought myself to watch it, but it's out there on the internet for the whole world to see." A sharp pain, as if he felt the hooves of the bull all over again, pierced him. "Like Nicholas I suffered from an infection. The trampling caused mine. I've been left with a limp, twinges that remind me of the accident, especially when the weather changes, and I can't have kids. Nicholas will be my only child."

"No children?"

"The scar tissue was extensive." He severed eye contact with her. "When my fiancée found out the extent of my injury, she hightailed it out of my life."

"I'm sorry, Zachary."

"You should have more kids. You're a good mother. I know you've always wanted more than one."

"That's why you pulled away?"

"Part of the reason. Our time together as a couple is over. Has been for years." *Don't pursue this. You need more than I can offer.* He flicked his hand toward the pad. "I see you're still drawing."

She peered at him for a long moment as though deciding whether to continue the conversation or not. "I don't do it as much as I used to. I'm trying to get back into it again."

He released a breath he didn't even realize he was holding until she dropped the subject of why they weren't suited together. "I'm glad. You were always so good. Can I see that?"

She flipped the lid over the drawing. "I'm not through. I'll show you when I am. How about some peach cobbler?"

"You know I'll never pass up one of your desserts." As she dished up his portion, he added, "Nicholas has been wanting me to take him to a rodeo. There's one next Friday in Bartlesville. I'd like to take him then. It'll be our guys' night out."

Her mouth tightened. "Sure."

"I promise I won't try and get him to pursue anything having to do with the rodeo."

"Next weekend will be a big one with the rodeo on Friday and HHH Junior Rodeo on Saturday."

He took a bite of the cobbler, the dessert melting in his mouth with just the right sweetness. "Mmm. This is great." After another scoop of it, he said, "I'll have Nicholas spend the night Friday and he can help me the next morning get ready for HHH Junior Rodeo."

"I'll be there early. I signed up to help set up the activities."

"Then come early and have breakfast with Nicholas and me. I'm sure he'll want to tell you all about the rodeo."

"Is that your roundabout way of asking me to fix breakfast for you two?"

"No, if you don't mind having cold cereal." He really did need to learn to cook now that he had a child part of the time. He still had a long way to go to be the father he wanted to be. He hated playing catch-up, especially with something so important as his son.

Jordan parked in front of Zachary's house early Saturday morning, just hours before the ranch would be crowded with families from the Helping Hands Homeschooling group participating in the HHH Junior Rodeo. Sitting and staring at the front porch, she couldn't bring herself to move from the car. When Zachary had picked Nicholas up yesterday afternoon to attend the rodeo, she'd wanted to go with them. She'd almost said something to them as they left. But then Zachary's words about it being their guys' night out stopped her. She swallowed the request, a heaviness in the pit of her stomach.

She was elated that her son and his father were bonding, spending time doing special activities. But she couldn't help feeling left out. The times all three of them had spent together made her want even more a complete family—a mother, father and child. Children, actually.

Zachary, though, couldn't have any more kids. His revelation had stunned her, but did it make any difference in the long run? Did it change her feelings about him? No, she wasn't like his ex-fiancée. She loved him no matter what, but at the waterfall, he'd hammered home where they stood. Friends only—and then that only because of Nicholas.

his silence when she'd asked him if he'd forgiven had been her answer. He couldn't get past what had happened eleven years ago. When he looked at her, he saw her betrayal—like his fiancée's. Nothing she would change that. It really wasn't because she deserved to have more children. Nothing he said really made her feel any differently.

It might as well have shouted it from the cliff surrounding the pool. She and Zachary would share Nicholas like a divorced couple. She had to move on.

Would her son begin to prefer his father's company to hers? Would she lose her child to Zachary? She hated thinking like that, but suddenly she felt in a competition for Nicholas's love.

The front door flew open, and her son ran out of the house, a grin plastered all over his face. By the time he'd reached the car, Jordan stood and grabbed the bag of groceries for breakfast.

"You're up early. Did you sleep any last night?" she asked Nicholas, who hugged her. She closed her eyes and relished the feel of his arms around her. How long would this last?

He walked next to her toward the house. "Nope. Too excited. Especially after seeing what real cowboys do."

"So you enjoyed seeing your first rodeo?"

"Yep." He hooked his thumbs into his jeans pockets. "One day I'm going to be as good at roping as Dad."

"Where is your dad?"

"He's trying to fix breakfast."

"He is? I thought I would cook for you two."

"He muttered something about having to learn. He called Aunt Becca and got some instructions, but I don't think he has the hang of it."

"Why?"

"You'll see." He tugged her toward the entrance.

The second she stepped into the house she knew why her son had said that. A burning smell drifted from the kitchen. "What's he making?"

"Pancakes. He used a box mix, but it isn't working very well."

"You think?" she said with a laugh and headed toward the back.

When she entered the kitchen, gray smoke poured from the skillet on the stove. On the counter sat a cookie sheet with burnt toast on it. Zachary snatched the frying pan off the burner and dumped its contents into the sink then turned the cold water on. A sizzling sound filled the silence, and steam bellowed from the skillet.

He whirled around. When he saw her, relief flooded his features. "I pulled the toast out of the oven and buttered the other side, then stuck it back in. That's when the pancakes I put on were getting a little too brown, so I flipped them. Thankfully they still looked edible. But everything after that went downhill. I was pouring the juice when I smelled the toast burning. Just as I took the pan out, the pancakes…" He waved his hand toward the sink. "All I want to know is how in the world do you coordinate putting a meal on the table with everything done at the right time?"

"Practice." She tried to contain her smile but couldn't.

"Yeah, like roping, Dad."

"So I get to look forward to more of these types of disasters?"

"Maybe you should take it in stages. One dish at a time."

He blew out a breath. "We'd starve at that rate."

"I'll clean this up and make some omelets. You can fix the toast while I do that." She opened the oven. "For starters you need to lower the rack so it's not so near the broiler." Taking the oven mitts, she adjusted it for Zachary. "That should help it not brown so quickly." She spun around. "Or better yet, buy a toaster. Much easier. You put it on a setting and leave the work to it."

"Can I help?" Nicholas asked.

"You can set the table." Jordan withdrew a mug from the cabinet, poured some coffee and took a sip. "Not too bad."

"I did something right."

Zachary's smile renewed the dreams she had about being a family. She quickly shoved them away. She needed to protect herself from getting hurt any more than she already was. *Friends only.*

Jordan sat across from Zachary later that afternoon at a picnic table under a pecan tree. All the races and competitions had been completed half an hour ago, and Nicholas had come in third in the barrel race. In his roping demonstration he'd managed to land his lasso around the sawhorse twice as he rode by it. When her son competed in the sheep race, she'd laughed so hard her sides had hurt. Nicholas didn't have one problem in his events and the grin on his face had made it all worth it.

Lifting a bottle, she took a swig of water. A sigh escaped her lips as she relaxed for the first time in hours. "It's a good thing we only do this once a year. It's a lot of work putting this on."

Becca joined her and Zachary, sliding in next to her

brother on the bench. "I heard Nancy and some of the others talking about doing this in the spring and fall. Everyone has had so much fun."

Zachary groaned.

"I'll do more next time. And Paul," Becca quickly said. "The ranch is a perfect place for it."

"I don't know about that. It may take me that long to recuperate from this one."

"Jordan and I did the food. You just had to organize the races."

"And line up all the animals. The sheep alone weren't easy to find." Zachary pressed his lips together.

Becca opened her mouth to say something, looked hard at her brother and frowned instead.

"Also think of all the extra lessons I had to give. I had to make sure people knew what they were doing. Riding a sheep isn't like riding a horse." A gleam sparkled in his eyes as he winked at Jordan.

Becca playfully punched her brother in the arm. "I knew it. You've had a great time. So can I tell Nancy it's a yes for next April or May?"

"I won't hear the end of it if I say no, especially from my son. So yes."

"Great. That's all I needed to know." Becca hopped up and headed off toward a group of people by the barn.

"Are you one of those brothers who relished making his sister's life miserable when you two were growing up?"

"Isn't that what a little brother is for?"

"I wouldn't know. All I had is a big sis like you."

Nicholas ran across the yard toward them.

"I'd like Nicholas to stay over again tonight. We decided to lie out in the pasture where there are no city lights and study the stars. See how many we can count."

Spend the night again? If she wasn't homeschooling her son, she would never see him anymore.

Nicholas skidded to a stop at the end of the picnic table. "We're going to be in the field." He waved his hand toward an empty pasture to the left. "Some of the guys are putting together a touch football game, and I'm going to play."

*Football?* Until her son had gotten to know his father, he hadn't wanted anything to do with the sport, and she'd been thrilled by that. "Hon, you've never played before. I think you should sit this one out."

"But I want to play. I'm going to be on Randy's team. If I don't play, the sides won't be equal."

Jordan glanced from Nicholas to some of the larger boys gathering near the field her son indicated. He and Becca's oldest son were the smallest two on the teams. "I don't think so."

"Dad?" Nicholas glued his attention on Zachary. "Touch football isn't like regular football. I'll be okay. Tell Mom that."

Zachary looked toward Jordan. "There's no tackling in touch football. It's mostly running and trying to evade the opposing player. Nicholas would be good at that. He's pretty quick."

"Yeah, Mom, remember how well I did when we played soccer?"

"They aren't the same."

"Please." Nicholas wore his puppy-dog look.

Rising, she glared at Zachary. "Can we have a word?" She walked a few steps away from the picnic table and turned her back on Nicholas. When Zachary

joined her, she lowered her voice. "He isn't equipped
to play something like football, even touch football."

"Quit smothering *our* son. Other kids play and are
perfectly fine. I used to play and there were no broken
bones."

"I don't like this."

"What? The football or me having a say in what our
son does?"

*Both!* She'd been the only caregiver for ten years
and now all of a sudden she was supposed to consult
and share the decisions with Zachary. Acid burned her
stomach. She skirted Zachary and marched back to the
table. "If your dad thinks it's safe, then I'll—"

Nicholas threw his arms around her neck. "Thanks."
Then he raced toward the field where the others were.

When Zachary approached, she muttered, "I've been
manipulated," then strode toward a group cleaning up
the eating area.

As Jordan stormed away, disconcerted, Zachary took
his cowboy hat and dusted it off against his jeans, his
hand clutching the Stetson. Everything had gone well
today. Nicholas hadn't had a problem in any of his competitions, and yet Jordan insisted on being overprotective. She needed to back off, and he was going to make
sure she realized that. He owed it to his son.

Then he thought of why Jordan was so protective of
Nicholas. She'd had to face almost losing him—alone.
He'd wished he'd been there to help her through the or-
deal. Hold her. Comfort her.

The commotion of the teams preparing to play in
the field drew his attention. Even though he understood
where she was coming from, she still had to realize he

was Nicholas's dad and had an equal say now in how their son was raised.

The participants of the touch football game formed their teams and lined up. Zachary stood against the fence, not far from the sideline they had marked with long links of rope. Two barrels at the ends of the pasture were the goal posts. Some of the parents, including Jordan, came to watch the impromptu scrimmage. She stood next to Becca several yards away from him and stared straight ahead. Her features formed a neutral expression, but even from this distance he felt her frustration and anger conveyed by the crossed arms and legs.

For the first fifteen minutes Nicholas hung back, not going after the person with the ball. Then suddenly one of the opposing players caught the ball near his son. He dashed after the thirteen-year-old and touched his arm. Nicholas jumped up and down. Randy came over and gave him a high five. His son's grin encompassed his whole face.

From that point on Nicholas became more involved. Several times he went after the ball carrier and once more tagged him. He was becoming more confident the more he did. First with riding, then roping. And now playing team sports like soccer and football. Zachary felt as if he'd accomplished something with his son— showed him how to play.

During the half his son ran over to him and took the bottle of water he handed him. "I'm not so bad."

"No, you're quick on your feet. You're doing good."

Nicholas made himself as tall as he could and raised his chin. "Mom worries too much."

"That's a mother's job." Although he had to agree with his son.

Nicholas glanced behind him. "Gotta go. We're starting the second half."

Zachary chuckled to himself. A month ago his son knew nothing about football until he watched some videos and read about it prior to the homecoming game.

The time flew by. The dad refereeing the game indicated a minute left. Nicholas's team had the ball and the quarterback stepped back to throw it. His intended receiver was delayed and Nicholas jumped up and caught the ball. When he came down with it clasped to him, he wobbled and paused to steady himself. An opposing team member running full force toward him noticed the delay and tried to stop. Instead he bowled right over Nicholas, flattened him on the ground. The ball shot up in the air. Someone snatched it and ran for a touchdown.

Nicholas remained down, not moving. Zachary's heartbeat accelerated as he jogged toward his son, Jordan a couple of feet in front of him. She knelt next to their son, Nicholas's chest rising and falling rapidly.

"Don't move." Her hands ran over his body. "Where does it hurt?"

"I'm fine," Nicholas said in a breathless voice, dragging air into his lungs.

"You don't sound fine."

Their son pushed his upper body to a sitting position. "Just winded. Did we get a touchdown?" Nicholas looked beyond Jordan to Zachary.

He stepped forward and knelt next to her. "Yes."

Nicholas grinned. "We won, Mom!"

"It's time for us to go home." Jordan put her arm around Nicholas's shoulders and helped him up.

"But I want to spend the night with Dad."

"Not tonight."

"Partner, why don't you go say goodbye to everyone."

"But, Dad—"

Zachary tossed his head toward the barn. "Your mom and I have something to discuss."

Nicholas heaved a sigh then trudged off the field toward his teammates near the fence celebrating their victory.

When their son was out of earshot, Zachary rounded on Jordan. "Why isn't he staying tonight? He's fine. Nothing happened to him."

"We don't know that for sure. He could have a mild concussion. I'm gonna keep an eye on him. If anything is wrong, I'm near the hospital. This isn't up for discussion." She pinched her lips together and narrowed her eyes.

"Yes, it is. He's my son, too."

"I've been his primary caregiver and that isn't gonna change."

He squeezed his hands shut then flexed them. He moved into her personal space, his face close to hers. "That's because you kept him a secret." He schooled his voice to an even level while inside anger boiled. He had so much time to make up, and she was standing in the way.

"There's nothing I can do to change the past and I'm tired of trying."

When she started to skirt him, he impeded her progress. "Do I have to speak to a lawyer about my rights as Nicholas's dad?"

The threat, unplanned, tumbled from his mouth, and the second she heard it, color drained from her face. Her pupils grew huge. One part of him wanted to take the words back. Another meant everything he said. Nicholas would be his only child and he intended to participate fully in his life.

Jordan froze for a few seconds then she backed away, her mouth hanging open, her eyes round. Whirling around, she fled across the field, grabbed their son and made her way toward her Camaro.

*What have I done?* He buried his face in his hands and kneaded his fingertips into his forehead.

Becca closed the distance between them. "What's going on? Jordan and Nicholas are leaving." She nodded toward them getting into the car. "What did you say to her?"

"I asked if I should contact a lawyer concerning my rights as Nicholas's father."

His sister drew in a sharp breath. "You didn't? Why did you say that? You two can work things out without bringing lawyers into it. How do you think Nicholas will feel?"

"This never should have been an issue. I should have known from the beginning. I could have married her. Nicholas would have had both a mother and father."

"Then do it now."

He stared at Jordan and Nicholas, his son's face set in a pout, her expression anger filled. "It's too late for us."

"Because you can't forgive her."

"I'm trying," he said, instead of explaining his turmoil over not being able to give her another child.

"Not hard enough."

Jordan backed up her car, then headed down the gravel road.

"Go after her. Don't leave it like that."

\* \* \*

*A lawyer! Zachary wants to get custody of Nicholas.* All hope of them ever working something out vanished when she heard those words. There was nothing she could do to earn his forgiveness, to make him understand all she wanted was for him and Nicholas to be her family. She didn't care if he couldn't have any more children.

"Mom, why are we leaving? I want to stay." Nicholas clicked on his seat belt.

Fury jammed Jordan's throat and something she wished she didn't feel—the pain of loss. She drove toward the entrance to the ranch, tears stinging her eyes. "It was time to go. You hit the ground pretty hard. If you get a headache, become nauseated or dizzy, let me know immediately."

"I don't have a concussion. I'm fine."

*Lord, I just want my old life back. At least I knew what to expect. I don't want to lose my son. I know I've made mistakes, but why couldn't Zachary, Nicholas and I be a family?*

She pulled onto the highway. "Hon, you've been gone a lot lately. Nana and Granny have missed you. I missed you."

Nicholas remained quiet. Jordan slanted a look at him. A pout thinned his lips, his arms folded over his chest.

She'd get home and talk to Rachel. She just needed to get things back under her control.

Out of the corner of her eye, she saw something large and brown, moving fast, crossing the road only yards in front of her. A deer?

* * *

Zachary jumped in his truck and started out after Jordan. He shouldn't have said what he had about the lawyer. He might be angry with her, but that was hitting below the belt, and she didn't deserve it. She'd been a good mother to Nicholas.

He pressed down on the accelerator to catch up with her. Up ahead he spied her Camaro.

Then he saw the deer leap onto the highway right in front of Jordan's car. She swerved to avoid the animal and plowed off the road. Her vehicle bounced across the rough terrain and plunged into a ditch near the field, a tree stopping her forward motion. The medium-size oak swayed under the impact. His heartbeat stalled for a few seconds as his gaze fastened onto her car, the front end smashed against the trunk.

With his pulse thundering in his ears, he sped until he reached the place where Jordan went off the road. He slammed on his brakes and jumped from his truck. He raced toward the wreck. His pulse racing even faster than he was.

*Lord, let them be alive. It can't end this way.*

Reaching the rear bumper, he climbed into the ditch on the driver's side, nearest him. A gray cloud billowed from the scrunched hood. He peered inside. Her head lay against the deflated airbag and steering wheel. He jerked on the door. He couldn't budge it.

Back up the ditch, he made his way to the other side and tried to get in. A fine powder floated inside the car. Nicholas, held up by his seat belt, sagged against the window, a spiderweb of cracks spreading out from the contact with his head. Blood ran down his face.

Panting, trying desperately to suppress the panic

churning in his gut, Zachary yanked with all his strength on the handle. For a few seconds nothing happened. Then the door creaked open half a foot. He wedged his arm through the crack and pried it open farther.

"Nicholas. Jordan." His voice shook as much as his body did.

Jordan moaned and looked toward him. Blinking, she raised her head and reached toward their son. "No. Nicholas."

He stirred, his eyelids lifting partway. "Mom?" He tried to move and collapsed back.

"Stay still, son. I'm calling 911." Zachary dug for his cell and clenched it to keep the trembling in his hands from showing. After he reported the accident, he turned back to Jordan and his son. "Help is on the way."

"My leg hurts." Tears filled Nicholas's eyes and spilled over onto his cheeks, mingling with the blood.

Zachary inspected his son and noticed his left leg was pinned by the dashboard. Kneeling next to Nicholas, he took his hand. "You'll be all right. Just don't move."

Jordan tried her door. When she couldn't budge it, she twisted back toward Zachary. "I'm stuck."

The fright on her pale face, in her voice, tore at his composure. She tried to unhook her seat belt but couldn't. She shoved again at the door but it remained shut. When she looked at him, her panic drove the terror away.

"Easy, Jordan. The paramedics will be here soon." He stood and stared down the stretch of highway then stooped again. "I hear a siren. Five minutes tops." *Hurry. I can't lose them.*

"I need to help my son. I couldn't stop. I couldn't avoid…" Her words faded into the quiet. She placed her hand on Nicholas's arm closest to her as though she could will her strength into him.

His own helplessness inundated Zachary. He rose again and watched for the ambulance. Flashing lights and the sound of the siren grew closer. The pounding of his heart nearly drowned out the approaching emergency vehicles. He'd never been so afraid in his life— even when the bull had crushed him.

"Everything is going to be okay," he murmured as much to reassure himself as Nicholas and Jordan.

Hours later, Jordan sat in the waiting room surrounded by family, Granny on one side and Rachel on the other. Her mother was nearby talking with Zachary and Becca, their voices too low to hear what they were saying.

Nicholas had just been taken into surgery to repair his broken leg. The scent of antiseptic knotted her stomach so tight bile clogged her throat. The sterile room, painted a light green, reminded her of the one in South Carolina. She'd almost lost her son then. This time he would be all right, but the feeling of being out of control bombarded her from all sides.

She leaped to her feet. She couldn't sit here any longer.

"Where are you going, honey?" her mother asked.

Glancing over her shoulder, Jordan locked gazes with Zachary for a few seconds before looking at her mom. "Out of here."

Zachary rose, concern in his expression. "I'll come with you."

"No!" She fled the room, tears shadowing her vision as she hurried down the hall toward she wasn't sure where.

The last thing she needed was Zachary to be kind to her, to say anything to her. Since the paramedics and highway patrol arrived on the scene of the wreck, everything happened in a blur as if she were watching it from afar. Separate. A spectator.

She wanted her old life back before she'd come to Tallgrass. Since her arrival home, nothing had been the same. Every day there was something new to deal with. She didn't know what to expect anymore—except that Zachary didn't really want to have anything to do with her. Only Nicholas.

The sign for the chapel drew her toward it. She entered and escaped inside the dimly lit room, nondescript, with several rows of chairs. The sounds of the hospital faded as she shut the door.

She collapsed onto the seat nearest to her and bowed her head. For the longest moment she couldn't think of anything to say to the Lord. Her son was hurting again because of something she'd done this time. She should have been able to avoid the accident. She should have been able…

The tears streaked down her face, released finally like a valve turned completely on unchecked. She let them fall into her lap. She'd walked away with a few cuts and bruises. Why couldn't she have been the one hurt, needing surgery? Not her son.

*Why, Lord? What are You trying to tell me?*

The door opened. Lifting her head, Jordan grew so stiff her muscles locked painfully. She needed to be alone. She needed— Granny slipped inside and came to sit beside her. Her grandmother patted Jordan's hands clutched together in her lap.

For minutes silence reigned in the chapel. The hammering of Jordan's heartbeat pulsated in her ears. Slowly her grandmother's presence blanketed Jordan in a calming mantle. God had sent Granny to comfort her.

"I've really made a mess of my life," she finally said, the heat from her grandmother's touch warming Jordan's cold body.

"Why do you say that? The wreck was an accident. From what Zachary said there wasn't anything you could have done. It happened so fast."

The mention of Zachary renewed her fear that he'd take her to court concerning custody of their son. The calming mantle slipped from her. "He wants Nicholas."

"Of course he does. He's his father. It's a good thing he wants to be in Nicholas's life."

"He told me he's gonna talk to a lawyer."

"When, child?"

"Today at the ranch right before I left."

"Do you trust in the Lord?"

"Yes." Jordan shifted toward her grandmother and saw the doubt in her eyes. "You don't think I do?"

"I believe you think you do, but you're always so busy trying to control everything in your life that you've lost sight of what's important. God knows what is best for us, and sometimes we have to just put our faith in Him. Trust Him, child, completely. He brought you back here for a reason. Quit fighting Him every step of the way."

"Control? Today I discovered I have no control really. Literally in a blink of an eye your life can change."

"My point exactly." Granny tapped her chest. "Take

it from this eighty-one-years-young woman who has been through a lot in that time. Just when you think you've got everything figured out, something changes. Faith is what has sustained me. It can for you, too." Pushing to her feet, she gripped the back of the chair in front of her. "I imagine you've got some thinking and praying to do. I'll be in the waiting room."

Jordan stood and hugged her grandmother. "I love you. I'll be back in a little bit."

After Granny left, Jordan sank back down and clasped her hands. "Father, I've been so wrong. I've been scared to trust anyone—You, Zachary. There's always been a part I've held back. Please help me. I need You."

"Nicholas is gonna be all right, Zachary." Becca paused next to him at the vending machine.

He punched the button for coffee. Its scent wafted to him as the cup filled. He'd always loved the smell of coffee. Now it seared a hole in his gut. "I'll feel better when the doctor tells me. Remember what happened to me when the bull trampled me?"

"This is different. Not nearly as complicated." His sister checked her watch. "In fact, the surgery should be over soon."

"I can't help wondering if what I said to Jordan right before she left didn't contribute to the wreck."

"You told me you saw it and it happened so fast there wasn't anything she could have done except swerve or hit the buck. Hitting the deer would have caused major damage, too. Remember that time Dad ran into a cow? The insurance company totaled our car."

"I know." He dragged his fingers through his hair, kneading his fingers into his taut neck muscles. "But I really didn't mean I would contact a lawyer. I was angry and lashed out at Jordan. She left upset…" He couldn't shake the image of her car going off the road or the picture of Jordan and Nicholas hurt and trapped. Helplessness flooded him again as if a downpour deluged him.

"Then talk with her and tell her you didn't mean it. Ask her forgiveness."

He flinched. "How can I ask her to do that when I've had trouble doing that myself?"

"What would have happened if Jordan had really hurt herself or worse—died? How would you have felt holding on to that anger over something that happened years ago? Does your anger make you feel better? Or is it Audrey you're really mad at? Forgive both of them."

His sister's words made him think about the unthinkable. Had his relationship with Audrey colored his with Jordan? What if Jordan had died today? The very thought chilled his blood. A world without her? He shuddered, one wave after another rippling down his body.

"You've got more than yourself to consider now. What are you teaching your son if you hold a grudge like you are? If she can forgive Mom, why can't you forgive her?"

Zachary took the coffee cup and sipped at the hot brew. A bitter taste coated his tongue that had nothing to do with his drink and everything to do with the picture of the kind of man he was showing his son.

Rachel came around the corner. "Zachary, Nicholas is out of surgery. The doctor is in the waiting room."

* * *

A few hours later Jordan stood outside Nicholas's hospital room. "Mom, I'm staying here tonight."

"Honey, I'm worried about you. You look exhausted."

"I couldn't sleep even if I was at home. If all goes well, Nicholas will come home soon. Then I can get some rest."

Her mother squeezed her hand. "I understand. I'll see you all in the morning."

Jordan watched her mom and grandmother get on the elevator before she turned back toward her son's door. Everyone was gone except Zachary. She'd been able to manage being in the same room with him as long as others were there, too.

She entered, her gaze immediately seeking the bed where Nicholas slept. He'd wakened briefly after the surgery but was now sleeping soundly. His bandaged head underscored what had happened earlier.

Again the picture of the buck flashed into her mind. It had been too close for her to do anything but swerve or hit it. Neither option had been good. The sounds of the crash—the crunch of her car folding like an accordion, the airbag exploding outward—and the smells of the leaking engine fluids mingling with the stagnant water in the ditch assailed her. Goose bumps rose on her arms, and she hugged them to her.

Zachary cleared his throat, reminding her she wasn't alone. Wouldn't be the whole night because he was staying with his son, too. Exhausted, aching, she didn't know if she could deal with another incident where they dueled over Nicholas. Why couldn't he leave and come back with the rest in the morning? She'd always been the one in the past to stay, holding vigilance. But wasn't that the problem?

Zachary should have had that choice all those years ago. She turned away, not wanting him to see the conflict that had to be written on her face. He couldn't forgive her, so as most things, this was out of her control. *Lord, Your will.*

With Zachary on the small couch, she moved to the chair a few feet away. She turned it to point toward Nicholas's bed. Taking a seat, her back to Zachary, she closed her eyes and inhaled deep breaths to calm her stressed body. But nothing relieved the tension that bunched every muscle.

The hairs on her nape tingled right before Zachary's hand covered her clenched one on the armrest. "I'll sit here if you want to lie down on the couch."

His warm touch shot up her arm, burning through any defenses she scrambled to erect. She couldn't take another rejection. Not today. "I'm fine," she managed to say through parched lips, her throat so dry the words squeaked out.

He moved in front of her and squatted. "No, you aren't. You were in a wreck, too. I imagine your body is starting to feel the effects of it."

"Don't do this. Don't make…" Her throat closed completely around any other words she tried to say.

"I think we need to talk."

"No, not now. I have enough to handle without you letting me know I put our child in danger. He's there because of me. I—"

Zachary drew her up and pulled her into his embrace. "You aren't at fault. Don't do that to yourself."

She resisted the lure of his arms, jerking back. "If I

hadn't left when I did or gone a little faster or slower, Nicholas wouldn't have been hurt."

"What-ifs don't change the situation and only make you upset. Freak accidents happen to people."

Her jammed tears swelled into her eyes. She blinked, releasing them. "I know. I can't control everything like I've wanted. That point has been hammered home to me today painfully. But why couldn't I have been the one in that bed? Not my son."

"*Our* son." He brushed his thumbs over her cheeks, erasing the tears only to have them replaced immediately. Framing her face, he inched closer. "We are in this together."

Not really and that was the problem. She wanted all of Zachary. She wanted the complete family. He didn't. She'd messed it all up. Straightening, she attempted a smile that fell flat. "I appreciate your concern. I'll be okay, especially when I can get Nicholas home."

He tugged her toward the couch, gently pushed her down then sat beside her. "We still need to talk. Earlier today I didn't mean what I said about getting a lawyer."

Tension, even more than before, whipped down her length. "Maybe for the time being, but will you use that threat later when we clash about Nicholas?"

"I know we can work something out. You want what's best for Nicholas, and so do I."

He hadn't answered her question, which clinched her stomach into a snarl of emotions. She curled her hands at her sides. She loved him. And couldn't have him.

He slid his arm along the back of the couch, loosely cocooning her against him. "I'm not doing a very good job of explaining myself."

"Oh, I think I know where you stand."

He leaned closer, putting his thumb under her chin and turning her head so she looked straight at him. "Do you? Because until recently I didn't realize what I was doing. How harmful my attitude was."

"What do you mean?"

"I let my anger purposely make you mad. You fled. If I hadn't said that to you, we might have been able to work everything out earlier today, and Nicholas wouldn't be lying there."

"Didn't you just tell me we can't play what-ifs?"

"Yes, but see how I can twist it around to be my fault? It really was no one's." He stared at his son for a long moment. "When you came back to Tallgrass and told me I was a father, I was furious at you. At first, all I could see was the ten years you'd stolen from me."

She opened her mouth to apologize again, but he placed his finger over her lips.

A lopsided tilt to his mouth filled her vision. "I know you're sorry for what happened, but I was being stubborn and not listening to what you really said. I was letting what happened with my fiancée affect us. You aren't Audrey. When I turn the situation around and look at it differently, I'm so grateful to you for giving me a son even if it was ten years late. You didn't have to tell me. Then I would never know the joy of being a father. You've given me that joy and for that I thank you."

"You forgive me?"

"More than that. I love you, Jordan. I've never really stopped. We were both young and said and did things we regret. I can't keep living in the past. I want a future with you and Nicholas. I want a family. I could have lost you today. That can change a person's perspective real fast." He cupped her face. "Can you forgive me?

Will you accept me in your life even though Nicholas will be the only child we have?"

His questions hovered suspended in the air between them for several heartbeats. For a second she wondered if she'd heard him correctly or was it her weary mind playing tricks on her.

"I know you have a right to be mad at me. I—"

Jordan placed her fingers over his mouth. "Shh." Winding her arms around him, she drew him toward her and kissed him with all her heart.

"I want to do what we should have done years ago. Will you marry me as soon as possible? Make me happy? Make our son happy?"

She combed her fingers through his hair and slanted his head toward hers again. "Yes." She planted a peck on one corner of his mouth. "Yes." Another kiss on the other side. "And yes. You and Nicholas are my life." Her lips covered his with the promise of more to come.

# *Epilogue*

~❧

"It's taken us a long time to get here, but we've finally gotten it right, Mrs. Rutgers." Zachary locked his arms around Jordan.

"Say that again." She cuddled closer.

"Mrs. Rutgers."

"I don't think I'll ever get tired of hearing that name."

He smiled. "That's great since you'll have it for say fifty or so years." Leaning forward, he kissed her thoroughly.

Someone coughed behind Jordan. She blushed and turned within her husband's embrace.

"Save that for the honeymoon." Granny winked. "Right now you two have guests to see to."

Jordan scanned the reception hall at the church. All their friends were crammed into the large room. The new ones she'd met through Helping Hands Homeschooling group and the old ones she'd grown up with. But besides Nicholas and her family, the two she was happiest to see attending her and Zachary's wedding were his parents.

"Oh, I see Doug is getting seconds. I'd better corral

him before his cholesterol shoots up." Granny shuffled off to the right.

"How long do you think it will be before Doug and Granny marry?" Zachary whispered against her ear.

"I hope soon. Her and Mom are fighting again."

"Speaking of mothers, are you really okay with Mom taking Nicholas to Arizona for the week while we're on our honeymoon?"

Jordan caught sight of her son, in a leg cast but mobile, talking with Zachary's parents. "Totally. Your mother and I had a long talk last night. All we both want is what is best for you and Nicholas. We're on the same page."

A twinkle sparkled in his eyes. "Good. Can we sneak away now? I want to start the honeymoon."

"Sounds like a perfect game plan."

\* \* \* \* \*

Dear Reader,

I had so much fun creating the story of Jordan and Zachary, high school sweethearts who parted and were forced to be together again because of their child. This is a book about forgiveness and trust, which are so important in a relationship. Both Jordan and Zachary had to deal with both of these issues.

Also in *Heart of a Cowboy*, Nicholas didn't flourish in school although he was very smart. He stifled his intelligence because the other children made fun of him. This is a reason some parents homeschool their children. In each book in the series I want to try to show a different situation that leads to parents deciding to homeschool.

I love hearing from readers. You can contact me at margaretdaley@gmail.com or at P.O. Box 2074, Tulsa, OK 74101. You can also learn more about my books at www.margaretdaley.com. I have a quarterly newsletter that you can sign up for on my website or you can enter my monthly draws by signing my guest book.

Best wishes,

*Margaret Daley*

## QUESTIONS FOR DISCUSSION

1. Zachary couldn't forgive Jordan for not telling him about his son. His past ruled his life. Do you have something that has happened in your past that has done that to you? How can you get past that?

2. Who was your favorite character? Why?

3. Why is it important to forgive others and ourselves? What happens when we live in the past rather than look forward to the future? Which do you focus on—past, present or future? Why?

4. Jordan was afraid of losing her son to the point she was overprotective. Have you ever done that? How did you handle it?

5. What was your favorite scene? Why?

6. Jordan knew she'd made a mistake concerning Zachary and Nicholas and regretted it. Have you ever made the kind of mistake you felt that you paid for more than most? How did you deal with it?

7. Jordan thought if she could control her life then she would be all right. She didn't realize there are a lot of things we can't control in our lives. What are some things that have happened to you lately that have been out of your control? How did you deal with them?

8.  Nicholas was very smart and learned quickly, but he hated to write and avoided it as much as possible. Have you ever avoided something you couldn't do well? What happened when you had to do it?

9.  Zachary loved taking risks like bull riding in a rodeo. Do you take risks? Why or why not?

10. Although Zachary knew he should forgive Jordan, that God wanted him to, he couldn't. Have you ever done something you knew you shouldn't? How did the situation turn out by avoiding what you knew you should do?

11. Granny was Jordan's mentor. Jordan turned to Granny for advice. Do you have a mentor? Who is it and why is that person your mentor?

12. Jordan kept a secret for more than ten years. Secrets often have a way of coming out. When she came back home, she had to face the secret she'd kept. When it came out, she had to face the consequences. Has that happened to you? What did you do?

13. Jordan's mom was treating Granny as if she were a child rather than her mother. How do you treat your parents? Do health issues affect your interaction with your parents?

14. Nicholas wrote an essay about the disappearing cowboy—an ideal from our past. Do you agree with him? Why or why not?

15. Both Jordan and Zachary wondered what would have happened if Zachary's mother had passed on the messages from Jordan. Do you ever wonder if something would have happened differently in your past, where you would be today? Is it good to wonder what-ifs in our lives? Why or why not?

# HOME FOR GOOD

Jessica Keller

Thank you to Mom and Dad, for all your support. To Lisa, who always believed in me. The Wunderlich sisters, who were never shy about feedback, and for both being as in love with Jericho as I am. Special kudos goes to Sadie, who urged me to write in the first place. Thanks to George and Wanda, for taking the time to answer all my questions about living in the country. Carol and Kristy, my beloved NovelSisters, your prayers made this book a reality. And to Matthew, I could never express in words how much your support and encouragement mean to me. I love you so much.

Hope deferred makes the heart sick,
but a longing fulfilled is a tree of life.
—*Proverbs* 13:12

# Chapter One

After what seemed like a lifetime of bad days, Ali Silver couldn't wait to share a carefree afternoon with her son at the city picnic. Sunshine washed through the valley, giving a glow to the rivers and casting shadows out of the sharp mountain canyons to the west. With the pickup's windows rolled down, the air drifted in, spiced with alfalfa and silver sage. Fields of bucking hay splashed across the landscape, juxtaposed with the occasional lone apple tree—relics leftover from once substantial orchards.

Ali drove with one hand on the wheel, the other cocked in the open window. "Hang on to that. We don't want to spill it before the soldiers get to taste it."

Her son, Chance, hugged the bowl on his lap. "I know. This is the special potato salad. The one you only make for special people."

"Like you." She winked at him.

After waiting in a line of traffic to enter the park, Ali maneuvered her beast of a truck into one of the last available spots. She took the potato salad from Chance, and they ambled toward the crowd near the food tables. A couple local firefighters manned the grills. They waved. The smell of sizzling brats tickled her nose.

Hannah, a shop owner in town, signaled to Ali. "Isn't this just the nicest thing? I do believe the Hamilton Civic Club pulled out all the stops to honor these troops."

Ali balanced the bowl against her hip. "Having a picnic to honor the local servicemen who have returned this year was a great idea. I'm glad the town is doing something. And Chance loves anything to do with the army, so he's tickled to meet them."

Hannah clasped her hands together. "Oh, yes. I like them teaching the young people to support the troops."

Chance yanked on Ali's arm.

Hannah chuckled. "That boy's eager!"

Messing up his hair, Ali smiled down at her son. "Go on and find Aunt Kate and see if you can snag an empty table for us."

Without waiting to hear more, Chance took off running. Ali's heart squeezed. He might mirror her brown-sugar-like freckles, but the thick maple-colored hair that stuck up on the side when he woke in the morning, his square jaw, the angular nose and intense pale blue eyes—all of that belonged to his father. Chance looked just like…

Ali shook her head. She did not want to think about *him*. Not today. Not ever.

Instead she chose to weave through groups of mingling neighbors, greeting them with a nod since her hands were full. She located an empty place for the potato salad on a table already loaded with deviled eggs, baked beans and desserts. Satisfied that the food situation was under control, Ali snatched a gooey-looking brownie and raised it to her lips.

"Hiya, Ali."

The voice from her past rocketed through her with the force of a kick drum. The brownie flew out of her hand, leaving a powdered-sugar trail down her shirt on its way to the hard dirt. She spun around.

Jericho Freed.

All six feet of him, clad in jeans and a fitted gray-striped button-down. His bold, masculine eyebrows rose as he surveyed her with look-me-in-the-eyes-if-you-dare blues. He wore a straw cowboy hat with unruly hair poking out, and a five o'clock shadow outlined his firm jaw. More than eight years later, and the man still made her mouth go dry.

It frustrated her that after everything, he still had that power.

So she did the only rational thing she could think to do. *Flee.*

In a fluid movement, Ali sidestepped him and took off sprinting at a breakneck clip. Her hat flew off.

He yelled out her name.

And just like in the past, his voice poured sweet and velvety, like chocolate over each syllable. Ali's nails dug into her palms. She didn't want to hear him. She never wanted to fall under his spell again. Tears gathered at the corners of her eyes as she ran.

Why was he here? Oh, why hadn't she moved away when she had the…chance? *Chance!* Suddenly she pounded faster, the narrow toe of her boots chafing against her feet.

Jericho couldn't see Chance. She wouldn't let that happen. *God, please!*

Ali zeroed in on her sister Kate milling next to the volleyball court.

She waved her arms. "Quick! We have to find Chance! Now!" Ali pressed a hand to the stitch in her side as she looked over her shoulder, scanning the crowd for the cowboy with impossibly blue eyes. He hadn't followed her.

Kate jogged toward Ali, her eyes wide. "Sis? I don't see smoke coming from your hair, so if it's not on fire—what is?"

She seized Kate's arms, clamping down on reality. "He's here. He's back. What am I supposed to... What if he... What about Chance?" Her voice rose in a frenzy.

Kate shook her gently. "Who's here?"

"My husband."

"Ali! Alison!" With his hands looped onto his belt buckle, Jericho kicked, sending a cloud of Montana dust into the air. Maybe he should chase after her, but his knees probably couldn't handle running at that clip.

*Great. Just great.*

He rubbed the back of his neck as Ali hightailed it like a spooked filly. At that speed, she might make the Canadian border by nightfall. It sure wasn't funny, though. A man couldn't laugh, not when the rejection felt like a sledgehammer hitting him square in the chest. The cold look in her hazel eyes told him where he stood. Unwelcome. Unforgiven. How could he have expected anything else? But her reaction rankled him all the same.

He rubbed his jaw and growled. Could he blame her? No. What kind of man envisions a warm welcome after eight years of silence? Jericho Eli Freed. *Stupid man.*

A young boy with floppy hair ambled toward him. "Are you really a soldier?"

Jericho cleared his throat, pulled at the fabric of his army pants and dropped to one knee. "I sure am." Or was.

"That's cool. I want to be a soldier someday." At this confession, the child looked down and dug his toe into the ground.

Keeping his voice low to draw the kid out of his shell, Jericho asked, "Do you feel funny around new people? 'Cause I sure do. When I was your age, I just had one friend in the world and she was the only person I'd talk to." Jericho laid a hand on the boy's scrawny shoulder.

Suddenly a shadow loomed over them. "Get your hands off of him."

Jericho jerked back and looked up—and his mouth fell open. Fire in her eyes, Ali Silver stood there, an arm wrapped around the boy as she pulled him close.

Jericho jumped to his feet, putting his hands palm up in surrender.

Even seething mad, beauty radiated from her. Sure, she had changed in the last eight years, but in a good way. Auburn mellowed her once fire-truck-red hair. The long tresses he remembered were now cut so they skimmed her ears. Cute.

*Ali.* His Ali. She'd been a slim thing, barely entering womanhood when he left. Now she had gentle curves that he had to school his eyes not to explore. Her hazel eyes held a soft sincerity that drew him in. A familiar tightening gripped his stomach as his pulse started to go berserk.

The kid pushed against her. "No, Mom, he's not a stranger. This is a soldier. We were becoming friends."

Jericho's mind raced like a mouse caught in a maze. *Mom?* The single word sent a zap through his body, like someone had dumped a vat of ice over his head. Ali was a mother? Had she remarried? Impossible. The kid was what? Six? Seven—?

"Ali?" He tried to meet her gaze, but she looked away.

"Hey, Chance." Ali leaned over to speak close to the child's ear. "I think I see your teacher, Mrs. McBride, over there. Can you do me a favor and find out how she liked those pies we made her?"

"Ali?" Jericho repeated. His mind latched onto the name *Chance* and filed it away for later.

Chance's brow creased. He looked at Jericho, then back at his mother. "How come he knows your name, Mom?"

Despite the sweltering day, a cold sweat pricked the back of Jericho's neck.


Her mouth went dry. No matter what, Ali had to get Chance away from Jericho. She placed her hands on her hips. "It doesn't matter, Chance. Now go visit with Mrs. McBride for a minute." After sending Chance away, she took a deep breath and turned to address Jericho, but couldn't make herself completely meet his gaze. "I don't know why you're here—"

"We need to talk." He shoved his hands into his pockets.

"There is no 'we.'"

He quirked an eyebrow. "I disagree. Unless I slept through signing some sort of papers, you and I, well, we're still married."

Her tongue suddenly felt like a dried-up riverbed.

*We're still married.* Fear skittered down her spine like racing spiders. Of course. As a teen mom on her own, she didn't have spare money to toss around on lawyer fees.

She balled up her fists. "I want you to leave."

He shook his head, reached a hand out toward her, then dropped it to his side. "I'm back, Ali—back for good."

"Why?" The word came out more whisper than force.

She stared into his intense blue eyes, her gaze dipping to the single freckle above his lip. Same dime-sized scar near his eye, the slight tug of his lips—always ready to joke.

He stepped closer. "I need to talk to you. Explain about being away."

"Just *being away*? How nice. Sounds warm and fuzzy, like you took a vacation."

He ran a hand over his hair, cupping the back of his neck as he tipped his head to the side. "I always wanted to come back. But—"

"Stay away from me. Stay away from my son."

"I need to—" He reached for her.

She slapped away his hand.

"Ali…" He grabbed her elbow, and a thrill skittered up her arm and down into her stomach. She let out a muffled cry. Why? Why, after all these years, was his name still branded across her heart?

Fighting the hot tears stinging her eyes, she jerked from him. "Don't touch me. Please, don't touch me." A sob hung at the back of her throat. "I can't do this. I can't handle being this close. I can't talk to you."

"But I have to talk to you. Give me fifteen minutes. Please?" His voice flowed, soft and reassuring.

"No!" She swiped at the traitorous tears squeezing from her eyes.

A warm, steady hand touched the small of her back. She turned to find Tripp Phillips, local lawyer, old classmate and friend, beside her. In his usual dress pants and polo, his stability brought an ease of calm to her shaking nerves. She gripped his arm.

"Alison, is something wrong?" Tripp's voice came out controlled and comforting. He had a manner that made even the most skeptical of strangers immediately warm to him. "Is Freed bothering you?"

"Tripp Phillips, I don't believe you were a part of our conversation." Jericho's voice hardened.

"Rightly so, but I'm not going to stand around while you make Alison cry."

"I'm not crying," Ali mumbled.

Tripp turned her into his shoulder. His hand cradled the back of her head as he wedged his body between her and Jericho.

Jericho growled.

Chance chose that moment to come bounding back. "What's wrong, Mom?" He wrapped his arm around Ali's waist and peered at her from under thick black eyelashes. "Mrs. McBride liked the pies, but I didn't tell her about the green worms we found in the berries. Did you think I did? Is that why you're crying?"

"I'm not upset about the worms, honey." Ali caressed his tanned face, and Chance rewarded her with an impish grin.

Tripp cleared his throat. "I think your mom's not feeling well today, buddy. We better take her home."

Jericho held her gaze. "Ali, I'm not done trying to talk to you."

Tripp turned and led her away from the monster of her past. Good old Tripp. At least one dependable man remained. If only Tripp had been the one to chase her in high school instead of Jericho, life might have turned out differently. At least Tripp stood by her now, always helping and advising her. His sound counsel lifted a weight from her shoulders, and she was grateful.

Chance twisted around, then cupped his hands around his mouth. "Wait! Are you going to be at the fireworks show tonight?"

A chill ran through her veins.

Then that voice from her dreams over the last eight years answered back. "'Course, Chance. I wouldn't miss it for the world."

Jericho wanted to hit something. No, he wanted a drink. A nice, tall amber malt with a high head of foam. Hadn't wanted that for five years, but there you go.

Looping a hand over the back of his neck, Jericho tensed as Tripp guided Ali away, like an auctioneer showing off a prized mare.

Could Tripp be Chance's father? Fear sliced through him.

Jericho stalked past the picnic and grabbed the door handle on the rusted Jeep he had found at his dad's house. So she ran into another man's arms when he left? And if he was right about the kid's age, she didn't even wait for sunset before finding comfort in Tripp.

He kicked the tire.

Maybe he had left Ali, but he'd always been faithful. Always loved Ali, and only Ali. Left because he loved her too much to stay and watch himself destroy her.

Jericho climbed into the vehicle and slammed the

door. He closed his eyes and pinched the bridge of his nose. What was a man to do? He came home to mend his marriage. After all his wandering, Jericho finally felt like a man worthy of being a husband.

Was he too late?

# *Chapter Two*

❧

As Ali drove under the American flags suspended above Main Street, panic welled up in her throat.

She'd have to see *him*.

"Mom, drive faster. We're gonna be late to the fireworks." Chance bounced in the back seat.

From the passenger's seat, her sister Kate laid a hand on Ali's arm. "Are you all right?"

Ali glanced back at her son. "This traffic's pretty bad."

Kate shrugged. "Everyone is just excited. A week ago we thought the show would be canceled like last year."

"I still can't believe the donations the city got at the last minute. Wish I knew who had purse strings like that. I could tap them for Big Sky Dreams." Ali bit her lip. The worry she felt over the financial problems of her nonprofit organization was never far from her mind.

"This is different. The Fourth of July. People get excited about patriotic stuff."

"You think blowing up a bunch of cardboard is more important than helping handicapped kids?"

"Now don't go putting words in my mouth, big sis. You know I think what you do is worthwhile. I'm just saying, the draw for something like this is more universal."

Ali bumped the truck along the grass-trodden lot being used to park overflow for the fireworks show. The three climbed out, scooped up their blankets and plodded across the fairground's field, looking for a spot to claim. Ali stopped often to chat with her neighbors, wave to her horseback-riding students and embrace folks she'd grown up with.

As the first explosion resounded in the sky, Ali relaxed. Propped on her elbows, she laid back, watching her son's face more than the Fourth of July display. His mouth hung slack as his eyes sparkled to match the show lighting up the night sky. He wore a giant toothy grin. She wished she could recapture that feeling in her own life. Would she ever again know that feeling of freedom, of trusting and letting go? Where had her joy gone?

Jericho Eli Freed. That's where. The man had successfully smashed her hope of a white knight when he ran off like a bandit with her dreams.

Standing there, ten feet away from the love of his life, watching her smile and sigh, an ache filled Jericho that reached clear to his toes. So his Ali wasn't all mountain lion snarls and rattlesnake warnings. As she watched her son, softness filled her face. *Beautiful.* Staring at his wife, his mind blanked out.

"Hey, lover-boy." A warm hand touched his arm, and he glanced over. Kate stood at his elbow. "Are you going to look at her all night? Or will you man up and do something?"

"You're talking to me? I figured all the Silvers hated my guts."

Kate motioned for him to follow her a few paces away from where Ali and Chance sat. She dropped her voice to a whisper. "Are you still in love with my sister?"

Jericho swallowed hard. *Bold little thing.* The last time he'd seen Kate, she'd been a skinned-knee kid.

"Well? Answer me, cowboy." Her eyebrow drove higher.

Jericho cleared his throat. "Yes. 'Course. I've always loved her, always will."

Kate nodded. "Bingo. Well, if that's the case, I'll help you."

"You wanna help me get Ali back?"

She let out a long stream of air, like he was daft for not tracking with the conversation. "Yes. When you left, Ali fell to pieces. You know better than anyone that she didn't have the easiest life. But with you, when you were there for her, all that other stuff didn't strangle her. Then you left, and…"

*You destroyed her.*

"I know. I'm sorry. I'd do anything to change the fact that I left."

"But I need to know, before we become partners in this, are you a better man now?" She jammed a finger into his chest, and he knew exactly what she meant. *You still a drunk? Ornery? Will you leave again?*

He lifted his hands, palms out. "I'm a man surrendered now, Kate. Still make mistakes. But I haven't touched a bottle in five years, and I've made a promise to God that I never will. I won't hurt Ali. I came back to make good on my wedding vows…to honor and protect her, to fix what I did. But she doesn't want me at all."

"I think you're wrong."

"But what about Chance?"

Kate held up a hand and shook her head. "Not my story to tell."

Sweat slicked his palms. "Don't know, Kate. I was watching her just now. She smiles for everyone but me. She started crying when I talked to her. I think she'd relish watching the buzzards pecking at me before seeing me again."

"That's because if she lets down her guard with you, she stands to lose the most."

"Meaning?"

"You cowboys are all seriously dense."

He rolled his eyes. "Continue."

"She's closed off to you because she loves you the most. That makes you the biggest danger of all. If someone else rejects her or betrays her, she can shrug that off, but you? That's everything to her. Has been since you two were kids."

Well, that was clear as mud.

"So here's the plan." She glanced back at Ali, then leaned toward him. "In a minute these fireworks will be done, and I'm going to ferret away Chance with the lure of some sparklers." She patted the bulge in her purse. "That'll leave you a good amount of time to talk to Ali."

"But what do I say?"

"If you can't figure that out, cowboy, then you don't deserve my sister."

Alone, lying back and scanning the night sky through the leftover smoke hanging in the air, Ali almost breathed a thankful sigh—but then *he* sat down next to her, took off his hat and tapped the brim against his leg.

"I don't want you—"

"I know." He wound his hat around in his hands, and the motion tugged at all the broken places inside her. "I know you don't want me. And after a time, if you still feel that way, I'll honor that. I'll leave you alone for good."

"Good, I want that. Now." She started to sit up, gathering the blanket Chance and Kate shared during the show, but his warm hand on her arm stopped her. He gently turned her to face him.

She sighed. "Okay, if I let you talk, we'll be done? You'll leave after that?"

"If that's really what you want." He ran his fingers over the rim of his hat.

"It is. So go ahead, shoot."

He gave the slightest sign of an outlaw smile. "Not a good thing to say to a cowboy."

She rolled her eyes. "Speak, rover. Talk. Say whatever it is you're so bent on telling me."

He shifted. "I should have never left."

"You've got that right."

He placed a hand on her arm and gently squeezed. "Let me talk, woman, please." Jericho removed his hand. "That day. You've got to understand that I had to go. I had no choice. I was so afraid that I'd hurt you, Ali. I loved you so much, and I sat there watching myself destroy the one person in the world who meant anything to me. That day when I lost it…tossed your lamp…well, I saw a streak of my pop in me, and it made me sick. I got in my car and just took off, kicking up a cloud of dust."

Blinking the burn away from her eyes, Ali moved to stand up. "I don't need to hear a replay of this. In case you forgot, I was there."

He stopped her with a touch of his hand. "Please stay."

Who was he to beg her to stay? But like a fool, she hunkered back down.

"I stopped at Pop's house and had an all-out yelling brawl with him, then lit for the state line. I got a job driving a tour bus at Yellowstone. They canned me a couple months later when they found out I hit the scotch before the rides. I spent the next year or two working as a ranch hand at different places, most of the time herding at the back, eating cattle dust and that's about all I felt I was good for. I thought about coming back—wanted to—but I was a sorry mess that you didn't need. I drank more than before. Drank all my money away. But God kept me alive, so I could come back to you and—"

"I hardly think God has anything to do with it. You were a drunk, lying, good-for-nothing boy."

He nodded. "I can't argue you about that. I was. And I took the coward's way. I just needed—" he closed his eyes "—escape."

Ali bit back a stream of words. Adults didn't get the choice of escape. They bucked up and dealt with it, like she had. "Escape from what? Me?" Her muscles cringed. *Never enough.* Her love couldn't heal him. She'd failed as a wife, and that's why he left.

"No. Never you. I needed to escape *me*." He thumbed his chest. "I was furious at God for taking my mom, hated Pop for becoming a cruel drunk—then hated my-self just as much for becoming everything I despised in him. I was angry that I couldn't be what you needed. I talked you into running away from your family in the middle of the night, into marrying me when you were only eighteen. I had nothing to give you but my heap of troubles. I was just a kid myself, and I didn't have the first clue how to take care of you properly. What kind of man was I? So I drank. I wanted to be numb. I wanted nothing to matter anymore, but I kept seeing your face, kept catching whiffs of pretty flowers that reminded me of you." His ratty straw hat flaked apart as he twisted it round and round in his hands while talking.

With a bull-rider's grip on her purse, Ali chewed her bottom lip. Jericho's humility unnerved her. He was supposed to be cocky. He was supposed to smell of al-cohol, combined with the cigar smoke from whatever bar he'd rolled out of at three in the morning. But no, he sat here emitting an intoxicating mixture of hard work, rain and alfalfa.

He paused, his soft eyes studying her. When she didn't respond, he continued. "It got worse, though. I found myself sneaking into barns at night just for a place to sleep away the hangover. Homeless…can you imagine?" He gave a humorless laugh. "The great ranch baron Abram Freed's son, homeless." He threw up his hands. "One night an old rancher found me, and I thought he was going to shoot me between the eyes, but he invited me inside. Let me sleep in his guest bed-room. He was a veteran, and when he talked about his time in the service he just became a hero to me. This man had been through so much terrible stuff, but he was even-keeled and kind. And I wanted to be him. So I enlisted. I owe that man the life I have now."

"You're really a soldier, then?"

He put back on his hat, steepling his hands together. "Ali, who's Chance's dad?"

The question froze every inch of her that had thawed during his story. "He doesn't have one. He's *my* son. That's it."

"Unless he's adopted…that's not really possible."

"Are you done?" She knew her harsh tone would wound his open spirit, but she didn't care. Not when Chance got pulled into the conversation.

He sighed and worked the kinks out of the back of his neck. "After I enlisted, I went through training and spent some good time learning what it means to be a man of discipline and determination. After a couple years my group got drawn for deployment, and I wanted to call you, wanted to say goodbye, but didn't feel like I had the right to. Not one person I cared about knew I was over there, knew I could die at any minute."

*Die?* Her head snapped up. Could he have died without her ever knowing? Wouldn't her heart have felt the loss? Regardless of her anger, she would never have wanted that.

Across the field, Kate and Chance picked their way toward her.

"…but then one day we were sent on this mission and—"

She cut him off. "That's great, Jericho. Sounds like life without us worked out just fine for you. Our lives have been good without you, too. I got some schooling and started a nonprofit that I really care about." She rose, hoping he'd follow suit.

"Without us?" He took the blanket from her arms.

"What?" Her tongue raced against the back of her teeth.

He quirked both eyebrows. "You said *us,* plural."

She pushed him away with her best glare. "Us…as in the Bitterroot Valley, your dad, the people here in Montana that you grew up with." Her hands shook. Almost gave it away. Foolish mouth.

Chance's rapid steps approached.

"Your story, well, it doesn't change much for me. I still want you to turn on those boots and do that walking-out bit you're so good at."

"I can't, Ali, not yet."

"But you said you'd leave if that's what I wanted, and I do."

"I came back because I have to ask your forgiveness. And if we can, I want to fix our marriage. Be there for you like I promised nine years ago."

"I don't want that."

"Hey, Mom! You found Jericho!" Chance frolicked around the two adults.

"How were the sparklers, buddy?" She dropped down and pulled her son into her arms.

Chance's gaze flew to Jericho, and his cheeks colored. The little imp wiggled free. "They were great. My friend Michael told this girl Samantha that he was going to put a sparkler in her hair and light it on fire. But Kate told him that someday he'll be sorry he ever talked to girls that way."

"I'm sure he will be." Still on her knees, she smiled.

Chance turned toward Jericho. "You're a guy. What do you think?"

"I think your mom and your aunt are right. A real

man is always nice to a girl." His gaze locked on Ali. "Always."

Chance grabbed Jericho's sleeve, pulling the man to his level. "Were you talking to my mom again? Do you know her?"

Ali jumped in. "Jericho and I did know each other, but it was a really long time ago, pal. His dad's ranch backs up to ours. We were neighbors."

Chance took her hand. "That's cool, so we can share him."

Behind him, Kate attempted to hide a laugh with a cough.

"Hey, Jericho, it's my birthday in two days. Will you come to my party? Looks like you already know where our house is."

"Chance! Did you ever think Jericho might have other things to do with his time?" Ali's eyes widened. *Please let Jericho have something to do that day.*

Jericho spread out his arms and let a low, rumbling laugh escape his lips. "I'll be there, champ. I'm free."

"Then will you promise to teach me to ride a ewe?" The child's eyes lit up, hands clasped together.

Jericho rose. He rubbed his jaw and looked to Ali. She shook her head. "I think you're too big for mutton bustin'. The kids who do that are five or six."

Chance crossed his arms. "It's not fair. Our ranch hand, Rider, won't teach me. Now you won't, either."

"I could teach you something else. How about roping? Do you know how to lasso a steer? 'Cause that's loads harder than riding sheep."

"You promise you'll come teach me?"

"I'll bring the dummy steer and everything." Jericho smiled down at Ali's son, and her heart squeezed—with panic or tenderness, though, she couldn't be sure. One thing she knew—Jericho Freed was back in her life, whether she wanted him there or not.

## *Chapter Three*

Scientific research said mint-and-tan-painted walls were supposed to soothe her, but each step Ali took toward her mother's room weighed her down like shuffling through deep mud. She nodded to other residents of the facility as they teetered down the hallway, gripping the railing that ran waist-level throughout the nursing home. She clutched her purse against her stomach. Mom didn't belong here. People in their fifties shouldn't be stuck like this.

Paces away from Mom's door, Ali leaned against the wall and sucked in a fortifying breath. It stung her throat with the artificial smells of bleach and cafeteria food. She pulled the paper out of her purse and read it again.

I saw you together at the Independence Day picnic. If you value what's important to you, you'll stay away from him. You've been warned.

Ali didn't know whether she should run to the police department or laugh. The glued-on magazine letters looked straight out of a cheesy television crime show. But was the threat serious? Who would leave such a thing tacked to her front door? Thankfully, her head ranch hand, Rider, found it before Chance woke up. Her son could pretend bravado, but with something like this, he would have dissolved into a puddle of tears.

She racked her mind, tallying a list of the people she remembered seeing at the picnic yesterday. Not one of them would have cared in the least if they saw her speaking with Jericho. Who wanted to keep them apart? Not that she minded. That's what she wanted anyway, right? All the more reason to steer clear of the man, but it grated to be threatened.

Unless… No, it couldn't be. Abram Freed had never been fond of his son's attachment to her, but she'd made her peace with the cantankerous cowboy years after Jericho left. Besides, with the paralysis on the right side of his body, the man couldn't move—he lay in a bed here in the same nursing home as her mother. He couldn't harm her, and he'd keep her secret about Chance, too.

A nurse wearing a teal smock broke into her thoughts. "You gonna go in and say howdy to your ma?"

"Hi, Sue. How's Mom doing today?"

The nurse's blond eyebrow rose. "No disrespect, but your ma's the most ornery patient we have. But we don't mind none. She's a fighter at that. I think most people would be gone already with what she's got, but she just keeps hanging right on."

Ali gave a tight-lipped smile. "She's a handful."

Jamming the menacing letter back into her purse, she smoothed down her shirt and ran a hand over her hair before entering her mother's room. The sight of Marge

Silver—weak with pale skin hanging in long droops off her arms and a map of premature wrinkles covering her face as she whistled air in and out through the oxygen nosepiece—always made Ali's knees shake a little bit.

"How you feeling, Ma?" She came to the side of the bed. Ali felt a deep emptiness. Her mom's eyes stared back, cold and hopeless. Shut off, like her spirit had already given up.

"Dying… Been better." The words wheezed out, stilting every time the oxygen infused.

Ali crossed her arms and buried her balled-up fists deep in her armpits. She wanted to take her mother's hand in both of hers, but she knew better. Never one to show affection, her mother wouldn't have considered the touch comforting. "You aren't dying."

"Want to.… Nothing left…here."

"You know that's not true. There is Kate and me and Chance."

"Not that any of…you…care."

"I wouldn't be here if I didn't care, and I know Kate visited just the other day."

"The ranch?"

Ali straightened a vase on the bedside table. "It's fine."

"The…lawsuit?"

Ali bit her lip. She should be used to this by now; her mom asked the same questions every time she visited. But somehow, the little girl in Ali who wanted to know her mom loved her came with expectations that left her drifting in an ocean of hurt every time. Besides, she didn't want to think about the deaths of that poor couple. It was an accident.

"Don't worry about that. Tripp's taking care of it. He always does the best for us."

"Has to…. None of the rest of you…have any thought…in your heads. Never…happen…if your father…still alive."

Ali pulled her purse tighter up on her shoulder, then gripped the bed rails. "I miss Daddy too, Ma."

"Your fault…he's dead."

"Don't say that."

"So…selfish, had…to ride. Had…to…rodeo."

"It's hardly my fault Dad got caught under that bull's hooves." Ali stared out the window, fanning her face with her hand to dry the tears clinging to her eyelids. She tried to block out the memory of her dad, the amateur rider Buck Silver, being crushed again and again by two thousand pounds of angry muscle and horns. She saw his body go limp, remembered trying to run into the arena but Jericho's strong arms held her back.

"Your fault…men leave. Your dad…your husband."

"You're wrong. Jericho's back," Ali ground out.

"If he finds…out. He'll…take your son. You'll…be alone."

"He doesn't know about Chance, and he has no reason to ever know."

"People…always leave."

"That doesn't have to be true. Chance will always be with me. And Kate's back right now."

"How long…before she goes…too?"

"I don't know, Mom. Here, I brought you some stuff from the house." Ali set a bunched paper bag on the nightstand. "I'll see you next week."

Ali barreled out of the doorway—and straight into Jericho Freed's solid chest.

* * *

"Whoa, there." Jericho grabbed Ali's slender biceps to steady her.

"I'm not a horse." She jerked away.

"Of course you're not." He tipped her chin with his finger, and her red-rimmed eyes, tears carving twin paths down either side of her face, made his stomach flip. "Why are you crying?"

She swiped her face with the back of her hand. "What are you doing here?"

"Pop."

"Oh, I knew that. I'm sorry. It was so sad—he was all alone. They aren't sure how long he lay there…"

"You're avoiding my question." He gave a smile he hoped exuded safety and reassurance. "Why the tears?"

She tossed her hands in the air. "Oh, just another invigorating talk with my mother."

"She's here, too?"

Ali shrugged and gave an unflattering grimace in what looked like an attempt to hold back emotion. "She has lung cancer. I mean, we should have expected it. She smoked three or four packs every day of my life, and only got worse after we lost Dad."

"And let me take a guess—she's still as bitter and mean as ever."

Ali met his gaze, and the tears brought out the gold flecks in her eyes. For a moment he couldn't breathe. "She's had a hard life."

"True, but she doesn't have to take it out on you. Don't blame her moods on yourself. It's fully her choice how she treats people."

"You're one to talk," she mumbled and he swallowed a growl.

Could she never forgive him?

He blocked her path when she moved to walk around him. "Are you going to be all right?"

She dug her toe into the floor, and in a small voice confessed, "She still blames me for killing Dad."

He wanted to scoop her up in his arms and feel her head resting against his chest, trusting his strength as he carried her away from all the people who tried to tie millstones around her neck. Quashing that desire, he settled for cupping her elbow and leading her outside, away from the oppression and doom of the nursing home. Thankfully, she walked right along with him, even leaned into his touch a little bit.

When they got outside, he led her to her truck then turned her to face him. He rested his hands on her shoulders. His blues met her sparkling hazels as he said in a soft, low voice, "It wasn't your fault. Your dad made a choice that day to get on that bull. He took a risk, and it turned out to be a disastrous one. But that's all it was, an accident."

She worked that bottom lip between her teeth. "But he would have been trucking. He wouldn't have been at the rodeo if I hadn't been so bent on barrel racing."

"He loved the rodeo. I'm just sorry we were there to see it that day."

Ali nodded in an absent way, then pushed up on his wrists. Jericho let go of her, but as he stepped back he noticed something curious. "Your tires are on their rims."

"What? I just drove here. They were fine." Ali turned around and then slapped her hand over her mouth.

Jericho bent down to examine the tires. Sure enough, each one bore a deep slash. Intentional. His stomach rolled. "Cut. Know why someone would want to make mincemeat of your tires?"

She dragged in a ragged breath and clutched her purse close to her chest. "Yes."

"Well?"

Her eyes widened. "I can't tell you."

"What? That's ridiculous. If you have a problem with someone, tell me and I'll take care of it for you."

Ali's brows knit together. "Why would you do that?"

He stepped forward, propping a hand on the truck above her head. He leaned toward her. She was so close. If he dropped his head, he could kiss her. Taste the sweet lips he'd dreamt about for the eight years he'd been gone. He wanted to, badly. Would she meld against him like she used to, or would she slap him and run?

"Nine years ago, I made a promise to protect you. I went and made a real mess of that, but I'm back. You can call on that promise if you want to. I'll be here for you. You hear me?"

"I'll be fine. I just have to walk to Mahoney and Strong—Tripp's an associate with the law firm. It's not that far." She looked around him toward downtown. Jealousy curled in his chest.

"I can drive you there." He hated himself for being any part of bringing her near Tripp, but he'd just made a promise, and he'd stay true to it no matter the personal cost.

"I'll walk."

"It's farther than you think, and it's hot as blazes out here. Let me drive you."

She shook her head.

"Can I pick you up from his office and drive you home?"

"I'm sure Tripp will drive me home. I'll see you around."

She brushed past him, but the sweet smell of her lingered—something flowery. Jericho walked back to his Jeep. His pop would have to wait another day or two for a reunion.

He needed to find four new tires and get them on that beastly truck before Tripp could swoop in with some kind of heroic act.

# Chapter Four

With his legs tossed over the edge of the porch, Chance swung his feet, banging them against the house with the rhythm of an Indian drumbeat.

Ali leaned an elbow on the armrest of the Adirondack chair, resting her chin on her palm. "Hey, little man, cut that out."

"Is that your truck, Mom?" He sprang to his feet and squinted in the direction of the driveway.

Her green monster of a vehicle rattled over the gravel. "Looks like it. I left my keys with Tripp, and he said he'd have someone fix the tires. That must be him." She pushed up out of the chair and crossed to the steps.

The man climbing out from the driver's side looked about the same size as Tripp, but that's where the similarities ended. Ali pursed her lips.

Chance jostled past her. "Jericho!"

"Hey, bud." He touched the brim of his hat. "Ali."

She narrowed her eyes. "Why do you have my truck?"

He looped his thumbs in his pockets. "You left it at the nursing home. It's got new tires. The old ones couldn't be saved. But these are good ones. You won't have to put chains on them in the winter."

"I'll go inside and get my purse. How much do I owe you?"

"Nothing."

"Nothing? The tires I had were almost bald. I priced out new ones weeks ago, and the lowest I could find from anyone was around a thousand. I can't…won't be able to give you all of that right now, but I can mail you the rest and—"

He shook his head. "Like I said, you don't owe me anything. But your engine's making an unnerving jangling noise, so I'm going to take a peek at that sometime this week."

She thrust out her hand. "My keys."

"Funny thing about that." He leaned a foot on the steps and rested his hands on his knee. "I didn't have keys so I had to hot-wire it." He scratched his neck. "Hadn't done that since high school. Remember how we used to drive Principal Ottman up the wall?"

Ali bit back a grin. "He never could quite figure out how he kept losing his car, or why the police kept finding it at Dairy Queen."

Chance leaped off the last two steps, landing beside Jericho. "What's hot-wire?"

"Well, it's how you can drive a car if you don't have keys. You see, first you take a screwdriver and pull the trim off the steering column. Unbolt the ignition switch, then—"

Ali cleared her throat.

Jericho's lips twitched with the hint of a smirk. "Right. Not something you need to know, bud."

The front door creaked, and Kate popped her head

through the opening. "Al? Oh hey, Jericho. Your hot chocolate's boiling over. I shut it off. Hope it's not scalded."

Ali slapped her hand over her heart. "I'd completely forgotten. Do you still want cocoa, Chance?"

Her son's affirmation propelled her into the house. She stuck a spoon into the pan full of liquid chocolate. She brought the hot cocoa to her lips, blowing on it before tasting. "Still good."

Kate set out three mugs. "Jericho can have my cup. I'm headed upstairs anyway."

"He's not staying."

"Guess again, sis. He and Chance are already out there, cozy together on the steps. It sounds like they're swapping tall tales."

The ladle rattled in Ali's hand. "He can't stay. I don't want him on our property, not near Chance."

"Too late." Kate drummed her fingers on the counter. "Did he fix your truck?"

"The tires."

Kate let out a long, low whistle.

"And he won't let me pay him back. Not like I have the money to anyway."

After wishing her sister good-night, Ali hugged the three mugs of steaming cocoa to her chest and strode back outside. Chance popped up, reached for his and then hunkered back down so close that he bumped knees with Jericho. She handed a cup Jericho's way, and his fingers slipped over hers in the exchange. Ali inhaled sharply.

He took a sip, then tipped the mug at her in a salute. "This is good."

She wrapped an arm around her middle and looked

out to the Bitterroot Mountain Range. The snowcapped peaks laughed down at the fading sunlight in the valley. The sides were blanketed in a vivid green tapestry of pines. Each canyon crag vied with the peaks for splendor. The Bitterroots calmed her. Taking them in reminded her that even when life felt topsy-turvy, purpose and beauty remained in the world.

"It's from scratch. Mom says none of the packaged stuff in our house, right?" Chance beamed at her, a whipped cream mustache covering his top lip.

"Right."

"Jericho told me he used to ride the broncos in the rodeo. Isn't that cool? But he said he never rode the bulls. He said it's too dangerous, just like you always say."

Ali leaned her shoulder against a support beam on the porch. "Yes, Jericho used to ride the broncs. He used to rope in the rodeos, too."

Chance plunked down his mug. "Sounds like you were more than neighbors, 'cause I don't know things like that about old Mr. Edgar, and he's lived right across the field my whole life."

Jericho shifted to meet her gaze. He raised his eyebrows.

She let out a long stream of air. "We used to be friends, Chance, that's all."

Chance tapped his chin. "Does that mean you're not friends anymore?"

Jericho kept staring at her. His intensity bored into her soul, and she looked down.

"Jericho's been gone a long time."

She wandered down the steps and into the yard. Their pointer, Drover, trailed after her. She scratched behind his ears, causing his leg to thump against the ground in doggy-bliss.

That had been a close call. Too close. But it's not like she could kick the man out right after that conversation. Doing so would only raise Chance's suspicion.

The low rumble of Jericho's voice carried as he launched into a story detailing an adventure from his days in the army. "We had to go in helicopters, only way to get there. We could hardly see through all the sand swirling around and—"

"So it was like a beach?" Chance peppered Jericho's monologue with a constant stream of questions.

"Naw. Beaches are nice. This was a desert. Hot. It'd be about one hundred twenty degrees, and we'd have to lug around seventy pounds of equipment on our backs without an ocean to cool off in. Ants all over our food. Not too much fun."

Ali coughed. "I think it's about bedtime."

"No way. C'mon, Mom. One more story."

Jericho laid a hand on her son's head. "Don't argue with your mom, bud. Go on up. You'll see me again. Promise."

With a loud groan, Chance shuffled into the house.

A pace away from her, Jericho rose to his feet, his masculine frame outlined by the light flooding from the house.

She crossed her arms. "I can pay you back."

He stepped closer. "I promised to protect you, remember? I made that pact, and I aim to keep it for the rest of my life. You owe me nothing."

She bit her lip.

He tipped his hat. "Sleep tight, Ali." Then he brushed

past her and strolled, hands hooked in his pockets, into the hay field back toward his pa's place.

Sweat trickled down Ali's neck as she lugged the last saddle onto its peg in the barn. The triangular posts drilled into the wall were genius. Much better than tipping the saddles on their sides and storing them on the ground like they had been doing. She made a mental note to thank Rider.

Ali placed her hands on her hips as her mind ticked over the accounting books for Big Sky Dreams. She'd never been great at balancing the ledgers, but even Ali could see that money was missing. But how?

Megan Galveen, the other riding instructor for Big Sky Dreams, sashayed through the back door in black designer jeans.

Ali smiled at her. "You're a lifesaver. Thanks for taking care of Salsa when he started misbehaving. I don't know what made the horse so skittish today. I know you've only been here a month, but have I told you how thankful I am for your help?"

Megan pouted her full, over-red lips and closed one eye, tapping her sunglasses to her chin. "Oh, only about every day. But please, do go on."

Ali laughed. "Well, enjoy your afternoon off. You know you're welcome at Chance's birthday party, right?"

Her coworker flipped her long, glossy black hair. "A party for seven-year-olds isn't really my thing."

"No, I guess not."

Why had Ali even asked her? The woman was more suited in looks to walk down runways than teach handicapped kids about horses.

Ali glanced down at her own mud-caked boots and dirty jeans. She grimaced. Maybe she ought to spend more time on her looks. She ran a hand over her flipped-out, short red hair. Yeah, right. She worked in hay and horse manure all day, and the only kisses bestowed on her came complete with animal cracker crumbs.

Someone cleared their throat, interrupting Ali's train of thought. She looked up to find her head ranch hand, Rider Longley. The man looked like his name—taller than he ought to be and scrawnier than a cornstalk. With his junked-up Levis, scuffed boots, a blue shirt with white buttons and a new brown hat, he looked the part. But he would have been just as comfortable in a cubicle, wearing khakis while programming laptops. He lacked the cowboy snarl in his face, but he made up for his failings with heart and determination.

He looped a rope over his shoulder. "Someone's been out messing with the fences in the heifer field again. I figure it'll take most of the day to round them up off Edgar's property and mend the cuts."

Ali's heart stopped. "What do you mean, messing with the fences?"

Rider adjusted his hat. "I'm not an expert on these sorts of things, but how the slices are, looks to me like someone snipped through our fences with wire cutters. Cows can cause damage, but not clean breaks like I'm finding."

"That's ridiculous." Megan plunked down her suitcase-sized purse and pawed inside until she fished out her lip gloss. "Who would want to mess with Big Sky Dreams?"

"Dunno." He shrugged. "I'm not a detective. Just know what I see."

\* \* \*

Pulling off her hat, Ali swiped a hand over her forehead. Now that Rider and Megan were gone, her thoughts swirled. The threatening note, slashed tires, money missing from the Big Sky Dreams account and now the fences—what was she going to do?

"I brought this for you." Kate came beside her, handing over a chilled water bottle.

Ali held the bottle to her neck, then to her cheek. "Feels good. It's really a scorcher out here today. I hope the old air conditioner in the house holds together for Chance's party."

"It'll be fine. If it busts again, those kids won't care."

Ali stepped forward so she stood in the barn entrance. The wind ruffled through the valley, kicking up the smell of the nearby river and drying the sweat from her body.

"How'd lessons go today?"

She unscrewed the bottle cap and took a long swig, catching dribbles on her chin with the back of her hand. Ali loved nothing more than talking about her handicapped horseback-riding program. "Good. Alan's coming along great. The movement's strengthening his core and helping build some muscle tone." It felt good to know that something she'd started made a difference. "Rebecca's parents told me that her test scores have improved since joining the program last month. Can you believe that?"

Kate squeezed her arm. "That's awesome, Al. How about those two?" She jutted her chin toward the sprawling side yard, near the practice corral where Ali usually ran her horse, Denny, through the barrels. Today two boys practiced their cattle roping. Ali gripped the barn wall. Well, if the broad shoulders and popping biceps of Jericho Freed could be classified as a boy. Okay. Man and boy.

Ali let herself breathe for a moment before answering. "I don't know what to think. First he takes care of my truck, then this morning he shows up on the doorstep with a rope in hand, asking for Chance. What was I supposed to say?"

"I think you did the right thing, Al, by letting him spend time with his son."

"But that terrifies me."

"What? Him being here? Or him with Chance?"

"With Chance. Both. I don't know."

"What did he say when you two talked after the firework show?"

Ali crossed her arms, propping her shoulder against the barn. "He said he wants forgiveness. He said he wants to repair our…marriage." A gritty lump formed in her throat as she watched Chance loop the rope over the fake horns and give a loud whoop. He clapped victorious hands with Jericho, whose deep laugh drifted across the yard. A person would have to be blind not to see the resemblance. They had the same eyes, same unruly hair, same slight swagger in their walk, same full-chested laugh. Ali rubbed at her throat.

Kate touched her shoulder. "What are you gonna do?"

"He's a drunk, Kate."

"I haven't smelled beer around him, and I sure haven't seen him staggering around. He might have been at one point, but it doesn't seem like he drinks anymore."

Ali closed her eyes. "If he'd walked out on you like he walked out on me, would you forgive him?"

"We're called to forgive everyone."

"He gets to turn my life into a nightmare. Then with a little 'I'm sorry,' we act like it never happened? Convenient."

Kate placed a hand over hers and Ali looked down, not realizing that her knuckles had become white from her iron grip on the barn door. She let go of the metal and flexed her hand, drawing the blood back into her fingers.

"I don't think forgiveness has to mean forgetting, Al. The consequences of sin will always be there, and I think he's suffered them. Forgiveness means you grant pardon for what happened. It's you saying you won't be bitter and hold those actions against him."

Ali hugged her middle with both arms. "I can't do that. He left. It bothers me that his life's been fine without me, while I had to struggle and scrape and wish each day he'd come back and rescue us." Her voice caught.

"I wouldn't say he got off easy. He's missed seven years of his son's life. Eight years with the woman he loves."

Ali snorted. "Right. He loves me loads."

"And he's back—maybe now's the rescue you waited for."

She shook her head. "I stopped believing in fairy tales a long time ago. There are no white knights, Kate. No one is riding in to save the day. Life is about pressing on when things happen. It's all about who has the most grit, and I think I've proved my worth."

"Maybe that's your problem." Kate's voice took on a sad tone.

Ali jerked back. "My *problem*?"

"You're right. Jericho's not your white knight, but he was never supposed to be. What chance did your husband have of succeeding with those kind of expectations? He can't be the one to rescue you. Not in the way you need. Just like Ma, you're letting hate and bitterness eat away at you, and you think your misery gained you some sort of badge of honor. You think you can punish Jericho for what he did by closing yourself off and holding him at a distance." Kate thrust out her hand. "But look at him. He's free, Al. You're the one still locked up and suffering. And you will be until you offer forgiveness."

Ali shoved the bottle into her sister's hands. "I have work to do. Thanks for the water." She stomped back into the barn. Twine bit into her hands as she grabbed a bale of hay.

Her sister could go chew on screws. Kate had no idea. She was so young when Dad died, and Ali had stepped into the gap to take Ma's wrath. What did Kate know of suffering and pain and the consequences of sin?

"Nothing." Ali yanked a razor from her pocket and sliced the twine. Pulling the hay into even squares, she placed a bundle in each horse's stall. Drover, playing supervisor, padded along, making sure each horse got their fair share. She caressed the dog's head and smiled when he yawned.

In the moments when Ali looked back at her short-lived marriage objectively, she could see the truth. The judge should have stamped *disaster* in bold red letters on the marriage certificate. In her needy state, did she drive her husband to the bar? In their small apartment, she'd watched the man who was supposed to save her morph into the man he most despised. Had it been her fault?

She swiped away treacherous tears. Infernal hay dust.

*I was so afraid that I'd hurt you, Ali. I loved you so much.*

Jericho Freed, hurt her? Not possible, not the way he imagined. If she thought the man possessed any tendency toward violence, he wouldn't be alone out there with her son right now.

No. She saw the man she knew. A memory of Jericho taking a beating from his father to protect a runt puppy flashed through her mind. Then one of him at nineteen years old, stepping in between her and Ma, telling her she won't be speaking to his wife *that way* anymore.

Even that last night, with clear eyes, she could see that he left to protect her then, too. In his own way, Jericho always had put her first, but then what kept him from coming home? Didn't he know how much she needed him the past eight years?

## Chapter Five

Ten children tromped like a herd of mustangs around the dining room, over the checkered kitchen floor and out the back door as Ali tried to pull the last of the food from the fridge to set out on the table.

"Don't let the door—"

The last child jumped the three steps down into the yard, and the screen door smacked against its hinges, tearing the hole in the screen a few inches wider.

"I'll fix the screen tomorrow." Jericho took the heavy pile of plates from her hands and set them on the counter.

Heat blossomed on her cheeks. He had no right to look that good in a clean pair of jeans and shined boots. His tucked-in, starched red button-down hugged the coiled muscles in his arms.

The sight made her wish she'd taken another minute to give herself a once-over before guests arrived. But the emotional mess Kate had tossed on her that morning made her work slower in the barn. By the time she came back to the house, less than an hour remained until party time. Enough time to shower, but not enough time for makeup or to blow-dry her hair. Jericho probably thought she looked like a wet prairie dog.

She waved her hand, dismissing his comment. "You don't have to fix that screen. It's been like that for months."

"I know I don't have to. But I don't mind. I have to come to tune that clank out of your truck anyway."

Kate stuck her head into the kitchen, a smile on her face as she looked between Jericho and Ali rearranging the table. "Need any more help in here?"

Ali surveyed the room. "I think I've got the food under control. If you want to get one of the games started outside, that would be great."

Kate saluted and meandered out the back door. Satisfied that everything was taken care of, Ali turned, nearly slamming into Jericho. She gasped. She'd almost forgotten he was in the room with her. *Alone.*

His gaze shifted down and up, then down again.

"What are you staring at?" She wiped her hands on a dishcloth and tossed the rag into the sink.

The hint of a roguish smile pulled at his lips. "You're beautiful. I didn't have a picture of you. For eight years I had to rely on my memory. Couldn't do you justice. It's nice to look at you." Ali wanted to accuse him of lying, but his voice wrapped around her, ringing with sincerity.

"Ha." She tucked a damp clump of hair behind her ear, only to have the doggone thing fall forward again. "Then you need to get out more."

Jericho raised a dark eyebrow. "Nope. I don't need to look anywhere else to know that this—" he swept his hand to indicate her "—is my favorite sight."

She harrumphed. "I'm all wet, and I don't have any

makeup on. And I'm pretty sure I'm wearing yesterday's socks. Still the prettiest sight?"

He leaned against the counter. "Yes, ma'am." Teasingly, he continued, "But if you want to get good and soaked, I saw a horse trough out front I could dump you in." He moved toward her.

Ali swatted at his hands. With a laugh, she bumped into the garbage can. "Jericho Eli! Don't you dare. I'm too old to get troughed." She dashed behind the table.

"Mom!" Chance burst through the door. "Can I open presents now?" A battalion of kids trailed in his wake.

"Sure, bud. We'll open presents in the front room right now, and then we'll eat."

"Did you make your chocolate cake? The one made with—" he leaned toward her, knowing he wasn't supposed to give away the secret ingredient "—mayonnaise?"

She winked, and her son's gray-blue eyes danced with merriment. As he clomped away, a wave of joy washed over her. Threatening letters, lawsuits and financial woes couldn't touch her today.

But an unwanted husband could.

Jericho took her elbow, turning her to face him.

"I may be asking you to kick me in the teeth, but I need to know." Jericho stopped and looked down at his boots.

Her heart lurched in her chest. The muscles on the side of his jaw popped, and Ali's gut rolled in anticipation of his question. A drunk she could keep secrets from, but a man who proved thoughtful, patient and kind? Everything a father should be?

But—no. He was still the same man who had run

off on his wife without looking back, discarded his responsibility to her when it suited him and left his child growing inside of her. The shrapnel in her heart from his departure still chafed, and she wouldn't open Chance up to that world of hurt. Jericho hung around for now, but he could still leave at any moment. A child deserved better than that.

Walking to the sink, she turned her back to him and rinsed off a plate. "I don't really have time right now."

His footsteps moved closer, but she didn't dare turn around. He was so near. Ali's breath caught in her throat. One look into his earnest eyes would unglue her resolve.

He took a breath. "I've been thinking. I did the math…being Chance's birthday today, and him turning seven…"

Her hands gripped the cool metal of the sink.

"It only leaves two options."

"Two?" Her voice came out small.

"Unless he was a preemie. But he wasn't, was he?"

Ali locked her gaze through the window over the sink, to the corral. "No, Chance wasn't a preemie."

She felt him take another step closer. "Then it happened when I was still around."

Spinning, she faced him, arms crossed. "It? *It* happened? I think you better go."

Her emotions reflected in his eyes. The same torment. The longing for everything to be right again.

"Is Chance…is he mine?"

"Chance is *mine*. I asked you to leave." Ali pushed against his chest, and he caught her wrists. She pressed her elbows into him. "Let go of me."

"Let go of her!" Tripp crossed the kitchen in three seconds flat. Jericho dropped the light hold he had of Ali as Tripp sidled up beside her. "I don't think you're welcome here anymore, Jericho."

"That true, Ali? If you want me to leave, I will." His lips formed a grim line.

Tripp slid his arm around her waist.

She nodded. "I can't deal with you right now. I need to take care of all the people here."

Jericho narrowed his eyes, almost like he wanted to say something more, but then he put on his hat and dipped his chin. "Be talking to you later, then."

When he left, Tripp took hold of her hands. "Alison, tell me what's going on."

"You saved me. I almost told him about Chance."

The pressure of his hands increased a bit. Besides Kate, Tripp was the only other person in town who knew for sure that Chance was Jericho's son. "You can't ever do that. You tell him about Chance, and he'll probably sue you for parental rights, or at least want shared custody."

She broke away from him and rubbed her temples. "What am I going to do?"

"You need to divorce him. Make the separation legal. Divorce is your only option." Tripp said it so easily. *Divorce.* The word tasted sour on her tongue. But the lawyer made it sound like going for coffee. His tanned arms showed from the rolled-up sleeves of his oxford, and his blue eyes seemed to take her in, while his wavy brown hair stayed perfectly in place.

She brushed at crumbs on the counter. "I don't see the point."

"I don't see the point of *not* divorcing him."

"I know him. He won't sign any papers."

Tripp shrugged. "It doesn't matter. He abandoned you. Didn't send word for eight years. No court will deny your petition."

An uproar in the front room drew her attention. She glanced at the door separating the kitchen from the rest of the party. "Doesn't a divorce cost a lot of money? You know about our financial situation."

He waved his hand. "I have a friend at the firm who can do the paperwork for you. I'll take care of everything. I'll need your signature, that's all."

She wrung her hands. "I don't know."

Tripp took her shoulders so she faced him. "But what if…what if another man wants to marry you?"

Her gaze snapped to meet his, and she didn't see a trace of mocking in his blues. Like a spooked horse, panic bolted down her spine. Another man? Did that mean…?

The door banged. "Mom! Look at what Jericho gave me. Where is he? I want to show him how I've been practicing." Chance thrust a lasso into her hands.

She slipped away from Tripp and took the thick bound rope, running her thumb over the rough surface. "He had to go home."

"Aw, man. I wanted him to show everyone. He's so cool." Chance started walking back toward his party, then stopped. "He'll be here tomorrow, right?"

"I think so, honey."

"Good. I like him the best out of all your friends."

She hugged her middle as she watched Chance leave the room. What was she going to do about his growing attachment to Jericho? It couldn't continue. For Chance to be safe, and her life to continue without any bumps, Jericho needed to leave town. Soon. Because if he didn't, Jericho was bound to figure out that Chance was his son.

Adrenaline tingled through Jericho's muscles as he walked the short length of the Silvers' hay field toward his father's expansive land—the Bar F Ranch. The pain in his knees throbbed, almost blinding him with intensity, but he limped without stopping to rest. He'd ice them at home.

He'd like to rub that smug look off Tripp's face. How dare the man touch his wife?

Scooping up a rock, he tossed the stone into the deep gully separating their properties and waited, listening for the *ping* of it hitting bottom. His heart felt about as jagged and bottomless.

No wonder she didn't like the sight of him. Ali hadn't cheated on him. Chance *had* to be his son. Not only had he left his teenage wife, he'd left her pregnant and alone.

Why didn't she tell him? He would have stayed. No. That was worse. To stay for the sake of the child when he hadn't been willing to stay for the sake of his wife? Cow manure ranked better than him right about now.

The army chaplain's voice drifted through his mind. *You are not your past errors. You are redeemed.* Jericho had rejoiced in that. He had learned to live in victory, but he wanted his wife's forgiveness, too. What would he have to do to prove to Ali that he could be trusted? Would he ever get through to her?

*Husbands, love your wives, just as Christ loved the church and gave himself up for her.*

The scripture whizzed through his head and stopped him cold in his tracks. He looked up at the sky as a burning Montana sun began to wrap purple capes over the mountains.

Love her. Keep on loving her.

That much he could do.

## Chapter Six

Jericho stared at the clock on the dashboard.

*Twenty minutes.*

He ran a hand over his beard. He needed a shave. Maybe he should do that first. No. He refocused his eyes on the front doors of the nursing home. It was now or never.

*Never sounds good.* But he pushed open the Jeep's door and climbed out onto the sun-warmed pavement.

The over-bleached smell of the nursing home assaulted his senses. The hollow clip of his boots on the laminate floor echoed along with the one word ramrodding itself into his head. *Failure. Failure.* Reaching the door bearing a nameplate reading Abram Freed, Jericho froze. He pulled off his battered Stetson and crunched it between his hands. Then he took a step over the threshold.

The sight of Pop tore the breath right out of Jericho's lungs.

Once the poster of an intimidating, weathered cowboy, Abram now just looked…weak. His hair, brushed to the side in a way that Jericho had never seen, had aged to mountain-snowcap-white, but his bushy eyebrows were still charcoal. Like sun-baked, cracked mud, cavernous lines etched the man's face. The once rippled muscles ebbed into sunken patches covered by slack skin.

Jericho waited for his dad to turn and acknowledge him. Or yell at him. Curse him. But he didn't move. What had the doctor told him about Pop? The call came months ago. Stroke. He'd lost the use of his right side. None of it meant anything at the time. But now he saw the effects, and his heart ached with grief for the father he hardly loved. Abram Freed looked like a ship without mooring—lost.

"Hey there, Pop." He hated the vulnerability his voice took on. Like he was ten again, chin to his chest, asking his dad's permission to watch cartoons.

Pop's body tensed, and his head trembled slightly. With a sigh, he raised his left hand off the white sheet by a couple inches. His dad couldn't turn his head. A stabbing, gritty feeling filled Jericho's eyes as he skirted the hospital bed and pulled out the plastic chair near his father's good side. His dad's eyes moved back and forth over Jericho's frame, and the left side of his dad's face pulled up a bit, while the right side remained down in a frown.

A nurse bustled into the room. "Well, now, look at this, Mr. Freed, how nice to have some company. Saw you had a visitor on the log—thought it was that pretty little lady always popping by." She moved toward his father as she spoke.

Pretty little lady? Jericho scanned the room. A fresh vase bursting with purple gerbera daisies sat on the nightstand next to a framed picture of Chance. The photographer had captured the boy's impish smile, crooked on one side and showing more gums than teeth as his blue eyes sparkled. He was holding up a horseshoe in a victorious manner.

*Ali?*

The nurse poured out a cup of water and set it on the bedside table. "And who are you?"

"I'm his son."

"Mercy me." The nurse leaned down near Pop, speaking loudly. "I bet you're glad to see this young man, ain't you?"

"Ith… Ith."

Unwanted tears gathered at the edge of Jericho's eyes as he watched his father struggling to speak.

Abram smacked his left hand on the bed and closed his eyes. "I dondt know. I dondt know."

Jericho searched the nurse's face. She offered him a sad smile. "That's the only understandable phrase we get. It don't mean anything. He says it no matter what's being talked about. But he can hear just fine. He likes when people come and talk to him. Don't you, Mr. Freed?"

Pop's drooping eyes slid partially open, and his head nodded infinitesimally.

Everything inside Jericho seized up. He clenched his jaw, blinking his eyes a couple times. His last meeting with his father whirled in his head—him screaming at Pop, blaming his father for all that had gone wrong in his life.

Over the last eight years, Jericho had pieced back together his world. He'd returned to Bitterroot Valley for two reasons—to repair his devastated marriage, and to restore his relationship with his father. But how could he do that with a man who couldn't speak? He wanted his father to tell him that he was sorry for the abuse and neglect after Mom died. But that apology would never come. And like it or not, he had to be okay with that.

"Since you're here, will you help me move your pa?"

"What?" Jericho scratched the top of his head. "I guess whatever you want me to do, just say."

"We try to move him every hour or so. Prevent sores. It helps to fight the chance of pneumonia, which is always a possibility." She leaned back to Pop. "But we'd never let that happen, sweet man like you. We take good care of you."

She motioned for Jericho to move his father, and after a moment of hesitation, he lifted Pop's frail body in his arms. The old man fit against his chest. Tiny. Breakable. His father's right side hung limp, whereas the muscles on the left side of his body pulled, straining for dignity. A flood of compassion barreled through Jericho's heart, burying all the anger he'd felt for the man who'd caused him such suffering. Abram Freed could never hurt him again. His dad deserved to be treated with respect, no matter their past.

The nurse indicated a beige wingback chair. Jericho recognized it from his childhood home. With extra care, he set Pop down. As he began to move away, his father touched his hand. Jericho turned, and Abram pointed to a nearby chair.

He looked back toward the nurse as she inched toward the door and raised his eyebrows. She smiled. "It's okay. Just go on and talk to him."

Clearing his throat, Jericho rubbed his hands together, eyes on the floor. He looked back at his father,

and the despair swimming in the old man's eyes unglued Jericho's tongue.

So he began to ramble. Told Pop about the past eight
years, and went on about still loving Ali. Told stories
about the war, and in the midst of it an emotion filtered
across his father's face that Jericho had never seen before. Pride.

Swallowing the giant lump in his throat, Jericho
leaned forward, and in a voice barely above a whisper
said words he hadn't planned. "Pop. I'm sorry I left that
night. I didn't just walk out on my wife. I walked out
on you, too. We had our bad times between us, but it
was never like that when Mom was alive. I understand
now why you drank. Losing the woman you love… I
get it. I forgive you."

Jericho waited, bracing himself for the backhand to
his face or the kick to his side that didn't come. Instead
a soft, weathered hand covered his and squeezed. He
looked up and his breath caught at the sight of tears
slipping from his father's eyes.

"Forgive me?" Jericho whispered.

With his good hand, Pop patted Jericho's cheek, trailing fingers down his chin as if memorizing every inch
of his face. His father sighed. He pointed, shaking his
finger at the top drawer of the nightstand.

Jericho shifted his chair and set his hand over the
handle of the drawer. "Want me to open this?"

"Yeth, yeth." Pop nodded. He opened the drawer and
found a single envelope with "Jericho" written on the
inside. Could Pop still write? Or had this always been
waiting for him?

"You want me to have this?"

His father waved his arm, motioning toward the

framed picture of Chance. Jericho scooped the photo up and handed it to him. Pop stroked the picture, tapped the glass then pointed at the envelope bearing Jericho's name.

Jericho gulped. "Should I open this now, or you want me to wait until later?"

Pop tapped his finger on the envelope and then pressed the packet into his son's hands. Jericho nodded and slipped his finger under the lip. Into his hand tumbled a gold watch and a very thin copper-colored key. The tag on the key ring bore the number 139.

"This is Grandpa's watch. You sure you want me to have it?"

"Yeth."

Eyes burning, Jericho slipped the watch onto his wrist. His dad had worn it every day that Jericho could remember. "And what's the story with this key?"

Pop jabbed his finger at the photo of Chance.

"It has to do with Chance?"

"Yeth. Itha. Tha. I dondt know."

Jericho covered his dad's hand and gave it a squeeze. "Don't worry about it, Pop. I'll figure it out."

Denny's rhythmic pounds worked the knots out of Ali's muscles as he galloped across the wide field near the grove of cottonwoods. The trees stood like a gaggle of old women with their heads bent together sharing gossip. Hunching, she avoided the low-growing branches as her buckskin horse carried her.

She sighed. If Ali could have her way, she'd stay on Denny's back and ride off into the horizon like the heroes did in those Old West movies. No stress. No responsibilities.

"You're better than any therapist money can buy. Know that, Denny?" His giant fuzz-covered ears swiveled like a radar to hear her better.

"What are we going to do, huh, bud?" Swinging out of the saddle, she stood beside him, tracing her fingers against the yellow-gold hair covering his withers. He nudged his forehead into her shoulder, and she laughed. "You know I have a carrot in my pocket, don't you?" She pulled out the offering, giggling as his big lips grabbed the food. The warmth of his breath on her fingertips was as comforting as a loving mother's arms.

What would she do about Tripp Phillips's attention toward her? Ali rubbed her temples. She didn't want that. Not with Tripp. Not with any man. Marriage? No, thank you. But she didn't want to lose his friendship, either.

She walked away a few paces, then leaned against the trunk of the largest cottonwood. She slowly let her body slump to the ground. Cocking her knees, she looped her arms on them and looked out across the river as it rippled past. The scene felt familiar, and she instinctively turned and glanced up at the initials Jericho had carved there so many years ago. Funny, the things that could fill her heart with peace. The crudely chipped *JF loves AS* shouldn't cause anything to stir in her, but it did nonetheless.

What was she going to do about that man?

Denny nickered, as if reminding her of her real purpose. "Thanks, bud." She pulled the now crumpled warning letter from her back pocket and smoothed it over her thighs.

If you value what's important to you, you'll stay away from him. You've been warned.

No more threats had arrived. But that morning, Rider had reported that their fence line bore malicious damage. This time it caused one of the heifers to tumble to her death in the gully. Ali couldn't afford to lose any of the stock so carelessly.

It had been alarming enough to find all the horses in the front yard yesterday morning, and she'd wasted hours catching them. One stall left unhitched, she could believe. But ten stalls unlocked and the barn door left wide open? No coincidence, especially since Ali had been the one to lock the barn last night. And, although she wouldn't give fear lease enough to voice it, she thought she'd heard *something* outside the house while she lay in bed.

*Nine years ago, I made a promise to protect you.*

Startled by Jericho's voice in her mind, she pushed it away and tried to focus on a solution. One he was not a part of. Wasn't his presence the cause of all the problems anyway? The answer was simple—get rid of Jericho. If he left her alone, this magazine-gluing maniac would stop pestering her.

What Jericho had to say didn't matter. It also didn't matter that he'd showed up this morning on the steps with a giant bouquet of her favorite flower—he'd remembered about the daisies. Nor did it matter that, even now, he buried his biceps in grease, putting her truck's engine back together. Nor that Chance's eyes lit up at the sight of the man.

Ali looked at the sky to keep the wetness from trickling out of her eyes.

She shoved the letter again into her pocket and clicked her tongue to call Denny back to her side. Running a hand down his glossy muzzle, she leaned her forehead against his face.

"And it doesn't matter that it still feels like my heart's a hummingbird stuck in my rib cage each time I see him. Or that he really does seem changed. The ranch. Chance and Kate. Protecting them. That's what's most important, right?" Holding his bridle, she stepped away. His gentle eyes, fringed with thick black lashes, surveyed her for one long moment before blinking.

Climbing back into a saddle that felt more like home than any other place on God's green earth, Ali gave Denny his head. He cantered across the field as if he knew she needed the easy back-and-forth rocking motion to cradle her lost hope one last time.

Jericho Freed needed to leave. For good.

Denny plunged his lips into the trough. "Go easy, big guy. No colic for you."

"Hey, Mom!" Chance showed up at her elbow. He gave Denny's thigh three solid pats.

"Hey there, Chance-man." She ran a hand over her son's hair that stuck up at all angles. "Where's your aunt?"

Chance rolled his eyes and grabbed the edge of the trough. He used it as leverage and swung side to side. "She's making rhubarb jam. Bor-ing. And I told her that, so she banished me from the kitchen."

"Banished you, huh?"

"Yeah, but Jericho said he could use my help, and he showed me how to fix your truck. Then we changed the oil. Good thing I was there to hand him all the tools. Did you know how dirty your engine was, Mom? Major gross-out. Jericho had to use lots of rags just to see stuff." His earnest little expression made Ali bite the inside of her cheeks to keep from smiling at him.

She nodded solemnly. "That sounds serious."

Handing him Denny's lead, Chance fell into step beside her toward the corral. "And then he fixed a bunch of stuff on our truck."

"A bunch?" Ali wrinkled her nose.

"Yes. You're lucky he had so many tools in his car. He said—" Chance dropped his voice to imitate Jericho's "—'We've got to keep your mom safe. Got to fix all these things.'" Chance shrugged. "Then he did."

*Great.* What was he trying to do, heap coals upon her head? He was supposed to leave, not make her truck purr.

"I know a secret, Mom. Jericho told me."

Ali grabbed her son's shoulder and clamped down. There was only one secret Jericho would have involving Chance. No. He wouldn't—would he? "Secret?" she croaked.

"You have to promise you won't tell him I told."

"I promise. What is it?"

"I told Jericho that I like Samantha."

Ali's heart started beating again. "Oh, honey, you told me that months ago."

"*That's* not the secret."

"What is, then?"

"Jericho said you were pretty."

Ali rolled her eyes. "Secret's out. He told me that, too."

"But then I told him if he thinks that, he should marry you."

"You didn't!"

Chance gave two nods. "He said he liked that marrying part."

She popped a hand on her hip. "And where is Mr. Jericho right now?"

"He had to clean up, so I told him to use the hose out back and not to go in the house because I knew you'd yell at him. Remember when Drover and I played in the puddle and then we went in the kitchen and you were so mad you turned red? I told Jericho about that, and he said he'd better take his chances with the cold hose."

"He did, did he? Hey, can you do me a huge favor and find Rider for me? Let him know I need to talk to him about the fences."

The ranch—and maybe Chance—were in danger. If Jericho wanted to keep them safe, he needed to leave them alone. That thought propelled her forward. Drover trotted beside her, banging into her leg as Ali rounded the back of the house.

Jericho crouched. With the hose pressed between his arm and side, water splashed out in front of him. He rubbed his grease-covered hands together under the stream.

The Silvers' dog, Drover, pounced forward, snapping at the fountain. "Crazy dog. You're going to get all wet." Jericho laughed and backed up, right into someone. He peeked over his shoulder and spotted Ali, her eyes wide as the moon in surprise. Looking all cute and startled.

"Oh. Sorry." He dropped the hose and it sprayed into the air like a geyser, soaking his jeans and shooting at Ali in the process.

He leaned toward the handle attached to the hose

and turned off the water. Then took his time standing. He needed to read her face. Was she upset with him for showing up at her house again? Hopefully not. When he turned, he stepped closer. Ali's mouth hung open, and she blinked a couple times.

Jericho couldn't help himself. Using one finger, he tucked a chunk of hair behind her ear. When he grazed her skin she gasped. The sound made a tight fist unwind in his gut. He had to start telling her what was in his heart. Now or never—or risk losing her all over again.

After another step forward, he cupped Ali's elbow. He licked his lips. "I'm so sorry. I've missed so much. Ali, I—"

"Al!" The back screen door smacked the house as Kate rushed down the steps. Jericho tried to think of a kind way to tell Kate to go away, until he saw the tears flowing down her cheeks.

"What's wrong?" Ali grabbed hold of her sister's forearms, and Kate shook her head several times. "It's Ma. Ali, Mom's dead."

Ali's knees wobbled, and Jericho steadied her. He wanted to hug away the pain in her eyes, but for now he'd have to make do with being whatever she needed.

## Chapter Seven

The gold letters on the white clapboard sign announcing Riverview Cemetery seemed a mite too cheery for Ali's taste that morning. Like sheep grazing on the peaks, clouds huddled over the mountains. The minister closed the small outdoor ceremony with a prayer. Blinking away the emotions that blurred her vision, Ali wrapped an arm around Kate, who rocked back and forth, the butt of her hand pressed against her mouth.

"It'll be all right." She rubbed small circles across her younger sister's back.

Tripp and Jericho stood on either side like self-appointed sentinels. Chance leaned his head against Ali's stomach, and she used her free hand to trail her fingers over his hair.

The minister moved toward them, hands clasped over his Bible. "I'll pray for your peace. Please don't hesitate to stop by the church if you need anything."

Ali nodded. "Thank you, Pastor."

Rider stepped forward. He lowered his head, touching the brim of his black hat as he passed. Three other ranch hands followed, murmuring their regrets before leaving.

After a moment of silence, Chance spoke up. "Where is she?"

"Who, honey?"

"Grandma."

Ali let go of Kate and knelt the best she could in her black dress and pumps. She traced a hand down her son's expressive face. Jericho knelt down beside her. He looped an arm around her waist.

She took a breath. "Grandma passed away, sweetheart. She's gone. But now she doesn't have to be in a bed anymore and can breathe on her own."

Chance scrunched up his face, tilting his head to the side in a manner that made him look just like Jericho. "But I saw her in that box." He pointed.

At a loss for words, she looked to Jericho.

He gave a slight nod. "That's not really her in there."

Chance pouted.

"Listen, buddy. There is a part of us, the *real* part, that can't be kept in a box like that."

Chance looked at the coffin, then back at Jericho. Ali wrung her hands together. Why hadn't she prepared Chance better?

Jericho rubbed his bent knee, and a flicker of pain crossed his face. "Do you know who Jesus is, Chance?"

A grin creased her son's face. "Oh, does he work at Taco Time?"

Jericho used his hand to cover his smile. "No. That guy's nice, but I'm talking about a different Jesus. The one I'm talking about created those mountains over there." He pointed toward the Bitterroots.

Chance crossed his arms. "But does he make good tacos? Because—"

Jericho dropped a hand on Chance's shoulder. "You hungry? If it's okay with your mom, I'll take you to Taco Time for lunch, and we can talk."

Chance grabbed Jericho's hand and tugged for him to follow. "I think I need to hear about this guy. If there are tacos involved, he sounds kind of cool." Jericho rose with some effort. He looked back over his shoulder at Ali.

*Thank you,* she mouthed, and tears gathered at the corners of her eyes. He'd make a good father. How could she keep them apart any longer?

Megan appeared next to her. She squeezed Ali's hand. "It was a nice service. I'm so sorry about your mom."

"I just wish we could have done more for her, you know? I feel so bad. All of ten people showed up. Kate and I were the only ones here because of Ma. Everyone else came to support us. It's so sad."

"I remember you saying once, didn't you, that your mom was happiest when your dad was alive?"

"I can't think of a day she's been truly happy since before the day he died."

"Well, look." Megan swept her hand to indicate the headstone—a large one, with the names Buck and Marge Silver engraved across the front. "She's beside him again."

The only place Ma wanted to be.

"Thank you. We haven't known each other long, but I value our friendship. I'm glad you joined the Big Sky team. I don't know what I'd do without you."

"Oh, you know. It was that or assist my dad at the

research lab. No, thank you." Megan smiled and started to walk away, then paused. "It does seem odd, though."

With one last look at the grave site, Ali turned and fell into step with Megan. "What seems odd?"

"That Rider came. I sure didn't expect that one. But stranger things have happened."

Ali stopped. "Why would that be weird?"

"But he… I guess it shouldn't matter to me if it doesn't matter to you." Megan shrugged.

Ali crossed her arms. "Just go ahead and spit out whatever you're hinting at."

Megan pursed her lips and raised thinly plucked eyebrows. "I just thought he hated your family. So it makes me wonder why he would show his face here today."

"That's absurd. What reason does he have to hate us?"

"Could you seriously not know?" Megan narrowed her eyes. "His parents…your dad's company…the accident."

A chill prickled down Ali's spine. "What?"

"The semitruck. It was Rider's parents who were killed in that crash. He and his sisters are the ones who cleaned out all the company's funds in the first lawsuit, and they're the ones who are now coming after you. Don't you do a background check on people?"

"I've never run a check on anyone. I didn't even call his references. What if they're all made up?" Ali's hands shook. "No. I can't believe that. That can't be true. Rider is the sweetest guy." How was she to know? She'd been too young when the accident happened. Mom and the lawyers dealt with everything. Tripp was handling the recent civil suit. She hadn't bothered to ask him the details.

"Listen. My sister works at the bank that handles their settlement account. I know it was the last name Longley. Isn't that Rider's last name?"

*You've been warned.*

Ali gasped. "Do you think? Could all the stuff that's been happening—the missing money, the fences, the horses turned out, the letter—you *don't* think he's capable of that?"

"He's who I've had pegged all along."

"I had no clue." She balled her fists. "I have to fire him."

Her friend grabbed her hand again as they approached the parking lot. "You can't do that. You need proof. Let's catch him at his own game. If he's lunatic enough to be doing stuff, don't you think he'll be even more dangerous if you make him angry?"

"You're absolutely right. I don't know how he'll react. We have to keep Chance safe." She latched onto Megan's arm. "I need proof. Then I'm calling the cops."

"We'll save your family's ranch yet."


"Guess what?" Her son's new dress shoes galumphed against the wood floor. "I invited Jericho to stay and have supper with us."

"Chance!"

"I told him about our camping trip too, and he said he used to go camping all the time when he was young. So I told him he had to come with us because you're just a girl and maybe you don't know as much about camping as he does."

"Chance Silver!"

"We're still going camping, aren't we? You said if I

got an A in summer school we'd go, and I did, Mom. You promised."

"I know, honey. We're still going camping. Now go upstairs and change out of those clothes. The potpie is almost done." He disappeared up the stairs. "And wash your hands, buster!"

"Camping?" Jericho ran his hands over the top of the couch.

He suddenly felt too close. All the emotions from the past two weeks waged war in Ali's mind. She stepped away from him and straightened a pile of magazines on the coffee table.

"He wanted to go with his Scout group, but each boy had to have a parent along. It was all fathers, and I didn't feel right about it being just me with all those men. So Chance didn't get to go, and he's been bummed ever since." She smoothed her hands down her skirt. "I told him if he did well in summer school I'd take him."

"He had to have summer courses? Is everything okay with him?"

"Yeah. He's decent in school, but it's hard for him to stay focused. Math and science seem more difficult for him to grasp."

Jericho tilted his head. "It was that way for me too when I was about his age."

She looked up. Their gazes locked, and her palms started sweating. *He knows.*

"Listen, I don't have to stay, Ali. You've had a rough day." His low voice tickled down her spine.

"It's okay. We have enough." There was no point sending him away. Chance would be easier to handle tonight with Jericho around. Besides, with the loss of her mother, Jericho's presence lent a comforting feel of days gone by.

The next few hours would give Ali a chance to recoup her defenses, and plot some sort of strategy to confront the doubt bubbling in her head like a whirlpool. All the problems in her life felt like rapidly growing monsters, hungrily slurping all her energy and time.

She turned to go into the kitchen, but stopped with her back to Jericho. "Thank you for talking to him today."

"He's a bright kid. He had a lot of questions." He gave a low chuckle.

Ali grabbed the back of the desk chair near the wall. "I haven't really been on close terms with God."

"You're a good mother. Chance is fortunate to have you."

Ali shook her head and backed toward the kitchen door. "I haven't even thought about all that stuff for a long time. The only thing from the Bible I can remember is some verse that says hope deferred makes the heart sick. I've clung to that phrase this whole time."

"I think there's more to that verse…"

She cut in. "Just…thank you. That's all I'm trying to say."

"You're welcome. And, Ali? You can always come back to God. He's waiting with open arms."

*He's free, Al. You're the one still locked up and suffering.*

She needed to get away from Jericho. For now, she left him in the front room.

Pushing through the kitchen door, she glanced at Kate then crossed to the oven and pulled out the potpie, satisfied with its golden top. Kate silently pulled out three plates as she began to set the table.

"Four plates. We'll need four settings." Ali dumped the boiled potatoes into the strainer, shook it and put them back in the pot. She pulled out butter, cream and garlic powder, and yanked open the drawer in search of the masher.

"Jericho?" Kate guessed.

"Yes." Ali swiped the back of her wrist against her forehead. "What am I going to do?"

"About Jericho?"

"I think he… I *know* he suspects about Chance. And I won't—I can't— Chance is my son, and I won't lose him."

"You think Jericho will take him from you if he finds out the truth?"

Ali huffed and tossed up her hands, splattering a glob of mashed potato against the rooster backsplash. "He's a cowboy. Chance is captivated. Jericho can rope and ride and wrestle cattle. He can put an engine back together in one day. Chance thinks he'll be more fun to go camping with than me. How can I compete? I'm not cool. I teach handicapped kids how to ride horses. I make Chance clean his room and scold him for not brushing his teeth."

Kate tapped a handful of forks against her chin. "Sure. Jericho's exciting to a seven-year-old. But it's futile to play a competition game in your head. Chance loves you. You're his mother. I wish you could see— could admit—that Jericho is trustworthy. That cowboy in there isn't here to lord anything over you. Actually, he put all the power in your hands when he asked for your forgiveness."

Ali rinsed off her hands and dried them on the kitchen towel. She brought it to her face and pressed the damp fabric against her eyes. "I don't know if I can. I feel so threatened by him—by what forgiving him could mean to my life and to Chance's."

"You think if you open up that cage of bitterness and resentment you've kept your son and yourself locked in, that Chance will run away? But think, Ali—maybe you aren't meant to live in a cage. None of you are."

But her mother's voice echoed deep in her mind. *If he finds out, he'll take your son. No one will stay. You'll be alone.*

The doorbell rang. Since the girls were in the kitchen busy gabbing, Jericho answered the door. The man waiting on the porch was not a welcome sight.

His lips curled. "Tripp? What are you doing here?"

Tripp looked him up and down. "I could ask you the same thing."

"Seeing as my *wife* lives here, I figure it's my place. Now, the town lawyer on the other hand…what business does he have bothering these women on the day they put their mama to rest?"

"Your wife, huh? We'll see how much longer that lasts." Tripp shoved past him, banging his shoulder on the way into the house. The man was the same height and build as him, but Jericho could trounce the loafer-wearer any day of the week.

He followed on Tripp's heels. "And what's that supposed to mean?"

"Tripp." Ali crossed the room. She rubbed her hands on her flowery apron. The gold flecks in her eyes sparkled as she smiled at their old schoolmate.

Tripp took Ali's hand in both of his. He rubbed his thumb over her knuckles. "I kept thinking about the ordeal you've been through, and I had to come over and make sure you were okay. Is there anything I can do for you, Alison?"

Jericho rolled his eyes. "No, I think we've got it about covered here." Ali tossed him a glare, and he had the strangest urge to stick out his tongue at her.

"We were just sitting down to dinner. Won't you join us?"

The group moved to the kitchen, and Ali asked Chance to pull out another place setting. Tripp slithered right into the spot next to Ali, so Jericho took the spot next to Chance and across from Kate.

Chance swung his feet, banging them against the bottom rung of the chair. "Yes! I get to sit next to Jericho." After slapping Jericho a high five, he turned to the rest of the table. "Do you know how to start a fire without a match, Tripp?"

Ali dished out potpie.

"Smells good, Ali," Jericho said in an attempt to recapture her attention.

Tripp rubbed his hands together. "I don't know how to do that. But I always have matches on me so I don't need to."

Chance thrust out his fork. "Jericho knows. And he's going to teach me when we go on our camping trip, aren't you?"

"Sure thing, short stack."

"Well." Tripp took a long swig from his glass. "Chance, some of us didn't grow up with all the free time in the world. I grew up in a trailer park. My mom didn't have enough money for me to join the Scouts or to buy fancy camping gear. I may not know rough-and-tumble stuff, but I know about working hard for what I want. I know about scrimping through life, unlike others here who had everything handed to them. Some people have an easy life because their fathers were wealthy ranchers. I may not have all that money, but there are more important things I can teach you about than a simple fire."

Jericho slammed down his cup, and water sloshed onto the table. Kate handed him a wad of napkins. He sopped up the mess.

Ali's gaze ping-ponged from Tripp to Jericho.

Jericho cleared his throat. "The potpie is good."

Chance leaned his chin into his hand. "A fire without matches sounds more fun, though."

"But that knowledge is unnecessary if you always keep matches handy. And I do."

"Eat your peas, Chance," Ali snapped.

Tripp laid down his silverware and patted his mouth with his napkin. "So it's true? You're going camping with Mr. Freed?"

"Mom, too."

"Alison?" Tripp's eyebrows rose.

Her cheeks blossoming, Ali pressed back from the table. "Nothing's been discussed yet. More lemonade, Tripp? You're empty."

Seated at the head of the table, Tripp crossed his arms over his pressed oxford shirt. "I hardly think it's appropriate, this camping business. If you need someone, I can hire a guide. They have those for the tourists. I don't think you need anyone else's help." Tripp looked Jericho in the eye, then reached over and stroked Ali's hand. "I still don't know why you're both so set on going camping in the first place. I wish you wouldn't go."

Jericho's heart pounded like a poked bull. His biceps twitched as he balled his hands.

Ali pressed her hand over her forehead. "Let's not talk about this right now."

"Of course. Whatever you need." Tripp rose from his seat. "I have an appointment this evening anyway." He squeezed Ali's shoulder as he passed. "But we'll talk about this later."

Jericho leveled his best cowboy snarl at Tripp. "Or maybe she'll make up her own mind without your say so."

Tripp ignored him. Waved goodbye to the rest of the family and left out the back door. Jericho caught Ali's gaze across the table, and the worried lines around her eyes made him soften his expression. He sent a wink her way, hoping to take away some of the stress in the room. She didn't need more grief in her life. No, Ali needed to laugh more. If he got his way, Jericho would play a part in bringing more smiles to that beautiful face.

## Chapter Eight

A week's worth of tension trickled from Ali as she sat in the living room with her family watching a movie. Kate sat with her legs thrown over the arm of the over-stuffed chair, while Ali sat on one end of the couch with Chance's now drooping head against her side. The boy's feet were at the other end of the couch, in Jericho's lap.

She sighed. For as far back as she could remember, Jericho and Tripp had always been like two rams with their horns locked in battle. Good thing she had been able to usher Tripp out of the house after dinner. Not that she didn't like Tripp—she did. He was dependable and successful and gave every indication that he cared about her well-being. And he was kind to Chance. What more could she ask from a friend? But that's not all Tripp Phillips wanted anymore, was it?

Kate made a stretching sound, pulling Ali out of her thoughts. "I'm losing the battle with my eyelids. I need to get to bed."

Ali looked at the clock—it was past ten. "We need to get you up to bed too, Mr. Chance." She turned, and his sleeping body slumped onto her lap. "Chance." She put her hand on his side to give a shake, but a warm, calloused hand covered hers.

"Shhh. Don't wake him. I can carry him up to his bed." Jericho scooted out from under the boy's feet. With great gentleness, he lifted her son into his arms. Jericho cradled Chance's head against his shoulder. Ali began to rise, but Kate stopped her.

"Stay. I'll show him. I'm going up there anyway."

They tiptoed from the room and padded up the stairs. Ali rubbed her eyes and looked back at the television, where *Peter Pan* was playing. The lost boys bopped across the screen, taunting the pirates in one of the final scenes of the movie. Captain Hook nicked some of the fairy dust and now zipped around in the air after Pan. For a minute it really looked like the red-coated pirate would actually be victorious, but then the tick-tock croc jumped out of the water, the colossal crocodile's jaw slicing through the air as it snapped. Suddenly, Peter trapped Hook just feet above the wide-mouthed lizard, and the lost boys began to chant about him being old and alone.

Ali rubbed her hand against her collarbone because the ache in her chest started up again. She wanted to charge onto her feet and yell at the lost boys. They were cruel. For the first time ever, she *felt* for Hook. She watched his face, the emotions transferring from confidence to despair as he let their words sap his happiness away. Feeling the fairy dust failing, he crossed his arms, bowed his head and plummeted into the croc's waiting mouth. The giant beast swallowed his prize and dove back into the water. The lost boys cheered.

Swiping away a tear, Ali hit the power button and chucked the remote across the room. She strode out the door, down the porch steps and into the yard. Taking two ragged breaths of chilled night air, she looked up at the mountains and clenched her fists.

She thought about her mother's funeral. It burned her. No one in the community had bothered to come, and Ali realized she didn't want to live the same life. She didn't want to end up alone.

The front door creaked. "Ali? What are you doing out here?"

*Jericho.*

She hugged her middle as he crunched toward her over the gravel driveway. Stepping in front of her, he tipped up her chin, looking right into her eyes, which were brimming over.

"Is it your ma?"

She shrugged from his touch. "More than that."

"It might help to talk."

"I'll be fine."

"What are you doing tomorrow? Can't you take the day off? I think you need to get away from everything. The loss of a parent isn't something you rebound from the next day." His voice dropped, and his eyes softened. She knew how much he had struggled with the loss of his own mother.

Ali blew out a stream of air. "I can't take a day off. I have riding lessons to teach tomorrow, and the 'Dream A Little Dream' event for Big Sky Dreams to plan, and—"

"Can't someone else teach the lessons?"

She shook her head. "You have to be certified. I'm already running on fewer volunteers than I need, and Megan took tomorrow off so I have to be there."

"I'm not needed at Pop's place. His staff works like a

machine without me. They're used to running the place. It's been just them since Pop went in the nursing home. I'll help you. I'll get here early and saddle all the horses and get them ready before you wake up."

"I wasn't asking…"

He held up his hand. "I know. But I'm offering. I want to see you doing what you love. I want to understand why this organization is so important to you."

She knew she should say no. But she did need the help. And his desire to know the woman she was now felt like a balm for all the raw spots on her soul. "Guess I'll see you tomorrow."

"Sleep in, Ali."

She'd regret it later.


Rolling the heavy wood out of the way of the barn door, Jericho ushered in the sweet tang of freshly cut alfalfa. He walked to the middle of the indoor arena, surveying the training area, impressed with Ali's work. Stalls lined both sides of the barn, and the dirt floor in between could accommodate a class on horseback. Hay and tack filled most of the stalls on the right side, but on the left side, heads bobbed, ready to start the day. The smell of manure, animal sweat, hay and oats swept him back to his childhood.

Thankfully, each horse had a nameplate on their door that matched a name tag on their saddle. The first one read Salsa. Propping the saddle against his shoulder, he lugged it to the corresponding stall. As he came closer, a horse down the line whinnied and pawed its hooves against the wooden planks of the wall.

"Dumb horse," he mumbled. "Wait your turn."

Jericho ran his hands over Salsa's muscular body.

He went through the motions, checking for injuries or signs of sickness before saddling the horse.

His thoughts drifted to Ali.

She loved these fool beasts. Especially her Denny. Jericho remembered the day her dad brought home the flea-bitten buckskin. Abandoned and malnourished, he'd come cheap. When Mr. Silver walked the scrawny horse out of the trailer, Jericho thought the best thing for it would be a bullet between the eyes. The pitiful creature had ribs protruding out of his torso like a row of knives, with deep gashes on his sides, and his spine plates stuck out visibly like a stegosaurus. But Ali jumped up and down like Christmas morning, squealing. For a full year she babied that horse back to health. To be honest, Jericho had been eaten up with jealousy over her attention to that horse. But Ali had been right—persistent love had turned Denny into a winner.

The horse at the end of the row whinnied again. No longer pawing at his stall, he gave a full-out kick to the door. Jericho charged down the aisle.

"Doesn't Ali teach you manners? If you were my—" His words dropped off when he read the name on the stall. He heard an eager nicker then saw the giant strawberry roan. "Chief?"

The horse—*his horse*—snorted and tossed his head as Jericho unlatched the stall door. He stepped in, and Chief shoved his muzzle into Jericho's chest, sniffing loudly. "Hey there, old friend. I would've come to see you sooner if I knew you were here." Chief lowered his head, butting it against Jericho.

"He remembers you."

Jericho jolted. He glanced over his shoulder. Ali

stood two paces behind him looking cuter than should be allowed at six in the morning.

Turning back toward the overjoyed horse, he scratched Chief's neck and the beast leaned into his touch, releasing a deep sigh. "I had no idea you kept him."

She shrugged then crossed her arms. "You didn't just abandon me when you left. Chief refused to eat. He started picking fights in the herd where we had them boarded. I couldn't afford the fees anyway, so I came crawling back to Ma. I begged her to let me keep them here. I had to work with him every day to bring him back, but I think it was the therapeutic riding that really saved him. Once he finished the training, he was our big confident guy again."

Looking between the woman he loved and the horse he'd ridden since he was a boy, Jericho felt the weight of his consequences heavy around his neck. His throat went dry. "Thank you for taking care of him when I didn't."

"Are you going to take him back, away from here?"

Jericho patted his old friend. "You said he does the therapy riding?"

"He's one of our best. The kids love him because he's so big."

"Then he stays."

"But he's your horse. You have the right to take him back if you want."

Jericho paused, choosing his words carefully. "When we got hitched, he became yours, too. The whole two-becoming-one thing includes possessions. He's yours. I'm glad he's an asset to your program."

She released a long drag of air. "Oh, good. It's hard

to find quality horses with the limited funds we have, and the kids love him. I'd hate to have to replace him."

"Naw. This is where he belongs, right, Chief?" Jericho patted the roan's red-and-white-speckled withers. "I might want to come ride him every now and then though, if that's fine by you?"

Ali reached up and brushed away the bronze-colored mane from Chief's glistening eyes. "I think that would be just fine."

Jericho worked his thumbs over the back of his neck.

"You'll do fine." Ali squeezed his arm. "You're going to be the side walker. You just keep your hand a couple inches behind Eddy's leg while he's riding." She waved to a girl rolling into the barn on a wheelchair, then continued her instructions. "Just don't touch Eddy and you'll be fine."

Walk. Don't touch. Seemed simple enough.

"Doc. Doc. Doc." The small autistic boy tapped his helmet. His eyes looked spacey as he gazed into the arena.

Ali hovered near the child. "Of course you'll ride Doc, Eddy. And this man here is going to walk beside you, if that's okay? Jericho is new, so you'll have to help him."

Kate led out a roly-poly brown horse with a white blaze down his face. The child's hand shook, and he started chanting the horse's name louder when the animal stepped in line with the mounting stairs. Worrying the horse might act up with all the noise, Jericho transferred his weight onto his better leg, just in case he needed to take quick action.

Did Ali really know what she was doing? An accident with one of these kids could be catastrophic. The children were unpredictable around the animals—and a horse needed strong, confident handling, which Jericho doubted the students would have. Ali said she had some sort of certification that gave her the ability to teach therapeutic riding. But was it safe?

She brushed up beside him and explained in a low voice, "Eddy was nonverbal when he started the program. *Doc* is his first word."

Jericho gaped. "He couldn't talk?"

Rounding the brown horse, Ali helped Eddy climb into the saddle. The small child started clapping. Ali's voice was bathed in patience as she talked to the child. After the two other riders in the lesson mounted their horses, Ali strolled out to the center of the arena. Kate and two other volunteers led the horses around the edge of the circle. Ali pulled out cards for a game, handing a stack to each side walker.

"Ride to the red barrel. Touch your horse's back three times." Jericho read the card out loud.

Kate smiled, looking over her shoulder for instruction from the rider. "Where should we make Doc go, Eddy?"

The boy pointed at the red barrel near the front of the barn.

"Excellent job, Eddy!" Ali called, then turned to offer praise to a student who weaved their horse through the striped poles.

After the lesson was completed, Ali waved goodbye to her students and stayed in the barn talking to parents. Jericho made himself busy, scrubbing out water buckets and putting away tack. When she finished, he ambled over to her.

"What did you think?" She beamed. Jericho's breath whooshed out of his lungs at the sight of her. Ali was incredible.

"I'm glad I came. I think I understand a little more why this means so much to you."

She shrugged. "I fit in here, doing this. I love horses and children, so it works. I'm just glad riding can be used to make someone's life better."

"I can tell they were all having fun, but I guess I don't know enough about the particulars to understand what the riding does for the kids." He looped a lead rope over his hand.

She peered into a horseless stall, checking the tack hanging inside. "Did you know that a horse's gait mimics the human gait? The strides are almost identical. So when the kids are riding, the muscles they need to strengthen are being used without them even realizing it. I've read stories of students who couldn't walk learning how because of the therapeutic riding."

"Sounds pretty cool."

An idea had been nagging him since the beginning of the lesson, and he decided to feel it out. "Is this just something for kids, or would the therapy work for adults with problems, too?"

"Therapeutic riding definitely works for adults with a spectrum of issues."

"What about an amputation?"

"Yes. Therapeutic riding has been shown to speed the acclimation to a prosthetic."

Bingo. His idea took root, and suddenly purpose surged through his veins. Since returning home, his dogged drive had been to win back Ali alone, but he knew he needed to figure out the rest of his life now, too. Would he ranch like his dad? He'd thought before that he'd stay in the army, but that wasn't an option now. But this new plan? It just might work.

Ali moved aside the curtain and peeked out the window as Tripp spoke. He'd come to discuss payment options for the rest of Ma's debt.

"I don't like it, Alison, not one bit. What is he after?"

She snapped up. "I'm not following. Who are you talking about?"

"Freed."

She leaned her head against the glass. "I don't think he's after anything. I think he's just back."

"But he's been here—at your home—every day since he's returned. You don't find that strange?"

Working her lip between her teeth, she scanned the horizon, so sure she had just seen movement. "We were close growing up. Jericho never really had many friends besides me because of how his dad was."

Tripp took hold of her elbow and made her face him. "I think there's more to this that you're not saying. You know better. It makes me sick to stand by and watch history happen again."

"Tripp, I guess I don't know why this concerns you."

He stiffened, like she'd slapped him. "If that's how you feel, I can leave. I just—I considered us good friends, and I'm worried about you."

She laid her hand on his forearm. "Sorry. I didn't mean to sound harsh." She laughed. "*I* don't even know what I think. How can I voice what I don't understand?"

Pushing up his sleeves, he braced both hands on the counter behind him. "I guess the situation nettles me. I mean, this guy brought nothing but trouble into

your life. And if that's not enough, then he leaves you
and you have to struggle and work sixty-some hours
a week just to survive." His voice rose. "Don't deny
it. I've watched you ever since we were kids. He's got
some sort of magic over you. He's trash, Alison. He's
never treated you right, and now you're just running
back to him."

Ali clenched her fists. "Jericho Freed is not and never
will be *trash*. And I am not running back to him. He's
just around."

"Sounds like a lot of heartache if you ask me."

"Then what would you have me do?" She crossed
her arms and leaned against the counter opposite him.

Tripp let out a breath and stepped closer, drawing her
hands into his. "I would have you choose me instead."

"Choose you?" she whispered.

"Let me draw up the divorce papers."

"But I—"

"I want to marry you, Alison."

A flutter of panic tickled her stomach. Marry Tripp?
But Tripp didn't love her.

"Hear me out. I'm trustworthy. I'll never leave you
like he did. I will always be here for you. And Chance."
He licked his lips. "I want to adopt him after we're
wed."

A loud *clang-cla-clang* made them jump.

"Sorry… I…ah…sorry." Megan dropped to the
ground, cheeks reddening as she scooped up the empty
popcorn bowl. "Kate and I…our movie is finished."

"It's okay, Megan. Tripp was just leaving, and I'm
heading to bed." Ali took the metal bowl from her and
rinsed it in the sink.

Tripp looked between them like a scolded boy. He

inched his way to the back door. "Remember, just say the word, Alison. I can take care of everything."

Even though he was a good friend, Ali was thankful when the door closed behind Tripp. Upstairs in her bedroom, she pressed her fingers to her temples. Marry Tripp? She didn't love him, and certainly didn't appreciate his controlling tone tonight. Then again, love had gotten her into trouble in the past.

## Chapter Nine

"Well, all your paperwork looks to be in order, Mr. Freed. We just need to run some numbers, and I'll let you know what else you need to do to get this corporation off the ground. It doesn't look like there'll be any problems."

"Thanks." Jericho fought the itch in his fingers to yank a gap in his tie. The fool contraption always choked like a tightened noose. He ran his palms against the stiff fabric of his dress pants. While the bank employee typed at the desk, he picked up her nameplate, and it fumbled to the floor. He lunged to pick it up, smacking his head on the edge of the desk on the way up.

The young loan officer hopped to her feet. "Oh, dear, are you all right, sir?"

Rubbing the back of his head, he smiled. "I'm fine. Smarts my pride the most." He read the nameplate before setting it back on her desk. "Miss Galveen." Jericho scrunched up his brow. "Why does your name sound familiar? Did you grow up around here?"

She blushed. *Oh, just great.* She thought he was feeding her a pickup line.

"No. We're new in the area. Maybe you know my father? He works at the Mountaintop Research Laboratory." Pride laced her voice, and her chin went up a notch.

Jericho rubbed his freshly shaved chin. "Aren't they helping with research for bioterrorism? They work with some pretty dangerous chemicals, from what I hear."

She nodded. "Oh, yes. Everything they do there is very top secret."

"Impressive, but I don't rub shoulders with the doctor types there, so I don't know why your last name would stick out."

She pushed up her glasses. Then resumed tapping on her keyboard. "I have a sister who lives around here, too. Megan? She works on this Podunk farm near the outskirts of town."

"It's actually a ranch. Not a farm. I know the owner pretty well."

She straightened the bracelets on her wrists. "Small world."

"Does it look like everything will work out? There's a lot of paperwork involved, and I want to get this rolling as soon as possible."

"For now, things look great. But you do know, with this kind of undertaking, you're going to need a lot more capital. Do you understand how much money this will take to run? That's even if you can get it off the ground. That alone will take a significantly bigger sum than this loan. I'd hate to see you under water before your business has a fair chance."

"Don't worry. I have money coming to me."

She stopped typing and quirked an eyebrow. "Coming to you? How intriguing, Mr. Freed. Well then, if that's the case, I believe you'll be able to start this project soon."

"That's good news." He hooked his ankle on his knee, set it back on the floor then crossed his legs again.

"And might I say, this is a worthwhile endeavor. Even without the capital, I think there would be many individuals and organizations willing to donate to something like this."

Jericho nodded. He didn't need their money, but it was good to know the community would be behind him.

"More chicken salad, please." Chance shuffled over, plate in hand.

"There's plenty here." Ali dished another serving onto one of the sweet rolls she'd baked that morning and handed him the sandwich. The branches of the cottonwood trees swayed above them as the river gurgled a calming tune. Chance squished against her side, and she slipped her arm around his shoulders. She dropped a kiss to the crown of his head while he munched.

"We should do this every day. I love our picnics."

"I do too, bud." Ali pulled a caramel brownie from the basket. "We have to eat these before they get too gooey to handle."

Chance popped to his feet. "Hey, someone's coming."

Ali spun around. "That's Chief."

"It's not just Chief. Someone is riding him."

"I see that, Chance." She squinted, then sucked in a ragged breath. "It's Jericho."

Chance charged into the clearing. Hopping, he waved like a distress signal. Jericho swung down from the giant strawberry roan and gave Chance's shoulder a squeeze before tipping his hat to Ali.

She slunk against the tree and drew her knees to her chest. Why was he here? Did he remember it was their anniversary? Of course not. He never cared about keeping track of dates. He forgot her birthday that year they'd been married.

"Hey, pal, can you help me find a place to tie up Chief?" His voice awakened a flock of butterflies in her stomach.

"You don't have to tie him up. Mom says Chief is better behaved than me sometimes. Isn't that right, Mom?" Chance bobbed forward, his hand clasped in Jericho's.

"That's right, Chance." She gave Jericho a stiff chin-up greeting. "If you loop his reins over the saddle horn, Chief will hang out near that clover patch. He's been trained not to wander off."

Jericho cleared his throat. "Good to know. You've worked wonders with him. I don't remember Chief being so well behaved."

Ali hugged her legs tighter. "Yeah, well, men like to take off."

The blanket shifted as Jericho sat down. "Then that means Chief's a testament that a man can learn to stay put."

She uncoiled her body and ran her fingers against the stiff seams of the basket. "He's a horse." She took a deep breath. "What are you doing here?"

"Kate told me you guys were out here."

"'Course she did."

His work-worn hand covered hers, and he dropped his voice to a whisper. "Do you want me to leave?"

Chance grabbed Jericho's hat and plopped it onto

his own head. "We're having a picnic, because today is our special day."

Heat raced up Ali's neck. She jerked her hand from under Jericho's.

He raised a dark eyebrow. "Is it now? Do you want to hear the strangest thing in the world?"

Chance's eyes widened, and he nodded vigorously.

"Today's my special day, too." He tapped Chance's nose.

Ali's gaze locked with Jericho's. His eyes softened. A wave of warmth rushed through her heart. *He knows. He remembered.* A string of goose bumps raced up her arms, but just as quickly they vanished. Kate must have told him. Meddling sister.

Chance dropped to his knees. "Well, if it's your special day, then you should share our picnic."

Jericho kept staring at her. "What do you have there, bud?"

A crunching sound announced Chance's effort to paw through the basket. "Chicken salad and pasta salad, but don't worry. Just because they have 'salad' in their names doesn't mean they have lettuce. I hate lettuce. And Mom says with all the mayo, they're not even good for you. We have brownies, but they're getting mushy. Maybe you should eat one of them first."

Ali looked down, breaking the spell Jericho had over her. She swiped away auburn hair from her face and grabbed the basket when Chance pilfered a second brownie. "We only brought out two sets of plates and silverware. I hope you don't mind using dirty ones." She made Jericho two sandwiches, scooping a generous helping of pasta salad on the plate before handing him her utensils.

Chance giggled around the brownie bits in his mouth. "Gross. You're going to get my mom's girl cooties."

With a wink that sent Ali's heart galloping, Jericho smirked. "I'm not too worried about sharing any of your mom's cooties."

Jericho lifted the basket and blanket from Ali's arms when they walked back toward the ranch house. Chance bounded between them, clutching Chief's reins in his hand. Jericho glanced over to Ali, but her gaze darted away. Discovering that she still celebrated their anniversary had given him cause to hope.

"What do you two have going on the rest of the day?"

"I have to go to Walmart with Aunt Kate." Chance shuffled his feet.

Ali sighed. "There are three classes to teach this afternoon. It's going to be a long day."

Jericho switched the basket to his other hand. "I can stick around and help if you need more volunteers."

Ali ran her hand over Chance's head as they neared the house. "Can you put Chief in his stall for me so he's ready for Brandon to ride?"

She started up the stairs to the house, then turned to take the blanket from Jericho. "I don't know if it's the best idea for you to stick around."

"Are you still down volunteers?"

"Well, yes."

"Then why not? I sure hope you don't say I failed last time, because I thought my side-walking skills were legendary." He tried to wink at her, but she turned and grabbed the railing.

Standing near the front door, she pressed her thumb

and forefinger against her eyes. "Do you even know what day it is? How difficult this is?"

She whirled to walk into the house, but he captured her arm and made her face him. Setting down the basket, he placed his hands on her shoulders. "Today is the nine-year anniversary of the day the girl of my dreams married me. It was the happiest day of my life. I could never forget."

Tears made her eyes look like melted chocolate. His gut twisted. He never wanted to be the cause of this woman's tears ever again.

She pushed up on his wrists. "You only know that because Kate reminded you."

"Your anniversary gift is in there on the table."

"My gift?"

"I owe you a heap more. I'll make up for the lost years too, if you'll let me."

Her eyes widened. "You got me a gift?"

"Don't get too excited. It's not much. Go on in there. I know how you can't wait to tear off the paper. Remember that Christmas when you found your presents early?" He chuckled at the memory of finding her in their front room with scraps of paper all over.

"I warned you that if I found them, they were fair game to open." She pushed through the front door and beelined for the gift. She lifted the item in her hands before meeting his gaze.

"Go on. Open it." He smiled.

She tore off the ribbons and shredded through the paper. Jericho laughed. Good thing he'd convinced the lady at the store to wrap it for him. Left to him, the thing would have been tossed in a bag and handed to Ali.

She pried open the box and peeked inside. Her gasp

caused warmth to spread through his chest. She pulled out the horse statue and examined the sculpture from every angle. "Jericho, this is beautiful."

He crossed the room and took a seat beside her on the couch. "I'm glad you like it."

She traced a finger over each of the three horses carved in stone. Her favorite beasts were captured in a steady sprint together, hair flying. Free. "What is it made out of? I've never seen anything like it. Not this shade of red or with bands in these colors. It's so unique."

"It's made from a block of jasper. I saw it and knew I had to get it for you." He'd searched for the perfect token for weeks. A diamond ring had been his first thought. As young as they were when they got married, he never gave her an engagement ring or wedding band. But Ali wouldn't have accepted anything like that. Not yet.

She set the statue down and moved back, surveying it.

Jericho picked it back up and turned toward her. "See, I chose it because there are three horses. I figured they could be like you, me, and God. That's what was wrong before. We left him out completely. But we can be like these horses. We can gallop together."

He only wished there had been one with a smaller fourth horse so he could let Ali know that he wanted Chance, too. Staring at the statue again, Ali fanned her face, making Jericho smile. Just maybe they'd become a family after all.

Ali performed rapid-fire blinks to keep the moisture from leaving her eyes. Jericho Freed sat inches away, going on about dreaming together as she fought an urge to toss her arms around his neck and beg him to come back and truly be her husband. She watched his lips move over the words. Did his kisses still have the power to set her brain spinning? She leaned a little closer.

The front door jerked open. Megan appeared. "Are you doing lessons today?"

Bolting up, Ali looked at the clock. "I'm sorry. I didn't realize—yes, I'll follow you out." She skirted the couch. Jericho rose and followed her through the front door.

Ali forced herself to breathe. She needed to be careful. She didn't know if she could handle any more time with Jericho without doing something she'd regret later.

## Chapter Ten

"Can't I go to Mark's house? Puh-leaze, Mom?" Chance walked beside her, the shiny pail smacking against his calf with every step.

Ali racked her brain, trying to remember which one of the kids was Mark. The one whose parents let them ride the ATVs? Definitely not happening.

"No, pal, I need you to help me." Straightening her glove, she swiped the back of her wrist against her forehead.

"This is the worst day ever. Mark's parents don't make him scoop poop." He slammed the bucket on the ground of the training corral, releasing a puff of dust into the air. She coughed into her elbow then raked up manure, tipping it into the pail.

"Well, I'm afraid Mark won't know a thing about running a ranch when his parents leave it to him, but you, sir, you'll be able to do everything."

"Maybe I don't want to work on a ranch." Chance stomped his boot, his eyebrows drawn.

Grabbing the handle, she pushed the bucket back at him. Her hands shook. Didn't want to work on a ranch?

"You can't mean that. All this property will be yours one day."

"I don't want it. I want to move far away and never scoop poop again."

"Who will take care of the horses and the cattle if you don't?"

"This stinks," he mumbled.

"Watch your attitude, mister."

With eyes blazing thunder, Chance dropped the bucket again. "If I had a dad, he'd be here helping us, and we wouldn't have to work so hard all the time."

"Well, it's just us so—"

"Where is my dad, huh? Why don't you talk about him?"

Ali bit down on her lip. She reached for her son, but he yanked away. "Honey, we've talked about this a million times. You know the story."

"No. Not really. You only told me you were too young and that my dad had to go. I heard you tell Aunt Kate that you should have never married him, that it was one big accident." Chance trembled. Ali tried to reach for him again, but he shoved against her with so much force that she winced.

"My relationship with your father was a mistake, but *you* are not. Do you understand me, Chance? You're the most important person to me in the whole world."

"Everyone else has a dad. Why can't I? Didn't he want me? Is that why he's gone?" He swiped at hot, angry tears.

Everything in Ali ached to take him in her arms, to kiss away the hurt and rejection revealed in the bent of his brow, but for once, she didn't know how to cool his temper. This was exactly why Jericho couldn't be told.

Look what perceived rejection did to her son. If Jericho walked away from Chance after they both knew, the destruction would be irreversible.

"Chance." She knelt down in front of him, the dry earth coating her jeans. "Your dad left because he didn't want *me*." The words sliced as they came out. "He didn't even know about you, sweetheart."

"Then maybe you should tell him. It's not fair. He might not want you, but what if he wants me?" He spat out the words.

His little fists shook. Thin as a reed in the wind, his chest heaved. "Why do Jericho and me have the same eyes, huh?"

Bile crept up the back of Ali's throat. "Blue eyes? A lot of people have blue eyes."

"Not like these." He jammed a finger toward the offending body part. "Our eyes are the same color as the slushies from the gas station. The electric blue ones."

"Cha-ance." She dragged out his name. "A lot of people have blue eyes. Tripp has blue eyes like yours, too. It doesn't mean anything special."

"But how come Jericho and I laugh the same?"

"You're not making any sense, honey. Now grab that bucket, and let's do the other side of the corral."

With a growl, Chance kicked the metal bucket, sending manure into the air. Ali rocked back, throwing her arms over her head to block the raining mess.

"Chance Silver! Get to your room this instant."

He started to stalk off, then whirled around. "Know what? I'm going to find my dad. He'll be nicer than you, and he won't lie to me like you do." With that declaration, he charged off toward the house.

Ali tried to stand, but her knees wobbled. The handle of the metal bucket shuddered in her hand.

It started already. She was losing her son, and she didn't know how to get him back. She slumped to the ground. Her hands dropped into her lap, and she just stared at them, numb with swollen emotions.

Head in her hands, Ali didn't look up from the kitchen table when the back door creaked open, followed by the telltale slap of the screen door against the house.

"Hey, I was looking for you. I want to talk… Are you okay?" Kate dropped into the chair beside her.

Ali sighed.

Kate ran her hand across the tabletop. "Huh. How's that for bad timing?"

Ali leaned her cheek on her hands. "Bad timing?" She lifted her eyebrows.

"I was looking for you everywhere. Couldn't find you or Chance."

"Chance is in his bedroom. I'm considering keeping him locked up there until his eighteenth birthday. What do you think?"

Kate's eyes widened. "Don't tell me you caught him yanking feathers out of the chickens again?"

Ali offered a slight smile. "Worse. He wants to know who his father is."

Kate whistled, long and low.

"That about says it."

Pushing up from the table, Kate crossed the room to the fridge. "Well? Are you going to tell him?"

"I can't. Chance doesn't even know who his father

is, and he already likes him more. Think if he found out for sure that it was Jericho."

Popping open a take-out container, Kate gave it a sniff and pulled a face. "Do you seriously think Chance isn't smart enough to find out? I mean, he might not figure it out today, but if Jericho is going to stay in Bitterroot Valley, and if he keeps hanging around here, Chance is bound to put it together."

Ali grabbed the edge of the table with wrought-iron strength. "He asked why they have the same eyes."

Dumping three offending containers from the fridge into the trash can, Kate shrugged. "I honestly don't see why you keep lying to both of them."

"I'm not lying." Ali ran a hand through her hair. She didn't like being called a liar twice in one day. "I'm just not telling them. That's not the same."

Kate rolled her eyes. "Whatever. If it makes you feel better to believe that, then you're lying to more than just them."

Ali rose. "Where do you get off, Kate? Seriously. You can't stand there and judge me. I'm sick of it. I'm sick of not living up to anyone's expectations. I'm sick of you and your perfect little life and you spitting out platitudes."

Kate jammed down the garbage lid. "Sick of it, huh?"

Boiling over with emotions that had nothing to do with her sister, Ali thrust her hand. "Makes me want to puke."

Kate leveled a glare. "Good. That makes my news easier to tell you. I found a job. I'm leaving."

"Leaving?" Ali stumbled back and blinked. "But why?"

Kate tossed up her hands. "This isn't where I belong,

Al. It's never been my world. You live and breathe these animals, this land. I don't. At all. I don't like working with the horses. I don't like doing manual labor in the heat. I don't like being able to see for miles and miles. The bugs. None of it."

"I don't understand."

"Ali, think about it. Unless you're too blind to see, your prodigal husband has returned. I've lived my life helping you long enough, and you don't need me anymore. Move on, sis. Forgive your husband and live a new life with your family."

Ali swallowed a lump the size of Montana. "Is that how you really feel? Like I've held you back?"

"Not in the terrible way you're imagining. But I took off more than a year before starting college to stay with you and help take care of Chance. I stuck close to home for school and came back right away, all so I could be here for you and Ma."

"I never asked that of you. You could have done anything you wanted. Don't blame me for—"

"I'm not blaming you for anything. It's just how it went. I don't regret staying behind with you. But now that I know Jericho is back, I'm going to move on. Finally do my own thing."

Ali searched her little sister's face, trying to grasp what she was saying. "You're really leaving?"

"Yeah. Sorry to tell you like this." Kate walked toward the back door. "But I found a job. I went to college for a reason. Better use that degree, right?" She opened the door and offered Ali a small, soft smile. Then she walked outside.

"Right." Ali stared at the door as it slammed shut.

\* \* \*

Pink light, the blush of the first kiss of sunlight, flooded the valley. Ali drank in a fortifying breath drenched with the sweet scent of wildflowers. She pulled herself off the dew-drenched ground and shook the clinging grass from the back of her shirt. Guess she ended up falling asleep out here last night. She stretched against a kink in her neck.

Arms draped around her knees, she relished a peaceful moment spent laughing at the prairie dogs popping in and out of their earthen holes. It made her forget for a short while about all the responsibility weighing her down.

She took a deep breath. "I don't know what You're doing, God, but something is happening and I'm not sure I like it. But at least I can say thank You for new starts."

First there was Chance's outburst yesterday, cured by two hours in his room. He emerged contrite and happy to trail Kate the rest of the day. All talk of fathers abandoned.

Ali still felt uneasy about her ranch hand, though. He didn't strike her as a person who was capable of harming anyone. Was Megan right? Could Rider Longley really be out to get her? Why would Rider give two bucks about seeing her and Jericho together at the picnic? The thought almost made her laugh.

Then Kate's big announcement. *Leaving.* She didn't know how to function without her sister around. Sure, she could be happy for her little sister, going out and making something of herself in the world. It's just that Ali had always counted on the fact that Kate would be *here*.

And what about poor Tripp? Ali wrung her hands. The man was everything she should want, but couldn't force her heart to love. His attention brought added stress.

Everyone chipped at pieces of her heart then walked away. Ali shivered and hugged her torso. She might be left with nothing.

"Miss Ali!"

She looked up. Across the field, Rider jogged toward her, his mouth in a grim line. Ali rocketed to her feet.

He reached her seconds later, holding his side, puffing out breaths. "Miss Ali, I've been looking for you everywhere. Megan said to get you quick. It's Denny."

## *Chapter Eleven*

Ali tore across the field on the toes of her boots. Her hat flew off. Grabbing the door of the barn, she used it to bank hard and round down the aisle. A couple horses snorted when she entered. Denny's stall stood open.

Megan sprang to her feet. "I don't know what's wrong with him. He won't get up and—"

Ali pushed past her. Denny lay on his side, eyes closed. His head rested in filthy straw. Dropping to her knees, Ali crawled to him. "Denny? Hey, boy. What's wrong, handsome?"

He didn't stir. Didn't open his eyes.

"How long has he been like this?" She groped her hands over his body, searching for an injury, hoping he'd nicker or snort. He felt warm. Much too warm. And he heaved more than breathed, as if he couldn't fill his lungs.

Megan stepped back. "I don't know. I found him this way."

Trembling, Ali looked over her shoulder to Megan, who propped her shoulder against the doorway. "How long until the vet's here?"

"I didn't call him yet."

"Do it now," Ali pleaded. Why hadn't she come out to the barn when she'd woken up instead of going out to the field? She should have known he needed her, should have *felt* it. If something happened to him...if he... She shook her head.

Turning back to Denny, Ali ran her hands along his neck, pressing her ear against his side. His heart raced, and her eyes burned. "C'mon, buddy. Stay here with me."

Ali got up and stepped to his other side. Blood pooled from his lips, and her vision went blurry. Kneeling near his head, she pressed her face against him. She drank in the smell of his skin, memorized the play of hay dust against his strong black muzzle.

"I love you. Please don't leave me," she whispered. Her lips brushed his jaw.

He made a weird noise deep in his throat, like he was trying to talk to her and couldn't. Ali pulled back. Denny opened the gentle, expressive eyes she loved, and his gaze locked with hers for a long moment. Ali held her breath. Her old friend gave one long sigh and closed his eyes again. Black lashes splayed out against his golden fur.

And just like that, he was gone.

*No!* The word rocked through her, and she wanted to hurl something. She grabbed at the side of the stall, but the moment she found her feet, she turned and looked down at Denny. Her beautiful friend, with his magnificent glossy buckskin hide and his perfect black stockings. She covered her mouth with her hand, holding back a sob as it shuddered, trying to get out of her body.

*Gone.*

Her knees buckled, and she came down hard beside him. Crawling over his middle, she ran her hands through his mane, cupped them over the soft hairs on the edge of his ears. His body was still warm, possessing the power to make her feel whole. What would she do without him? Riding Denny was the only thing that had ever made her forget the ache inside.

"Denny. I'm so sorry." Her tears exploded one after another on his neck. She moved to lie against his back. A deep moan escaped her lips, and the sobs came then. She wrapped an arm over the top of him and pulled herself closer, weeping.

Kate stepped toward her. "Al. Hey. Let's get you out of here."

Ali lifted her head and shook it. Choking on her emotions, she sat and pushed her sister away. Then she leaned back over her beloved horse, running her hands across the length of his body. She stroked her fingertips down his face.

"After Jericho left, I used to have trouble sleeping. I'd come in here and crawl up on Den. I'd sob into his back and whisper 'come home' over and over again. Denny would breathe even and steady, as if to tell me no matter what—no matter who left—he would always be there for me. I used to come out here and just hug his neck for hours when Ma got bad. And he'd let me, just loop his head over my shoulder and rub his muzzle on my back like he was saying that he loved me, even if no one else did."

"Come on, it's not good for you to stay with him like this." Kate beckoned to her.

Ali curled back down against Denny's back. "Leave me alone."

"Al…"

"I mean it. Just leave me alone with him. Please."

Kate backed out of the stall, motioning for the others to leave the barn.

Feeling like her insides had been ripped out, Ali sobbed into Denny's lifeless body. "I'm so sorry I wasn't here for you. I'm so sorry, Denny."

The Jeep churned the gravel, kicking up a cloud of dust as Jericho pulled onto the Silvers' property. He was late for the riding lessons, but there were no cars, none of the usual bustle. He parked the vehicle, got out and strode toward the barn.

Rider skirted around the side. "Wouldn't go in there if I was you."

"Where is everyone?"

Rider's gaze shifted to the door. "Classes were canceled today."

Ali didn't cancel classes for anything. Jericho grabbed Rider's arm. "What's going on?"

"It's Denny. Ali's in there with him. She won't come out, and won't let any of us in."

Jericho saw it in Rider's eyes. Her horse was dead. *Oh, Ali.*

Pushing the ranch hand aside, Jericho raced into the dark barn. In the commotion, the lights must have never been turned on, and he wasn't about to now and risk startling Ali. He walked into the fifth stall and froze, the air catching in his chest. She lay with her arms around the horse she loved, whispering into his unhearing ears.

Tears stung Jericho's eyes as he knelt, running his hand over her red hair. Ali blinked up at him, and for a moment, he thought she would shove him away. Yell at him to leave. Instead, she sat up inch by inch and cupped her hands over her face. Thinking she was ready to leave Denny's side, Jericho took her elbows and drew Ali to her feet. She let out a loud, mournful whimper that made his insides run cold. He pulled her against his chest, but she crumpled. He went down to the ground with her, holding her while she shook.

"He's gone. He left me." One of her hands shot out, and she stroked the animal's now-cold leg. Jericho took both her hands and ushered her beside him as he sat, leaning against the wall of the stall. He wrapped her in his arms, trying to offer his warmth and his strength. She turned into him, grabbing fistfuls of his shirt as she cried, "Why does everyone leave me?"

"I'm here, Ali. Shhh." Jericho stroked her hair and rubbed circles on her back. He dropped a kiss against her hair. "I gotcha." Blazes of pain raced up his knee, but he wasn't about to risk shifting his weight. Absolutely nothing short of the barn catching on fire would convince him to do something that might force Ali to move. Pulling her closer, he nosed into her hair, smelling the trace of something flowery like the outdoors. *Smells like the sunshine.*

All too soon, Ali put her hand to his chest and pushed a little. She sat back, eyelashes damp, nose blotchy, and eyes red-rimmed.

He'd never seen someone more beautiful.

He wanted to kiss the tears from her cheeks. Instead, he settled for wiping them with the side of his finger. "I'm sorry about Denny. I know what he meant to you."

*Uh-oh.* That got the floodgates started again.

The next breath she sucked down rattled on the way in. "He was *everything.* I don't know what I'm going

to do without him. It hurts. Right here." She laid both
of her hands over her heart. "Could I be having a heart
attack?"

Pulling up his knee, Jericho finally found a moder-
ate amount of relief. "I think it's heartache, sweetie,
not a heart attack."

"It's too much. Why is so much happening at once?"
Using the back of her wrist to wipe her nose, she closed
her eyes.

He took a deep breath. What comfort could he offer?
Her beloved horse lay dead as a stone inches away. No,
he wouldn't make light of the loss by trying to tie it up
with pretty words, even if he could find something eloquent to say.

When she opened her eyes, her gaze locked with his.
The gold specks in her eyes sparkled, and he couldn't
breathe for a second. He broke the trance, more out of
necessity than anything. He would *not* kiss this woman
next to Denny's body.

He cupped her shoulders. "What's too much?"

"Ma just passed away. Now this. You showed back
up, and Tripp is stressing me out. Chance is angry with
me, and Kate is leaving." Using her fingers, she ticked
off the offenses. "The ranch isn't turning a profit, and
I'm afraid Big Sky Dreams might not be able to meet
our fund-raising goals, and then I'm so scared…"

Concern prickled down his skin. "Scared about
what?"

Her mouth opened in an O. "Just all this. Everything
that's going on."

He could see it. She still didn't trust him. Fine. He
could live with that for now. At least she wasn't so bent
on pushing him away anymore.

"Don't know how I feel about making it on your list."

"You can't deny that your presence is adding a lot of stress."

"It doesn't have to."

"Jericho, what am I going to do without Denny? I had this big plan. He was going to save us. I had us signed up for six rodeos this summer." She fingered Denny's ear. "I know it sounds stupid, but I had it all planned. We were going to take first place at all six races and use the prize money to pay off the debt and help keep the doors to Big Sky Dreams open. And now?" She shrugged. "Now that hope is gone, and I don't know what I'm going to do."

His heart wrenching at seeing her beside Denny, Jericho scooched over and placed his hand atop hers where it lay on the horse's neck. "Maybe," he whispered. "Maybe you need to look to a different savior."

Her eyebrows rose. "You?"

Shaking his head, he gave her hand a squeeze. "No. I want to help you, if you'll let me. I'd love to be beside you for all that stuff you just said, and do my share of fixing. But I'm no hero to put all your trust in. I'm talking about God."

She snorted. "Now you're starting to sound like Kate. She keeps leaving these three-by-five cards all over the house with verses scribbled on them. Supposedly it's so she can memorize them, but I think she's trying to leave hints for me."

Jericho smiled. "Like spiritual bread crumbs? I knew I liked that girl." Just then, Ali's redheaded sister tiptoed into the barn and Jericho caught her eye, giving her a nod.

"Hey, Al, you okay?" Kate's voice came low as she ducked her head into the stall.

"I don't think I'll be okay for a long time."

"Well, we called the vet and he's making arrangements to have Denny picked up. I don't think you should be here when they do it."

Neither did Jericho. Growing up on a ranch, he had seen his share of dead animals. Often, Pop moved the carcass to the edge of the property and let the mountain lions, bears and wolves have at it, but the few he'd seen hauled away, well, he didn't want Ali to witness it with her beloved pet. The companies were respectful, but seeing them wrap chains around Denny's body and drag him into the truck? No, thank you.

He stood, offering a hand to her. She surprised him again by taking it.

Her lip trembled. "I want an autopsy. Tell Dr. Hammond… I have to know what caused this."

Kate's brow wrinkled. "Al, that's expensive."

Wrapping his arm around Ali's waist, Jericho ushered her out of the stall and slowly down the barn aisle. "I'll pay for it."

Sure that she was going to argue, he racked his brain for a way to convince her, but she just said a quick and quiet, "Thank you."

# Chapter Twelve

Ali trailed Jericho toward the café. He held open the door. After they were seated, she excused herself to the washroom. Grasping the cold sink counter, she searched her reflection. Were her eyes as empty as she felt inside? How terrible was it to mourn a horse more than her own mother? Splashing water didn't improve the puffy redness on her face, nor did it take away the lingering barnyard and manure smells. Yanking paper towels out of the temperamental dispenser, Ali wet them and rubbed the worst of the grime off her forearms.

"This is as good as it gets." She meant to walk out and join Jericho, but her feet didn't move. Why was she here? Alone with *him*. Okay, the café might be pretty full, but it wasn't like Kate or Chance could walk in and interrupt them. She should have stayed at the ranch. There was work to do. Maybe he'd take her back if she asked. Filling up her day with a bunch of tasks would minimize the pain. The hole in her emotions would split open and she would bleed inwardly when she lay in bed tonight, but she'd worry about it then.

As she walked into the eating area, Jericho's blue

eyes seemed to drink her in. She tried to remind herself that she didn't like the man with the disarming, crooked grin seated at her table, but that was becoming harder to believe. Honestly, he terrified her—for herself and for what he had the power to do to Chance.

Her trail of thoughts halted when she spied the glass in his hand. An amber liquid with the telltale trace of white froth. Stomach recoiling, she slammed her purse on the table, and he spilled some of the brew on himself. *Serves him right.* She'd been wrong to trust him at all. What was the saying? A leopard always shows his spots. Drunkard. That's all he'd ever be.

Pulling a wad of flimsy napkins from the basket on the table, Jericho dabbed at the wet spot on his shirt. "Got me good." He laughed, and it grated her nerves.

"Hitting the hard stuff a little early, huh?"

"Pardon?"

Giving her best I'm-not-stupid glare, she pointed to his glass.

He stopped dabbing. "You have a problem with that?"

"Yes, actually, I do. *That stuff* ruined our marriage, and you have the audacity to order it and swig it down in front of me like the good old days? Take me home, Jericho." She rose to her feet, but he just leaned back, crossed his arms, and gave her a searching look.

"Taste it."

"What?"

"Taste it."

"You know I don't—"

"Take a drink." He grabbed the glass and thrust it into her hand. She gave a cursory sniff. Well, it didn't smell strong, more sweet, more like… Heat rushed to her face, and Ali set back down the glass as she stumbled into her seat.

Jericho raised a dark eyebrow. "You got something fierce against apple juice? 'Cause if you're gearing up to ask me to sign a petition for some apple cider temperance group, I'm not doing it."

She fanned her face. "You know what I thought."

An emotion filtered across his face, something deep and sad that made Ali want to take his hand in hers. He straightened back up and rested his arms on the table. "Yes." It came out as a miserable sigh. "I know what you thought. I guess I just wish that wasn't the first thing that came to mind for you."

"I'm sorry." She bowed her head.

"Don't be. In the past, I did nothing but hurt you. You have every right to doubt me. But I promise you, I'm going to do everything in my power to gain back your trust. If it means anything, I haven't touched the stuff in more than five years."

"It's all so weird. You're *supposed* to order a beer. That's the man I remember. But you, like this, I don't know what to do with."

A woman who matched Dolly Parton in voice and hair-height stopped at the table to take their orders. Jericho asked for the chicken club, but Ali declined food.

"Just some iced tea, if you have it."

"Not hungry?" Concern thickened Jericho's voice.

She shook her head.

He cleared his throat. "So you don't know what to do with me, huh?"

"You're so different."

The food arrived, and Jericho bowed his head. Wow, praying in public. That was new, too. When he picked up his silverware and looked at her, an easy peace filled his eyes and made her swallow against her own hollowness.

"Would it be okay? Could I finish what I started telling you at the firework show?"

"That feels like forever ago."

He shook his head. "Just twenty days."

"Come again?"

He gave a little-boy smile, like she'd caught him stealing penny candy. "I've been counting and thanking God for every new day I get with you."

It sounded sincere, sweet even. And that blasted hummingbird came back, banging against her ribs. She narrowed her eyes. "Okay, so talk. I'm listening."

After wiping his mouth with the napkin, he let out a long breath. "It's hard to know where to begin. But I told you about the stuff that happened to me, Yellowstone and the ranches and the army. But I didn't tell you how I changed in here." He touched his chest.

"When that war veteran took me in, he sobered me up. Wouldn't let me leave, and wouldn't let me touch the drink. For a while I was furious. I tried to call the cops on him a couple times, report that he had kidnapped me or something, held me against my will. But then, after the poison got out of my system, it all hit me. I was a coward, and by not facing my troubles, not dealing with the pain in my past, I let it destroy my future, our marriage and I was terrified I'd destroy you."

Ali wanted to say something. Everything in her wanted to ask him why he didn't come home. Why hadn't he been able to work through the issues with her beside him? But she held her tongue.

"Then one day when I mulled it all over, I picked up

the guy's Bible and flipped through the worn pages. The first thing I read was this verse telling me that my body is a temple, and I should honor God with it. I made a pact that day that I'd never touch alcohol again, and I haven't."

"Just like that?" Ali snapped her fingers.

"No. It wasn't magical or anything. It was hard work and a lot of almost big-time mess-ups, and yeah, even tears if I'm being honest. But once I got over that, I tried to figure out what to do next. Ali, you've got to understand that at that point I wanted to come home. Badly. I even made all the travel plans, but I couldn't do it."

"Why?" she whispered.

"I wasn't a man worthy of you. In our whole relationship, I only took from you, so I couldn't come home with nothing to offer. I didn't know how to be the husband you needed and deserved. After the stories the vet told me about his time in the army, I decided I'd join and make something of myself, or so the saying goes."

Ali dropped her head into her hands and mumbled, "So like a man."

"Huh?"

"I only ever wanted *you*. I didn't need you to become anything. I just wanted my best friend beside me."

His hand snaked across the table and took hold of hers. With his thumb, he traced circles on her palm while he spoke. "I know. I get that now, but I had this inner drive to prove I was good enough. That, and I didn't think I was ready for the real world. I figured it would be easier to stay sober in the army, but boy was I wrong. It's just like anyplace else. You can find whatever experience you're looking for. It's whatever you want to make of it. So, while the guys went out celebrating, I spent all my time with our chaplain because he was the only person around my age not going out to the bars every free night."

"I'm glad there was someone there for you." The rhythm of his touch to her palm proved too tempting, so she closed her hand around his to make him stop.

"He was. And I told him everything about us and about my life. He didn't do the whole preacher thing on me. He told me that my identity was not the makeup of my past mistakes. He said that I had a clean slate. Man, that changed my world."

"Sounds very convenient though." Ali shrugged away from him. "I mean—what? You're suddenly not accountable for anything in the past? Just—*poof*—pretend it didn't happen?"

"I have to live with a lot of regrets, but I can't let them own the future."

His words reminded Ali of something Kate had told her weeks ago. "You're free."

"I guess I am." The corner of his lip pulled up. "I'm also done with this sandwich. Should we head back?" He looked at his gold watch, once owned by his father. "I think it's been long enough."

As he maneuvered the Jeep out of the parking lot, Ali reviewed their conversation. She tipped her head to watch Jericho out of the corner of her eyes. The man had changed completely; no one could deny that. But then again, he was still her same Jericho. *Her Jericho?* She adjusted her seat belt. Where had that come from? Jericho came back, yes, but not in that way in her life. She had Chance to think about, and Tripp's offer still lingered in her thoughts.

She sighed. Jericho and Tripp. Besides their blue

eyes and build, they couldn't be more different. With Jericho, it was like going on the world's biggest, most heart-pounding roller coaster. Tripp? Tripp was the tour bus around the park. But between the two, if an accident occurred, a person was less likely to get hurt on the bus.

It still wasn't okay that Jericho had been gone so long, but she understood his absence a little better now. She couldn't argue the fact that he had become a better man. *Good for him joining the army. Never saw that coming.*

She tensed. As an army man, Jericho was bound to leave her again. Maybe not by choice next time, but did that matter? Even if he wanted to be with her, one day he would leave, and he might never come back. She couldn't—*wouldn't*—open herself or Chance up to that.

"All the streets are blocked off." Jericho rubbed his jaw.

She hadn't been paying attention. But a look down Main Street showed it was empty, and blockades barred the way. Jericho looped the Jeep around in a three-point turn and went down another road.

Ali propped her feet on the dashboard. "Daley Days. With all the commotion, I completely forgot. Looks like they're getting things ready for the street dance this weekend." She loved the celebration that commemorated the town's founder.

"Please tell me they still have the kiss-the-pig contest?" He gave his full-chested laugh as he turned onto the side street that led to her family ranch.

Ali smiled. "Of course! Only the best for our great town."

"Are you taking Chance to all the activities?"

"I really shouldn't. I have a fund-raising event for

Big Sky Dreams that I need to finish planning, and I'm really not feeling up to it with all that's happened, but I probably will. Chance loves it. What kid wouldn't? We always did."

When he didn't say anything, she looked over and noticed a small, soft smile on his lips. He slung an arm over the steering wheel as they bumped up the gravel driveway.

"What? What are you thinking with that look on your face, Jericho Freed?"

"I like talking to you the way we used to."

When he tossed the Jeep into Park, Kate ran toward them, waving her arms, with Megan and Rider on the front porch. Dread brought a crop of goose bumps to Ali's back. "Oh, no. I think maybe they haven't gotten Denny yet."

Breathless, Kate grabbed Ali's arm the moment she stepped out of the vehicle. "He's gone! We've looked everywhere. We can't find him!" Kate's eyes were wild.

Ali's stomach plummeted.

Jericho rounded the Jeep and laid a hand on Ali's shoulder. "Who's gone, Kate? Spit it out."

"Chance. Chance is missing."

# Chapter Thirteen

Jericho's mouth went dry. He worked his jaw back and forth. "What do you mean, *missing*?"

"In all the commotion, he disappeared. One second he was here digging in the mud with Drover, and the next he was gone. We've looked everywhere." Kate wrung her hands. "Megan searched the house. Rider searched the barn, and I looked in the yard."

Ali tore across the driveway toward the house. Screaming her son's name, she burst into her home, running from room to room with Jericho in her wake. Her high-pitched voice echoed up the stairwell. Jericho's heart lurched into his throat. Was Chance prone to wandering off? Ali's terror signaled that it was completely unexpected.

"Chance! C'mon, partner—come out of wherever you're hiding." His loud voice drowned out Ali's.

Her eyes blazed. "Chance Silver! If you are hiding, come out right now. This is not funny." Ali's lip started to tremble, and everything in Jericho wanted to pull her into his arms and make her pain go away. But they needed to find Chance.

He grabbed her and tugged Ali along after him, back toward the yard. Her hand felt cold and clammy, forming a weight in his stomach.

He stopped on the porch and scanned the countryside. "Boys wander. It's just a fact. I used to take off all the time when I was young. I was never in trouble, and I always moseyed back home soon enough."

She worked her bottom lip between her teeth. "Just like you." It was only a whisper, but it made his heart pound harder.

Spinning, he pointed at Kate. "Stay at the house. Check all the rooms again in case he's hiding. Think of places a boy would find neat to explore, like the attic. Megan, stay near the barn and holler if you see him. Rider, take the truck and check out by all the cattle pens. That boy has been more interested in bull riding than I'm comfortable with, and if he decided to try it on his own, you'll find him there. Ali and I will check the rest of the property."

Ali stayed rooted to her spot, her eyes raking over the yard. Jericho placed a hand on the small of her back and propelled her forward. "C'mon, I need action right now, not fear."

She nodded, then started jogging beside him.

Unlatching the corral, he called for Chief. "Is there any other horse here that'll let us ride bareback?"

"Not quickly. The rest are pretty old."

Jericho nodded. Like the old days, he grabbed Chief's mane and hurtled onto the horse. He reached down, grabbed Ali's hand and hoisted her up behind him. When he kicked Chief into motion, she wound her arms around his torso, her cheek pressed against his back. Her tears dampened his shirt.

"Chance!" Making Chief tear across the fields like a young buck, Jericho scanned the horizon. His mind ticked through the options. What on this property would entice a seven-year-old boy? That's where they needed to go.

"I'm so afraid," Ali whispered.

Jericho unwound a hand from Chief's mane and placed it over the one of hers that rested near his heart. "He's just a boy. Don't worry. He's probably off having the time of his life, and we'll laugh about this later."

"But what if someone took him?" Her voice trembled, along with her body.

"Took him? Who would take Chance?"

"Someone is doing bad stuff to the ranch, Jericho. Someone threatened us." Ali wept, her hands fisting the fabric of his shirt. "Chance! Chance, baby, where are you?" Her body shook so much, Jericho worried she'd fall off the horse. Taking Chief hadn't been his best idea, but nothing could get to every nook and cranny of a ranch as quickly as a horse.

"I need you to calm down, Ali."

"Calm down! Didn't you hear me? What if he's been kidnapped? What if… Dear Lord…please don't let anyone hurt him."

A chill ran down Jericho's back. "Think. Where can a kid hide on this property? What place is maybe a bit dangerous? That's where Chance will be."

"The gully."

His stomach dropped. The gully was more than just a bit dangerous. Urging Chief to head west, he took his hand away from Ali and tangled it back into the horse's copper mane. Jericho leaned forward as Chief plunged ahead faster. With each hoof pound bringing the gully closer, Jericho prayed for Chance's safety.

*Someone threatened us.*

Anger boiled in him. If anyone dared bother Ali, Chance or anyone here, they'd have to answer to him.

*Threatened.* What on earth could she mean?

Nearing the spot, Jericho slowed the horse's pace. Before he could halt Chief completely, Ali jumped off and raced toward the jagged ravine that split Silver property from Freed property. Jericho leaped down and jogged after her. They yelled the boy's name, scanning the deep niches of the gully. Ali's calls were strangled out between choked sobs, each one wrenching at Jericho's heart. She stumbled on the uneven cliff face, but Jericho caught her around the waist before she fell.

"He's gone," she wailed with her hand cupped over her mouth.

Craning his neck, Jericho hushed her. He thought he heard… *Yep.*

Dropping to his knees, Jericho scooted to the edge of the craggy rocks and looked over. Sure enough. "Right there, Ali. Look, he's down here." He pointed.

Ali lunged forward. Jericho held up his hand to keep her from tumbling off the side.

She swiped the back of her arm over her face. "Where? I don't see him. Chance?"

"Mom!" Chance gulped in air then whined.

"Chance! Chance, baby, come back up here."

"I caaann't." He sniveled.

She squeezed Jericho's arm. "Something's wrong. I think he's hurt."

Reaching out, he cupped the back of Ali's head, making her look him in the eye and hoping she saw something that would make her trust him. "Everything will be okay. I'll go down there and get him. I'll bring him back to you."

Nervous energy prickled his muscles, but he schooled himself not to show it. Jericho licked his lips and dropped his feet over the edge. Growing up at the foot of the Bitterroot Mountains, a man learned to free climb before he could walk. Then again, it had been a while and he was never all that good at it, but Chance needed him.

He worked the muscles in his jaw. *Find a handhold.* He shifted, fingers shaking as he clung to the cliff face. He wished he'd thought to bring a rope. The rock dug into his skin, but hearing a whimper from where Chance hunched in a crevice pushed Jericho to move faster.

"I'm coming, buddy."

He felt down with his foot, and his toe touched on the small rock shelf beside Chance. Knowing better than to trust the crumble of boulders the boy perched on, Jericho kept a tight hold of the wall as he angled closer. "Hey, bud, you okay?"

Chance shoved out his bottom lip. Red rings circled teary eyes. "My arm hurts. Bad."

"Did you fall in here?"

The boy nodded, and a wash of chills raced down Jericho's spine. He looked up. "Ali. I need you to take Chief and bring back rope."

Her head peeked over the side. "You can't bring Chance up?"

"Not safely. And, Ali, be quick. These rocks are crumbling."

Her head disappeared. Seconds later, Chief's hooves pounded thunder.

Jericho found a small ledge a few feet away and hunkered down. "Your mom'll be back soon. I need you to be very brave, okay?"

Chance peeked at him. "But my arm."

"Why were you down here, anyway?"

"Megan said there were kittens crying by the gully. I heard her tell Aunt Kate."

Jericho dragged in a long breath. "And you didn't like to think of them stuck in here, did you?"

"No. What if they couldn't find their mom?"

Jericho craned his neck, but didn't hear any mews.

A truck roared across the field. Rider's head appeared over the gully wall. "Mr. Freed?"

"Rider. We need help."

"Me and Miss Ali brought some rope. I'm going to tie it to one of these trees and toss it down."

A cable snaked over the edge of the cliff face, and Ali dropped another bunch of rope down the ledge. Jericho caught it and gingerly worked his way over to where Chance stooped.

He constructed a makeshift climber's harness around Chance then, binding it with more knots than necessary, he attached it to the dangling rope. "I know your arm hurts, but I need you to be really strong, okay? I need you to hold on tight, even if it hurts and you want to let go." He tugged the rope, certain it would hold. "Rider, go on and hoist him up."

He patted Chance's head. "You're secure, but I still want you to hang on to this rope like it's that bull you always wanted to ride."

Chance bit his lip and nodded.

Jericho smiled and lifted his chin. "Win the buckle, kid."

* * *

Swirling her cup of lukewarm coffee, Ali leaned back against the cool hospital wall.

Jericho laid down the magazine he'd been reading. "What's the verdict?"

She sighed. It had been a long day. First with Denny, then an emotional conversation with Jericho, then Chance—her heart seized. She should have been there. "He broke his wrist. They're casting it right now. He picked the camo plaster because he wanted to match you, Mr. Army."

"Thank God that's all it was."

Sliding into the waiting room chair, she set down her coffee. "Do you need a doctor, Jericho? Were you injured climbing? I saw you limping afterward."

"I'm fine. I'm more worried about you."

She sipped her coffee. "Me? I'm not the one who free-climbed into the gully."

"What did you mean earlier, when you said someone's threatening you?"

"I don't really want to talk about it."

"Ali." He grabbed her hand. "Remember, I promised to protect you. If someone has done something that makes you think Chance could have been in danger of being kidnapped, then I need to know."

How much to tell him? *The truth.* She swallowed hard. "Things have been happening around the ranch lately that make me think someone is trying to harm me."

His eyebrows knit together. "What sort of things?"

"Money is missing from the Big Sky Dreams account, and someone has been tampering with our fences and letting out the cattle. We lost three heifers in the ravine so far. You knew that someone slashed my tires. The horses were set loose twice now. And I found a note."

"A note?"

"Yeah, someone left a creepy note tacked to my door saying that if I valued what was important to me, I'd stay away from you." She twisted the lid on the coffee cup.

"From me? It named me specifically?"

She nodded. "It said something about seeing us together at the Independence Day Picnic. That I'd been warned."

He rubbed his thumb over the top of her clenched knuckles. "Why didn't you tell me sooner?"

"Because it's not your problem." Ali jerked her hand from his and crossed her arms.

"If I'm named as the reason these things are happening to you, then I'm already involved."

"If I had told you, would you have stayed away?"

"Absolutely not. I'd have been around more, like I'll be now. We'll get to the bottom of it. I'll figure out who's behind it and—"

"Hey, Mom. Hey, Jericho." Chance crossed the room with a nurse at his side. "Look how cool this is. I could hide in the woods, and no one would see me. Will you both sign my arm?"

Jericho's laugh failed to calm Ali. The tight lines around his eyes were still present, and she knew they meant trouble for her. He wasn't about to drop their conversation about the note. If she heard him right, he was about to say he'd take care of whoever wanted to cause them harm. But that didn't sit well with her, because she didn't want Jericho in danger, either.

\* \* \*

How the fool man convinced her to come out to the street dance, Ali had no idea. She shook her head as she walked beside Jericho. The rowdy twang of country music filled the air. Laughter and the clips of boots against Main Street bounced off the buildings lining downtown.

Chance cupped his cast and looked at Jericho with round eyes. "Can I ride on your back?"

"Sure thing, partner." He bent down so her son could scramble up. He grunted. "Watch the kidneys, kid."

Chance scooped off Jericho's hat, giving it a new home swimming over his small head. She smiled at the way Jericho's hair stuck up in all directions, but the rough-and-tumble look only increased his appeal. The man looked too tempting for his own good—clean-shaven, in his pressed denim shirt and muscle-hugging jeans.

The sun would dip behind the Bitterroot Mountains in the next hour, but warmth remained for the black tank top and gauzy skirt she'd donned. Ali always liked the way boots looked with a knee-length skirt, especially while twirling during a country dance.

As if reading her mind, Jericho glanced over. "I'm glad they've kept this a family thing. Real friendly, with all the old-timers and kids involved."

She smoothed down her hair and moved toward the sidewalk, away from the crowd already line dancing. "They've stayed pretty true to the innocent olden days."

"Hey, look." Jericho jutted out his chin. "There are Kate and Rider dancing together. When he's not working, that guy sure follows her around like a homeless hound dog. Is something going on between them?"

"I sure hope not." Making sure Chance wasn't paying attention, Ali leaned close and whispered, "We think Rider might be our saboteur."

Jericho laughed. "Rider Longley? Absolutely not. He loves your family."

"I've heard differently."

He shot her a look that said they'd talk about it later.

Up front near where the deejay and square-dance callers stood, children of all ages moved to the beat. While most knew the steps, one freckle-faced boy spun in helter-skelter circles, ricocheting off other dancers.

Chance tapped Jericho on the head. "Will you take me up there?"

"Sure thing, pal."

"Will you stay and dance with me?"

Jericho yanked on his collar and widened his eyes at Ali. He mouthed, *Save me.*

She laughed. The cowboy had never been much for dancing, but he could use a little torture all the same. "I think that's a great idea, Chance. You and Jericho go on up there, and I'm going to find me some huckleberry lemonade."

"You owe me!" Jericho called over his shoulder with a full-chested laugh.

She liked that about him—when he laughed, he did it completely, none of that chuckling stuff. Pulling out of the crowd, she took in the sight of all her friends and neighbors enjoying the evening. A teen with long black hair slow-danced with arms fully extended, swaying side to side. A father with dimples danced with his daughter perched on his toes.

Ali's eyes lingered on an elderly couple, gnarled hands entwined over their hearts as they barely shuffled to the music together. At the song's crescendo, the elderly man leaned forward and kissed his little white-puff-haired wife right on her firecracker-red lips.

Ali's eyes welled up at the sight. A lump the size of Montana formed in her throat, as if all her bitterness and regrets had risen and now she wanted them gone. She wanted freedom from the weeds growing like man-acles, restraining her heart from hope and forgiveness. She wanted love like *that*.

Sliding her gaze, she bit down a laugh. Good to his word, Jericho stood up front surrounded by a crowd of kids, attempting to dance and making a complete and adorable fool of himself. As if embarrassed, Chance kept stopping him, and then he'd demonstrate a move and make a hand motion inviting Jericho to try. Jeri-cho looked more like he was trying to shake a prairie dog off his back than any dancing Ali had ever seen.

"Care to dance?" Tripp touched the small of her back.

"Tripp. You startled me." She spilled a bit of her lemonade onto the straw bales lining the street. She surveyed the tanned lawyer. "I didn't know you owned boots."

He shrugged. "The event seemed to call for them. Got your attention turned elsewhere, I see." He jutted his chin in Jericho's direction.

"Yeah, Chance broke his arm a couple days ago so I want to keep a close eye on him."

"Are you okay? I heard about Denny."

Tears stung Ali's eyes. She shook her head.

"I understand if you don't want to talk, but I want you to know I'm here if you need anything. I'll do anything for you, Alison. You know that, right?" He flashed a made-for-Hollywood smile.

"You've been such a good friend to me these last few years. I don't know what I would have done without you."

"I haven't seen you out there yet." He took the cup from her hand and set it down on the steps leading to the bakery door. "Mind if I'm the first tonight?" He offered his hand.

Ali shrugged. "I guess that would be fine." With the rest of her family occupied, a dance with a friend sounded harmless. Although, Tripp didn't just want to be her friend, did he? Ali swallowed hard, regretting accepting his hand already.

Jericho froze and watched that man pull *his wife* out onto the street. Tripp put one of his hands on Ali's slender waist. Then he entwined his fingers with hers. Tripp looked up, meeting Jericho's stare. He gave Jericho a crooked smile, then turned his face into Ali's hair.

"Jericho." Chance tapped his arm. "I think you're too old for this because your face is all red, and the vein on your neck looks like it's going to pop out. You should sit."

Scooping his hat off the kid's head, Jericho took a few deep breaths to calm himself enough for rational thought. "You're right, Chance. I need to slow down a bit, but I'm not sitting this one out. Not on my life." He stalked through the crowd, bumping into a couple and making them miss their dance steps. "Sorry," he muttered. Nothing would deter his course. Not when it concerned Ali. He'd fight for her until she told him flat-out to stop.

Zeroing in on the pair, he tapped her on the shoulder. "Mind if I cut in?"

Tripp scoffed. "Actually, we do."

"I asked the lady."

Both men looked at Ali. She bit her lip. "It's okay, Tripp. Thanks for the dance."

Jericho puffed out his chest, heart swelling. He took Ali's hands and pulled her against him.

The corners of her mouth twitched as if she fought a smile. "You shouldn't have done that. An angry Tripp isn't worth one dance."

"Don't like seeing another man with his mugs on my wife." Holding her this close, he whispered against her ear. The silky strands of her hair tickled his mouth. He shut his eyes.

She trembled against him.

He pressed her closer. "Shhh. It's okay, Ali. Please be with me like this."

"Jericho... I'm not... You can't..."

The pain in his knee made their dance more like a shuffle-stop-walk, but he didn't care. "I want it to be just you and me, Ali. I've always wanted that."

She pushed back a little, but still in his arms. "It's not just me anymore. I have Chance. We're a package deal."

He stopped dancing and tipped her chin to hold her gaze as he spoke. "I want you both."

"But what if—"

He put a hand on either side of her neck, cradling the back of her head with his fingers. "I don't care who his father is, Ali. He's your son. But if you let me, I'd love him like he was mine."

"Even if...?"

"In fact, I might already."

Her eyes searched his. "You do?"

"Of course I do." He smiled, waiting for her to open

up and confirm that Chance was his son. Instead, she nodded once and laid her head back on his shoulder.

Jericho sighed. Maybe in time she'd trust him enough to tell him the truth.

## Chapter Fourteen

"I hardly think it's necessary for you to stay here." Ali jammed her hands to her hips and tapped her foot against the floor.

Kate wrinkled her brow. "I don't know, Al. I think it's wise to have a man here until stuff blows over."

Ali shot her sister a glare. *Traitor.*

"It won't work. We don't have any extra beds so—"

Jericho shook his head. "While in the army, I learned to sleep anywhere. I slept leaning against a tank wheel in the middle of mortar fire once. I could curl up on the kitchen tile in there and be just fine."

Chance slurped on the last of his firecracker Popsicle. Blue and red colors painted his face. "That's gross. You could sleep in my room, but my bed is small. Mom said I'll get a bigger one soon, though." He looked up at Ali with hopeful eyes, as if she'd spring for a new bed after his benevolent offer to Jericho.

"Appreciate that, but this couch in here will work just fine."

"Yeah, I don't need you in my room 'cause I'm strong. I'm a guy." Chance chewed on the Popsicle stick, thinking hard. "You should sleep in Mom's room with her. She's got a big bed."

Kate ducked, hiding a chuckle behind her hand.

Heat crept up Ali's neck, but seeing the full-out fire on Jericho's cheeks made her feel better. "Enough, Chance. Get upstairs, wash your face and throw on your jammies." She pointed toward the stairs.

The boy set down the stick on the coffee table. When he faced Jericho, he shrugged. "I'm just saying. I'm brave, but she's a girl, and girls get scared easy. And she has the biggest bed. It makes sense."

"Put it like that, and it sure does make sense. But between you and me, I think it's safer for everyone if I'm down here on the couch." He shot Ali a look.

"To bed, Chance."

He harrumphed but obeyed, albeit with loud, drawn-out steps on the stairs.

Ali chuckled. "I'll be up in ten minutes to read the first chapter of that book with you. Be ready when I come."

Jericho set down his cup of milk and stretched. "You know what? I'm going to go up there and search all the rooms."

"You can't be serious." Ali inched toward the stairs to block his progress.

He took her shoulders and gently moved her aside. "Listen. When we were looking for Chance, you really believed that someone might have taken him. If you're that afraid of whatever is going on, then yes, I'm going to take it seriously. And I'm going to go up and check all the rooms so I know for sure that nothing's lurking that shouldn't be."

*Lurking?* She hadn't thought of that. Now she

wouldn't get a wink of sleep. She stepped back. "When you put it like that…"

He disappeared up the stairs.

"You okay with all this?" Kate dropped down on the couch, sprawling her feet on the coffee table.

Ali sunk into the side chair. "Not like you offered much help."

"Oh, c'mon. You know that having him here is probably the best thing right now. Who's going to try to mess with the ranch when they find out he's standing guard?"

"I just… It's not proper."

"Proper? He's your husband. What could be more proper?"

Ali leaned her head on the overstuffed armrest. "I haven't slept under the same roof with that man in more than eight years. It's unnerving. I was just getting used to him being back in my life. But not like this, not all the time and not in our house."

A devilish smile pulled at Kate's lips as a mocking gleam lit her eyes. "Well, if Chance had his way, your husband would be…*in your bed.*"

Ali burst out laughing. "What am I going to do with that child? He's set on pairing us up. I was mortified."

Kate crossed her arms over her stomach and closed her eyes. "You sure you're okay?"

"Besides this stuff, I'm pretty stressed out for the 'Dream A Little Dream' event I have for Big Sky Dreams. I mean, if we don't get the money, I don't know what we're going to do. And this is the first event we're having here on our property." Her sister nodded off, so Ali stopped talking.

Finishing the last of her water, Ali looked up at the ceiling, listening for footsteps. Silence. Ali crossed her

legs, jiggling her foot. How long did it take to peek into
a couple of rooms? Losing the battle with her curiosity, she tiptoed past Kate and crept upstairs. A small
sliver of light trickled from under Chance's bedroom
door, but not enough to illuminate the hallway. Shadows painted the second floor. Ali peered into her bedroom. Negative. Then she turned the corner at the end
of the hall and gasped.

*Oh no!* Jericho Freed stood in *that* room. An unwrit-
ten rule in the house was that the door to that room, the
small room at the back of the house, stayed shut at all
times. Her heart pounded so loud, it reverberated in her
ears. He shouldn't be in there.

She stayed in the hall, grabbing the cool door handle
for support. She was thankful, at least, that Jericho's
back was to her. Ali cleared her throat, nice and loud.
"Are you done checking the rooms?"

When he whirled around, Ali noticed that it looked
like he was trying very hard to keep his composure. "All
my stuff. You kept everything," he whispered.

She gave what she hoped came off as an indifferent
shrug. "It was that or toss the junk."

Jericho rubbed his jaw, then reached out and trailed
his fingers over a box full of his old paperback West-
erns. "But you kept it. For eight years. Why?"

Giving a little growl, Ali stalked to the stairs. "I don't
know, Jericho. Just leave me be about it. And get out.
That door is supposed to stay closed."

He brushed past her, his voice husky. "But it's open
now."

*Crunch.*

Okay. The first sound could have been his imagination, but that one? No, that was real. Stealing across the grass, it whooshed a bit in the still night as Jericho investigated the source of the noise. With deliberate steps, he came to the front of the barn and craned his neck to listen.

The sound—a horse, maybe? Blame it on a year experiencing the harsh realities of war, but Jericho Freed didn't like to leave a strange noise unexplored. Sure, that same fact cost him his army career, but this was Ali's safety. He wasn't about to take any chances.

His fingers grazed the barn door. Just as he feared. *Unlatched.* With it hanging open, he squeezed his body through then faded into the shadowed area near the stall doors.

He squinted into the darkness. A person in dark clothes hunched over something in the stall used for storing hay. A chill washed over him. Ali was right. No other explanation existed for someone being in the barn at this time of night. Despite the slicing pain in his knee, Jericho pressed against the wall and slunk toward the wrongdoer. His footfalls undetected, he grabbed the dark figure by the arm and flung the intruder around to face him, pressing them hard against the wall.

Jericho clamped his hand over the perpetrator's mouth. "I'm gonna lift my hand in a minute, and you're going to tell me two things. Why are you here? And why are you hassling Ali?" As he spoke, his eyes adjusted to the darkness, and recognition poured through him. He took the slender but firm arm in his hand, the petite frame and long, dark hair. "Megan?"

She shoved away his hand from her face and wiped her mouth with her sleeve. "Of course. What are you doing here?"

Peering around her into the stall, Jericho saw a gas can, an ax and some rope. He narrowed his eyes at her. "What are *you* doing?"

She ran a hand over her hair. "Didn't Ali tell you?"

"Tell me what?"

"Huh. Guess she doesn't trust you."

"I'm calling the cops."

"Easy there, Trigger. I'm doing a stakeout. Helping Ali catch the person who's been doing stuff."

He raised his eyebrows. "Which is why you're putting gas in a highly flammable room? Are you crazy? There's hay dust everywhere. This place is one step from an inferno."

"I will have you know—" she crossed her arms and stepped away from him "—that Rider Longley left these next to the house. Pretty suspicious, if you ask me. I was moving them, and I didn't think it was dangerous in here. It's just hay dust." She shrugged.

Jericho grabbed her biceps in one hand, and the can of gasoline in the other. "I don't buy a word of this. Let's go see if Ali gives the same story."

He dragged her with more force than necessary across the yard and up the front steps. A wild, howling fear bit at his ankles the entire walk to the house. Rope? Gasoline? An ax? At least now the gas can was clear of the hay dust.

"How do you know Rider left that stuff near the house?"

"Who else? He's the one with a vendetta against this family. Will you *let me go?*" She shoved at his hand as they tripped up the porch steps.

Jericho thought about the implications of the items

Megan found. Who made a big to-do about always carrying matches?

*Tripp.* It all made sense. The letter—he was at the Independence Day picnic. He didn't want Ali near Jericho. He probably banked on the fact that Ali would run into his arms for protection. *Think again, Tripp Phillips.* Jericho wasn't about to let that happen.

He released Megan, and they entered the house.

Ali bolted from her chair. The book she'd been reading tumbled to the ground. "Megan? Is something wrong? What are you doing here?"

He spoke before Megan could. "Is Megan supposedly trying to help you stake out the place?"

Ali looked slowly from him to Megan and then back to him. "We had talked about it. Yes. Trying to catch Rider."

"That's all I need to know." He turned to Megan. "Sorry if I scared you, but I had to be sure."

"Whatever. I'll see you both tomorrow. Sorry for trying to help." Megan elbowed past him, her voice dripping sarcasm.

Ali trailed Megan out to the porch. "Hey, wait up."

Her friend turned, palming at her cheeks.

"What just happened?"

"Are you going to marry Tripp? I heard, that night when he asked you in the kitchen."

Megan's question jarred Ali like a bear trap crushing her leg. Marry Tripp? She didn't want to think about that right now.

She sighed. "I don't know."

"Why not? I mean, Tripp's a good guy."

"You're right, Tripp's an amazing guy. He's been

there for me when I had no one. He's been my closest friend the past couple years."

"But you're already married."

Ali's shoulders slumped, and she looked out at the mountains. Married? Okay, but only in the legal sense, really. "You're technically right."

"I think you should stay with your husband." Megan rubbed her hands up and down her arms. The evening carried a distinct chill, despite how hot the day had been.

Ali swallowed hard. "You do?"

"He's a nice guy. I don't know what happened between you two in the past, but he cares about you, Ali. You should have seen the way he rounded on me in that barn when he thought I was there to do something nefarious. He loves you."

Later, with those words etched in her mind, Ali stared up at the ceiling of her bedroom, unable to sleep. Drover gave a giant puppy yawn and eased tighter against her in the bed. She turned and splayed her hands into the dog's silken fur, running his floppy ears through her fingers as he gave a little harrumph and closed his eyes.

"I don't know if I can handle it all. Do You hear me, God? It's too much," she whispered. But it didn't feel like the prayer penetrated the walls, let alone made it all the way to heaven.

The ache in her heart had begun as a throb the moment she was alone. Now, hours later, it felt like open heart surgery without anesthesia. Denny was gone. *Dead. Forever.* Someone was after her. Jericho was here. Ali squeezed her eyes shut.

She felt like a pocket turned inside out with nothing left to give. Using the edge of her blanket, she dabbed at the tears sliding down her cheek, hoping the sniffling wasn't as loud as it felt. Ali turned into Drover, using his back to muffle the sobs that threatened to rake through her body at any moment.

Bolting up, Jericho's gaze scanned the room. The bags of frozen veggies he'd put on his knees slid to the floor with a plop. With the steps of a practiced hunter, he stole to the stairs and heard a sound that made the hairs on the back of his neck prickle. The subdued moan came from upstairs. *If anyone hurt Ali, or Chance, or Kate...*

He took the stairs two at a time. Bending an ear near each door, he listened for the haunting sound again. All he heard were soft snores from Kate's room. Nothing by Chance's, so he pushed open the door. The child lay sprawled on his bed, his chest rising and falling with deep sleep. Jericho backed out of the room. Finding Ali's ajar, he peeked in, and his heart constricted. No evil Tripp stood over the bed with an ax, but the sight of Ali crying sickened him all the same.

Leaning against the wall in the hallway, he prayed for guidance and for Ali's peace. She sniffled, and his gut told him to do something to help her. Without thinking, he went back downstairs and put on the cast iron kettle. As the water warmed, he fumbled through the drawers and the pantry looking for mint tea. While they were married, Ali had experienced trouble sleeping. The only remedy had been mint tea—and him rubbing circles on her back until she drifted off.

Regret formed a lump in his throat. How had she fallen to sleep after he left? Lost in the alcohol, he'd never thought about it before, and the totality of what his leaving had done to her rocked through him.

Hands shaking, he poured a cup and let it steep.

The floorboard creaked behind him. Dressed in over-sized sweats, Ali blinked. "What are you doing?"

Jericho crossed the room and held out the cup to her. "It's mint. I heard you crying."

She bowed her head and took the cup, blowing on the warm liquid before sipping. "You remembered."

"'Course I did. I haven't forgotten anything about you." He motioned for her to join him at the table. "Do you need anything else?"

"No." She straightened. "I should go back to sleep."

He sighed. "I'm here…whenever you need me."

Ali surveyed him through the rising steam. Her eyes searched him, almost caressing his face. Cautiously, Jericho took a step forward and pressed a kiss to her forehead. "Sleep well."

As she left the room, he heard a very quiet "Thank you."

## Chapter Fifteen

"Please, Mom, please." Chance's dress shoes left skid marks on the clean kitchen floor as he hopped up and down.

Ali scrubbed the same serving platter with a Brillo pad for the third time. "Oh, I don't know. There's so much to get done around here, and if you all are leaving, I'll need to do double time."

Kate captured the plate and yanked it away, rescuing it from another round of scouring. "If you don't want to come to church with us, it's okay, Al. Just say so, and everyone will leave you alone."

The scrape of Jericho's chair as he pushed back from the table drew everyone's attention. He nodded his head once, real slow. It seemed to be some sort of secret signal because Kate grabbed Chance's hand and headed out the back door.

Ali wrung her hands, puckered from dishwater.

Jericho rose and clomped toward her. All dressed up in a tucked-in button-down, a tie and suit coat—but the jeans and boots still screamed cowboy. "No one's interested in forcing you to do anything you don't want to. You know that, right?"

She bobbed her head.

He came closer. The spicy, woodsy trace of his cologne drifted over her, and she fought the urge to close her eyes and breathe deeply—that, or bury her nose against that place on his neck where she knew he sprayed the enticing nectar.

She swung toward the oven and snatched the dirty skillet.

He followed her. "I wanted to thank you for letting me bring Chance with me today. Thank you for trusting me with him."

She batted hair from her eyes. "He's thrilled to go."

He eased the skillet out of her hand and dropped it into the sink. A little water sloshed onto the counter. When he reached for the dishcloth, she leaned out of his way. He mopped up the spill on the counter, then dropped the cloth into the dirty dishwater.

She looked down, straightening the rug with her foot. "I want to go, too." She met his eyes—his soft, pleading eyes. "I know it's stupid, but I feel like God will shoot lightning bolts at the church or something if I dare to darken the doors."

His lips creased into an easy smile. "It'd be more like fireworks celebrating a daughter's homecoming. But I understand. I've felt that way before."

With a sigh, she rubbed her elbow. "It would just feel strange walking in there, after all this time."

"They're holding the worship service in the park today in lieu of a church gathering. And so far, it looks like God hasn't tampered with you whenever you're outside, so I think you'll be in the clear today." Jericho winked.

"It's out in the park?"

"You can get up and walk away if you feel uncomfortable."

"I think I'll come, then. Shouldn't you guys have left already?"

"If Kate's hot to trot she can leave, but I'll wait. I'll always wait for you."

Her eyes locked with Jericho's. He thought she was worth waiting for. Warmth flooded through her, and suddenly she couldn't think of another reason in the world to stay away from him.

On the drive over, Jericho eased her discomfort. He promised the service would be casual, and he complimented her outfit twice. When the Jeep halted in the parking spot, she looked down at her white capris, strappy sandals and sapphire V-neck crew. A necklace or some sort of embellishment would have been nice, but it had been the best she could scrounge up in seven minutes.

Jericho rounded the car and opened the door for her, offering his hand to assist her down. "Don't want you twisting an ankle in your fancy shoes."

"They don't even have heels." She took his hand all the same.

Chance bounded over from the truck Kate drove. His tie was already missing, and his sleeves were rolled to his elbows. "Mom, Aunt Kate says we get to sit on the ground and that there will be cake and juice afterward." He caught her hand and swung it as they picked their way through the crowd together.

Jericho's laugh washed over them. "Church isn't out-side all the time, bud, but they do usually have treats after service."

The group located an open spot on the side of the gathering. Before they sat down, Jericho shrugged out of his suit coat and laid it on the ground, motioning for Ali to sit on it while the band on the platform started singing.

Her eyes widened. "I don't want to get your coat dirty."

One side of his lips lifted, and something twinkled in his eyes. "I don't want your white pants getting ruined."

"Good point." She lowered herself onto his coat. He did the same and edged closer. Chance plopped down on her other side, and Kate sat on some grass at the end of the line.

When the service ended, Ali rose and gathered Jeri-cho's coat in her arms. Before she could bolt to the Jeep, neighbors swarmed her with hugs.

Mrs. Casey, one of Ali's high school teachers, squeezed tight. "You dear thing. Why, I'm so pleased to see you out today. Does a heart good to see my old students. And who might this strapping young man be?" She peered at Chance over her glasses. Ali introduced them.

"Is that Alison Silver?" Linda Smeer, a sleepover sis-ter from days gone by, shook Ali by her shoulders. "I can't believe it. I'm so excited to see you. I think about stopping by your ranch all the time, but I know you're so busy. Let's plan a time to catch up."

"I'd love that." Ali smiled at her, and they exchanged cell phone numbers.

Two families with students in her program stepped

forward and greeted her. Ali swapped a high five with Ned. He'd come a long way since joining the Big Sky Dreams program. Seeing him so comfortable around the large crowd, and able to handle contact, made moisture gather in her eyes.

Jericho poked her in the side, his eyebrows raised. He offered her a red velvet cupcake from the dessert table. "Looks like you've got a lot of friends here."

She plucked at the wrapper. "More than I realized. I think next week I'll come to church with you guys again, even if it's inside the building. I've missed this."

"No lightning?"

"Not yet." She couldn't help the smile that bloomed on her face. Nor the sigh that escaped after she bit into the delicious treat.

Jericho patted Salsa's neck and checked the horse's water. Full. Good. A barn cat slunk into the stable. He scooped up the furry intruder, then latched the door shut.

"Don't let Drover see that you found the cat," Ali called from down the line. He watched her. She stopped near the empty fifth stall and trailed her fingers over the door. Denny's stall. Ali wrapped her arms around her middle and turned away.

Jericho picked up his speed. "Anything else need doing?"

She pressed her lips together. "No. All the horses are in and fed. We just lock up the barn, then I spend some time with Chance before bed."

"He challenged me to a game of Battleship." He set the cat near the tower of hay bales.

They walked together out of the barn, and Ali

stopped to turn the lock. She checked twice to make certain the door was secure. "Are you prepared to be sunk? He's insanely good at it."

He caught her gaze and held tight. The gold flecks in the hazel pools shimmered. *Sunk? More like hook, line and sinker. What are you doing to me, Ali?* He cleared his throat. "So what's on the menu for dessert tonight?"

"I made cookies-and-cream cupcakes earlier. They should be cool now, so they only need frosting. They'll be ready by the time your ships are destroyed."

"Such a vote of confidence."

"Oh, you don't know how Chance gets when he's playing board games."

He rubbed the stubble on his chin and laughed. "You forget. I've lost to him in Clue twice now."

Looking out across the corral, Ali crossed her arms and sighed.

He touched her hand. "What's on your mind?"

"Sometimes I wonder if starting Big Sky Dreams was one enormous mistake. I mean, it takes so much of my time away from Chance. Not just the lessons, but I spend so much time looking for donations and planning fund-raisers, too. I wonder sometimes if it's all worth it."

"You take good care of Chance. Don't doubt that."

She started walking toward the house again, and he fell into step with her.

Ali gave a quick nod. "You know you don't have to keep staying here. I'm sure you're needed at your dad's place."

"I'm not. His staff took care of the place before I came home, and they can take care of it just fine without me." Jericho grabbed the front door, holding it open for her. She smiled at him, and his heart hammered against his rib cage. The past week spent around her only strengthened his determination to win back his wife. "Believe me, I'm right where I'm supposed to be."

## Chapter Sixteen

$A$li waved as her last student left, then wiped her hands on her jeans. With the "Dream A Little Dream" fund-raising event tomorrow, she needed to finish polishing all the tack, make the barn shine and hose down a couple of the dustier horses. Beyond that, calling vendors for confirmation and checking to make certain the attractions she planned to offer to donors were set ranked top on her list for today.

Chance popped up beside her elbow. "Know what, Mom?"

She smiled. In his scuffed black boots, jeans and T-shirt, the bandanna tied around his neck *like Jericho's* made him look like a cowboy-in-training. "What, Mr. Chance?"

"I reminded Jericho about camping, and he said we can go this weekend, as long as you say it's okay." He jumped beside her as he talked.

"Did he, now?" Ali rolled the ends of a set of reins in her left hand. "How much work have you accomplished today?"

"We did everything you asked. Cleared all the weeds,

and Jericho mowed the yard. I swept the porch, and I even helped Megan rake the corral. It is *so* clean, Mom."

She laid down the tack and walked to the barn entrance, pretending to scrutinize her crew's work. To be honest, the property hadn't looked better since before Dad died. The guests for tomorrow's event would find Big Sky Dreams shining with a professional polish.

She turned back to her son. "Everything looks amazing. So you win. It's okay with me if you go camping with Jericho this weekend."

"Aren't you coming?"

"Oh, honey, I think it'll be better if just you two boys go." Jericho proved capable enough and trustworthy. She could relax with Chance under his care for one night. And besides, it would give her some time away from the man's intoxicating presence that threatened to throw her well-planned life off-course.

Yes. She welcomed any excuse to get him away for a while, even if that included time alone with her son. Which frightened her too, but somehow she trusted Jericho not to tell Chance about their marriage now—even more than she trusted herself around him.

"You hafta come. It won't be fun without you." He grabbed her hand and tugged a little, yanking her toward the corral. Jericho crouched nearby, giving the fence a new coat of white paint. "Jericho!" Chance bounced on the balls of his feet. "She said we can go camping. But she said she won't come with us."

He took off his hat and scratched his head. "Not coming?"

"I thought it would be good if you guys went alone, made it just a boys' thing."

"You have to talk her into going. I'd even help with

the fence. See, Mom." Chance grabbed Jericho's abandoned brush and smeared the next post so the paint ran down in goopy globs.

"Aw. Come with us. We want you there." Jericho cocked an arm on the rail, tilting his head to her with a half smile. "I think it'd be good, the three of us together."

"I just think it's better—"

Chance jumped back to his feet, flinging a long stream of paint across the lawn. "Who will tuck me in if you're not there?"

"Well, Jericho, I guess."

"He can't. Only a mom can do it. That's the rules. You have to come."

"Hey, Al? I need you over here," Kate called from the maintenance barn.

Ali cupped her hands around her mouth. "One second, Kate!" She turned back to Chance and plucked the dripping brush from his hand. "You are so helpful, sweetheart. Could you maybe use just a little less paint?"

Jericho appropriated the tool and winked at her. "I'll show him how to do it. This'll be the best fence from here to Canada. What do you say, Chance?"

Her son scratched his chin. "Probably."

Shaking her head, Ali bit back a chuckle. She started to walk away, but a cold damp tickle went up her arm. She looked down at the white stripe. "Aw. Sick, Jericho." She swatted at him. His eyes gleamed with mischief. "This is outdoor paint. It'll take forever to wash off."

"I know." He bit back a laugh.

Ali scooped at the dollop running down her arm and raised an eyebrow at him. He backed up, bumping into the wet fence. When he craned to look at the damage to the back of his shirt, Ali smeared her handful across his jaw and neck.

He pounced, missing her. She squealed and took off running. His full-chested laugh echoed after her. She glanced over her shoulder and smirked. Jericho turned his attention back to Chance, smearing two streaks like war paint onto her son's cheeks.

She reached the run-down green barn panting. It housed broken equipment and old, busted tack. Rustic to the core, no modern conveniences graced the old building. The only light trickling in came from cracks in the side walls and holes in the roof. Birds roosted on the rafters. Ali hated the maintenance barn and avoided going inside it. But it also housed the large wagon occasionally used to give hay rides to the Big Sky Dreams students. She planned to offer rides to donors tomorrow, so she plunged into the musty building.

Squinting to locate Kate among the piles of unwanted items, Ali found her sister on her hands and knees next to the wagon.

"Need something?"

From her prone position, Kate huffed, then sat back on the heels of her feet. "What were you talking about with Chance and Jericho?"

"I said they could go camping this weekend, and they were trying to convince me to go along. I don't think it's a good idea." She rubbed at the smear on her elbow.

"Al, your family wants you. Why would you say no to that?"

"My *family*?"

"Your husband and son. What else would you call that?"

Tracing her fingertips along the grooved wood on the side of the wagon, Ali shrugged. "Just sounds weird." She straightened. "You didn't call me over to ask me that, did you?"

Kate paused. "No. When was the last time you looked at this thing?"

Ali worked her bottom lip between her teeth. "Yesterday morning. Why?"

"'Cause you can't use it. The axle's busted."

Dropping down beside her sister, Ali craned her neck to look under the wagon. Sure enough, the back axle hung in two splinted pieces. "But I checked every inch of this thing yesterday. It wasn't like that. Kate, it looks like…like someone *sawed* through the axle."

"That's what I thought, too."

Fear, now a gnawing companion, ignited Ali's nerves. "Who would do such a thing?"

"Besides us, who has keys to the barn?"

"Only…"

"Rider." They spoke the name in unison.

Charging from the barn, Ali spotted Tripp Phillips climbing out of his Subaru. She called to him. A lawyer was exactly what she needed. With quick, long strides, they met each other midway in the yard. From the corner of her eye, she saw Jericho stop talking to Chance and stand, watching her. At least he remained out of earshot. He'd flip if he knew about the wagon.

Tripp placed his hands on her shoulders and squeezed. "What's wrong, Alison? You look like you've seen a ghost."

"I might as well have. Someone's been doing stuff, really bad stuff, to the ranch and—"

"Doing stuff to the ranch? Why didn't I know about this?" His grip tightened. "Are you okay? No one's hurt you, have they?" His gaze drifted to the right, Jericho's way.

She shook her head. "No, not like that. Someone's been playing mean tricks the last few weeks. And I have proof that Rider Longley's the one doing it."

His eyebrows knit together. "Why does that last name sound familiar?"

"Someone in his family is suing Dad's company. His parents were the ones who died in the crash... He hates me."

Tripp's mouth pulled into a sneer. "And he's *here*? You let him work on your property? Oh, Alison. This is all worse than I thought."

She bunched up her hands, her nails digging at her palms. "I didn't know before, but I'm going to fire him. Right now. I think it'd be better if you came with me. I don't know what he's capable of."

Tripp gave a wide smile. "Of course. I'm really happy that you asked me. That you trust me. Let's do it now."

She nodded, and he took her hand. Jericho called out her name, sounding wary, but Ali waved him off as she climbed into her truck. At a jaw-rattling speed, she drove to the upper heifer field where they found Rider checking the new calves.

"Need something, Miss Ali?" The lanky cowboy looped his hands around his belt buckle as she and Tripp walked toward him.

"Yes, actually, I do. You're fired. Leave my property and never return."

Rider staggered backward, his shoulders sagging

like she'd delivered a physical blow. "But why? I know I'm still learning."

"How can you stand there and pretend you haven't done anything? Did you think that little prank to my tires was funny? How many of my cows have died because of your *unfortunate* fence clipping?" She brushed off Tripp's restraining hand and advanced toward Rider, challenging him.

Rider's eyebrows climbed above the brim of his hat. "I'm trying to catch that person. Ma'am, I'm willing to sleep out here and—"

"Oh, that's rich. Sleep out here so you can successfully set my house on fire? Was that your little plan last night?"

"A fire?"

"Cut the puppy-dog sad-eye act. Your family is suing me. Do you deny that?"

"Well, no, but—"

"Right. So get off my property before I give you a real reason to sue me."

"Miss Ali, I—"

Tripp stepped in between the pair, blocking Ali. He crossed his arms. "I believe the lady's said her peace. If I were you, I'd get on out of here without another word. Remember, I'm a lawyer, and I'll make sure any words you say now come into the courtroom should this escalate."

Giving one stiff nod, Rider turned and barged toward his red truck. Relief rushed through her veins, and for a moment it felt like the world was right again. But then she remembered the sabotaged wagon.

"What am I going to do?"

Tripp snaked his arm around her shoulders, turning her toward him. "About what?"

"The wagon we use for events, you know, the hay cart? Rider sawed through the axle. We have a couple hundred people coming here tomorrow, and nothing besides food booths. I promised a ride to donors." She covered her face with her hands. "The entire fund-raiser is going to be a failure."

"Leave everything for tomorrow to me."

The morning of the "Dream A Little Dream" event rolled in with a cloudless sky and an over-enthusiastic sun. But despite the heat, Ali flittered from group to group with a giant smile plastered on her face. Really, her cheeks had started to hurt.

The makeshift parking lot—a plowed-over field on the east side of the ranch—couldn't cram in another car. The tantalizing, sweet smell of kettle corn saturated the air, almost covering the equally enticing burgers sizzling on the giant grill. People mingled together in small groups scattered across the lawn. Some stood near the therapy horses, which were latched to posts in the corral, looking their finest with braided manes and ribbons tied to their tails. All thanks to the Big Sky Dreams students who had showed up early to decorate. The horses stomped from time to time, flicking away flies. Attendees petted their noses and took their pictures. A demonstration, complete with students of all riding levels, would close the event in the next hour.

The hum of a local band performing on the front porch drew a ready crowd. Some of her students clapped out of rhythm, but no one seemed to mind. Most of all, people who didn't even know Big Sky Dreams existed showed up because they spotted the hot air balloons floating above the ranch.

All thanks to Tripp Phillips.

"Ready for an adventure? You promised to go up with me." The very man reached out his hand to her and led her to the front of the balloon ride line. Tethering ropes tied to the baskets allowed them to be hoisted up and down, giving each paying group a ten-minute ride into the skies. Well, more of a hover than a ride. The tethered balloon only rose a hundred yards or so over the ancestral ranch house, but guests still filled the queue, tittering with excitement all the same.

She bit her lip and peeked over her shoulder to try to spot Jericho in the crowd. "You sure these things are safe?"

Tripp grinned, tugging her into the wobbling wicker basket. She yelped when the balloon pilot turned the level on the fuel tank, enabling three-foot flames to dance within the rainbow-themed balloon. She worried her hair might catch fire. With a jolt, they started to rise. Ali stumbled back against Tripp, laughing. He wrapped an arm around her waist.

"Thank you." She turned to Tripp, who watched her and not the scenery. "This is amazing. I don't know how you worked it out in one night, but thank you for making this happen."

His lips spread into an easy smile. "I had some favors to call in. I'm happy to help you." His expression changed. "Chance tells me you're going camping this weekend?"

The wind whipped hair across her face, and she brushed it away. "He's pretty set on it."

"I don't want you to go. It's not safe. Not if Jericho

is going. I can't understand why you'd leave him alone with your son, either."

"Well, I can't go back on my word now. Chance'll freak."

"Who cares what he thinks? He doesn't need to get what he wants all the time. You're the parent. Act like it."

"Excuse me?" Ali narrowed her eyes.

Tripp took her gently by her upper arms. "I'm sorry. That came out wrong. I just don't like the idea of you and that man out there alone together. Don't I have the right to voice that?"

She pulled away. The basket swayed. "We won't be alone. Chance—the whole reason we're going camping—will be there." Turning her back to Tripp, she bumped into a fuel tank, stubbing her toe against the hard metal. "Ouch! Okay, that's it. I'm ready to go back to earth now."

With a fire in his belly, larger than the one shooting from the burners on the balloons, Jericho waited for Ali's ride to finish. He forced his clenched fists to open. Punching Tripp Phillips, as pleasant as it might be, couldn't happen. Not in front of a crowd. Not while Ali thought he hung the moon for orchestrating this event overnight.

A thought kept coming back, like a mosquito in a closed room. It didn't seem possible for Tripp to have planned all this in one evening. If the man had known that Ali's wagon would be sawed through and had worked out the balloons and band weeks ago…now that made more sense.

When their basket touched down, Ali exploded out

of the doorway, and Jericho strode forward to meet her. He warred with himself for a moment. Should he tell her about the phone call and the horrible news right before the riding demonstration? The set of her brows told him to wait.

Clamping his mouth shut, he walked beside her. While she stomped her boots and gave orders, he helped the students mount the horses. Jericho quieted the crowd with a shrill whistle, then handed a microphone to Ali.

"Welcome to our first annual 'Dream A Little Dream' event. Is everyone having a good time?"

A round of applause and a smattering of cheers erupted. Jericho unlatched the corral, parading the first horse and rider into the arena by a lead rope while Ali explained the methods used for therapy riding. After three students demonstrated more advanced techniques, the last kid, astride Chief, performed a very slow barrel race.

"Well done, Ned! I don't think I want to try racing against you anytime soon. You'd give me a run for the winner's purse for sure." Her voice sung through the speakers, and the crowd chuckled good-naturedly. As she closed up the event, thanking everyone and giving special recognition to the companies volunteering time and supplies, the crowd clapped, then began to disperse with a rumble of chatter.

Later in the evening, after picking up the trash littering the ranch and unbraiding horse hair, he had a chance to inch up next to Ali again. "I think everything went well. What do you think?"

Hair limp from sweating all day, Ali tipped her face his way as they walked toward the house. Her nose and cheeks were red from being sun-kissed, and the cara-mel coloring in her eyes glowed in the fading sunlight.

*So cute.*

"It did go well. I don't know the money count, but I have to believe we raised enough to get us over the latest hump. Beyond that, it was just exciting to see so many people learn about therapeutic riding for the first time. If anything, we opened up some eyes to a need."

Jericho decided to start in on his news in a slow, deliberate way. "It was a wonder. Tripp sure has a lot of connections around town. Powerful connections. I feel like, after seeing this today, that man could get his hands on just about anything he wanted."

"Tripp saved us. Without him, there wouldn't have been an event today. Even if we still had the wagon, it would have been Podunk at best."

Catching her arm, Jericho brought her up short be-fore the porch steps. "I think he's dangerous."

"Dangerous? Funny—he said the same about you." Her eyes narrowed.

"I don't know how to say this kindly, but I got a call today from the vet." Jericho looked up into the purple-dusted evening sky, wishing he didn't have to tell her. "He gave me the findings on Denny, because I paid for the necropsy. Ali, Den was poisoned."

"Po-poisoned?" Ali's knees buckled.

Jericho lurched forward, catching her by the elbows. "Yeah. Not by eating the wrong plants, either. The doc-tor said it was some pretty strong stuff called Ricin. He was amazed that anyone besides a medical researcher would have access to it. Guess the stuff's been used in warfare to kill people before." Sliding down, he helped her sit on the porch steps.

She pulled away, her head in her hands. "Someone did it on purpose? Killed Denny? Why?" Her voice caught.

Jericho wrapped an arm around her shoulders and pulled her against his side. "Yes. I'm so sorry. Someone killed him—someone who's around this ranch from time to time, who has the kind of pull around town to get his hands on strong experimental medicine."

## Chapter Seventeen

Ali scanned the Blodgett Canyon, pulled in by its beauty. Even after a last-minute attempt to beg off joining the boys on the camping trip, one look up the wooded trail told her a hike would slough away her worries more effectively than staying at home would have. At least Kate wasn't home alone; thankfully Megan had volunteered to stay with her.

"I'm just saying, this doesn't seem like enough stuff." Jericho pulled the last of the three backpacks from the truck bed, looping the largest over his shoulders.

"You're the one who told me not to pack any dinner." She bent, adjusting the itchy string of bells Jericho had forced her and Chance to tie around their ankles before exiting the truck. "Seriously, these bells are overkill."

Chance danced around, jingling like a Christmas elf.

Jericho grinned. "They'll ward off wildlife. You know that. Lions and bears."

"And tigers, oh, my." Ali stood and adjusted the straps to her backpack.

With a laugh, Jericho tilted his head toward the

mountains. "No tigers in these parts that I'm aware of, but plenty of other dangerous critters."

"Right, with all the rabid carnivores we'll encounter on our hike in broad daylight." She rolled her eyes.

"When the huckleberries ripen late like they did this year, we could run into a black bear or two. Why take the risk?"

Chance grabbed a bag from Jericho's grasp. "But they're scratchy."

Jericho tweaked Chance's nose. "Then you, my boy, should have worn longer socks."

Ali took the bundle out of Chance's hands. "I still think you should have let me pack more food."

Jericho's eyes widened. "Are you kidding? Why lug a bunch of weight when the streams are bursting with rainbow trout?"

"I don't know how to fish." Chance latched on to Jericho's hand with his cast-free one.

He patted her son's head before adjusting his pack. "That's because I know your mom is secretly afraid of fish. She won't even swim in a lake because she thinks they might bite her."

Chance giggled.

"You know I can hear you, right?" Ali pushed back her hair, a line of perspiration already dribbling down her back.

Jericho winked at her over his shoulder. "You just stick by me, Chance. I spent most of my weekends growing up in these mountains."

She kicked a small rock on the path, and it rocketed into the field. "It wasn't that they would bite me. I don't like when they get too friendly and rub their slimy fish bodies against me."

"And how many times have you had that happen to you?" At least he had the decency to hide his wicked smirk behind his hand.

"Lake Como. You were there. Once was enough."

The tall grasses surrounding the entrance to the path popped with the color of wildflowers. The buzz of bees filled the air. Following Chance's excited but inexperienced pace, they completed the short stint through the densely packed forest on the trail. The damage from the great fire, more than ten years ago, still showed dominance with charred trees, many felled, poking out through the glasslike surface of Blodgett Creek. She remembered the terror of the days the fire ripped across the Bitterroot Range, flames licking the night sky and making national news. Such destruction, and it still had a deep hold on this land. Yet new growth flourished, green sprouting out among the ashes.

The resilience of the mountains made her wonder if she too could rise through the ruins, or if that kind of rebirth remained reserved for nature alone.

Her eyes trailed over to Jericho. Did he remember she used to think the jeans and crisp, white T-shirt he donned was the most attractive outfit any man could wear? With two days' worth of soft cocoa-colored stubble on his jaw, he *knew* that drove her crazy in a good way. *Aggravating man.*

Midway through the climb, as the creek narrowed, the trail became talus with large, loose, shaky rocks.

Ali wobbled on a ledge. "This is getting steep quicker than I remember."

Jericho reached out to steady her, taking her hand to guide her over a treacherous lean of boulders. "Want me to carry your pack for you?"

She shook her head.

Chance puffed beside them, hands on his knees. His face flushed. "You can carry my stuff."

Jericho patted his head. "Naw, you're strong. If I remember right, there's a waterfall just up the bend here that we can rest by."

Chance pouted. "I don't think I like hiking anymore."

Jericho laughed. "Here. I'll take your bag, but then I need you to keep an eye out for any little sticks you see because we'll have to find some kindling along the way. Does that sound fair?"

Chance's shoulders slumped. "How big do the sticks have to be?"

Jericho held his thumb and pointer finger a couple inches apart. "Just like this. Not big at all. We won't have a fire for dinner tonight without kindling. See, it's sometimes the really small stuff that's the most important."

Chance jabbed a finger into his own chest. "Like me? I'm small."

Jericho squeezed his shoulders. "Like you. You're really important to both of us. We wouldn't be camping if you hadn't wanted to go, right?"

Chance looked up for a moment, shielding his eyes with his casted arm. "Okay. So how long until the waterfall?"

"Five, maybe ten more minutes." Jericho shrugged.

When Chance bounded ahead, Jericho tried to stand, but stumbled a little. He winced. Ali caught his arm. He used her as leverage to get to his feet.

"Is your leg hurt?"

He smiled. "No more than usual."

They trudged side by side until a cool mist settled on Ali's hair. "Wait. There really is a waterfall?"

"'Course. Why would I lie to him?"

"I don't know. To get him off your back. To stop him from asking questions. People give kids false promises all the time."

"Not me."

Chance jogged back. "Hey, Mom. There's a stream. Can I go in the stream?"

"Let's make sure your bells are tight." Jericho leaned over and adjusted his bells, which proved a difficult task with Chance wiggling so much. When the boy's bells were secure, Jericho turned and grabbed Ali's foot. "Let's make sure your string's on good, too."

She set her foot on his thigh while he adjusted her bells. "Wow, thanks. Sure wouldn't want those beauties to go anywhere."

He stood. He shook his head at her, but the crinkles around his eyes betrayed that he fought a smile. "While we're at it, my little sass-mouth, let's make sure everyone drinks a lot of water when we're resting."

As the afternoon sun baked the backs of their necks, the troop struggled up the long, steep pitch. Jericho continued to encourage them along and asked often if Ali or Chance needed anything. When the sun began its plunge into the western sky, Jericho deemed a small piece of land where the rock met the forest the ideal spot for camping.

"Watch those cliffs for mountain lions, okay, buddy? That's your job right now."

"And if I see one, jingle my bells, right?" With his back to Jericho, Chance kept his gaze on the granite cliffs.

Pulling the three-man tent from her bag, Ali hid her grin. The probability of a lion waltzing around on the craggy canyon walls before nightfall rivaled that of an African elephant plodding up to their campsite and asking for a cup of tea. After dusk could be a different story, but then a roaring fire in the rock pit that Jericho constructed would keep animals away.

Jericho took the tent from her and limped over to the small clearing. As he pulled out the wrapped canvas, his brows drew together. "This thing's as thin as a fly's wing."

"It's ancient. That's Dad's old tent. I had to dig around in the maintenance barn to find it."

"Where's the ground sheet?"

She set aside the frying pan and mugs. "I didn't bring one."

"I don't see a rain tarp in here, either."

"It's pretty sunny."

He stood. His mouth pulled into a grim line as he rubbed his forehead. "You didn't bring one? The weather changes here every ten minutes. C'mon, Ali."

His tone propelled her to her feet. "*You* said pack light!"

Hands tossed in the air, he rolled his eyes. "That doesn't mean don't bring essentials. What are we going to do if those clouds let loose? There isn't shelter for miles." He thrust a hand toward the ominous sky cover rolling across the mountains.

Ali gulped. "It'll miss us." Feigning nonchalance, she resumed unpacking her bag.

"Sure hope so, or else we're all gonna get a good soaking."

"Oh, drop it already and put up the tent. Or put it aside and I'll take care of it."

Leaving his mountain lion patrol post, Chance joined them, with a pink bitterroot flower that looked a little like a water lily cupped in his hand. "You two sound just like Mark's parents."

Heat spread up her neck. Ali pretended not to hear.

"That blush looks good on you, Ali." The tease thickened Jericho's voice. He went about setting up the small tent, a task that took him a total of six minutes. Chance offered unneeded instruction, but said he couldn't help because of his cast.

"You know the story behind that flower you're holding?" Jericho asked Chance.

"Yes. The mountains are named because there are lots of these."

"Well, there's more to it than that. Why don't you ask your mom to tell you the story? Then you and I can go catch some dinner."

"Mom? Do you know why this is called a bitterroot?" Chance crossed their makeshift campsite and plunked the flower into her hands.

Ali cradled the deep pink petals against her palm. They were too beautiful for such a terrible name.

"If I remember right, they were called something else, but then when Lewis and Clark came to explore this area, the Shoshone Indians cooked up some of the roots and Lewis and Clark spit it out, saying the food tasted bitter to eat."

Jericho joined them and spoke in a low voice. "To the Shoshone Tribe, the bitterroot flowers were a delicacy. They were honoring Lewis and Clark by feeding them the root, but the explorers didn't understand. The Sho-

shones valued the flowers because they were a source of nourishment, but the same exact thing made Lewis and Clark gag. Kind of interesting how people can experience the same thing and yet view the outcome so differently."

As the sun dipped below the horizon, they spent the waning hours around the fire. The smell of cooked fish permeated the air as Jericho told stories that had Chance giggling until bedtime.

The evening air, spiced with the sweet hint of paintbrush flowers and blue beardtongue, drifted over where Jericho lay. The trace of a fresh rain smell worried him. He bunched an arm under his head like a pillow. A night spent on the hard-packed ground would cause him pain tomorrow, but Ali wouldn't welcome him in the tent. When the first couple drops of rain hit his face, he didn't have much of a choice.

Crawling, he bit back a howl as his left knee wrenched the wrong way. The hike up proved more difficult than he'd realized. Jericho sighed. What else in his life would he have to eventually give up because of his injury?

The zipper on the tent stuck, and he had to play with it a moment before scooting inside. He fumbled in the absence of starlight, but a quick perusal showed Ali lying on the left side with Chance in the middle. Jericho shuffled to the boy's other side.

*"What are you doing?"* Ali's voice came out as a demanding whisper.

"It's raining outside."

Ali took a loud, deep breath. She rolled onto her other side, her nose probably touching the tent wall.

Jericho gently moved Chance over a bit, then edged into the foot of space along the canvas wall. The light pitter-patter of rain sprinkled against the sides.

Ali's hushed voice jolted his eyes open a moment later. "'Fess up."

"Come again?"

"What's wrong with your legs? You've been limping like a cowboy straight off a cattle drive all day. Tell me straight, or sleep outside."

Licking his lips, he considered a lie. But at some point she would have to know the truth, and a lie now would only make things worse. "I got hurt while stationed overseas." It was easier confessing it quietly into the darkness of the tent than having to look at her.

"Got hurt?" Her voice went up a notch.

"I was on a mission, and we heard someone calling for help in a building. So I went in with some of the guys from the unit. As we searched the third level, a suicide bomber ran into the ground level."

"Oh, no."

"We had seconds before the place exploded. It happened so quickly. I lit for one of the windows and jumped to the ground. Landed on my feet and ran to safety. Shouldn't have been able to do it. Guess it was the adrenaline and all. We lost the rest of the guys in the blast." He paused, choking back the emotions that surfaced every time he thought about his dead friends.

Silence hung between them.

"But you…you weren't hurt?" Her voice cracked.

"God only knows how I got back to base. I reported what happened. But then the pain hit me, made me double over. I collapsed and woke up the next day in a dusty army hospital, both of my knees swollen to the size of basketballs."

"Broken?"

"No, just ruined for good."

"What exactly does that mean? For good?"

He shrugged. "Means I'm not what I once was. I'll have to have knee replacements on both legs before long. And even after that, my legs will never be what they once were."

"Then you're not *ever* going back?"

"No. My army career ended that day, and as I realized that while lying in the hospital bed, I almost gave up. They thought they'd lose me to pure dehydration and depression because I wouldn't touch anything. I nearly died during recovery. But the one thing that kept me going—the single thought that gave me any hope—was you."

The pitter-patter of rain became a rattling, full-out bucket-toss against the tent.

He exhaled. "I had all this time to think over everything that had happened between us. I just wanted to come home and be with you. Each night I dreamed, picturing you running to me when you saw me for the first time. Wishful thinking." He chuckled.

She snorted. "Instead I ran away from you. Sorry about that."

"You gave an honest reaction. I see now, more than ever, how much I deserved your censure. What kind of creep walks out on his wife?"

"Jericho—"

His voice hardened. "If you let me, I promise I'll spend the rest of my life making it up to you."

"I'm just sorry. Sorry you had to go through all that

to become the man you are now. I'm sorry I wasn't enough, as your wife, to help you through everything." Her voice caught, and in the closed-in area he could sense her shoulders shaking with tears. He reached out, draping his arm over Chance, who moved a bit. His little feet dug into Jericho's side. Jericho shifted, then ran his hand up and down Ali's exposed arm.

"Shhh. Don't say that, honey. You were everything I needed, and I was too blind and lost to know it. You were faithful and marched around my walls, trying to tear them down, trying to get inside to reach me. But just like my namesake, I was too stubborn. It took a lot of horrible things to make my walls crumble from the inside out. It was the only way."

"I forgive you." He barely heard her muffled words. Heart jackhammering against his chest, Jericho squeezed her arm, then left his hand lying on her shoulder as he fell asleep.

"Nooooo!"

A frightening wail woke him. Jericho bolted up, smacking his head against the low side of the tent and sending a rush of water through the canvas in the process.

"Mom-maa-aaa-aa!" Chance lurched as a crash of thunder shook the ground.

Jericho's skin prickled. He scooped up the boy and rocked him against his chest as Ali sat up, looking at Jericho with wide eyes.

"Hey, buddy, we're here." She pushed out of her sleeping bag and laid a hand on the child's arm.

Chance twisted away from Jericho, wrapping his arms around his mother's neck.

The cracks of lightning made it possible for Jericho to assess their damage. Water flooded the bottom of the tent, and the triangular top threatened to cave under the sag of water at any moment. The trees surrounding the area made their campground unsafe to ride out a storm. They couldn't stay here.

A rumble shook more rain onto them.

"We're going to die! I hate camping. We're all going to die!" Chance sobbed into Ali's neck as she ran her hands over his hair, trying to soothe him. Jericho felt helpless to deal with the howling boy, but he could go find them a safer location. He inched toward the door. Chance's small hand sprang out and stopped him.

"Don't go. Don't leave us here alone."

Jericho's heart poured out with love for him. Everything inside him wanted to go and take both his wife and her son in his arms. He wanted to form a shelter around them that nothing could break apart. Meeting Ali's eyes, his heart seized, because written there he found Chance's same plea: *Don't leave us.*

Crawling back to his loved ones, Jericho worked the watch off his wrist and pushed it into Chance's hands. "My dad gave me this watch, and my grandpa gave it to him. I'm giving it to you to hold for me. That's how you know I'm coming back. Okay, buddy? All I'm going to do is find somewhere safer for us and then come back for both of you."

Biting down on her lip, Ali nodded.

"But I dooooon't want you to goo-oo." Chance broke into a fresh torrent of tears. The tent drooped lower under the weight of gathering water.

"Chance. Hey, I need you to be extra brave for me.

Your mom needs a guy to protect her while I'm gone.
Can I trust you to do that?"

Sniffling, Chance gave one little nod. Jericho turned
to leave, then went back to Ali. He cupped the side of
her face, and she leaned into his hand. "I *will* come
back for you guys."

Sloshing out of the campsite, Jericho lost his balance and grabbed for a nearby tree. Missing it, he went
down hard into the gathering mud. As he rose, a ball of
pain scorched his knee. His muscles screamed at him to
crumble to the ground again, to weep against the ache.
But *they needed him*.

That thought pressed him forward through the tor-
rential downpour into the canyon.

The minute Jericho slipped out of the tent, doubts
assaulted Ali's mind and dared to yank away any hope
rooted by their earlier whispered conversation.

No more army. No more leaving.

As she leaned her chin on Chance's head, her husband's words danced through her mind. *I just wanted to
come home. The single thought that gave me any hope
was you. If you let me, I promise I'll spend the rest of
my life making it up to you.*

Her poor Jericho. All he had been through in the
past eight years wrenched at her heart. The same experience might have produced an angry and bitter man
in someone else. Instead he had grown compassionate,
patient and confident.

And he had *nearly died*. That halted her thoughts. In
all the years of his absence, the fact that he could die
never really occurred to her. Goose bumps rose along
her arms—whether from the chill of the rain pouring

into the tent, from Chance's quiet sobs, or from the thought of losing Jericho, she couldn't be certain. She did know that she never wanted to feel this way again. Raw from eight years of bitterness. Could offering forgiveness really heal her, too?

*Pop. Pop. Pop.*

The top of the tent began to shudder, ripping from aged seam to aged seam under the weight of the water pooling at the top. Chance screamed as a trough full of rainwater gushed down, drenching them. Shivering in the huddle of torn canvas, Ali peeked at the storm. The violence of the striking lightning shook the small cliff face they camped on. She prayed the forest wasn't dry enough to ignite like it had ten years ago. A powerful wash of rain sent their pots and pans crashing and clanging over the edge of the mountain. A scream lodged in her throat, Ali yanked Chance out of the way.

She worked her lip and brushed the damp hair from her face as she cradled Chance tighter against her. Should they get up and leave? Seek shelter on their own? Something might have happened to Jericho. He had bad knees, after all. Ali shouldn't have let him go out onto the slippery mountainside.

"Chance! Ali!" The man's voice boomed through the forest. His call thawed out her nerves, and with shaking legs she pulled Chance to his feet.

"Over here, Jericho!" she hollered.

Lightning sliced the night sky, illuminating the outline of Ali's protector, his white T-shirt clinging to ready muscles. He slogged toward them, and she could tell from the set of his brow what all the climbing today cost him.

"You came back." She breathed as he drew near.

"Always, Ali." He crouched down, scooping Chance into his arms. "Follow me." He pressed his lips close to her ear so she could hear him over the howling wind. "I found a place that'll keep us safe."

## Chapter Eighteen

The rush of rainwater formed a thick rut along the mountain path as Ali ducked her head, trying to follow Jericho's steps while he carried Chance. Wind whipped over her, threatening to toss her off the cliff's edge. Rain plastered her hair and stole her sight. Blinking, she slipped, her legs splaying out at awkward angles in the mud as a shriek caught in her throat. Tumbling forward, her foot caught, and she slammed down onto her chin. A warm metallic taste registered on her lips. *Blood.* Pressing up onto her knees, she wiped her mouth and bit back tears. She couldn't see them anymore. Gone.

"Hey. There you are." Jericho appeared through the tree line, Chance clinging to him like a burr. "You hurt?"

She shook her head. "I'll live."

He bent and offered his hand. Knees wobbling, she rose. He laced his fingers through hers and led them to a natural stone staircase. They splattered up and tripped on the slicked rocks a time or two before reaching the top of the climb. The scent of decaying leaves and wet moss clung to her nostrils.

"Almost there," he said.

Jericho hesitated, but when a flash of lightning lit the sky, he jerked to the left and tugged Ali along. Traversing over a mound of jumbled rocks, he motioned to a small chasm in the mountain wall. Not quite deep enough to be called a cave, an overhang blocked the small area from the worst of the storm's wrath.

Stooping, he shuffled into the den and dropped down. "We're safe now, bud."

"I want my bed. I hate camping." Chance stomped his little foot.

"It's not so bad. You'll have an adventure to tell Kate and Megan about, won't you?"

Chance stuck out his bottom lip. "I'm not ever doing this again."

"Come here, Chance." Her son needed no more invitation to climb into Jericho's lap.

Scooting onto the dry earth, Ali leaned her head against the rock wall. They were closed in tight. Leaving a foot of space between herself and the boys meant half her body still got a sprinkling of rain from the unprotected opening.

Jericho lifted his arm, making room for her. "Come here. I promise I won't bite."

Running a hand over her drenched hair, she gave him a wary look then slid over a fraction of an inch. He leaned over, hooked her by the waist and pulled her against his side. She shouldn't be this near to him. His presence, even waterlogged and cold, had the power to throw her off course. But did that even matter anymore? Not tonight. Not when it felt like they were a hundred miles from another person. Not with her family tucked tightly together. For the first time since Denny's death, warmth spread through her body, almost alleviating the ache inside.

Chance motioned to her. "Come closer, Mom."

Kate's words replayed in her head. *Your family wants you. Why would you say no to that?*

Pressing herself along Jericho's side, she reached out to her son. Chance looped his arms around her neck and pressed his downy cheeks against her neck. The bottom half of his body draped across Jericho.

"I love you, Mom," he whispered.

Words caught in her throat. "You too, Chance."

"And you, Jericho," Chance mumbled against her hair.

Jericho tightened the hold he had on Ali's shoulder, his heart doing a double-time march.

He wound his free arm over Chance's legs and swallowed against the gritty lump in his throat. "Hey, love you too, bud."

As the child's breathing evened, Jericho shifted to look at Ali. His stomach catapulted into his throat. Turned to the side, her face was only inches from his. It would take a mere second to lean forward and brush his lips against hers, to test her response. But Ali's eyes searched his with such intensity that he looked away. He could tell by the tilt of her head that she considered telling him the truth.

*He's my son. Isn't he?* The words almost reached his lips, but he reined them in. He could never be satisfied without his wife and her son in his life. His insides seared like hot metal. He wanted it all. But he'd forfeited all those privileges eight years ago.

He didn't even know what to do when the child cried.

Weeks ago, Ali had been right to say that Chance had only one parent, her. Jericho sure didn't know how to take care of Chance. It wasn't like he had had a stellar example of a father.

*But I am.* The words from his memory flooded his heart.

Jericho squinted out into the storm. *God?* The voice sounded so real. So he silently prayed, asking God to protect his family as they rode out the storm, and that their return hike tomorrow would prove uneventful.

"Tripp wants to marry me."

Her words jarred him worse than a slap upside the head. He swung around, trying not to disturb Chance. "What?"

She brushed the hair from Chance's forehead.

His lips tightened. "You can't. We're married. You can't." Not his most convincing or eloquent argument, but it's all he had.

Leaning the side of her head on Chance's, she locked gazes with Jericho. "I don't know anymore. I don't know anything."

"Are you in love with him?" He hated his sudden shortness of breath.

Lifting her head, Ali offered a tight-lipped smile. "He's been very good to us."

"But—"

"He's handled all the stuff with the lawsuit. Then, even though it's not in his realm of practice, he found answers to all my other questions about setting up Big Sky Dreams, and he found someone at the firm he works at to go over all the paperwork when Ma got admitted to the home. Then when your dad had his stroke,

Tripp seemed just as upset about it as anyone, and he came to tell me first."

"That doesn't make any sense. He's always hated me and Pop." Jericho tried to keep the growl out of his voice.

"Maybe hate's not the right word." She looked up and to the left, one eye squinting a bit in thought. "Jealous? That fits better. I think, for some reason, he was always jealous of you. I mean, look at it. From the outside, all he knew was that you grew up the son of a rich rancher, while he had a single mom who struggled to make ends meet. Maybe, I don't know, maybe that's why I have a soft spot for him—the single-mom part."

Jericho didn't like talking about soft spots in her heart, not if they had anything to do with Tripp Phillips. "No. I think it's just that he's always been smitten with you and now he thinks he has his chance to move in for the kill."

She looked out at the steady cascade of water flowing down the rocks.

He jerked his bum knee to the side. "I don't want you around him. He's dangerous."

She turned, and her eyes flashed. "I'm grateful to you for watching over us these last few weeks. But you can't tell me who I can and can't spend time with."

He gritted his teeth together. Technically, he could do exactly that. "I think he's behind the stuff that's going on at the ranch."

Ali shook her head. "No. You're wrong. It was Rider. I fired him. Nothing's happened since."

"Nothing's happened in two days. So that means you're in the clear?" He cocked an eyebrow.

"Maybe."

"Let me tell you what I think. Tripp Phillips has always been sweet on you, and none of this started happening until I came back in town. If Rider Longley had some vendetta against you, don't you think he would've done something about it sooner?"

Her brow formed a V. The patter of rain began to lessen, signaling the end of the storm.

"Connect the dots. We know for sure that Tripp saw us together at the picnic. You said that he has access to your organization, so that explains the missing money. He knew you'd be at the nursing home the day your tires were slashed. And he's the only person I know with the kind of pull to get his hands on medicine that would down a horse—"

She covered her ears. "Stop!"

"I'm just stating the facts."

Ali blinked a couple times. "Why does everything have to change all the time? Why can't people be as they seem? I hate it."

He adjusted his position, pulling Ali tighter against him. "Not all change has to be bad."

Her head drooped against his shoulder and she shifted, snuggling into him. "It sure feels that way lately—only bad changes. It's all I've known these last few months. With Ma, and Kate, and you, and Tripp and Den."

Jericho rested his chin on her head. "The stuff that matters doesn't change."

"Like what?" Her breathing began to ease.

"Like God. He's always constant. And Kate might leave, but it won't change the fact that she's your sister and she loves you. One day, when Chance grows up, he'll want to move out of the house, but it won't change the fact that he'll always be your son and he'll always love you."

Jericho stopped and glanced down at her face. Eyes closed, her long lashes splayed out against her sun-kissed cheeks. In sleep, she nuzzled against his chest.

He whispered with the side of his face resting on her head. "And nothing in this world can change the fact that I love you, Ali. I've loved you since we were kids, and I always will. You can tell me to get lost, and I will, but it won't change my love."

Ali cuddled closer to the warmth of the body next to hers. And for a moment she imagined herself home, in her own bed. But the protecting sensation of arms encircling her and the jabs of rocks at her back suddenly brought back last night's escapade.

The golden fire of sunrise crept its way along the granite cliffs when Ali stirred. At some point during the night, they'd slumped down. Jericho lay on his back, and Ali curled like a happy cat beside him. Chance, who'd always been an active sleeper, ended up in the shallow end of the crevice, his head on Jericho's thigh.

Scooching out from under her husband's arm, she tried not to wake him. On her knees, she looked down at the two males, and a smile tugged at her lips. They looked one and the same—mouths open slightly, hair rumpled, soft expressions on their faces.

Pushing out from under the overhang, she tiptoed down the jumble of rocks and the natural stone stairway. A damp mossy smell flavored the morning air, and from her position, she could see the lake below glittering like a sea of diamonds in the first flood of sunlight.

Their late-night conversation came back to her, and

she had to admit that Jericho might be right. Change didn't have to be negative. Each morning ushered in newness, whether the world wanted it or not.

*Nothing in this world can change the fact that I love you, Ali.*

If only. But the words had been dreamed. Jericho hadn't spoken them. What would she say to that, anyway?

Wandering across the open plane, she chose the path back into the woods. She stopped near their campsite, and her worst fears were confirmed. The tent and most of their belongings had become waterlogged, and a rainfed river had washed it all into the ravine more than fifty feet below. Good thing they got out while they did, or that could have been them down there. Chance's hatred for camping suddenly sounded entirely rational.

Not ready to return to her sleeping guys, she brushed aside a branch and squished in the mud on a path leading deeper into the woods. The fresh scent of pine engulfed her.

Jericho said God didn't change. But that unsettled her. Because if God didn't change, that meant Ali had been wrong in her anger these past eight years. She'd always pictured God getting upset with her, saying *Enough!* and walking away. And she wouldn't blame Him, either. She'd railed against Him. Spit her rage in His face.

She gasped. "*I* changed. Not you. I walked away."

Ali swiped at the tears on her cheeks. Did God hurt as much when she turned and walked away from Him as she had when Jericho left? And yet, He waited with open arms. She felt it. Flipping the image, realizing that she was the one who had left, not God, changed everything in her mind. Her knees felt weak. "I'm so sorry. Forgive me. Please forgive me," she whispered.

When she opened her eyes, her breath caught. Not twenty feet away, a mama moose and her calf grazed on the damp forest grass. They seemed to glide on their stiltlike legs, nosing the ground for tree roots. The sunlight dappled through the canopy, lending a glossy sheen to their black coffee-tinted coats. The cow could charge at her if the mama sensed any threat to her calf, so Ali tried not to move.

But at the sound of a guttural growl, she spun on her heels. Ali found herself face-to-face with a mountain lion crouching on a rocky ledge. In a millisecond she saw that the size of his paw matched the size of her head, and his teeth looked longer than her fingers. Fierce yellow eyes surveyed her, and his muscles coiled beneath a shimmer of golden hair.

Her blood ran cold. *I'm going to die.*

# Chapter Nineteen

A chill against his back, Jericho stretched. The pressure of Chance's head resting against his leg made Jericho's lips pull into a smile. His hip burned from digging against the rocks all night, but it seemed like a small price to pay for snuggling with Ali and her son. He groped to the right, his fingers fumbling across rocks. His eyes jolted open.

No Ali.

He sat up, easing a backpack under Chance's head. Jericho crawled to the edge and peered down the path, but found no sign of her. He turned back to her son, and with a growl picked up the bells that should have been tied around her ankle.

He shook Chance's shoulder.

The boy rubbed his mouth. "Whaa?"

"Up, Chance. I need you to wake up and help me."

Chance sat up, blinking his eyes. His brows drew together.

Jericho turned to the side and withdrew the gun from his pocket. He jiggled it, hoping the rain last night hadn't caused any damage. He put it back, then thrust a string of bells into Chance's hands. "Here's the deal. Your ma went for a walk and isn't back yet, so I'm going to go try and find her. I need you to stay here and count to one hundred, then rattle these. Keep doing that until I get back. Okay?"

On his knees, Chance scooted so he could lean against the back wall of the cave.

Jericho squatted beneath the rock overhang. "Now what are you supposed to do?"

Chance yawned. "Count to one hundred, shake this." He jiggled the strand of bells. "Then repeat."

"Good boy. I won't be gone long."

"Why can't I come?"

"What if she comes back while I'm gone? You don't want her to be sad, thinking we left without her, do you?"

Chance shook his head.

"Right. So your job is even more important than mine." He squeezed the boy's ankle and gave a wink as he scrunched backward out of the small cave.

Chance cocked his head. "Are you going hunting while you're gone?"

Jericho raised an eyebrow.

"You have a gun in your pocket. I saw you look at it when you thought I was sleeping."

"Good eyes." He didn't answer the boy's question. No use making him even more scared about his mom. "Start counting."

"One…two…three…do I really hafta?"

"One hundred." Jericho hollered over his shoulder, and Chance resumed his count.

He gritted his teeth. Knee burning with hot fire, Jericho limped down the stone staircase, praying his leg wouldn't give out altogether and send him tumbling over the edge.

What was she thinking? Any person with half a mind who lived by the mountains knew that a stroll at dawn meant borrowing trouble. Dawn and dusk were the most active hunting times for the predators here.

He picked up his pace.

Ali was the most incredible woman ever created. Strong and independent, but willing to accept help, she let a man feel like she needed him. Beautiful, even when drenched to the bone. Laughing and open often, but guarded when necessary. He didn't understand what was happening between them, but the last few days felt different. Ali seemed to trust him more. Confusion reigned sovereign in the stampede of emotions, but he'd take whatever she wanted to offer.

Nothing remained of the original campsite. The tent and all the belongings they'd left last night had tumbled down the side of the cliff. His stomach lurched. That could have been them down there at the bottom of the ravine. A prickle ran up his neck. Where could she be? He inched toward the edge of the cliff. She wouldn't try to free-climb to their stuff, would she? Nothing down there was worth risking her neck for.

A throaty cat cry ripped the still air.

*Ali? Please, God, no!*

With strength born out of terror, he sprinted toward the source of the sound, yanking the small revolver from his pants pocket as he ran. He swung around a tree, and the sight before him made his blood freeze. Not three feet from Ali, at eye level, a male mountain lion crouched. The animal spit hate in her direction. One swipe of his paw, and she'd be gone.

Aiming the gun into the air, Jericho pulled the trigger, and the crack of the shot resounded against the cliff face. Flinching, the lion dropped back, leaped on a higher rock and scampered away. On the other side of the small clearing, a moose cow and calf took off in a wild charge.

Weak with relief, he dropped the hand holding the gun to his side. On legs wiggly as rubber, he crossed to where Ali stayed rooted, mouth open.

The moment he was at her side, she came unglued. Ali bolted into his arms with a force that almost knocked him over. She burrowed her face into his chest. "He was going to kill me."

Jericho rested his chin on her head, breathing in her sunshine smell. He let his fingers go to the tips of her hair. "Shhh. You're fine. You just got in the way of his breakfast is all."

She trembled. "Th-they don't usually go for moose."

"He looked young. Probably still learning. A pretty string of bells would have saved you."

Her hands came up, entwining around his waist as she laid her cheek right over his heart. "I thought he'd kill me. I kept thinking, what would happen to Chance…to you?"

Fear echoed within his racing heart. Every moment with this woman was a gift, and she needed to know it. Jericho licked his lips, relishing the feel of her body melding to his. "I love you. I don't know if you heard when I said it last night. But I love you, Ali. Always have, always will. You know that, right?"

Sniffling, she nodded against him. He placed a kiss on top of her head and left his hand cupped against it.

* * *

Despite the morning chill, Ali's entire body blazed. Jericho loved her.

Questions zinged through her mind. Should she say something? Did he only tell her that because she almost died?

As much as the words filled her with longing, they also terrified her. Her life with Chance was so routine. What if it bored Jericho after a time? What if he left again?

Thinking of her son brought her back to reality. A lion had almost ripped off her head. She trembled again. Who would care for Chance if something unexpected happened to her?

She sucked in a breath. "Chance is your son." Had she really just said that?

Jericho went rigid. "What?"

She pushed back from him. "He's yours."

Grabbing her shoulders, his mouth hung slack. "I thought… But… You're certain?"

Ali laughed at his shock. "Of course. You're the only man I've ever been with."

"Did you know? When I left?"

"That's why I stayed up that night. I wanted to tell you, but you came in and—"

He pulled her back into his arms, wetness gathering around his eyes. "I'm sorry. All these years, you were all alone. I'm so sorry, Ali."

She clung to him like a life preserver, needing his strength in that moment just as much as he seemed to need her. "Silly man. I forgave you already."

"He's my son."

"Didn't you already know? You two are mirror images of each other."

"I thought. I hoped." He let go of her, raking a hand over his matted hair. "But hearing it—this is wild." Jericho's hands shook. "What will he say? What if he doesn't want me?"

Joy bubbling up, Ali laughed. "Want you? You're his hero. He already loves you."

"But I'm just flesh and bones. I'll let him down someday. Then what? Maybe we shouldn't tell him. What do I know about being a father?" He paced away, hands in his pockets.

"Jericho. Look at me."

He obeyed.

"You're already the best father he's ever known. Hear me? You're amazing with him. There's nothing to worry about."

They agreed to wait and tell Chance back at home, but the entire climb down the mountain, Ali caught Jericho staring at her. For the past month she'd been so worried about him finding out; now she wondered what took her so long. Ali snuck another glance at Jericho. Hope sung in her heart, but she silenced it quickly. Just because he loved her didn't mean he'd stay forever. He supposedly loved her last time, too.

Ali knocked on Kate's bedroom door.

"Come in."

She pushed inside, and Kate stopped toweling off her hair. "Look at this. Our fearless adventurer back from her travels."

Flopping down on her sister's bed, Ali groaned.

"On a scale of one to ten, the camping trip would rank around a two."

"You looked tuckered out when you got home yesterday. I think you set a sleeping record. Was it sixteen hours? Jericho's been here already to collect Chance. He said he had your permission."

Ali sat up quickly, her hand flying to her head. "I did the stupidest thing. Oh, Kate."

"I'm sure you've done stupider."

"No. Seriously. I told Jericho that Chance is his son. Why did I do that?"

"I'm proud of you, Al. You did the right thing."

Ali sprung to her feet. "He scared off the mountain lion, and then I thought about what would happen if I died and I just blurted it out."

"Mountain lion?" Kate met Ali's eyes in the mirror.

"What should I do? I told him he could take Chance for the day. Now it starts, this joint custody stuff Tripp warned me about. At least we live on properties that touch. That'll make everything easier."

"I think you're missing the obvious solution."

Ali jammed her hands onto her hips. "Being?"

"Take Jericho back. Live together. Be a family."

"No. I can't—I'm not ready for that. *He* still terrifies me." Ali hugged her middle.

"Does Chance know?"

She shook her head.

Kate stopped putting on foundation and faced her. "When are you planning on telling him?"

A half laugh, half sob escaped from her lips. "Today."

Her sister jumped up, crossed the room and hugged her. "This is huge."

"We're supposed to tell him tonight, together."

A truck, kicking up a cloud of dust, bumped up the driveway. Ali watched from the window as the delivery man jogged to the back and pulled out a package. Megan trotted from the barn and signed for the box. As the truck pulled away, Megan hurried toward the house. Ali left Kate's room, pounding down the stairs.

"Special delivery!" Megan waved the package.

Ali joined her in the kitchen. "Who's it for?"

"You, sleepyhead." Thrusting the package into her hands, Megan smiled. "Open it."

Pulling at the tape, she pried open the long box. When she peeled back the top, a heady perfume infused the air. She peeked inside and gasped at the colorful bouquet of roses.

She motioned to Megan. "Hold the box for me while I pull these out."

"Oh, they're stunning! Who are they from?" Megan buried her face into the flowers, breathing deeply.

Ali fished out the pink envelope and peeled it open. She read the card out loud. "'Missed you. Waiting for an answer. Tripp.'"

"Here. I'll put these in water for you." Megan grabbed a vase from on top of the fridge and began to fill it at the sink. She looked at Ali over her shoulder. "You know about the stud bull, right?"

Ali pulled a knife out of her pocket, cutting off an inch of the stems. "I know he's ornery as an old schoolteacher."

Megan handed her the vase. "Wait, no one told you?"

"Just say it, Megan." Dropping the flowers into the water, Ali gave them a fluff before placing them on the table.

"He's gone."

Ali cocked an eyebrow. "Define *gone*."

Megan tossed up her hands. "Vanished. Missing. Snatched."

She grabbed the back of a chair. "Did anyone see anything?"

"No. We searched his field. There are no openings in the fence. No sign of tampering."

"Someone can't abduct a two-thousand-pound beast without being seen. I've had enough. I'm calling the cops."

Megan caught her arm before she could get to the phone. "I don't know. Don't you still want to catch Rider in the act?"

"I think it's out of my hands. I thought when I fired him, it would stop."

"I don't like this any more than you do. But let me help you. I'll stick around later the next couple days and try to get some evidence on him. Then we'll have something tangible when we go to the cops. We want them to take us seriously, after all."

Ali rubbed her temples. "Two days. In two days, even if we find nothing, I'm calling the cops."

Chance gave Jericho a toothy grin as they bumped up the driveway.

"So I'm a real cowboy now?"

Jericho winked. "Certifiably."

"Can we tell Mom what I did?"

"Always." He threw the Jeep into Park, and Chance burst out the door and up the porch steps to his mother before Jericho could unbuckle his seat belt.

A smile pulled at his lips as Chance rushed over everything they'd done that day. The kid had his mom by both hands, giving little jerks when something in the story really excited him. When Jericho joined them, Ali looked up and mouthed "thank you."

She propped her hip against the porch railing. "Slow down, sweetheart. You sat on calves? No wonder you look like you haven't bathed in a week."

"Yeah. The ranch hands caught them. Then I'd have to sit on them and hold them real still because Jericho took a knife and castled them—"

"Castrated," Jericho offered.

Chance made a face, and Jericho lifted his hands in surrender.

"The calves didn't like it."

Ali smirked. "I'd imagine not."

"But, Mom, you can ask Jericho. I am very strong. He said I had to be to hold the calves down. And I thought they'd hurt me, but I was too tough for them."

Her eyes meandered over Jericho. "That so?"

He squeezed Chance's shoulder. "He turned green for the first fifteen minutes or so, but he held it together. Took a second to find his cowboy grit is all."

"I have it, Mom. Jericho said in spades, which sounds like a lot."

Ali caressed Chance's face. "Sure does. It seems like you had a good time today. Are you starting to like ranching?"

"Yes! Jericho said he'll teach me all the cowboy things that I don't know. They don't use horses for stuff on his ranch. He said I have to go on the dirt bike and ATV before then so I can help. Right?" Chance looked up at him, and Jericho fought wetness in his eyes. His son.

Jericho cleared his throat. "Yep. You'll have to ride

with me until you're older, but I'll need you trained by the time I have to sort the herd in the fall."

"Cool. I like spending time with you."

His eyes skittered to Ali's, and she nodded. "Hey, Chance, Jericho and I need to talk to you. It's something very serious, okay?"

Chance spun, grabbing him by the hand. "I'm sorry. I didn't mean to do it."

Mind reeling, Jericho hunched over. "Do what, bud?"

"I broke a tool at your barn today. I pretended to be a knight and used it like a sword, but it got stuck in the tree bark and bent, then I put it back and didn't tell anyone." His small chest heaved.

Dropping into an Adirondack chair, Ali laughed.

Jericho chuckled, too. "I don't care about that. But c'mere." He pulled Chance onto his lap. "Don't ever be afraid to tell me something like that. You can talk to me about anything."

"Okay. Then what do you wanna talk about, 'cause I didn't do anything else wrong today."

Ali took a deep breath, then leaned over and took her son's hand. "Do you remember when you asked about your father?"

Chance nodded. "You said he left because he didn't like you."

*Because he didn't like you?* Jericho bit down hard on the back of his teeth. Nonsense. He wanted to root that lie right out, but the blush blooming on Ali's cheeks made him hold his tongue. He'd wait till they were alone.

"Yes. But you still want to know who he is, right?"

Chance licked his lips. "Yes. Because even if he

doesn't like you, he might like me. Right? Do you think he'll want me?"

Jericho tightened his hold on the boy. "I know so."

"Sweetheart. Jericho is your father."

Chance stiffened in his arms. Jericho's mind whirled. Then his son's little shoulders started to shake, and Chance covered his face.

Jericho stared at Ali, who met his look with wide eyes. "Chance, hey, baby, what's wrong?" She ran her hand over the child's head.

Sucking in his bottom lip, Chance faced Jericho. "You're my dad?"

"Are you disappointed?"

His son sniffled. "No. You're my favorite person in the whole world." He flung his arms around Jericho's neck, choking him.

But Jericho reveled in it, bear-hugging his son back. "I love you, Chance."

"Can I call you Dad?" Chance whispered against his neck.

Jericho swallowed down a lump the size of the Bitterroot Range. "I'd like that a lot."

Ali's eyes swam with tears. She pressed her hand over her mouth as she watched them.

His son pulled back. "Are you going to live here? With us?"

"Well, I'm staying on your couch until we're sure you guys are safe here."

"But you don't want to stay with us forever? Is it because you still don't like Mom?"

Jericho's heart squeezed. He wanted to reassure Ali so badly. He set Chance back so they could make eye contact. "I love your mom."

Springing to the ground, Chance gave a loud whoop. "This is the best day of my life. So you'll live with us and we can be a real family?"

"I'd like that. I'd like that a lot. But that's between your mom and me."

After sending Chance up to take a bath, Ali moved to leave, but Jericho caught her hand. "Sit out here. Watch the stars with me."

He pulled her down onto his lap. He smelled like hard work and country air. He smelled like home.

She tucked her head against his neck. "I think that went well."

Jericho ran his fingers into her hair. "Yep."

A calf in a yonder field bayed as they sat there holding each other. With her eyes closed, Ali listened to the steady thump-thump of Jericho's heart. Her stress was lost in the dependable rhythm.

Tracing his fingers up and down her arm, he broke the silence. "What do you think about what Chance said? About being a family?"

She pushed away from him and stood to grab the railing. Then she looked out across the mountains. "I'm not ready for anything like that. I can't—"

Jericho came beside her, his shoulder pressing against hers.

"I'm so afraid," she whispered.

"I won't hurt you again, Ali. I promise. I won't leave."

Swiping at her eyes, she turned away from him. But he caught her arm. "Hey, don't run off. We don't have to talk about that right now. I want to be by you is all. We can talk about something else. Anything. Tell me about your day. What did you do with Chance gone?"

Warmth spread through Ali as she stared into his soft eyes. He wanted to be by her. He cared about the mundane happenings in her life. He loved her.

"I had two riding classes. Went to the bank to clean out my mom's safe-deposit box—"

He snagged her hand. "Safe-deposit box?" Then he laughed. Scooping Ali against him, he spun in a circle. "You're a genius."

He set her down. He fished into his pocket and pulled out a small key. "Pop gave this to me when I first went to visit him. I've been carrying it around all this time wondering what it opened. Go figure. I never thought about a safe-deposit box."

"Do you have any idea what your dad would put in it?"

"No, but I'm going to find out tomorrow."

## Chapter Twenty

Ali blocked the sun from her eyes as a car maneuvered down the pothole-ridden driveway. She batted at a horsefly.

Chance scampered up beside her. "Is that Dad?"

Ali's heart fluttered. *Dad.* Chance found every opportunity to say the word.

"No, honey. That's Tripp's car."

"Aw, man."

Ali rested her hand on his head. "We like Tripp."

He shrugged. "He's all right."

Before Tripp could climb out of the car, Chance raced to his window and popped his head inside. "Hey, Tripp. Guess what?"

The man slid out of the car and smiled at Ali. "What, Chance?"

"I have a dad."

Tripp's smile disappeared, and his brows plunged. "That so? Well, we all have fathers, but some of us never get to have a relationship with them." He leaned down and tapped his chest. "I had a dad too, but I didn't get to know him or live with him, either. He never claimed me as his. But know what? I had other people in my life instead, like you do."

Chance scrunched up his face. "But I *have* one."

Tripp walked around Chance, briefcase in hand. "Hi, Alison. Hot day. Do you have a moment?"

Chance trailed after him. "My dad is Jericho Freed."

Tripp stopped. "Wh-wh-what did you say, son?"

"Jericho is my dad, and we wrestled down calves together. He took me camping and said I'll like it better next time. And he's living with us now." Chance started to spin.

Tripp's eyebrows arched. "That so, Alison?"

Ali closed her eyes. "He is not *living* here. He's just sleeping on the couch for the time being. Until we know all the threats have stopped."

"Stopped? But you fired Rider?" He raked a hand through his hair, then motioned for her to follow him to the porch. "Why didn't I know about all this?"

Megan stepped out of the barn to wave at them. Chance sprinted over to join her.

At the base of the steps, Ali laid a hand on his forearm. "We'll be okay. Don't worry."

When they reached the porch, he captured her wrist and tugged her into the house. "You told Jericho about Chance? They both know?"

"I couldn't lie anymore. It didn't feel right. Besides, Jericho's a great father. I was cheating Chance out of something special by not telling them." She pulled away from him and crossed to the sink. She started rinsing the plates from breakfast.

"How could you? You have no guarantee he isn't going to pick up and leave again. Now you have a child who's going to be damaged by that. Do you know what it's like to not have a father, then to find out who he is and have him not want you?" Tripp's voice caught, and he turned his back to Ali.

"Tripp?" She wiped her hands on her jeans. Stepping near him, she touched his shoulder.

He took a deep breath. "It'll devastate Chance when Jericho rejects him. He'll leave, and Chance will wonder his whole life what he did wrong to warrant his father's abandonment. And Jericho *will* leave. I can promise you."

"I'm tired of basing my decisions on fear. I had to tell him. What if something happens to me?"

Tripp thumped his chest. "You don't think I would take care of Chance? Didn't I tell you I'd adopt him? I'd be a father to him. But that wasn't good enough for you. *I* wasn't good enough for you, either."

"Oh, no. Tripp, no. It's not like that." She moved toward him, but he stepped back.

"Don't you realize? You've ruined everything. Everything."

With his lips pulled into a snarl, Ali didn't know how to soothe Tripp. Why was he so angry? They both knew he didn't love her. But then what would make him so upset?

"Good morning, Mr. Freed. Are you here about your business?" Miss Galveen, the loan officer, greeted him as he entered the bank.

"No. Everything is set there." Jericho looped his hand around his neck. "Actually, I'd like to look at a safety-deposit box, if I could."

The spikes on the heels she wore echoed against the marble floor. "Are you interested in getting a safe-deposit box, or do you already have one and need to check it?"

Fishing the key from his pocket, he held it out to her. "If this looks familiar, I need to see this box. If not, I need to figure out which bank uses these keys."

She hovered over his hand. "That's one of ours all right." A single eyebrow quirked. "But you didn't know you had a box? How remarkable, Mr. Freed."

"It's not mine. It's my pop's box, and he gave this to me. He wants me to open it."

"What's the number on there?"

"One thirty-nine."

Miss Galveen crossed her arms. The tight bun on top of her head made her look twenty years older than she was. "I'll have to see if you're authorized." Snatching the key from his hand, she disappeared behind the employee area of the bank.

Jericho rocked on the balls of his feet and resisted the urge to whistle while he waited for her to come back. He dropped down into a leather chair and adjusted his watch.

The click-clack of heels against the floor announced Miss Galveen's return. Using the arms of the chair, he heaved up his body to stand. Working with Chance on the ranch had made his knees numb.

"You may follow me, Mr. Freed. According to the paperwork, you're fully authorized to open this box. I'll take you there now."

He shadowed her across the hall, down a flight of stairs, through some twists and turns and onto the lower level. She pointed at the metal boxes sunken into the wall.

Jericho shuffled forward. "How does this work?"

"I need you to sign this paperwork." She thrust a clipboard and pen at him. "We'll unlock it together, then you may do whatever you want with the contents. When you're done, we'll lock the box together, as well."

After she left, Jericho held the metal container in trembling hands. What could Pop have in here? The latch creaked, and a single piece of paper rested inside. He unfolded it and started to read.

"'This is my Last Will and Testament. I, Abram Freed, being of sound mind and body, leave the entirety of my worldly possessions, my ranch and my wealth to the father of Chance Silver. This Will revokes all prior Wills and Codicils.'"

Jericho's hands shook, and his eyes darted down the page. According to the date, Pop had made the new will a year after Jericho left town. He licked his lips. But then that meant...

"He forgave me. All those years ago." His legs threatened to collapse. The area lacked a chair, so Jericho wobbled over to the wall and leaned against it. "I should have come home so much sooner."

Dropping his head, he squeezed the bridge of his nose. So many wasted years, while a family waited.

Smoothing out the paper, he scanned the information again. Not that he needed the money or cared about Pop's land. But the gesture of mercy rocked through him. How many times had he told his father he hated him? Hated the Bar F Ranch. But it would be his.

He rubbed his jaw. An emblem at the top drew his attention. *Mahoney and Strong.* That was the firm Tripp worked at. Ali told him that Tripp worked as an associate there.

But then that meant...? His mouth went dry.

Jericho charged up the steps and ran through the bank lobby while Miss Galveen called after him about locking the box. The heavy front doors smacked behind him as he yanked out his keys and roared his Jeep out onto the street.

Swinging into the driveway, his wheels spit gravel. He squinted, trying to identify the car near the house. Tripp's. His grip tightened on the steering wheel. He was surprised his teeth didn't bust at how hard he clenched them.

Throwing the Jeep into Park, he hopped out and charged toward the house.

Chance appeared, bouncing at his elbow. "Hi, Dad."

He stopped and dropped down to hug his son. "Hey there, buddy. Where's your ma at?"

The boy rolled his eyes. "Inside with Tripp. He's real angry."

Jericho bolted up. "I need to talk to him. Stay out here. Okay, Chance?" He shoved through the front door.

Tripp's voice carried from the kitchen. "Sign it, Alison. It's the only way to keep Chance safe."

"Safe?"

"Freed can't be trusted. Look at his past record. Your troubles didn't start until he got here. I hate even suggesting it, but have you thought that he might be the one causing problems around here?"

"He'd never—"

"He's always been a master at playing you, ever since we were kids. These occurrences have given him ample opportunities to gain your trust. He always seems to be around at precisely the right moment. You don't find that odd?"

Jericho hovered near the kitchen entrance, a tickle running down his spine. Would Ali defend him? Or had he shattered her trust?

Silence. His stomach dropped into the toes of his boots. Wishing he could see her face, he pressed his palm against the door.

Tripp cleared his throat. "Divorce is your only option. He has been nothing but heartache for you your entire life. Cut the dead weight. Choose a new start. Choose me."

*Enough.* Jericho burst into the kitchen. He bounded toward Tripp and ripped the papers out of his hands. "Like fire that's her only choice!" He whirled toward Ali, shaking the divorce papers in his hand. "Were you gonna sign? Be straight with me."

Her eyes widened. "What are you doing here?"

"Know why he wants you to sign these?" Jericho crumpled the legal documents. "He wants to marry you. And let me guess, he wants to adopt Chance after the wedding. Am I right?"

Tripp and Ali spoke at once.

"Don't answer him, Alison."

"Well, yes."

Jericho's lip pulled up. "'Course I'm right. Know why? Because Tripp here knows about my pop's will. Don't you, Tripp? Found yourself a bit of a loophole. Didn't tell Ali that little tidbit, did ya?"

Ali's gaze ping-ponged from Jericho to Tripp, back to Jericho. "Will someone just spit it out? I don't know what you're talking about."

"He's the one who's been manipulating you. You and Chance are as good as dollar signs in his eyes." Jericho tugged the will from his pocket and shoved it into

Ali's hands. She folded back the page, her eyes scanning the paper.

Tripp growled. "How'd you get your hands on that, Freed? That's not public knowledge until your dad's death. How'd you weasel it—did you break into the firm? I could have you arrested."

"My dad's smart enough to secure his own copy."

Ali shook her head. "I don't understand. Why would your dad…?"

Jericho took his wife's hand. "Don't you see? Pop figured Chance was mine. Plus Pop knew, before I even knew, that I'd come back. But Tripp just wanted my dad's money. He doesn't love you, Ali, not like I do."

Tripp made a lurch for the will, but Jericho jerked it away. "I wanted it because your dad's money is rightfully *mine*." His face reddened.

Rocking back, Jericho crossed his arms. "And how do you figure that?"

With a deep breath, Tripp clenched his fists. "Because, as the oldest, I'm the rightful heir. That's how these things work, and Abram just disregarded that, after everything."

Ali squeezed Jericho's arm. "Heir?"

Bracing his hands on the counter, Tripp looked Jericho in the eye. "Meet your older brother."

Jericho's mind spun like a carnival ride. Being plowed over by a charging heifer would have hurt less. "I don't have a brother."

Ali jammed her finger at Tripp. "So it was you all along. You killed Denny, didn't you? You stole money from Big Sky Dreams. You know what that means to me—to the children. How could you?"

Tripp's eyebrows dove. "Absolutely not! Freed's turning this all around. You can't trust him. How long has he had the will in his possession? How can you be certain he's not the one manipulating you? It seems like quite the coincidence. Funny, he came home when Abram is close to dying, and there is a will naming him sole heir if he wins you back. He simply has to get you to say Chance is his son. When something is that convenient in the courtroom, we call it what it is—guilty."

Jericho crossed his arms to hide his fisted hands before he struck the man. "I'm finding one problem with your logic. There's no motive. I don't need the money, and I could care less about that ranch."

A wicked gleam lit Tripp's eyes. "I heard that you *do* need money. Lots of it, actually. For a little business venture you're doing. Bet he hasn't told you a lick about that, has he, Alison? He told the people at the bank weeks ago he had *a lot of money coming to him.* Interpret that for me."

Ali gasped.

Jericho seized her arms. "Don't listen to him."

"Did you say that to someone at the bank?"

"I did. I have no clue how Tripp would know that. But—"

She yanked out of his grasp. "I want you both out. Now."

"Ali. Let me explain." Jericho took a step toward her.

She stopped him with her palm to his chest. "I don't want to hear it. Get off my property. I don't know who I can trust anymore."

Tripp rounded the counter, but Ali put a hand up to him, as well. "I'm serious. Both of you leave right this second, or I'm calling the cops. You're not welcome on my land."

\* \* \*

Jericho snatched the divorce papers from his passenger seat and ripped them until it looked like snow. Would she have signed? It rankled him that she could disregard the entire last month. Like it meant nothing that he'd told her he loved her.

But she'd never returned the words.

His muscles ached like after a hard run. He scratched his head.

*Meet your older brother.*

Tripp? Jericho did the math—they were what, three months apart in age? Tripp and Jericho had the same build, the same piercing blue eyes. Why hadn't he noticed before?

He stumbled out of the Jeep and into the nursing home. Swirls of over-musked perfume and cafeteria food rushed past as his boots clapped down the familiar hallway. He trudged into his father's room.

Jericho took a deep breath and dropped into the chair beside his dad's bed. "How you doing today, Pop?"

Pop's brow wrinkled halfway.

"Yep. I'm having that kind of day, too. I figured out the key you gave me."

His father pointed at the picture of Chance on his nightstand. Jericho scooped up the photo and ran his thumb over the glass. "You knew all along that I had a son. Why didn't you try to find me?"

Pop grabbed Jericho's knee and gave a gentle squeeze.

"I know. You can't tell me. But, Pop, I missed out on seven years. All the time, I had a family waiting."

He took off his hat, placing it on the end of the bed.

"I found out something today. I want to check it with you first."

Pop nodded.

The words stuck in his throat. Jericho licked his lips. "I'm just going to spit it out plain." He took a breath and worked his jaw. "Is Tripp Phillips your son?"

Pop bowed his head for a moment. "Yeth."

Lightning rattled through Jericho's chest. "But then, that means you cheated on Mom before she got pregnant with me?"

Pop rubbed his eyebrows. "Yeth."

"Why didn't I know? Why didn't you tell me? I should have *known* I had a brother."

"Ith. Ino. I dondt know."

Jericho closed his eyes. "No wonder Tripp always hated me."

Elbows on his knees, Jericho buried his head in his hands and blew out a long stream of air. Life had been perfect yesterday. How did it go all topsy-turvy in less than twenty-four hours? Feeling the touch of his father's hand on his head, he glanced up. Pop's eyes brimmed with tears, and Jericho's mouth went dry.

He took his dad's hand again. "Don't worry. I'm still here."

## Chapter Twenty-One

Ali ached like blood pooling behind a bruise.

She flipped on the faucet, letting cool water trickle to fill her hands. She splashed her cheeks then scrubbed her face on the hand towel, hoping to wash off the blotches and the empty look in her eyes. But a glance in the mirror sent her gripping for the counter.

Scanning her red-rimmed eyes, rumpled hair and drooping mouth, she sucked in a ragged breath. "Pull yourself together, girl."

But this time sapped her more than last. *He's gone.* She'd sent him packing with a threat of the police, and he hadn't loved her enough to stay and fight. *Like last time.* She failed. Failed as a wife when he most needed her to stand beside him, trust him. She knew with bone-deep certainty that Jericho Freed hadn't manipulated her and yet, in the split second that mattered, she'd doubted him.

Ali shoved the towel into her mouth, biting down a sob. Just because she prowled the house at two in the morning didn't mean the rest of the family needed to be woken up.

Would another eight years pass before she saw him again? He could be halfway to Mexico by now. Gone for good.

Without Denny, Ali didn't know what to do with the grief washing over her. If she could, she'd wander out to his stall and climb up on his back again. A twilight ride would have soothed her enough to sleep.

But without him, the pain dared to drown her.

As she tied her robe, a piece of paper taped to the mirror caught her eye. Kate. One of those three-by-five cards she loved to scribble on and stick all over the house.

Before, Ali had ignored them, but now she squinted to read it.

*Some trust in chariots and some in horses, but we trust in the name of the Lord our God.*

She snatched it off the mirror, clutching the verse to her chest. Trust in horses. Jericho had accused her of that. Of treating Denny like a savior.

"Oh, God. I'm so sorry. I'm not good at trusting You, or anybody for that matter. I messed up big by not trusting Jericho today. What's going on? I feel so lost. Is it supposed to hurt like this? I thought freedom would be safe. No more pain. Aren't You supposed to protect me?"

Stumbling out of the bathroom, she stopped to let her eyes adjust to the darkness. She crept downstairs.

Her mind meandered like a lost calf, and each thought cried for attention. Hadn't life been better before Jericho came back? At least then her emotions had been packed floor to ceiling with crates labeled Resent-

ment, Bitterness, Anger. It had been ordered. She had
known who she was and what drove her. But now, after
offering forgiveness—after yanking the weeds out of
the garden of the soil in her heart—an empty patch of
dirt remained.

On bare toes, she padded across the living room,
but she stopped to trail her hand across the back of the
empty couch. Jericho's couch. She swiped at her cheeks.

Flipping on the kitchen light, she grabbed the tea-
kettle and filled it with water. Mint tea. That would
help her sleep.

Ali smoothed aside her hair and slumped down into
a chair.

If only she could think of a way to regain the reins
of her life. She sighed. Even before, the control that had
been in her grasp had been based on lies. The boy who
ruined her life didn't exist anymore. No. Jericho oozed
regret. Every action proved him now to be a man of
compassion, humility and patience.

Chance needed his father. She couldn't separate
them.

She needed her husband.

Ali rubbed her palms against the cool laminate wood
on the table.

But the biggest lie had been her own. All these years,
she had viewed herself as strong and independent. *Lies.*
Ali ran a hand through her hair. She didn't want to be
alone. And not just anyone would do. She wanted Jericho Freed.

The kettle rattled with steam.

She poured some water into a mug and leaned her
hip against the counter, crossing her arms while the tea
steeped. Lurching forward, she spied another of Kate's

verse cards taped to the window above the sink. She
snatched it and smiled. Like a treasure hunt. What had
Jericho called them? Scripture bread crumbs.

"Bread crumbs to lead me home," she mumbled as
she shuffled back to the table with the mug and card.

*Bear with each other and forgive one another if
any of you has a grievance against someone. Forgive as the Lord forgave you. And over all these
virtues put on love, which binds them all together
in perfect unity.*

Perfect unity. She could use some of that.

Kate bumped into the door as she opened it, squinting. "What are you doing up at this hour?"

"Sorry. Did I wake you?"

Kate rubbed her eyes and yawned. "I heard the kettle whistle."

Ali squeezed her hand as Kate took a seat at the table.
She rubbed at her eyes and jutted her chin toward Ali's
mug. "Do you have any more? It smells good."

Scooting her mug across the table to Kate, Ali got
up to pour herself another.

Kate blew away the steam from her tea. "Why are
you up?"

"A lot on my mind. I couldn't sleep."

"Are you nervous something bad will happen without Jericho here?"

"No. What if I lost him, Kate?"

Kate slurped her tea. "Huh."

"I love him."

Her sister slapped the table. "Well hallelujah and call

it Friday! It's about time you admitted it, even if the rest of us have known for, oh, ten years."

"I think I was afraid. Because owning up to it makes things worse. I think I was safer pretending that I didn't care about him. For that matter, we can lump God in there, too. Depending on Him feels like waiting in a desert for rain."

"But when the rain comes to a desert, it floods with abundance."

"True."

"What are you so confused about, Al?"

She finished the last of her tea but still cupped the mug in her hands, letting the warmth radiate into her chilled nerves. "*Confused* isn't the right word. *Confronted* might be better, or *convicted*."

Kate raised her brows.

"It's your stupid note cards." Ali pushed the two she'd collected across the table. "It's like you planted them special for me tonight. There are little verse booby traps all over the house."

Kate looked over the cards and smirked.

"I've been so stubborn and foolish for *years*. Then I forgave Jericho and told him about Chance. I figured that counted for something."

"It's not like that—"

"I even had this revelation on the camping trip. I did to God what Jericho did to me. I walked away from someone who loved me without looking back."

"That's *huge,* Al."

"But tonight I realized there is something I haven't done. I've never actually surrendered to God. I've never acknowledged that He's in control of my life."

Kate's hand snaked forward and clasped hers. "Do you want to?"

"I'm terrified about what that entails. But yes. Will you pray with me? You're better at this kind of stuff than I am."

She shook her head. "No. I think you need to be the one talking. But I'll hold your hand while you do it."

Ali bowed her head. "I've been in charge of my life for too long and have almost run it into a gully. I'm handing over the reins to You. Amen." She looked at her sister. "Do you think that was okay?"

Kate rubbed her thumb over Ali's knuckle, her eyes shimmering. "I think it was perfect. We're sisters for eternity now."

Ali nodded. "What do I do next?"

"Get to know Him better. Stand firm in His promises."

"His promises?"

"Sure. The Bible's full of them. Like—" Kate popped up and grabbed a card from under a magnet on the fridge "—try this one on for size."

Ali took the card.

*Hope deferred makes the heart sick, but a longing fulfilled is a tree of life.*

"Oh, Kate. I'm such a terrible person. I threw this verse—well, the first half of it—in Jericho's face weeks ago."

Kate tapped the card. "Okay, so you've lived that first half, but the second part is the promise. That's what you should cling to."

"A longing fulfilled?"

"What are you longing for, Al?"

She licked her lips. "For my family. For us to be to-gether." Her voice came out hushed.

"Tree of life. Sure sounds to me like there's going to be a downpour in the desert." Kate grinned. "I'm going to bed. Don't stay up too much longer."

As Kate's footfalls grew distant, Ali splayed the three cards out in front of her. The empty place in the patch of dirt in her heart could be filled. A tree of life, blos-soming with love.

That night, for the first time in eight years, Ali fell asleep full of peace.

The screen door slapped against the back of the house. Ali glanced up from the floor as she mopped.

Megan put up her hands. "Sorry. I didn't know the floor was wet."

Ali leaned the mop against the cabinets. "Don't worry about it. If stuff stays clean for ten seconds around here, I'm amazed." She opened the fridge and pulled out a bottle of water then tossed it to Megan. "I'm sorry I didn't help with classes today. I've got a lot on my mind today."

Megan brushed off the comment with a flick of her wrist, bracelets jingling. "Don't worry about it." She took a sip of the water. "You've got so much going on. Believe me, I'm amazed you haven't said 'enough' and closed the place down."

"I'd never do that. It's too important to me. How did the classes go? Was Hank able to ride for the en-tire lesson?"

Megan set the bottle of water on the counter. "Yeah,

having him lie on the horse with that special saddle was genius. The more contact he has with the horse, the calmer he is."

Ali smiled. "It's the warmth. Hank's tight little muscles against the horse's heated ones loosen him up in a way other physical therapy can't. I'm glad it worked. It's worth the cost of that saddle, then."

Megan nodded. "Bungee's gone lame again, so we won't be able to use him for another week or so. Chance and I mucked the stalls so they're all set for the horses tonight. Do you want me to stick around and help with anything else?"

Ali slipped across the kitchen floor and hugged Megan. "You're amazing. What would I have done without you?"

"Oh, you know." Megan shrugged out of her hug then pointed at the bouquet from Tripp. "Have you sorted out your man problems yet?"

Ali smiled and plucked dead petals from the flowers. "I have. Oh, Megan, I'm in love."

Megan laid a hand on the back of a kitchen chair. "Wow. You made your decision?"

"I did. And I can't believe it took me so long. I mean, he's been so faithful for so many years." The phone rang and Ali grabbed it, reading the caller ID. "Oh, look. It's Tripp. I'm going to take this."

Two days. Too long.

Jericho did a full circle, taking in his childhood home. The lodge-style house did nothing to console him. It stood as a monument for a wealthy man's attempt to feel important. He wanted nothing to do with it.

Pacing, he stepped into the master bedroom. There was a place near the entry to the bathroom where the carpet used to smell like Mom. A bottle of perfume had shattered there, and no matter how many times she scrubbed, the feminine scent lingered. Jericho leaned against the wall and scooted down so he could sit with his hand on the spot.

Wetness gathered in his eyes, so he looked up at the ceiling.

Whenever Pop walloped him good, he'd come here and press his nose into the carpet, remembering his mom. Missing her. Sometimes he'd even tried to talk to her.

But now, more than anything, Jericho wanted Ali. With one last caress of the carpet, he rose to his feet.

He would have walked across their adjoining fields, but the Jeep could bring him there faster. After yanking on his boots, he locked the door and barreled out to his vehicle. Roaring it to life, he sped onto the country road that formed an L around their properties.

He flipped off the music. "Let her call the cops. But she isn't keeping me away any longer."

When he turned onto Ali's property, he rubbed his jaw. He had a brother? It still baffled him. Tripp had tried to use Ali as a tool for revenge. Jericho bit back a growl. How dare Tripp?

He jumped out of the Jeep and crossed to the barn where he figured Ali would be. But he only found Chance tossing a ball to Drover.

"Hiya, Dad!" He trotted over, dog in tow, and flung his arms around Jericho's waist.

"Hey, Chance-man." He squeezed back. "What are you up to?"

His son's shoulders sagged. "Not much. Everyone's upset or crying around here."

"Everyone?"

"Girls. I tell ya." Chance shook his head. "At least Drover's not a girl."

"Has your ma been crying?"

Chance rolled his eyes. "All the time." He chucked the ball at the corral and Drover barked, taking off at high speed. "She said you won't be around anymore, but that I could still spend time with you if I wanted."

"She said that?" Jericho wiped his clammy palms on his jeans.

"Yeah. Guess you made her really sad because she's never not wanted me around, and I do all sorts of dumb things. Did you try saying you're sorry? That usually works. Well, she'll still make you sit in your room for a time-out, but not for that long."

"I'll try to remember that."

"And you don't have a room, so you'd just have to sit on the couch 'cause that's been your bed. It wouldn't be bad because the TV's right there."

"Hear anything else she said about me?"

"Well, she didn't say your name, but the other night she thought I was asleep, and I wasn't. I heard her saying 'I just have to do it' over and over again. Then I *wished* I was sleeping."

A tingle, like ghostly footprints tiptoeing on his skin, walked up his back. *I just have to do it.* But that could only mean...

Jericho gripped the barn door. "Where's your ma, buddy?"

"In the house with Kate and Megan."

"Is it okay with you if I go in there and talk to her about the crying, without you?"

Chance popped the ball out of Drover's mouth. "I don't want anything to do with crying."

Jericho didn't bother with the front door, because the Silvers were always in the kitchen. He came up the back steps and heard Ali talking to someone. He opened the door slowly to prevent the loud slam against the house.

Ali. Pretty Ali. She stood with her back to him, one hand cradling a phone to her ear and the other wrapped around her middle. As he stepped into the kitchen, Megan arched her eyebrows.

Ali played with a magnet on the fridge. "Sure. To-night would work."

Megan tapped him on the arm. He looked over at her, and she mouthed "Tripp."

It took all his self-control not to storm across the kitchen and wrench the phone from Ali's hand. After everything, she'd entertain a call from the man?

His mind zoomed like an off-road race. *Tonight would work? For what?*

Ali stuck the magnet back in place and walked to the pantry. "I know the place. An hour?" Pause. "Good. It's a date then."

*A date? With Tripp?*

Jericho jolted back, grabbed the door handle and rushed outside.

Barreling around the house, he heard the back door smack the clapboard, probably leaving a dent. What did he care? Not like anyone wanted him here.

When he was almost to the Jeep, Chance called out. "Hey, Dad! Where are you going? Don't leave."

But he dropped into the driver's seat and slammed

the door. Rage poured through his veins. He threw the vehicle into Reverse and made it howl the whole way into town.

Ali set the phone on the counter. "Was that just— did he…?" She raced to the front room in time to see Jericho's Jeep peel out of the driveway.

Kate came down the stairs. "What in the world was that noise?"

"Jericho bolted out of here without talking to me." Ali rubbed her arms. What had he heard? "Can I use the truck, Kate?"

Kate shook her head. "Sorry, sis. I'm already late for work. I need it."

Ali huffed. "Can you drop me off along the way?"

"If it's on the way, then sure. But hurry up."

Ali popped her head into the kitchen. "Megan? Do you mind sticking around and keeping an eye on Chance for a couple hours? I wouldn't ask, but Kate's busy."

Megan tapped her nails on the table. "So you can go on your date?"

"So I can go to dinner, yes."

"You know that's why your husband left. He heard you say 'date,' and he took off like an escaped convict. You can't keep stringing along two men at the same time. There are always consequences."

"I'm not stringing anyone… Oh, can you just watch Chance for me? Yes or no?"

"Love to." Megan smiled.

"Thanks. I owe you big-time."

On Kate's heels, Ali left the house. She bumped into Chance, who was slumped down on the porch steps, palming away tears.

"He left me, Mom. Dad left without talking to me."

Ali gasped and clutched her neck, her heart wrenching as if someone drove a nail through it. She stopped to cradle her son in her arms. Smoothing a hand down his hair, she spoke in a soft tone. "Sweetheart, listen to me. Your father loves you. I want you to keep thinking that while I'm gone. And Chance, I love you, too."

Ali wanted to be angry with Jericho for leaving Chance so upset, but she reminded herself to have patience. He was new to being a father and would learn in time. Besides, if she got her way, Jericho would never leave them again.

Now she just had to locate the man.

# Chapter Twenty-Two

Jericho leaned against his Jeep. He scowled at the neon Open sign as the last rays of sun grasped the tips of the mountains. The raucous beat of an old rock song drifted from the door along with wafts of fried food, beer and human sweat. Girls in miniskirts giggled as they sauntered through the entrance together.

He gripped the vehicle's bumper to keep himself from going inside.

One drink. Just one cold, tall lager would ease his mind. Numb the hurt. But one drink would become five. He could embrace sweet escape for one night. But then what? He'd just be back at the start again, with one more mistake to tally against him.

The song switched to a country ballad that baited him to join them inside. He took two steps toward the door and reached for the handle. Then he fisted his hand and paced back to the parking lot.

He'd been so certain they were on the path to reconciling. So sure.

*What had Chance said he heard Ali say? I just have to do it.* Divorce.

He stomped away from the vehicle, then walked back and pressed both hands against the side. If she went through with a divorce, then what? Shared custody? Chance for one weekend a month, and three holidays a year? Jericho punched the Jeep.

He wanted to be an everyday part of his son's life. He'd already missed too many milestones. There were so many things he wanted to teach Chance, experiences he wanted to share with the boy. Holidays and weekends wouldn't cut it.

Beyond that, he needed his wife. He longed to hold her against him as they slept, and sit across from her at the dinner table each night. He wanted to do everything in his power to support her chasing after her dreams. But he couldn't do that if she didn't want him.

A truck bumped into the parking lot and stopped a few feet from him.

He glanced over his shoulder. Ali. She looked so pretty that it seared his chest.

She jumped down and waved to Kate. "Don't worry about picking me up. Jericho will take me home." Ali sashayed toward him. "Hey, stranger." She beamed.

He glanced at the bar, then back at Ali. His shoulders sagged. She'd come looking for him at the bar, and he'd proved her assumptions right. Why was she even here?

She snatched his hand as she came near. "Grab some curb with me?"

They sat down, and she scooted closer. Her legs touched his, and their shoulders in contact made every inch on that side of his body burn. He reminded himself to take a breath. "Aren't you going to be late for your date?"

"Naw." She turned his wrist over, tapping the watch. "I still have thirty minutes."

The wind picked up and her scent wrapped around him, tempting him more than any bottle of beer ever could. Yet he couldn't have this woman.

His eyes started to sting. "I didn't go inside."

"I know." She captured his chin and turned his face to look her in the eye. "I believe you. I trust you. Hear that, Jericho Freed? I know you'll never touch the stuff again."

"But you knew to look for me here." He snaked away from her, hiding his face in his hands.

"Sure. You're human. You'll always be tempted, but I know you're too strong to give in." She bumped her shoulder into his. "So why the long face?"

Jericho studied the gravel at his feet and steepled his hands. "Are you gonna divorce me?"

"Why would I go and do a fool thing like that?"

He swung his head toward her. His mouth went dry. "You're not going to sign any papers?"

Her lips pulled up slowly. "That would make it a whole lot harder to be married to you if I did. And being married to you is what I want most of all." She looped her arm through his. "It just took me a while to realize it."

"Talk straight to me, woman."

She turned and framed his face with her hands, pulling their heads so they were inches apart. "Listen to me. I love you, Jericho Freed. You're the only man who's ever been in my heart." She bit one side of her lip, and her eyebrows darted up. "Straight enough?"

His heart started up like a hoof kicking his chest. He searched her face. The gold flecks in her eyes shimmered. He'd never seen anything more stunning. Incapable of stopping himself, he leaned down and brushed his lips against hers.

Not wanting to startle her, he moved to break the moment, but she brought her arms around his neck. Pulling herself against him, she deepened the kiss, her lips warm and melding to his. He sifted her soft hair through his fingers. His hands explored the curve of her neck and traveled down her spine.

When they parted, a chuckle rumbled in his chest. She leaned her forehead against his, and their eyes locked like partners in a dance. Ali had a goofy grin pulling at her cheeks.

"I love you, Ali Silver."

"Ali Freed. I'm going to change it back. Has a nice ring to it." She sighed, lacing her fingers through his. Her head rested against his shoulder.

"Ali Freed. I do like the sound of that." He stiffened, sitting straighter. "Okay, but then I don't understand why you're going on a date with Tripp."

Her eyes widened. "That's why I'm here. I want you to come with me."

"On a date with him?"

"No. I only said yes because I want to confront him. But I'm afraid of what he'll do if you're not beside me. After everything he's done, I can't trust him. Will you come?"

He tucked her hair behind her ear. "I'd go to Africa right now with you if you asked."

"Do you think you can face him after everything you found out?"

"You mean since learning he's my brother?"

"Yes. Do you know for sure if that's true?"

He nodded. "I talked to Pop, and he confirmed it. It's wild. I'm half pleased to know I have another relation in the world, but the other half of me wants to kill him for what he's put you through."

She rose, offering her hand. He took it and stood, but then tugged her to a stop. "Hey. I wasn't after you for the money, either. You know that, right?"

"It wouldn't matter even if you were. I love you and want to be with you, so we'd both win."

Jericho clutched her shoulders and gave a small shake. "It matters to me." He led her to the Jeep. "I knew nothing about that will until the other morning. And I could care less about the ranch and Pop's money."

"What about the bank stuff?"

"I did have meetings with the bank, and I have set up a business. It's a little nonprofit operation, and I'm hoping you'll consent to helping me get it up and running."

"A nonprofit?"

"Yes. It's tentatively named A Soldier's Dream, but if you don't like it, we can change that. I'd like to couple it with Big Sky Dreams and offer therapeutic horseback riding for injured soldiers and for soldiers' spouses while they're overseas."

Ali screamed. She hugged him so tight his back cracked.

"Jericho! That's the greatest idea I've ever heard. I'm already certified to do that. We can start classes right away. I'll have to do a little bit of research and plan different lessons."

He smiled down at her as she rattled off information, loving the way her lips moved over the words. "Whoa there, sweetheart. I still have to finish filling out paperwork with the government so we can be recognized

as an approved program for servicemen. Then I want
to join our companies and help with all the expenses.
Add horses to the program, maybe another arena and
riding barn."

Her face fell. "That's a lot of money."

He shrugged. "I have enough."

"But how? I don't think the army pays an injured vet
a lot of money, and I know you haven't been working
anywhere since coming home."

"My mom had a separate will. Hers stipulated that
my father didn't get a dime of her money. Instead, it
was held in an account until my twenty-first birthday,
when the totality of the funds became available to me.
The only problem was, I didn't have a clue. Pop never
told me. When I got back in town, Mom's lawyer con-
tacted me. I couldn't believe he hadn't retired yet. It
took a lot of paperwork, but the funds are now free and
clear and mine."

"I thought your dad was the rich one."

"Me, too. But I guess they basically had an arranged
marriage. Their parents were business partners. The
Freeds had land but were low on money, and the Aus-
ters had money but no land. So they merged."

"Do you think she did it because she was angry with
your father?"

Jericho opened the door and ushered her inside. She
climbed up, and he stood in the open area, drinking in
the sight of her. He sighed. "Yes. I think she knew he
cheated, and that's why she changed her will. I'm sure
she justified her actions because she was angry."

She put a hand on his forearm. "Bitterness can do
that to a person."

"I love you, Ali."

"I know. Now get your hide in action, or we'll be late."

Unable to resist, Jericho kissed her cheek before closing the door. Her giggle worked its way into all the broken places in his heart.

With her hand clasped in Jericho's, Ali walked into the restaurant and spotted Tripp. "Let me do most of the talking," she whispered.

When she stiffened, Jericho slipped his arm around her shoulders and pressed his lips close to her ear. "Did I ever tell you you're the perfect height?"

She swatted at him, but her smile fell when she met Tripp's gaze. The lawyer's mouth pulled into a grim line as he rose. "Well, I asked you here to give you my side of the story, but I see you've decided which man you trust."

Jericho tensed. Ali gave his side a squeeze and sat down. She folded her hands on top of the linen tablecloth. "I'd like to give you the benefit of the doubt, Tripp. I've learned the dangers of jumping to conclusions." Her eyes darted to Jericho, and her husband's lips tugged to a whisper of a smile, but the crease in his brow stated his true mood.

Tripp pulled at his collar. "This is going to be awkward saying everything in front of him." He gestured to Jericho.

Ali laid a hand on her husband's arm. "Jericho and I are a package deal. It's your choice. Talk to both of us, or neither."

Tripp raked a hand through his hair. A shock of it fell forward onto his forehead. "All right. I knew about the will. I've known about it since the day I started my internship with Jeb Strong. But you have to understand, Alison, I'm not an ogre."

"Did you slash my tires? Did you kill Denny?"

Tripp's eyebrows shot up. "No. Absolutely not. I care about you. That's what I'm trying to say. I'd never do anything like that to hurt you. I admit, I saw the will and realized the loophole—that if you married me, and I legally adopted Chance, then when Abram passed away, I'd stand to inherit everything."

"You would have faked a marriage with me?" In an effort to draw strength from Jericho's touch, Ali groped for his hand under the table. His strong fingers closed around hers. His thumb traced a pattern on the back of her fist.

"No, nothing like that. You've been a good friend to me for years, Alison. I don't have many people in my life who genuinely care about me. Our friendship means a lot. I care about your well-being. I know you've been hurt deeply, and I would have been an honest and faithful husband to you. It killed me seeing Chance without a father when I would have gladly stepped into that role." He toyed with the coffee mug on the table. "You see, I know how terrible it is being a boy without a dad. I didn't want that for him. I thought I was doing something noble, but you're looking at me like I'm the leftovers from gutting a deer."

"Not when you put it like that. You're a good man, Tripp. You'll be an amazing husband to the right girl, and a devoted father." She leaned over and squeezed his hand.

"I'm not a monster," he whispered. "My mother and I, we really struggled. Dinner wasn't a daily event, if you catch my drift. She told me I wasn't allowed to tell anyone Abram was my father. Said it would shame her. But after she died, I confronted him." He let go of the mug and looked up. "How do you think I made it through college and law school debt-free?"

Jericho leaned forward. "That still doesn't explain why you would send a threatening letter to Ali and then sabotage stuff around the ranch."

"I didn't."

"He's right, Jericho. It's clear now. Rider did it all along."

Tripp swirled the water in his glass. "No. Rider Longley's innocent as a pastor on Sunday."

Ali gasped. "But you helped me fire him."

"I hadn't figured it out yet. Everything finally clicked this morning, or I would have told you sooner. It's that girl you have working with you, Megan Galveen."

Ali reached for her purse under the table. "No way. I can't believe that. Megan is my friend. She's helped us above and beyond what I expect from her on many occasions."

Jericho cleared his throat. "And what would her motive be? Didn't the letter say something about seeing me and Ali together at the Independence Day picnic? Why would she care about us?"

Tripp closed his eyes. "No. It's me. She's after me."

Ali yanked the crumpled threat letter from her purse, smoothing it on the table. "It doesn't say your name, Jericho. I just assumed it meant you. But it could mean Tripp. She could have seen him walking me away at the picnic. She may have meant stay away from Tripp."

Tripp nodded. He scanned the note. "That *is* what it means. I wish you had shown this to me because I received a couple of these glued magazine cutout letters, too."

"But she's never said anything. You honestly think she did all those things?" Ali rubbed her hands back and forth over the tablecloth.

"Think about it. She has access to your bank account for Big Sky Dreams, and money keeps disappearing."

Jericho jolted. "Her father works at the Mountaintop Research Laboratory. Her sister told me when I got my loan. They mess around with real heavy-duty drugs for bioterrorism purposes."

Tears rushed to Ali's eyes. "Denny."

Jericho reached over and stroked her hair.

Tripp drummed the table. "She's been stalking me since they came to town. At first I was flattered, and I'll admit I used her to gain information about you. That's how I knew about your loan, Jericho." He rubbed his jaw. "But then the letters started, and she kept showing up wherever I would be. She crossed the line when she showed up in my house in just her robe last night. I went to the police at that point to document everything." Tripp unbuckled his briefcase and pulled out a file. "The detective I worked with looked into her past. That's what's in this file." He pushed the manila envelope toward Jericho.

Jericho pawed through the papers, a deep scowl marring his face.

Tripp pulled out one of the reports. "Scary reading. She fell in love with her high school math teacher and become obsessive. She ended up tinkering with the engine of his wife's car. It caused an accident. The man's wife suffered massive injuries. Megan did a stint in juvie for it. She's also been arrested in another case for stalking and violating a restraining order. There's an incident of battery where she attacked the girlfriend of a man she liked, too."

Ali's pulse pounded in her throat. She shoved to her feet, hands shaking. "Chance."

Jericho touched her elbow. "Ali, what's wrong?"

"Chance is at the house with Megan. She thought I had a date with Tripp." She grabbed Jericho's shoulder. "We have to go. She could hurt him. He trusts her completely." Tears rushed to Ali's eyes. "If something happens to Chance, I'll never forgive myself."

# Chapter Twenty-Three

Jericho stayed zoned to the road. His Jeep's headlights tore through the darkness. Tripp's car trailed their bumper by inches.

The wheels smacked into a pothole, jarring Ali's spine. "What if she does something to him? He's so vulnerable. What if he's hurt?"

Jericho's hand shot out and clasped hers. "Pray with me, Ali. God, protect our son."

Rounding the bend, an orange glow sliced through the onyx sky. Ali squinted. Across the fields, mammoth flames licked the underbelly of heaven. Smoke traced puffy fingers up into the stars.

Reality struck like a sucker punch.

Her throat clogged. She grabbed Jericho's arm. "Fire."

Flames consumed the ranch house. Splashes of lava-orange and sunburst-yellow erupted, ravaging everything but the structure's skeleton, which stood a somber black against the blazing backlight. Smoke burned in the air as a million glowing ashes hung suspended, eerie lightning bugs in the gloom. The fire leaped from the building, devouring the hay and feed piles in the yard, spilling over into the corral.

A swarm of firefighters and police officers filled the driveway. The lights from their emergency vehicles bounced blue and red off the barn.

Wrenching open the door, Ali jumped from the still-moving vehicle. "Chance!" A sob choked her as she shoved past the rescue workers. Ali fought against the waves of heat rolling from the house.

An iron arm seized her waist and jerked her backward. "Ali. No." Jericho dragged her away from the inferno.

With a moan, the structure's roof caved. Ali screamed.

Fighting him, she yelled over the roaring flames. "Let me go! I have to save him. He could be burning to death in there. Chance! Let me go." She kicked, trying to twist from his unyielding grasp.

Jericho spun her to face him, chin jutting out. "No. You're not going in there. I'll go in. It doesn't matter if I get hurt. But he needs you."

Jericho set her back a step and elbowed through a group of firefighters lugging a hose. Jericho bent to charge into the fire, but an officer stopped him.

Ali bit her nails. She blinked, trying to see the house through the haze and her tears.

The police officer approached with Jericho. "Are you the home owner, miss?"

Ali latched onto the man's arm. "Our son. I think he's in the house. Please let us go in. We have to save him."

The cop's eyes softened. "Let me guess, a freckled thing about yea high who can talk the wheels off a wheelbarrow?"

Jericho looped his arm around Ali's waist. "Sounds about right."

"He's safe. Follow me."

Leaving behind the unholy music of crackling fire, splitting boards and crumbling dreams, they stepped toward three police cruisers parked near the barn.

The breath whooshed out of Ali's lungs when Chance raced around the last car and bounded toward them. "Mom! Dad!"

She dropped to her knees, and Chance launched into her arms. Rocking back and forth, she wept into his hair. "I love you so much."

Jericho's arms encircled both of them, pulling his family against his chest. He rubbed at his own glistening eyes. "I love you both. Thank God you're okay."

Chance trembled in her arms. "Our house. Mom, our house is gone."

She stroked his back. "I know, sweetheart. But it's not important. You're safe. That's all that matters to us."

The police officer cleared his throat. "I'll need some statements from you folks."

Ali coughed. "I don't understand. How did you know to come here?"

Chance pushed back against her. "That's easy, Mom. They followed Rider."

"What does Rider have to do with this?"

Her son pointed his thumb in the direction of the ambulance. "He's over there."

She rose, Jericho and Chance right behind her. Ali rounded the ambulance to where Rider sat under a paramedic's steady hand. His face was a patchwork of soot as rivulets of sweat carved paths that dripped from his jaw. He'd lost his tell-tale hat, so his hair fell damp and tangled on his forehead. His button-up and jeans were torn and charred, with a burnt hole where fire had tried to nip at his chest.

The cowboy straightened. "Miss Ali, I know I'm not supposed to be on your property, but I ran into Kate at the town square and she told me what's been going on. I got to thinking that Megan was always around when bad things happened. And some of the things she'd told me didn't line up right with what Kate said. When she told me Chance was here, I called the cops and—" he shrugged "—seems they already knew her name and about some trouble in her past, so they were quick to follow me. I hope you aren't upset that I disobeyed you about staying clear of your property."

Ali reached out and placed her hand on his arm. She locked eyes before he could dip his chin. "You saved my son's life. How can I ever thank you?"

"Can I have my job back?"

She engulfed him in a tight hug, her head buried against his neck. "Of course. I'm so sorry I doubted you."

Jericho placed a hand on her shoulder. "Did you go in the fire after our boy? Is that how you got burned?"

Chance stepped between his parents, tears dried, ready to be the center of attention. "Oh, no. It wasn't on fire yet when he came for me."

Ali squinted at Chance through the fading light. "*Yet?* What happened?"

Her son leaned against the ambulance's bumper. "Megan said we were going to play cowboys and Indians. She said I could only be the cowboy if she got to tie me up. But she said not to worry because cowboys are strong and can get out of the knots. So I let her, and she went outside to do a rain dance. I reminded her that we got a bunch of rain the other day. But she still went out, and I saw her walking around the house for a long time. I don't think she did the dance right though, because it smelled like a gas station instead of rain."

Ali gasped. Jericho's grip tightened.

Chance rambled on. "And she was wrong about the ropes, because I couldn't get them off. And I really tried. Maybe if I didn't have a cast? But then Rider came in and said it wasn't a good game to play. He brought me to Denny's stall and told me to stay hidden."

Tears rolled down Ali's cheeks as she turned to Rider. "Then how did you get burned?"

"When I came out of the barn, Megan had torched the house, and I saw her run inside. Don't know about you, Miss Ali, but I don't believe even the worst of folks deserve a fate like that. Couldn't have lived with myself if I hadn't gone in after her."

Chance patted Rider's leg. "He should enter the calf wrestling contest at the next rodeo. I think he'd win. He pulled Megan outside and she tried to get away, but Rider took her down in four seconds flat. Even with her biting him."

"Hush, Chance." Rider grunted. "I'm not getting my chest all puffed up over tackling a lady."

Ali met Rider's gaze. "But I thought you hated us."

"Are you talking about that lawsuit, Miss Ali?"

She nodded.

"I'm not a part of that. I don't have a thing against you. My older sisters are suing you. They're stuck in the past, in that moment when our parents died. They're so bitter. They can't let go." He rubbed his palms back and forth on his jeans. "But I've never agreed with them.

It wasn't your fault that the truck hit them. Never was. That's why they call it an accident. I'm trying to talk them into dropping their fool vendetta. It's hotheaded. Nothing can bring our parents back."

Ali paced away from the men. Her gaze landed on the hissing leftovers of her home. Her hand clapped over her mouth.

Anger and being unwilling to forgive could bring such destruction. Granting bitterness reign caused heartache. Her own mother, Jericho's mother, Megan and Rider's sisters all stood testament to it. And she had almost been like that, too.

The gravel crunched as Jericho stepped up beside her. He opened his arms.

She leaned against him. "What are we going to do?"

He kissed her forehead. "Rebuild. You and Chance are safe. That's all that matters to me. We'll clear this rubble and build a new home. A fresh start, together. That is, if you'll have me?"

Ali rested her hands on his chest, smoothing her thumbs against the fabric. She tipped up her eyes, her voice husky. "Are you asking what I think you are?"

His eyebrow rose. "Need me to go down on one knee?"

"I'd rather you keep holding me."

His arms tightened. "Ali, I love you. Let me be beside you for the rest of my life. Raise our son together. Marry me, again?"

Little hands shoved against their legs. "What are you guys doing?"

Ali laughed. "Your dad's asking me to marry him."

Chance scrunched his face. "But you can't, Mom."

She met Jericho's alarmed look and winked. "Why not, buddy?"

He rolled his eyes. "'Cause it's silly. You're already married."

Jericho placed a hand on their son's head. "The kid does have a point."

Ali turned in Jericho's arms as Tripp approached. She smiled at him.

He stopped a few feet away, shifting his weight from one foot to the other. He kicked at the gravel. "I took the liberty of speaking with the police and giving them a detailed account of all that's happened at the ranch. I hope I didn't miss anything. They'll require a written statement from you tomorrow, but you're free to go tonight. They're transferring Megan to the county jail tomorrow. I suggested a psychological examination."

"Thank you for taking care of that, Tripp."

He slipped his hands into his pockets. "I guess I'll be off, then."

Breaking free of Jericho, Ali touched Tripp's forearm. "I want you to know that you're always welcome on my property. I understand why you did what you did, and I appreciate what you were willing to be for Chance."

"No problem."

Tripp started to turn, but she stopped him. "If it's not too much to ask, I still want you to be a part of his life." She looked over her shoulder at Chance and Jericho. Her son leaned against his father. Jericho had his arms looped around their boy.

She looked Tripp in the eye. "I mean, you're his uncle, after all."

"You'd let me be a part of his life like that? After everything?"

"Yes, Tripp. Please, be part of our family?"

He pressed a hand against his face. "I've never— No one's ever—"

Jericho cleared his throat. "I'll be needing some lawyer advice from you, too."

Tripp's gaze darted between Jericho and Ali.

"Seems that someday I'm going to be left a heap of property that I don't need, or want. See, I'm planning to build a house right here for my family. But this property that's coming to me in a will, well, I'd like to make sure that I can legally pass it to my brother. Think you can help me?"

Tripp's jaw dropped. He worked to close it, then opened it again. "If you're sure?"

Jericho draped an arm around Ali and snaked the other one around Chance. "I'm sure."

"Then, in a legal sense, I think I might be able to help you. Thank you. I'm not really sure what to say."

"And like Ali said, I'd be proud if you'd be Chance's uncle."

Tripp blinked a couple times, looked at the ground then nodded.

As the last of the fire engines and police squad cars rolled off her property, Ali batted her hand against the smell of smoke in the air. She couldn't look at the rubble that had once been her childhood home.

Jericho slipped a cell phone into her hand. "Call your sister. Tell her not to come here tonight."

She took the phone, but didn't use it. Ali wrapped her arms around her middle. "But where will we go?"

"My dad's house is across the ridge, and I plan on bringing my family home there tonight, if that's fine by you." Jericho trailed a finger down her cheek.

She reached for his hand and pressed a kiss to his palm. "It's fine by me. I'll call Kate and let her know to meet us there."

Chance latched onto Jericho's hand. "We're going to live in your house now?"

"Only for a little while. We're going to build a new house with plenty of room for all your sisters and brothers." He winked at Ali.

She tossed back her head and laughed.

Chance bolted ahead in the field and spun around, Drover leaping behind him. "First a dad, then an uncle, and now sisters and brothers? Whoa. This family is getting huge!"

*Tree of life.* Ali smiled.

She laced her fingers with Jericho's and they walked across the field, whispering their dreams to each other as Chance and Drover ran ahead.

\* \* \* \* \*

Dear Reader,

Do you ever feel like God is far from you? I know I've felt that way before. Ali sure did.

Because of all the bad that happened in her life Ali assumed that God walked away from her. In the end, she faces a choice. She can stay hidden behind her wall of bitterness and be alone, or she can find hope in forgiveness. I'm so glad she chose the latter.

Life is hard. It's easy to let difficult emotions and struggles consume us. Ali pictures God slamming the door of her heart and yelling, "Enough!" as He walks away. But she was wrong. God was with her the whole time, waiting for her to come back to Him.

If you feel far from God, I pray you will take the chance now to return to Him. I promise He's strong enough for whatever you are facing today.

Thank you for reading Ali and Jericho's story. They've lived in my heart for the past two years. I'm tickled to see them finally on paper. I love interacting with readers on Facebook. Look up my author page and say hi!

Much love,
*Jessica Keller*

## Questions for Discussion

1. Ali has understandable reasons to be angry and bitter toward Jericho. Did you find Ali's transformation believable or not? How come?

2. Ali keeps Chance's parentage a secret because she's afraid Jericho's still dangerous. Do you think this was right or wrong of her? Is there ever a situation where deception is acceptable? What are some stories in the Bible that include deception?

3. Jericho feels that God told him to go home and fix his marriage. Ali shoves him away at every turn, and Jericho starts to wonder if he heard God wrong. Have you ever had a strong feeling that God wanted you to do something but found all sorts of obstacles in your path? Jericho presses through the obstacles and wins back his wife. Have you ever felt God wanted you to do something specific? Were you able to accomplish that, and if not, what changed your mind?

4. Kate tells Ali that she holds all the power because Jericho asked for forgiveness. What do you think Kate meant by this? Do you think it's true that forgiveness gives us power?

5. Because of his father's stroke, Jericho will never receive an apology for how he was mistreated when he was a child. Jericho has to learn to forgive his father without knowing if his father is truly sorry.

We all have people who have wronged us in our lives. When was the last time you forgave someone when they didn't deserve or ask for it? Is there someone in your life like this right now?

6. Instead of going straight to the police when she receives a threatening letter, Ali tries to solve the problem herself. She could have been saved a lot of grief if she would have asked for help, but not having police assistance afforded her and Jericho time to bond that might not have happened otherwise. Have you ever attempted to manage a problem on your own that got out of hand? Do you wish you had sought help, or are you glad with the end result?

7. Jericho tells Ali that she's made her horse, Denny, into her savior. What did he mean by this? Have your priorities ever gotten out of whack? What happened to set them right again?

8. For the past eight years, Ali assumed God had abandoned her, but on her camping trip she realizes that she's the one who walked away from God. This one moment changes Ali's life. Can you point to an "Aha!" moment or a perspective shift that had the same impact on you? What was it? What were the circumstances surrounding it?

9. Ali is afraid that if she darkens the door to a church, God will send lightning bolts at her, but when she finally attends, she's greeted warmly by friends who have missed her. Have you had a similar ex-

perience where you were expected to be treated one way and found grace instead? What were the circumstances? How did other people's unexpected reactions impact you?

10. In the story, Ali's mother and Rider's sisters are eaten up with bitterness. It stops them from moving on after tragedies. Have you ever experienced something like this? How difficult was it to let go of bitterness?

11. Jericho loves his wife and goes out of his way to show her. In what ways did Jericho's love for Ali resemble God's love for us?

12. Tripp says he's making a noble choice when he offers to adopt Chance and marry Ali. Given his past, do you believe he's sincere?

13. In the end, Jericho and Ali invite Tripp to be a part of their family. Does this seem like a wise choice? What would you have done?

14. If you could write an epilogue, what hurdles, if any, do you see in Jericho and Ali's future? What do you imagine would happen to Kate, Tripp and Rider?

# WE HOPE YOU ENJOYED THESE TWO
# LOVE INSPIRED®
## BOOKS.

If you were **inspired** by these **uplifting**, **heartwarming** romances, be sure to look for all six Love Inspired® books every month.

*Love Inspired*®

LIHALO2016

# Love Inspired®

## Save $1.00

on the purchase of any
Love Inspired® book.

Available wherever books are sold, including
most bookstores, supermarkets, drugstores
and discount stores.

✂ - - - - - - - - - - - - - - - - - - - - - - - - - - - - - - -

# Save $1.00

**on the purchase of any Love Inspired® book.**

Coupon valid until July 31, 2018.
Redeemable at participating retail outlets in the U.S. and Canada only.
Limit one coupon per customer.

52615199

5 65373 00076 2  (8100)0 12313

® and ™ are trademarks owned and used by the trademark owner and/or its licensee.

LICOUP0318

# Get 2 Free Books,

## Plus 2 Free Gifts—

### just for trying the Reader Service!

*Love Inspired*®

## Inspirational Romance to
## Warm Your Heart and Soul

---

Join our social communities to connect with other readers who share your love!

Sign up for the Love Inspired newsletter at **www.LoveInspired.com** to be the first to find out about upcoming titles, special promotions and exclusive content.

---

### CONNECT WITH US AT:

Harlequin.com/Community

 Facebook.com/LoveInspiredBooks

 Twitter.com/LoveInspiredBks

LISOCIAL2017